THE GRAND WORK

"You've every right to be angry," Persephone allowed. "The Grand Work places you at the threshold of life and death, endangering your lives and the lives of those around you. But for all The Grand Work takes, it also gives. It saves the lives, hearts and minds of many whom it touches."

Beatrice's small voice stopped her at the door. "Couldn't The Grand Work have *asked* us if we wanted this? Couldn't you ask for volunteers instead?"

The goddess stared at her. Hard. "If we did, what would you say?"

Beatrice wanted to denounce the Work, to say that she wanted nothing to do with it.

Persephone shook her head. "You were chosen because you'd say yes."

Other books by Leanna Renee Hieber:

The Strangely Beautiful Saga

To Ruth,

LEANNA RENEE HIEBER

Fulfill the prophecy!

The Perilous Prophecy of Guard and Goddess

DP

Dorchester
Publishing

DORCHESTER PUBLISHING

May 2011

Published by

Dorchester Publishing Co., Inc.
200 Madison Avenue
New York, NY 10016

ISBN 13: 978-1-4285-1116-3
E-ISBN: 978-1-4285-1203-0

The "DP" logo is the property of Dorchester Publishing Co., Inc.

Printed in the United States of America.

Visit us online at www.dorchesterpub.com.

To Marcos, *Rey de mi corazon.*

ACKNOWLEDGMENTS

As always, huge thanks to Richard Jones, my foremost resource on London ghosts and an all-around stand-up gentleman. To Marijo Farley, who read it first, I love you. To Mom and Dad, for all kinds of unfailing support. To Hope Tarr for the crucial writing/commiserating dates along the way. To Mary Rodgers for smartly picking sentences apart, among myriad vital things. To Hasna Saadani, for making sure I navigated many worlds with truth and heart. To Reverend Heidi Neumark, who inspiringly has me thinking of all faith in all ways. To True-Blood.Net, eternal gratitude for your support, along with the many book bloggers who continue to champion this series and my work—I couldn't do this without you. To my agent, Nicholas Roman Lewis, my personal rock star. To RWA NYC for honoring me and this series last year, I am still so moved. And last but never ever least, thanks to my editor, Chris Keeslar, who lets me write the books of my heart and makes them live, and the whole Dorchester team for believing in me and in these books.

The Perilous Prophecy
of Guard and Goddess

Prologue

The goddess stood on the Liminal edge, the boundary of the Whisper-world, a precarious place where guardian angels are appointed and fates are sealed, a space where beautiful or terrible things are set in motion depending on what is required.

It was time to choose the new Guard. She'd seen the previous Guard onto the field, saw to it that their spirits were happy and at peace. They now rested with their fellows while she stood at a new beginning. This moment was an important one. Vital, critical. And yet the past overtook her, wrapping its claws around her throat in the way it always did. She had seen this once for every mortal day that passed since the first:

Ah, light! Running across the grass, she laughed. The sound brought spring. Nearby the Muses frolicked, rejoicing in the sudden newness of life. Her beloved would be waiting here, too, beautiful, winged and warm. Not cold and horrible like he who'd stolen her away.

In centuries to come, she would curse the day she had been so careless. She would forever curse the day she failed to look behind her to the cave opening where burning eyes watched and hardened. But the call of a great bird sounded and a warm wind surrounded her. Strong arms cradled her and laughter greened the trees. The Muses rushed into the field, delighted. It was a reunion of dearest friends.

Her beloved kissed her deeply, the spring breeze entwining his black hair with her own prismatic tresses. Trailing the line of her body with his fingertips, he pressed against her, aching, desperate. He, winged and eternal, the Keeper of Peace, the Balance, the true husband of her heart. Phoenix. He drew back and stared at the woman that should not have become another god's bride. His body burst into flame.

She should have foreseen the danger. She had not heard the growl from the distant shadows. Phoenix's form exploded, his feathers scorched and smoldering. From him came an unforgettable, ungodly shriek of agony. She screamed, too, a noise that rent the heavens.

Her terror made the rain come, dousing Phoenix and muddying the ground with water and blood. But it was too late. Hysterical, she cradled the charred and reeking body of her true love. The Muses watched in horror.

The wind picked up. It lifted a huge feather with gentle hands, consoling, murmuring sweet sympathies; it knew the depth of their love, as did all that was divine. The feather moved as if with a life of its own, seeming to float of its own volition. Five Muses ran toward it. Four ran away.

Her true love's corpse crumbled to dust. Backing slowly from the body, she felt madness overtake her. Wailing, she beat her fists into the ground until her hands bled. "This is far from the end!" she shrieked. Gathering up his ashes, she cradled them in her skirts, pieces of bone, feather and hair; her tears moistened the wretched fragments. "The world will not release you. I do not release you. It will not end this way. We will return."

She turned to face the cave where the murderer lurked. Behind him stood a host of the restless dead. They had gathered, cackling and shrieking, bloodlust rising in their tortured hearts. These were the wretched dead that she could not reach, could never reach; they were hopeless cases that needed higher, more powerful salvation than her grace and light. These were the dead who tormented the living.

"Come. Home." Darkness growled.

"You are not home," she spat.

His red eyes narrowed. Her stomach heaved and she doubled over, helpless. A sickening, rotten pulp flew from her lips, and Darkness snickered. Damn him for tricking her all those years ago. If she'd never eaten those seeds, sickly sweet and insidious, he'd never have gained an advantage.

She stared at him in fury, rising unsteadily to her feet. He might have power over her body, as the Whisper-world had truly infected her, but he couldn't control her entirely. She always stood back up.

The dead rushed out into the field, floating over the earth, gallivanting in their ghoulish fashion, their bones disjointed and their forms horrendous. "Frolic, friends," Darkness gurgled. "Feed. Me. Misery."

But, no. From the still-burning ashes of Phoenix came new flame. The ashes in her hands and skirts stirred, and the bloodred colour shifted to a cerulean blue, a force emanating forth that was peaceful and full of music. Replacing the red conflagration was a low-burning azure flame.

It took the shape of a feather, then a veritable pillar of fire, and the goddess gave a choked cry. Phoenix was not bested, nor was he alone. Here were the Muses, those who'd stood by him, gossamer and glimmering angels, five beloved companions who were the best of friends. They stood apart from this horrid scene, and alongside the flame of Phoenix they stared down the restless dead with unforgiving eyes.

"You will feed Darkness nothing," came a ghostly whisper. That phantom voice rumbled like thunder, and the undead paused. "Henceforth know to fear me. My friends and I shall turn you back, all of you who terrorize the living. My murderer will pay. We will starve his restless bones until they are dust. Restless dead, meet the guardians of the living. From this day forward we wield righteous justice. We can no longer leave the Balance to the Earth herself. Her children need aid against the likes of Darkness, who seek to enlarge their empire of misery. Tremble in our path, you who seek to grow shadow."

The host hesitated, unsettled. From deep within the cave, lightning flashed. Darkness seethed.

All light vanished from the sky. In return, blue fire covered the ground like a flood. Two worlds were shifting, creaking, opposing each other in earnest, and only one could be the winner. But the victor would not be proclaimed that day. The barrier pins between life and death shimmered, and the Whisper-world acknowledged that battle as right.

Balance would be maintained despite the violence that had been done. Darkness could not reign triumphant. A Guard was necessary.

Darkness gazed about the field and growled.

She whom many called Persephone approached her husband slowly. Those red eyes retreated into the cave, widening in apprehension as a great and burning light began to emanate from her, white like a dove. Persephone gazed upon the new force that had gathered, at the five friends who had in that moment pledged to fight an eternity at her lover's side. She blew the fiery ghost of her lover a kiss and bowed her head to the attendant Muses, knowing now was not the day of their triumph, knowing many days of sadness lay ahead.

She turned back to Darkness and narrowed her eyes. "In time dawn will come, and you'll bow to our light," she declared. Then she clutched the remaining ash, feathers and bone of her beloved, lifted her diaphanous robes and stepped back into her Whisper-world prison.

★ ★ ★

That had been long, long ago, but The Guard still fought the good fight.

"It's time, my love," called a voice, a whisper at Persephone's cheek.

She blinked back tears and stared into a floating orb of blue fire, all that remained of her one true love. "You are a ghost. Dust and vapor," she choked.

"Yes, darling, I know," he replied, all too accustomed to this exchange. "But it's time. Time for a new Guard."

"Yes," she echoed, her voice hollow. She did not want to go through this again. And again. For such as her, fate was a slow-turning wheel. "And where do you and the Muses wish to fly this time?"

"Cairo, I believe. Let them confer."

The ghost of great Phoenix hovered beside her at the Liminal edge and directed her attention beyond. Here, upon this unique threshold, a window upon a great proscenium with curtain lifted onto the world, anything could happen.

At the crest of the proscenium arch, a vast clock of mortal time ticked musically, the movements of its intricate metal hands and barrel of numbers denoting the year, ever changing but slow and subtle. This place had been born near the dawn of humanity, back when the purgatorial Whisper-world first separated from the mortal one and left a single flexible portal between. For a while the Whisper-world was a dank grey empire born from the misery of humankind, Darkness its incarnate lord—the Liminal edge would always be vested in the needs of the living.

Because of that, the place favoured the work of The Guard. And because of its favour, from this precipice of possibility The Guard were chosen time and again by Phoenix and his Muse attendants.

The Muses in their timeless forms, iridescent and beautiful, vaguely humanoid shapes floating luminous as one might imagine angels, each a whirling wind of song and stars, joined the two great divinities that awaited them. They flew across the Liminal border in a dizzying, sparkling display of light and beauty, and Persephone smiled. She could not help but smile whenever she looked upon such good friends, and her oft-laboured breathing eased. But there were only four of them.

"The Heart was overeager," the Muse of Intuition cooed, its iridescent form neither male nor female. "Heart found a perfect soul in Ahmed Basri and has already gone ahead. The rest of us must catch up."

"Great One, Our Lady," acknowledged the Muse called Memory, nodding a shining head first at Phoenix, then Persephone. "We come wearied from war and yearn for less burdened soil."

The cerulean fire of Phoenix shifted to entwine his Muse friends in a wide embrace, a binding circle. His voice held regret. "Show me, friends, one ounce of soil turned by mortal hands that is not burdened. I will gladly send us there."

Intuition spoke: "Would that such soil existed. But, no, Heart has fallen for Ahmed and his visions and was off to Cairo in a shot. I daresay Cairo's a good choice, with its grave-robbing and such. There's great unrest around the tombs of that civilization, which first worshipped you, Great One," it informed Phoenix. "We've found powerful mortals who match our need. And their myriad backgrounds will make our Grand Work . . . quite a challenge."

The four Muses chuckled. Truth be told, they enjoyed unsettling mortal lives. There was a bit of playfulness in each that remained from their pasts, holding on to humour and heart at all costs, lest they fall to Darkness's traps.

"I've already touched my chosen," Intuition continued. "He would have died in a fire this morning if not for me. We are known for cursing mortal lives, perhaps, but so should we be known for saving them."

The fiery form of Phoenix gestured with an armlike appendage. "Precede me, friends, and I shall seize my own host."

"The Power and the Light," the four Muses murmured in reply.

As Persephone watched her friends leave, tumbling out into a blue sky spread vast before them, she remembered how they'd all once lived less troubled lives. She remembered bitterly how she'd sworn to be again with her beloved and not just his ghost. But that had never happened. And off they were to fight the good fight, and to fight it through eternity.

The Liminal, ever mercurial, ever mysterious, perhaps sensed her mood. Above, on the Liminal's proscenium arch, the clock that gently ticked away mortal life whirred and its intricate metal arms spun. The numbers on the barrel shifted, and the wide window suddenly revealed a scene from the past.

Persephone and Phoenix saw no longer the sparkling Muses careening down onto Egypt toward their chosen ones but a gaslit street shining elegant at dusk, homes and town houses full of Romanesque details with candles burning welcome in windows. German-speaking servants readied two carriages.

Phoenix did not need the language gifts of Persephone to translate, for the Liminal made all language comprehensible. A well-to-do family here had their belongings packed, and they turned to gaze fondly at a grand town house. Turning back to the line of carriages, the mother and father ushered their dark-haired daughter into one fine conveyance, but two persons lingered behind.

One, an exceedingly severe woman in an elegant black dress, her black hair streaked with silver and wound tight upon her head, clamped her hand firmly upon a young boy who looked older than his age in his fine dark suit. His black hair hung loose around his face, and his dark eyes shone uncannily sharp.

"Once we're in London, child, you'll see. A great future will unfold," the woman promised. Her voice was thick with an accent. "Alexi," she said sharply when the boy did not respond.

"Yes, *Babyshka?*" He looked up at her, his face impassive, his voice strong.

"What symbol crowns the alchemical pyramid?"

"The firebird," he replied.

"Exactly. And what will you do with him?"

"I shall harness him in my hand."

"So you shall," she promised. "There is more to our folklore than mere stories, my dear child. There are two worlds, the mundane and the mystical, and I've called them both down upon your head." The woman shifted her hand from his shoulder to brush a lock of hair from his face, cupped his cheek in a gesture more authoritative than kind. "You'd best do something with them."

The boy looked at her, unflinching, with unspoken agreement.

"Who is *that?*" Persephone breathed. The Liminal window had gone a bit glassy with the time shift, as if to keep them distanced, and she could see her form reflected inside. Every colour of her was shifting subtly, as if her body were a prism held to the light and turned by a gentle hand.

"I'm not sure," Phoenix murmured.

The grandmother spoke again: "Someday, my boy, you'll light the darkness with your fire and all the world will bow before it. I'll stake my life on that." She helped the boy into the carriage, then turned and stared directly through the Liminal, though that was of course impossible. She stared as if she were addressing Phoenix and Persephone, *daring* them. And then she held out an arm, deigning to allow a footman to help her into the carriage.

Persephone gasped. The scene faded to black, and the timepiece of the Liminal stirred, whirred and presented the current mortal year.

Persephone felt her excitement rise. Although she could no longer see herself and her multicoloured form, she knew she cycled through hues more quickly; she always did when her emotions were high. "Phoenix, my love. That boy . . . I've never seen a mortal so like you, an elegant young king of wisdom. Why, you've even been called down to his hand. Surely that's a sign. He'll be your Leader!"

"No. He's too young," Phoenix protested, his fiery form floating upward to the Liminal clock and doing the math of the elapsed years. "It doesn't add up. We take our mortals as late teens. The Grand Work at his age would break him. Besides, you saw: we've already chosen Cairo, and the Taking has already begun. He will be in London, and there can only be one Guard at a time."

Persephone stared at the Liminal window. Its light had

changed, and that Germany of years prior had faded to a metropolis of towers and domed temples, the morning call from muezzins lifting prayer up into the bright sky from the slender spines of pearlescent minarets. She squinted at the brightness, her eyes having not quite adjusted from the shadows she hated, though she rejoiced at the feeling of the sun upon her face.

"Go on, love, you've an annunciation to make with the Muses and their new Guard. I must find my Leader—of appropriate mortal age. In fact, I believe I know just the one, and she has little inkling how her mortal life will change. But, tell me one thing before you go." He wreathed phantom tendrils of flame around her, as this was the limited interaction they were still allowed. "I must know how you fare."

How did she fare? She worsened every year. The corner of her diaphanous robe was stained with blood and pomegranate juice, a sickly, rotting combination she'd been coughing up for centuries.

"The pain comes and goes," she murmured, giving a valiant smile and suppressing the rattle in her lungs. "But I always feel better when I meet my new Guard."

Stepping to the threshold, as if she were a bird ready to fly from a branch, she added, "But you must find out about that boy." Then she stepped through the portal and disappeared in a blaze of light.

Phoenix paused before he set off behind her.

Chapter One

Eighteen-year-old Beatrice Smith stared into Jean's deep blue eyes and really, truly wanted to be in love. Wholly in love. It was a fitting time for it; the breeze was warm, the Egyptian sun bright, and the ties of her bonnet were undone. She had stolen a few moments away from the ever-present eye of the housekeeper that her father had hired to not only clean their rooms but also keep watch and be a female presence in Beatrice's male-dominated life. For the moment, she was gloriously without scrutiny. Beatrice liked that best; when she was on her own and could make her own decisions.

"Will you ever get back to England?" Jean asked, his French accent as delightful as that bouncing lock of his sandy-brown hair in the breeze. "Do you even remember England? I'll bet you don't remember it like I remember Paris."

Beatrice looked out over the city. They'd hidden themselves above it all, sitting on the anterior ledge of a tower at the Church of Abu Serga from which they could survey their own little kingdom. Old Cairo's minarets pierced the uneven skyline, spires calling to heaven, cupolas and spherical forms above intermittent brick complexes, graceful curves among rectangular blocks, a feast of shapes and varying heights. Along the stones far below strode both the wealthy and poor, robed and suited, veiled and open-faced; there were the bronze and pale, the native and foreigner.

"A little I remember," Beatrice replied, finding it hard to think of any world that wasn't Cairo. "I remember how different the colours are. Perhaps the distance of memory mutes England's hues, but it seemed a gloomier palette. There's so much work here, I doubt Father's thought one whit about Oxford. He hopes to find out everything about the pyramids before everyone else. I'd like to help him."

Jean grinned. "Ah, yes, that's right. He's too busy grave robbing."

"No, Jean." Beatrice scowled. Jean was always teasing, but he should know better than to jest about a most passionate subject. "Father isn't like that."

"What's wrong with it if he were? Valuable stuff, antiquities—and I'm sure your museums will do a much better job of preserving them than the natives."

"You can't think like that, Jean. That's the whole trouble," Beatrice scolded, easily sliding into the role of lecturer or professor. "Just because a way of life died doesn't mean you can go tromping around their graveyards and taking souvenirs. Father's interested in the culture, in learning about the hieroglyphs, about elaborate burials, rituals and daily life. Civilization began in Nile soil. It's fascinating."

After a moment of reflection she turned to Jean and reiterated, "He's not just here to take things. He's a gentleman, you know. Though, I daresay most Englishmen are less refined. Some of the things he's suggested be stopped are quite . . ." She trailed off. "And then there are the tourists. They'll come to ogle his discoveries once they learn of them. They've already begun. Have you seen the guidebooks? Entitled people with money to throw away, thinking they can learn everything about a faraway place and its people in a few unthinking moments."

"You've heard too many of his lectures." Jean elbowed her, yanking at a bonnet tie.

Beatrice readjusted her ribbons. "Just think if someone were to go into your Notre Dame and overturn the vaults just because they were curious. There'd be hell to pay—"

"The recently dead are different than the ancient, Bea," Jean interrupted. "Your father might be standing in the way of a great discovery."

"He's trying to stand in the way of *looters,* Jean. It's very different. I daresay your father wouldn't mind a nice trundle of loot," she muttered. She'd been attracted to Jean because he was carefree and jovial. But if he didn't have a serious bone in his body, how could she ever talk to him about what was meaningful?

Jean held up his hands, the cuffs of his white linen suit ruffling in the breeze. "My family remains firmly rooted in the good, clean, honest work of banking. Father wants nothing to do with cursed mummy gold. But in a few years, none of this will matter. I plan on stealing you to Paris as soon as I've the chance, and I'll make you Mrs. Jean Pettande before your father can say Book of the Dead. God willing."

Beatrice blushed and cocked her head, giving him the first challenge of their young relationship. "But what if I don't believe in God?"

Jean twitched his nose, amused. "You're too young to be an atheist."

"And you're too young to know the truth. You grew up surrounded by Parisians. I grew up here. How can Coptics and Arabs, Sufis, Sunnis, Jews and everyone else who lives here, mildly disgruntled yet vaguely at peace with each other in the districts of this mad city, all believe different things and all be right? They must all be wrong."

Jean shrugged. "Someone's got to be right."

"Who, though?"

Jean grinned. His ruddy cheeks dimpled. "Might as well be me."

Beatrice snorted, not sure if she was amused or disgusted. "Why, Jean, I do believe you've succinctly stated the very heart of conquest."

He grinned. *"Oui."* His dive to place a kiss on her neck made her giggle. "But unlike Napoleon, all I'm interested in conquering is you."

Shifting his precarious position on the ledge, he pulled her into a real kiss. Then a thought occurred to him, and he raised an eyebrow. "If you don't believe in God, why do you care about anyone's mortal remains, like those musty old Egyptians?" He gave a mock sneeze, and she glared at him.

"No, I don't believe in the Book of the Dead and I'm certainly not convinced about our Bible, but that doesn't mean I want to steal anyone's bodies and put them out for a show. I respect what I see. What I'm not sure about are all the things I can't see: gods, demons, ghosts, curses—"

"You know, you really are too opinionated for your own good. I'm going to lock you away in a Parisian flat," Jean said. "That's what you really need." He scrambled to his feet, standing precariously on the ledge.

"Jean, be careful," she snapped. She was annoyed by his words, even if he was joking. Was he joking? He had a bent for carelessness. It would serve him right if he hurt himself, she thought in a moment of unkindness.

"Do you hear that, Cairo, Beatrice Smith shall be Mrs. Jean Pettande, stolen away like an antiquity, never to be seen again!" He stood shouting, flailing one hand and holding on to a gritty, sand-bitten window frame with the other. "I'll protect her like her father protects the ancients!"

"Stop that. Stop talking like that. I don't want to be stolen away or protected, I love Cairo."

And, she did. More than Jean. It was beautiful, complex and fascinating, its cultures, its histories and people . . . She even found some young locals attractive, which went very much against general British sentiment. Considering the abyss that stood between ever really getting to know any of them, such attractions were foolish. Someone like Jean, foreign as he was, was still European; safe, accessible and right. He was someone she was *supposed* to care for. This was what women her age did: they were courted, they fell in love and raised families. But his brash tone of conquest rode her sensibilities roughly. Her sunny, lovely day had soured.

Jean still played the buffoon upon the ledge. "Oh, Bea, your father may have let you read books and taught you ridiculous rituals of useless dead people, but you don't seem to grasp your place in this world. Look at you right now; you're just where a girl's supposed to be." He waved and giggled, shifting his weight. "At my heel, as I stand above and survey our kingdom!"

There came a cry from downstairs. A wind gusted, a powerful gale focused like a presence, like a person storming in as if in protest that Beatrice would not, in fact, be stolen away and trapped. Sand was kicked up at the same time Beatrice's blood chilled. Women and priests cried out phrases she recognized as scriptural exclamations, and she pursed her lips, passing it off as superstitious fancy.

But, suddenly she couldn't see Jean. And she couldn't quite feel her own body.

All within her gaze went blue. Beatrice's hands pressed hard against the tall window frame, and it was as if a great force collided with her body. There came a burst of angelic music and blinding light, a thrilling jolt through her blood, and a firm male voice said: "You'll not hear my voice again. You'll only feel my fire. But you, Beatrice Smith, have been chosen for The Grand Work. You are now more than humanity could ever offer alone, and you will fight on the side of angels for a better world. You are the Leader of the Guard."

A blinking image of a circular room and a bird fluttered

before her gaze. The wind was all around her, inside her. Beatrice was too shocked to utter a sound, too taken with this cataclysmic event, but at last the moment faded. Her senses returned to the present.

It was just in time—or just too late. Beatrice squinted past her blowing bonnet strings to see Jean's wide eyes and the top of his mussed brown hair vanish from view. He fell from the ledge upon which he'd been so reckless. He fell many stories, and Beatrice shouldn't have looked down. But she did. So much red against so much white. She wasn't sure she believed in God, but now, maybe, the devil. What had spoken within her? Whose voice had graced that terrible moment of pain and euphoria?

Tears streamed down her face as she peered down from the ledge. People ran to Jean's body and swarmed over it, though they were careful to keep out of the widening pool of blood. Beatrice ducked back, avoiding the upward gazes, gasping, wishing to see no more.

Coldness poured over her, one overwhelming sensation after the next. An icy draft? Something transparent appeared, grey and shimmering.

Jean. It was Jean! He floated before her, greyscale in his linen suit, his luminous face wearing an expression of confusion. He opened his mouth and spoke words she could not hear. She blinked. She'd stopped breathing moments before, and only now a gasp tore from her throat. She was staring at his ghost. She didn't believe in these things; she'd just said so. She was being proven woefully, horrifically wrong. He was holding his hand out for her, as if everything would be all right.

Beatrice reached forward, an unreleased scream threatening to tear her in two. Her world and sanity were both crumbling. Jean stared at her sadly. Seeming to realize something, he shook his head, disappointed. Then he blew her a kiss and faded from view.

Sound finally tore from her lips. Beatrice fell forward, turning her head and retching on the cool stone floor until she felt warmth on her hand like a ray of sunlight. Turning, she found a woman of unparalleled beauty beside her: glowing, majestic, full of colours. A glowing, floating woman whose hair was black, then brown, now blonde; her skin was pale, then olive, now dark—

She'd gone crazy. That, or this was a wretchedly cruel dream with an avalanche of events and sensations.

"I'm sorry," said the woman hovering before her, tears falling from her ever-changing face. She blinked blue then brown eyes. "I'm so sorry. I lost my lover, too. He was murdered. He burned to death before my eyes." Her tears were silver like mercury, and they rolled like beads down her cheeks and dripped to the floor.

"Who are you?" Beatrice asked, choking, wiping her mouth. "*What* are you?" She knew that sounded rude, but clearly she'd gone mad. She didn't need manners when she'd gone mad.

"I'm whatever you want to call me, and I have a job for you," the magnificent creature said.

Beatrice stared at her diaphanous layers and shifting colours, trying to sound brave but knowing she didn't. "Wh-what do you want with me?"

"I want you to know that death is not the end. I'll even show you it isn't."

Beatrice was suddenly full of fear and guilt. "I was saying I didn't believe in God but . . . I don't know. Please don't tell me Jean was punished for my blasphem—"

"I'm not handing out punishments," the woman interrupted. "But I am here to help set you on a path. You have been chosen for The Grand Work."

"I've been chosen as a nutter," Beatrice murmured. "And you can't be real." She rose shakily to her feet. All she wanted to do was weep, alone.

"Just outside," the woman said. "In a place that's neither here nor there, at the edge of time, between two worlds, you have friends waiting for you."

Beatrice stared. Her mind struggled. There was something inside her now, something warm and full of power. The sensation was making her dizzy, but it wanted her to be strong. Resolute. A leader.

"If you say so," she whispered, dazed, moving awkwardly to the stairs. She descended, her bonnet askew, her blonde locks mussed, and she didn't bother to wipe her eyes.

At the foot of the landing, looking similarly dazed, was a group of four young men and women. They were all about her age, and they were looking up at her. Waiting.

Chapter Two

Ibrahim Wasil stared at the smoldering foundation of his home. He'd watched it burn for several hours. He'd hung back from the crowd, his keen ears picking up all the murmuring about the dead bodies rumoured to be inside. His own, too, they thought. His, and the body of the man who had acted like his father. Not his true father. Only Allah knew where his real parents were, or if they had ever felt guilty for abandoning him as a baby on the stoop of an Englishman's home.

"Like Moses," his friend Isaac had once said when they were children, playing in a university courtyard. Isaac was a Jew, but there wasn't anything obstructing a friendship. The Fatimid Caliphate had held a relative tolerance for other religious groups, and while that ancient empire was long ago fallen away, some of its basic principles remained in Masir, in Al-Quahira, in this city the Europeans called Cairo.

There were tensions, of course, between faiths, races, classes and intentions. The pale skin of colonial interest could never entirely be trusted, whether it be French or British. However, one kind and gracious example of pale skin had raised him unquestioningly as his own yet with respect for his birthright: James Tipton had made sure that Ibrahim was heir to his rightful Arabic language and faith. He'd named him Ibrahim Wasil and made sure that he was proud of the name. But he'd also taught Ibrahim the Queen's English and escorted him to just as many Christian services as Muslim calls to prayer. A professor of religion at the University of Cairo, Mr. Tipton had encouraged him to be whatever he wished and had given him a place to call home while he learned what that might be.

Ibrahim wasn't sure what he prayed to as a tear rolled down his face, staring at the unfair demise of the one true good man he'd ever known. He supposed as many gods as would listen. Perhaps none. No one should be burned in his bed. Just like no child should be orphaned a second time.

He'd begun the day as a creature of two worlds, English and Arabian. Now, a man alone at the age of eighteen, he wasn't sure which world would take him, or if he would have to choose. James Tipton had managed to blend his life effortlessly in a loving mix of faith, culture and sensibility. Others he met, both English and Arabian, made it seem one had to cling to specific viewpoints and reject all the rest. Some of his own people had rejected outright the honest intentions of James and others at the university and had accused Ibrahim of abandoning his true self by living among them. For a boy who never for a moment forgot he'd been abandoned on a doorstep, this was a deeply painful accusation.

Ibrahim wasn't sure how to be the sort of man Tipton was, a man of his own faith and culture utterly welcoming of and unthreatened by all the rest. To be entirely his own man, regardless of others' approval, seemed far from his grasp. What should he aspire to, and how should he present himself? The truth was that he now had no home, and home was often where one truly found oneself. The Cairo streets could be hard.

Uprooted, he could be anything now, anyone. He could choose to be a ghost, he realized. The crowd assumed him dead. He could be invisible, no longer existent. Was that the answer? To be a ghost? Wondering and wandering? Something had pushed him out into the market this morning. Some instinct had told him there would be ripe, glorious pomegranates in the market and that he should get some. That strange, pressing urge, he realized, had saved his life. Would that it had saved the life of the man who'd provided a home for him.

A sudden violent wind knocked him forward, and a furor rose within him as if a bird loosed from a cage flapped madly at his insides. The pomegranates he held in each hand fell to the ground, rolling away and bleeding onto the sandy stone. And he knew then that nothing would be the same.

When he looked up again, he saw that was true. For, in thinking he had become like the dead, he now saw them. Ghosts stared back from every few feet; greyscale and luminous, spirits from Cairo and the spectres of nomads, ghosts of all faiths and races, eras and classes. The city was thick with them, and he felt an overwhelming wish to follow each and every one, to understand why they were driven here, to Cairo's streets, eternally wandering in and out of shops and homes and down brick lanes.

He heard a strange new voice, speaking in a language he'd never before heard and yet miraculously understood: "Hello, my torchbearer, Intuition. I saw the measure of the man you could be and had to save you from your fate. I'm sorry for your loss, but you gain new family and a new future today. I have plucked you from an early death to learn a story and fight the good fight. In the beginning were two lovers, beings of light who fought the dark. We are their continued struggle, and it is in their name I welcome you to The Guard."

Ibrahim heard these words within him, all around him, and they were confounding. The proclamation touched a numb part of himself and created a hollow echo there, for his eyes looked elsewhere—at the ghost of James Tipton.

Puzzled, the man floated over his home, staring down at its cremated remains. He cast his grey eyes everywhere, and at last they fell on the young man he'd lovingly and unquestioningly called son. It was then that he smiled his small, consistent smile, as if in seeing Ibrahim safe he had determined that all was suddenly well.

His adoptive father waved. Ibrahim bit back tears. His senses could not be trusted, and he would not show such womanly frailty. Yet, he was overwhelmed. The bird kept beating in his chest. There was something urging him to move forward, to travel, to seek out a new destiny, and this tension mounted as he began to hear more heartbeats than his own.

He had the uncanny sensation that he was now tied to beings other than himself and that he would never be alone again. But was that what he wanted? The sensation was both terrifying and wonderful. He had always been alone. Was this comfort or madness?

There came a blinding light beside him. Turning, he beheld a luminous woman, the flawless epitome of many types of beauty made from shifting colour. It was as if she stood before a prism and all light circled round.

"You are not Allah," he said, uncertain.

"Correct, I am not," she replied.

"Or one of the saints. Or prophets. You are an angel, then?" Ibrahim blinked, wondering if she would vanish when he opened his eyes, if his mind had been entirely torn asunder by the day.

"If you like. Come, Ibrahim," the woman entreated. "I'm sorry for your loss. Let me show you where you belong."

She held out a shimmering hand. Ibrahim looked down at it, and then he looked at the burning rubble. James Tipton had vanished. Ibrahim hoped that his Christian saints would take and hold him close. He was a good man. Allah would take him. While different words were used, the two faiths weren't too terribly dissimilar when one stripped away the trappings. Someone would take care of his father.

And, there was another matter at hand, the matter of the hand at his side. The hand of a stranger, patiently held out for him. Would it be proper to touch her?

"Do not be afraid," the woman said. "I'm here to take you home."

Ibrahim gulped. She lowered her hand, not offended that he did not take it. She did glance at the pomegranates lying bruised and dribbling onto the stones. She frowned and kicked the fruit aside, then turned and began to walk.

"Come," she bade him. He began to follow her through the city.

As they headed to a destination unknown, Ibrahim opened his mouth to question his guide, but the surety with which he'd felt that nothing would ever be the same stilled his tongue. He had inherited a new life in place of the old shell. Whatever had spoken to him—something that was now within him—was inherently good, just like the man who'd raised him. His senses were sharper now, and he'd never felt so alive. The world was at his fingertips.

Here was, perhaps, the only thing to ease grief and loss: community. Ibrahim had never been a social creature. He liked books, grand architecture and quiet spaces. His brain was nearly bursting with strains of poetry, texts in their entirety, and he was suddenly made happy by the certainty that he was on his way to meet friends?

"My mind is changing," he murmured. "Why?"

"You'll see," came the answer. The multicoloured angel would reveal no more.

Chapter Three

A part of Ahmed Basri's consciousness knew that he was dreaming. And yet, the hazy knowledge that he lay napping in his bed was little comfort when witnessing something he could not wholly understand but was terrible nonetheless. It was a war. A horrific war. In the ground. There were monstrous metal machines, roaring screams like angels plummeting from heaven. Or demons. He was baffled by these doomful abominations on an unknown shore under a colourless sky. This grey, muddy struggle in the ground had no kinship to anything he'd experienced in the golden warmth of Cairo. He did not want it to.

He had always held joy in his soul, since the very day he learned what it meant to do so, but these scenes of foreign terror shook him to the core. They caused bone-chilling cold, and he had to tell someone. This was a warning, surely; why else would such portents be shown to anyone? And the dead. So many dead. Too many. Fear began to seep into Ahmed's buoyant heart like water into a punctured boat.

"The dead have no place to go," he heard himself murmur, though he was not yet awake. "Help them," he urged. "Help the dead pass."

Into the grey air he called, exhorting the soldiers around him. The noise of those horrific mechanical beasts filled his ears, one growling nearby. No one responded. They were too busy dying and becoming grey, themselves; transparent shades, luminous yet sad. The air was grey not because it was a cloudy day in whatever country this was—France? He thought he heard French. Cairo had been overtaken by the French in the previous century; a bit of the language lived on in various instances in the city. But it wasn't clouds causing these thick grey swirls. The air was grey because it was filled with the dead. The dead choked the sky.

Ahmed feared for the joy in his soul. It was in danger. Who could see such horrors and retain hope or love? Who could gift happiness to others when such perils were in store?

He fought back and was rewarded. Words sounded in a new language he'd never before heard but somehow understood: "Yes, beloved, foster your joy," murmured a song of wind and stars, a divine voice. "For you are the Heart. You are a visionary, meant for great things. And you will attain them. In the beginning there were two lovers. These beings fought greedy shadow that sought to spread misery across the land. We carry on their ancient quest to light the darkness. This is the last you will hear me speak, but I welcome you to The Guard."

A gust of wind whipped through his small room, making chaos of the modest flat that his parents kept immaculately tidy. He shot up in bed, awake. The morning sun fell warm and assuring upon Ahmed's face, and something climbed into his soul like a man slides a silken tunic over his body. Ahmed was the tunic. Music and light filled him to the brim.

Had his vision called this herald, or had this herald caused that vision? He did not know, though they seemed linked. Neither was how he might expect mystical revelations to come, nor did they use the words of his Sufi teachings. But Ahmed had always known there was more to the divine than any man might grasp. He was sure that whatever he now carried within him was inherently good.

Yet, wasn't he too young for such a gift as this? He had not studied long with his teacher and it seemed premature for such spiritual grandeur. He reeled from equal parts of desire to accept this intrusion as divine and a longing to reject it and reclaim familiarity and some sense of himself. But no guidance came to him. His questions remained unanswered.

Ahmed blinked, suddenly desperate to look out his window, its pale curtains whipping about in the unusually forceful breeze. When he did so, his eyes met ghosts. Spirits, spectres, visions of all sorts mingled in the busy Cairo streets. Floating amid the thronging life were the dead, their grey forms a stark contrast to the golden hue of his city. He resolved to go out to them.

"Mother, I'm going for a walk," he called out as he passed. She sat hemming a robe in their dwelling's main room, lit brightly by the sun. He recognized her as beautiful, her layered, thin robes splayed around her like the petals of an open flower. He recognized her as someone he loved. Yet, it was as if he were suddenly looking at her through an inverted spyglass. She was as distanced as he was changed, and today would forever separate them.

She nodded, her black eyes glistening with the soft peace she'd always had, and he knew he would always cherish that about her, if now from a distance. Detached, he realized that whatever had taken up residence inside him was changing how he interacted with all he met—the world of the dead, and also clearly that of the living.

They were calm realizations, and he was delighted when he was bidden to join new friends. Like faraway strains of music he felt their distinct heartbeats, feathers against his ears pleasantly drowning out the bustling sounds of the city. At the same time he felt linked to the thrum of humanity. Five other souls he heard. With himself, six. The terror of the earlier vision faded, replaced by his usual joy, followed by an entirely new sense of power and wonder. His heart even seemed to grow a new chamber, expanding to heretofore unknown proportions.

Cast from the nest, he walked out into the world to test his wings. Whom would he meet? And should he tell someone about the vision of war that had first woken him to this new glory?

Though he didn't dare question his new gift directly, he hoped along the way there would be one, just one logical and reassuring voice, to assure him he'd not gone mad.

Chapter Four

Beatrice felt that her mind and body were suddenly, drastically different. No, they were still distinctly her own but . . . they were more. She was suddenly more. And so were the four people standing before her. On the ground floor, in a side portico of Abu Serge, were four young strangers all staring at one another as if they'd seen not one but a thousand ghosts. Perhaps, she realized, they had.

Beatrice stared at each in turn, first at a young man in robes she thought was possibly Sufi; her father had educated her on local cultural dress. Beside him stood a round-cheeked, buxom girl dressed in something quite French, her face white as a sheet. A tall British boy with strawberry blond hair stood close to this girl's left—he had to be British with those at once handsome and utterly ungainly features, and last was a stunning young woman with golden skin. Beatrice recognized her.

Her father had insisted she attend church with him here, for while Abu Serge's Coptic service was a world away from the Church of England, he had satisfied himself that it was Christian. Beatrice didn't care one way or another; she'd developed a fondness for the building and for watching those who worshipped within. She'd seen the girl here but never spoken to her; their worlds had felt so very different, even though this space should have brought them together.

The quintet all looked at one another in alarm. Beatrice finally asked, "What's going on?"

"Haven't the foggiest." The boy shrugged, his accent

confirming him British, from the north, likely, scratching his head.

The youth in dark Sufi robes spoke up, in Arabic. He said that he was suddenly seeing ghosts. He grinned as if excited.

Beatrice replied, her Arabic nearly perfect. "I saw a ghost, too." She choked on her words. "I just lost my . . . my beloved. He just . . . died."

The golden-skinned girl stepped forward. "I'm so sorry," she said in faltering English. After a moment: "I'm Verena. Verena Gayed."

"Verena like the saint," Beatrice murmured, clearing her throat and straightening her body. Unraveling would not do. The girl smiled proudly and nodded.

"George," the Brit murmured, taking the cue for introductions.

"Belle," said the girl beside him in a thick French accent, looking nervously up at George. The boy blushed, and all of him was suddenly as red as parts of his hair.

The young man in Sufi robes smiled beatifically. "And I'm Ahmed. My eyes are open now to wondrous things." His radiant expression faded. "I've seen terrible things too, though, and I hope to gain their meaning." After a moment he said, "We're missing one. We are supposed to be six, aren't we?"

It was true. Beatrice felt a sense of these young men and women gathered from all walks of the city. She could feel them like echoes of her own heartbeat, and there was one thrum more distant than the rest, as if it was getting closer.

"Come." Ahmed gestured. "We must await the sixth."

Not knowing what else to do, they all followed. Out the front door of the church they traipsed, and turned down a lane in a spot with a mosque equidistant. Their small circle was comprised of different faiths, and it seemed important to recognize both. But also, to remain unseen.

A thousand questions and concerns fled Beatrice's mind

when she sensed the strong persona that neared, and with it came a sinking sensation that her life was about to change profoundly yet again.

"I'm here," said a rich voice in Arabic.

Beatrice could not deny it. He was a tall, golden-skinned youth in a long, fine tunic, the sixth of their coterie. His gleaming black hair was neatly trimmed but curled around his ears beneath a beige cap. He was, she admitted, distressingly handsome, and his wide black eyes immediately pierced her to the core.

He released her from his weighty stare and took in the rest of the company. "My name is Ibrahim Wasil. I was led to you by an angel."

Around that same corner she came, all light and colour, the same creature who had comforted Beatrice earlier, and Beatrice could feel the others hold their breath at her approach.

"Hello, my beloveds," she said, her quiet voice a compelling music.

Beatrice wanted to scream for everyone and everything to stop, that nothing made sense. The world was spinning too quickly; these new things happening inside her were not tenable, not when her heart was broken. She needed a moment to—

"Leader," the multicoloured angel prompted, staring at her. "Your fire."

Beatrice stared back. What on earth did the woman mean?

"Oh, look!" Verena breathed, staring at Beatrice's hands.

Beatrice looked down to find that her hands were glowing blue. Cerulean fire wreathed them, fire apparently harmless to her skin. It was cool, energizing, tingling and full of song. The voice in her mind had said she would carry fire, but for what purpose? What did it do?

The moment she needed to clear her mind was apparently not to be granted. Instead, a wind whipped up, and Beatrice's blood froze in recognition: this wind was violent—a murderer . . . No. Jean had been precariously balanced and foolish, standing there on that ledge telling her she was too intelligent for her own good. The wind could not be blamed for his death. And, suddenly he seemed very far away. A whole lifetime apart.

She stretched out her hand, moving her fingers in amazement as azure flame danced about their tips.

The angel gestured, insistent. "Leader, send forth your fire to open the sacred space."

Beatrice set her jaw. If she was being called a leader and held fire in her hand, she might as well do as this supernatural being instructed; any heretofore unknown powers were about as sensible as every other mad thing happening at present. She cast her arm forward, and a door appeared where there had been none before.

The company jumped. The portal was tall, and beyond was dim; this was a doorway that hovered in midair, bordered by hieroglyphs written in shimmering blue fire. Then light beckoned them downward, inviting. Stairs appeared.

Beatrice had cast fire from her hand and opened an impossible, two-dimensional door into another world. A part of her trembling body wanted to faint, but she was too fascinated to dare lose consciousness. Had she not, in some way, asked for this? Had she not always hoped her destiny would be grander than that of an everyday Englishwoman?

"The sacred space is neither here nor there," the angel spoke up. "It is eternal, and it exists only for you. Its time and dimension are relative. So, come. Join me."

Ahmed was the first into the void. He practically charged. Beatrice threw a hand forward as if to halt him, but gasped as an arc of flame leaped to life around all the rest of their feet. It licked harmlessly at the hems of their garments while joining them in a circle of flame.

"We've bloody all gone stark raving mad," George murmured. Beatrice was glad someone else had been brave enough to say it.

"Come!" called Ahmed's voice from below. "It's beautiful!" he added in English.

"I don't know what's down there. Mr. Wasil, do you?" Beatrice asked the last member of their party. She spoke in Arabic. When the dark-haired youth shook his head, Beatrice turned to the prismatic woman. "How do we know it is safe? If I am Leader, am I not now responsible for these persons' welfare?"

"You are," came the reply, "and it pleases me to hear it. This place exists to keep you safe."

Beatrice waited for more, but the angel did not continue. "That isn't an answer," she protested.

"I'm afraid you'll have to grow accustomed to that." The multicoloured woman loosed a strangely bitter laugh.

Though her words caused them uneasiness, the group moved to the threshold. It hummed with energy, and they heard it singing. They were glancing in perplexity at one another when they heard Ahmed's gasp. He appeared below and ran back up the stairs.

"Come!" he insisted. "It's truly grand!"

It was hard to say no to Ahmed's enthusiasm, or to his ineffably contagious smile. Giving a communal shrug, the more reticent members of the party descended with him into the darkness.

The six found themselves in a circular stone room lined with pillars and lit by the light shining through a great bird above shaped from stained glass and mosaic tiles, a fiery halo constructed around its feathers. Beatrice, Ahmed, George, Belle, Ibrahim and Verena stared up at it, gaping. Beyond the pillars lurked a thick darkness that seemed to pulse and shift in the same way stars shimmer in a nighttime sky.

The colourful angel had followed them down, and she stood beaming at the foot of the stairs. "What are you?" Beatrice demanded of her. Verena and Belle looked over as if her tone had been too sharp. Beatrice closed her eyes, fighting a wave of anxiety. "Please tell us."

The creature eyed them singly, staring as if examining each of their souls. "Given your collective backgrounds, you may feel most comfortable thinking of me as an angel. I'm certainly not human, though I feel as you feel and care as you care. I even bleed like you bleed, almost. I've been called many things, and truly names don't matter. The Guards that have come before you call me their Lady, out of affection. But of all my names, Persephone is my favourite."

Their young eyes blinked away many seconds of silence. George coughed in discomfort, his cheeks again red. Everything the six thought they knew was now being redefined. Moreover, though she had not said so, none of them could quite get past the feeling of being near a goddess.

"Why have you called us?" Ibrahim asked.

"For The Grand Work," the woman replied, in Arabic much like his own. But her words echoed in translation to the rest.

Beatrice, while compelled by this divine figure, was also confused and upset by her. She felt Ibrahim's cool and intense gaze alternating between Persephone and herself, and it was a gaze fraught with both distrust and attraction. Beatrice resisted the urge to look back.

Ahmed spoke up. "What is that?" he asked. "What is your commission?"

His words resonated off the walls, were translated from Arabic to French to English. It was as if the room knew them, or was learning them. This place was alive with all of their hearts and souls.

The goddess threw forward a hand, her lovely face grimacing as if the act hurt her dearly. It was not without effect, however, and a black square became a rectangle and then a doorway. Another doorway in the air. Portals within portals, was this an endless iteration?

"Look. Learn," the goddess said. "But never go in."

Through the doorway were long corridors, each dark and dank. Endlessly grey. Beyond were whispers and murmurs, if nothing intelligible. But there were shades. There were hundreds—no, *thousands*—of shades, each floating listlessly down the endless corridors. Death. It was death, and so much of it.

Then, deep down one corridor, a moving shadow drew close. Tall, it had a vaguely human form, but it glided with unearthly grace. With it came dread, rancor, decay, it wore all of these like a cloak. Red, burning eyes glowed in its tenebrous face, two terrible lamps that Beatrice was sure would cause madness if stared at for long.

There came a hiss. At the base of the corridor opened hundreds of red eyes, as if something had just woken up to see them. There followed a terrible, dread growling, and such despair, such darkness, it was too much.

"What is that?" Beatrice exclaimed. Glancing at her companions, she found them pale, all colour drained from their faces, and shivering with fright.

"That is Darkness," replied Persephone, and they all heard the venom in her voice.

She twisted her arm, drew her hand into a powerful fist, and with a ripping sound the portal snapped shut. Beatrice and her companions could breathe normally once more.

"He and his desires are what you fight. Fear him and his domain, but do not fear your Grand Work. Here, on Earth, you have power. You are the mortal arbiters between life and death. You have gifts, each of you, to help."

She turned to Beatrice. "You, Beatrice Smith, are the Leader. As you know."

Beatrice's face remained expressionless, though her nostrils flared. Her posture straightened in the way her mother—resting in peace—had always required. She set her jaw. While she wasn't sure about Persephone, she was certain that, because she was a woman, if she didn't accept the title of leader with authority and confidence, the rest would share her lack of faith. They wouldn't be able to help it. This was a life-changing moment, Beatrice realized, and she determined to accept it. She set all fear of madness aside and accepted the mantle of power.

Whatever had taken residence within her also reacted to this call. Suddenly, all fears of a purposeless existence were gone as well.

Persephone turned to Verena. "The Healer. You will all face draining spirits, some of whom are truly dangerous. They will manifest violence upon those they've subjected to their possession. You will need Verena's hand."

Verena lifted her hand in amazement. It glowed with a faint, warm light that limned her golden skin and glinted in her dark eyes, heightening her already prominent beauty. Still, there was a fear in her that the girl didn't bother to mask. Beatrice couldn't blame her. Only one hour ago they had been normal mortals going about their daily lives. In an instant, it seemed they were the agents of the gods and they would soon look every moment upon death.

Persephone turned to Ahmed, who was staring at Verena in awe. "And you, Ahmed. The Heart." The Sufi smiled widely, his expression as radiant as the Healer's hand. The other five found themselves smiling in conjunction, even though they hadn't thought it possible in their odd circumstance. His joy was, as his smile, contagious.

"How do you know our names?" Ibrahim asked, his tone careful.

"Because you are my beloveds. You are the chosen. The

Muses, my old friends, chose you to join with my love to fight hungry Darkness, who would blanket the earth with his miserable, restless dead. They are ancient forces, and they have selected you to help them. I will help you in return." She gazed kindly at Ibrahim. "You, Ibrahim, are Intuition. You will be the first to feel the Pull, the exact point of each spiritual disturbance. You are your Leader's right hand. Your clarion voice, and your strength, will be critical in the fight."

Ibrahim turned toward Beatrice, his face blank. He was withholding both judgment and, she couldn't help but feel, acceptance.

"You, George, are the Artist. Evil won't acknowledge the importance of art. Make it."

George opened his mouth, blushed again, and closed it.

"Belle." Persephone turned to the round-cheeked girl, speaking now in French that was translated by the walls. "You are the Memory. Our mentalist. You will alter the recollections of those affected by malevolent spirits. You will turn the innocent away from poltergeists and terrors they ought not see, wipe their minds with but a wish. You shall find that you can see each past with but a touch, and your will works wonders upon others. You allow your fellows to move more easily through this world. Take care with this gift."

The young Frenchwoman nodded, a host of varied emotions playing over her face.

"How long are we in your service?" Ibrahim asked. Again, his tone was careful.

"You're not in my service. You are in the service of mortality, in the service of all life triumphant over death. You are soldiers of this world against the onslaught of the next, and you'll be soldiers until the Muses decide it is time to release you." The divinity's tone was matter-of-fact, easy off the tongue, as if she'd said the words many times before.

"What if we refuse service?" Beatrice asked. She was not

doing so but was simply curious. Out of the corner of her eye, she noticed that Ibrahim's lips twitched, either disturbed or heartened by her boldness; she couldn't guess which.

Persephone smiled. "Would you rather answer to him?" With a violent gesture, she ripped open the portal again. Those terrible eyes, the weighty dread, the utter, soul-sapping misery. Nightmare walked there. Nightmare was born there . . . *No!* No, she did not want to answer to that.

"That's enough," Beatrice said, seeing how her companions save Ibrahim quailed.

Persephone closed the portal with a fluid gesture, satisfaction on her face. "Then go forth. You'll know when you're needed. And you can return to this place—known only to you, made only for you—to renew your flagging spirits. Bless you for your work. This world needs you. Otherwise Darkness will take over, city by city, land by land. If his minions are not checked . . . Believe me, none of us want that fate."

Ibrahim glanced uncomfortably at Beatrice, but his words were to them all. "There is an oath upon my lips; I feel a burning need to speak it. What has taken up residence within us demands that I offer this incantation, but when I do so, I assume it cannot be undone. It may bind us eternally to these forces within. I do not know if we have a choice in this destiny, or what that destiny entails, so I'll not say this oath if any here object."

"You are wise, Intuition," Persephone murmured after the walls had finished translating his words. "Sensible and measured, you should rightly ask such questions of those who serve with you. And of those who command you. Your minds and hearts shall be sorely taxed, and so you must understand *why.*" She made her way to the centre of the sacred space, onto a spot where a great feather carved in the floor reflected her colours. "Let me show you how the Great Vendetta began, why The Grand Work is *my* war. Thus can it be yours."

She opened her palms wide. Suddenly the six saw through her eyes, and felt with her heart more powerfully than all human hearts combined. She showed them her history, channeling it from her soul into theirs. They experienced that horrific memory she relived every day of her divine existence, and their very essence bled in remorse. Darkness was guilty of vile, unforgivable deeds indeed, and they could help keep him in his place. They would join this sacred fight.

Beatrice felt the vision, and her connection to it, fade back to the cool air of their sacred space. She shook herself, traumatized further after what had already been too much. Without the new force inhabiting her, this sacred fire, the day's events would be certainly enough to sunder wits. Her companions all wept.

Persephone wept as well, her tears liquid silver like mercury. They fell and merged with the blue fire that threaded the floor, seeped into the stones, strengthening them, making the place entirely more luminous and full of resolve. This sacred space was built by tears, perhaps. Beatrice could imagine nothing else.

The goddess walked among them once more. "Fire, light and love shall fight against shadow, misery and eternal restlessness. We can never eliminate the enemy wholly, for misery clings stubbornly to the human soul. But we can keep the Balance just to this side of the light. To let Darkness tip the scales is to lose every last mortal mind. So take to your duty, *please,* and wield the powers we have given you. Do so for all of your kind."

"Say the oath of The Guard, Mr. Wasil. Please," Beatrice murmured. She and the rest of them had stood. "I doubt any of us has the capability to walk away."

Ibrahim cleared his throat. His words were choked. "Tipton. Ibrahim Wasil-*Tipton.*"

Beatrice cocked her head. "I'm sorry?"

"My name. It's Ibrahim Wasil-Tipton. James Tipton was not my birth father, but he took me in. Before I came here, I was wondering who I should be. Now I know. I shall take his name, for he was a good and an honourable man. As I make an oath to fight on the side of angels, I do so in the name of the man of faith who died today." Ibrahim turned to the goddess, and his face was that of one who had seen great loss. "He, too, died in fire. Unfairly."

"But you, my beloved, were spared," the goddess said.

The others were nodding in empathy, and she turned to them. "All of you were chosen for a reason your Muses know more than I. Some of you would not have lived had you not been chosen. Some of you would have lived much different lives." She glanced at Beatrice, her face grave. "Some of you asked for there to be more, and I hope you remember that. For what The Grand Work demands of you, you must give. But now I must go. As deeply as I regret it, the Whisper-world has its hooks in me, and to struggle is to prolong my agony."

Ahmed spoke, using a mixture of Arabic and a new tongue that they all recognized as intrinsically their own, a language of friends, the language of The Guard. "And you—why do *you* not choose a human host and join the fight? If the Muses did so, couldn't you? Would you not then be free?"

There was a profound helplessness on the divinity's face. "Ah! You, great Heart, you feel mine. You feel how I ache to love again. How I ache to be held again. But for me to come here . . . it would not be the same as the Muses. I've never been mortal, and I'm terrified of it."

She had a sudden thought, and her sad face brightened almost madly. "We have fought Darkness for so long, and in the same way, but . . . we have begun a new age. A gilded one. It may be time to move against Darkness at last. Who can tell? There have been odd shiftings in the Liminal."

While her words made little sense, the shifting colours of

her face made the goddess's emotions more profoundly visible. Her eyes sparkled with a sudden playful delight that Beatrice found so inviting she supposed it must have the power to enslave mortal men, though Persephone seemed too innocent to use it so. Or perhaps she was too distracted to remember how.

"Be well, beloveds, call upon the Power and the Light, and they shall aid you. I shall return, yet until then you must fight on your own."

She opened her palm. That dark maw of that shadowed, whispering world opened once more, a portal with dank shadows beyond and the murmurs of pain from thousands of years. Goodness, did she really live in that hellish darkness? It was clear she did not want to return.

Persephone turned her head and coughed as demurely as she could, but a spot of red dribbled from the corner of her lip. Blood? Was she ill? The goddess turned again, suddenly earnest, her face that of an excited child as she addressed her newfound friends. Yes, it was blood on her lip. That drop fell to the stone floor where it vanished, but when she took a deep breath, The Guard heard her lungs rattle.

"You'll forgive me, won't you? You'll allow me a moment of beauty before I go back? " she begged, then gave an odd, off-balance laugh. "I shouldn't, time ticks and so does Darkness. But to walk the streets among you dear human beings, to feel the pulse of the Earth, how its beauty sustains me . . . How I love you mortals and the marvels you create! I'll go and look upon something grand, something awe inspiring, before I turn my face to shadow once more."

She threw her shining garments over her body and vanished. Presumably, Beatrice decided, to Giza.

Chapter Five

Beatrice reeled from the divinity's sudden shifts of mood and intention, and the room seemed suddenly empty for the lack of her.

Ibrahim stepped into the breach. Clearing his throat, the young man began the oath he'd been pondering. Much like a call to prayer, it was clarion and regal, but it was in the language of The Guard and formed from those raw, seminal moments they'd watched through Persephone's divine eyes, writ now into their communal memory: "In darkness; a door. In bound souls; a circle of fire. Immortal force in mortal hearts. Six to calm the restless dead. Six to shield the restless living."

"The Power and the Light," Beatrice murmured.

"The Power and the Light!" her new fellows chorused.

No, Beatrice, she urged herself, hearing their unity. *Say it like a Leader.*

"The Power and the Light!" she cried, and she felt the whole of her body surge with pleasure and power. It was as if the very phoenix above was proud of her exclamation and warmed her with the hearth in its wings. There came a formidable result: Cerulean fire rose around them, leaping from the floor to burst high into the air. Chords of heavenly music tuned by stars roared in their ears, and the hearts of the six burned hot and intense; there was no other moment in the world but this, no other force, no other reason for living.

It was a delirious, beautiful sensibility that Beatrice didn't want to end. It was a moment that defined and defied existence, as close as she would come to heaven without dying. In this fire, by this light, they had become demigods. They would walk this land of Isis and Osiris, among the sands of ancients, banner-bearers of the culture's ancient god. They were being reborn here, and with them, Phoenix. Once more an old mythology was being made new. In their image. In their blood. In their hearts. For she was still Beatrice Smith. She was also *more.* They all were.

They bathed in the sort of warm light one imagines from heaven, that which banishes the darkest nights of the soul, and only Guardians of Time could know how long they stood drinking in this ambrosia. When at last the symphony of stars hushed to a whisper, when the column of celestial light faded and the sacred space became hazy blue-grey again, when the stained-glass bird was only dimly luminescent, not ablaze like a sun, they all stared at one another.

"That was right bloody incredible," George exclaimed.

Ahmed laughed, which gave all of them permission to join in. There was really nothing else to be done. In indescribable wonder, a strange family had been born.

Belle addressed them, her voice tremulous but clear, and brought them back to reality. "We'll need to go to our families one by one. We're not likely company, so we need to make introductions. Moreover, we need to come and go as we please. My gift urges me to make us transparent to those we love: we must become ghosts in our own lives so that The Grand Work is never undermined by the particulars of mortal life. It . . . it will not be easy."

They each stated the location of their homes, and Beatrice began sorting out an order in which to visit. Ibrahim was last to speak, and they turned to him, awaiting his answer.

"I've nowhere to go," he said in softly accented English. "I told you before. My house burned this morning, and the man who raised me. I have no one else and nowhere to go."

Beatrice felt her face grow hot with embarrassment. "Of course, I'm sorry." They were fellows in loss. Fresh loss.

When he stepped away from the group, deflecting all pity, Beatrice couldn't help moving forward and speaking for his ears alone. "I lost my betrothed this morning. This very morning. We are brother and sister in loss, Ibrahim Tipton," she stated.

Murmurs of apology flew from the others, though they had not heard her words. She felt Belle's hand reach out, trying to make a connection with a sister, attempting sympathy through touch. How could such terrible and wonderful things happen so suddenly? Did she truly now have such good friends who could feel her pain without words? And, when would she grieve for Jean? Would The Grand Work let her?

Ibrahim stared at her. "We are not related," he replied. His tone was cool, though she could tell he did not intend to be rude; he was simply stating fact. "We cannot truly know how one another feels. Despite what's happened here, hearts are too private, too individual. Do not assume."

Beatrice was stung. She straightened her shoulders and turned to walk away, almost careening into the figure who had approached them from behind.

It was Ahmed. "Ibrahim, our family has a spare room. I know they would gladly take you in, and Belle's powers can assure it. What say you, brother?"

Ibrahim nodded. "Thank you," he murmured.

Beatrice thought she saw emotion in his eyes, and she bristled. Ahmed, with that shining, engaging face that could warm the coldest stone, he could call Ibrahim brother and she could not. Why? Perhaps because she was a woman and not of his race. She was an invader, and female; even supernatural circumstances could not change that. Why, then, of all people, did he have to be her second-in-command? Why was she Leader? Such a pairing seemed ill-suited.

The group was quiet as they traversed the city that afternoon.

One by one, home by home, they made dutiful stops. First came the stately rooms where Belle had been raised as an only child, and the dazed, comely matron who was her mother.

"Bonjour, Maman—et au revoir," the French girl said softly, tears streaming down her face. The others stood in the doorway, watching. Belle shook badly until Verena stepped forward, placing a hand on her shoulder. Then Belle spoke with mounting confidence. There was an aura of light about her. Magic was at hand.

"These are my friends, and I have a new purpose. I shall come and go as I please. As will these friends. We here obey new masters, not those of our respective households. We will do The Grand Work without question. You will not stop us."

"Of course, daughter," Mrs. Montmare agreed, her eyes fluttering under the weight of magic being worked. "None shall stand in your way."

Next came Ahmed's family's simple, tidy flat. The announcement was much the same, though in the Basri residence Ahmed added the introduction of Ibrahim like a new relation. He was greeted with polite distance and an invitation to stay. Ibrahim's face was emotionless, but he bowed and thanked the family with what Beatrice recognized as genuine sincerity.

En route to George's home, which was farther south, Beatrice, still feeling a bit disjointed and rebuffed, determined that as Leader it was her duty to rise above any personal affront. In order to coordinate her new battalion, she needed to know the various needs of each member. "Mr. Wasil-Tipton," she began. "Do you imagine there will be services for your father? Would you like us to arrange something? Is there a way we may be of help?"

The group paused, not wanting to seem insensitive by journeying on without contemplation. Who could be sure what Ibrahim was thinking, other than perhaps Ahmed with his new talents? His face was like a mask.

"I appreciate the sentiment," he replied. "I believe the university will have a memorial. But truly, with this odd destiny, I don't believe I shall go. If I'm thought dead, isn't it better I remain so? All of you, look what we're doing here. You're all becoming ghosts to your families. So shall I be to the world."

They all reflected on his words. This single day had aged them all by years.

They began again down the street. As they did, Verena hurried to catch Beatrice, whose long strides made it difficult. "And your . . . companion? What of him? Can we do something for you? For him?"

Beatrice felt all eyes upon her. She choked back a wave of tears, grief just under the surface but recently supplanted by fear, power, wonder—at leadership, at their new language— and myriad other sensations. "No, I . . . I'm sure Jean's family will take care of . . . I'm not sure I want to see the body. I witnessed his ghost move on. That will suffice. No one knew we were together today, and I daresay he was prone enough to trouble that his death mightn't be a complete surprise. Now, enough on that. George, how much farther?"

"Another few streets," George replied. "Just south of the square here."

It did not take long for Ibrahim's stride, similarly long-legged, to bring him abreast of her. "I should have asked after you in turn," he said. "I am sorry."

Beatrice shrugged. "We've all had a trying day, to say the least. We must forgive any slights."

He evaluated her expression, seemed satisfied that she meant her words, and fell back to walk beside Ahmed.

The Sufi took one look at him, murmured an Arabic benediction about grief and placed a hand over his heart. Beatrice glanced back to see this happen, and she was surprised by Ibrahim's reaction.

"That's wondrous," the young man breathed. "Offer it to Miss Smith, too."

The Sufi did, and Ibrahim was right. Ahmed's jolt of healing power enveloped grief, lifted it free from the body and gazed at it subjectively, as one might examine a captured dove. Then it set it free with open hands.

"Thank you," Beatrice breathed.

"My pleasure," Ahmed replied, and they all knew that was true.

A fine residential complex housed the Tyler household. The Guard were mostly without siblings, but George had a brother, Bob, who was sour in contrast. Beatrice was glad she'd gotten George of the two. She also wondered if some distinct quality, of either leadership or independence, was more present in only children. Or perhaps they'd been selected as such so that there would be fewer persons to whom they would become ghosts.

"None shall stand in your way," echoed George's parents and brother, as had Ahmed's and Belle's mothers. Ahmed's father had gone to the mosque, a meeting with his Sufi teacher that Ahmed should also have attended, but each of The Guard now had a new faith, a new demand and claim upon them in addition to their old beliefs, and that claim was perhaps more immediately relevant than rigorously learning written scripture.

"None shall stand in your way," said Leonard Smith when his daughter at last clasped his hand.

It was odd, because she had always feared her father *would* stand in her way, would oppose her desire for a career, would pack her off somewhere, would find her help at grave sites or in academia unladylike. While she had no doubt he loved her, she had never been sure if that love wasn't, in part, conditional. Now, apparently, the only conditions were those of The Grand Work.

"These are my new friends," she had said, gesturing to the

other five as she tried to keep her voice level and strong. "We shall come and go as we please. All will be well." Her dazed father simply nodded and returned to his desk, a wide wooden surface ever piled with papyrus, beads and shards of clay.

Her heart ached. The closeness she and her father had known when she was little would never be regained. Perhaps it had fled years before and she was only now seeing the distance. But there was no time for sentimentalism, for that was the first time they felt the Pull.

★ ★ ★

Within the endless layers of shadow that made up the Whisper-world, around Darkness's throne flocked his minions. His favourites tended their master, who was in a foul mood. He'd drawn dread curtains to sit entirely wreathed in blackness, his robes thick around him, no outside light penetrating. Red eyes blinked slowly, two deadly rubies glinting in the darkness.

Outside paced his dog, one pair then two hundred bloodred eyes glimmering to life; less like precious jewels than its master's, their shifting numbers glowed more with fire than intelligence. The guardian creature drooled and whined, shifted its protean form, became a roiling mist, flickered, then again became a hundred-headed hound. Bored, Darkness tore open the curtain and tossed the hound bones that clattered onto the dais below. The mass of vaguely canine heads pounced. Countless teeth gnawed the offering, those infinite fangs now and then gleaming in a bit of reflected light.

"Just let me follow her," Luce the Gorgon whined nearby, folding her arms over the swaths of black fabric wrapped around her lithe body and head. Onyx snakes writhed beneath, hissed and snapped beneath her thin veil. "Let me prove myself to you."

"Leave. Me. Alone," was Darkness's reply, a low murmur in his usual halting cadence, thick and wet, the sound of storms.

"It isn't going to get any better. It's been centuries," Luce said in a conversational tone that seemed out of place in such bleak surroundings. "You'll not break her until you find whatever she's hiding. She disappears places. I think she's got something she'd like you not to know about. Some private treasure."

"She'll hate me. All the more. If I begin rooting around," Darkness replied. Robes shifted. Bones clicked together as Darkness adjusted.

"She'll never *not* hate you," Luce replied. "She always has."

The shadows moved, a whiplike thrash at nothing in particular that hit some sad passing spirit who wailed in pain. Luce could hear Darkness's teeth grind.

"*I* don't hate you." She sashayed up to where the shadows were thickest and knelt before him, running her hands up into the impenetrable blackness. "I adore you," she murmured, fumbling blindly at his robes. When visible, they were bright crimson, the only colour in this grey wasteland. That, and *her* wretched colours. Persephone.

"I. Am aware. Of your sentiments," Darkness replied, and the shadows kicked her away.

Luce scowled. "You're a fool."

"You. Are brash. For a servant."

"How else can I lift myself in your esteem?" the Gorgon asked. "It isn't like the olden days. We're all falling apart, us great ones. We're splintering. We're weakening. Humanity slips farther from our command. She's beyond hope, all mewling and retching. This may be her last century before she's nothing but pulp. You remember, just mortal decades ago, when she bled herself all over these stones in that pathetic attempt to break free, to end it—"

Darkness whipped his robes and shadows again, this

time casting Luce backward upon the stone. "Of course. I remember."

"Well, it could have consequences," Luce said, unruffled, picking herself up and glaring at his tall and potent form, at the red fires of his eyes. "Her pathetic attempt unwittingly opened huge holes in your kingdom. Who knows what, in her desperation, her powers might do? You must admit that she was never meant for this place, would stop at nothing to destroy it if she knew how. She's nothing but a hindrance—"

"STAND. DOWN," Darkness roared. Luce cringed and retreated, expecting to be struck. But she was not. Instead, Darkness beat his chest, rattled his bones; he turned his despair inward. The water of the nearby river crested, and its murmuring voices wailed and wept. "She is beloved of the dead!" he wailed. "And why shouldn't light couple with shadow! We are two sides, day and night! Together since time began!"

"*Separated* since time began," Luce insisted calmly. "Day departs. Night takes over. They cannot sit side by side. You are of one kind, she is of another. Her light hurts you, does not strengthen you. Your darkness decays her. Isn't it obvious it's a poor match after all these years? *I* am of your kind. I am trying to help you!"

"Why. Do. You. Insist? You torture me with your words," Darkness muttered.

Luce dared again to kneel at his feet, to again place herself partly into his abyss. "My liege. You've lost your strength. I hardly recognize the master I came to serve. You might want to start listening to me rather than wallowing in self-pity like all the spirits you command. Leave *them* to miserable uselessness. You're meant for something greater. You need to remind them all that you're the lord of the land; that light, in the end, bows to shadow. All life ends in darkness."

Darkness growled, and Luce breathed, delighted at the sound.

"If," the shadows rumbled. "I have my way. It ends. With me."

Chapter Six

The Guard stood outside Leonard Smith's apartments on the busy Cairo street, the sun dipping behind the minaret-spiked skyline. Beatrice last, the six of them were fully detached from the various watchful eyes of their families. The afternoon had seen it done in one fell swoop, but now Beatrice felt an odd rustling in her blood, a burning sensation that had her itching to move.

There was no time to question, to grieve, to scream, to run; there was only time to think what must be done. The new physical sensation felt like a sandstorm under her skin, a gathering of disparate elements into a whirling vortex. A pin on an inner map.

"What is this?" George exclaimed, clutching at his heart. "Tell me you all feel something, else I'm dying before you at the tender age of eighteen."

Belle laughed nervously.

Ibrahim shook his head and spoke with quiet confidence Beatrice admired. "The Balance is like a tapestry. When a thread pulls, we feel it. When a member of the restless dead tears free from that fabric, we must smooth it down once more. West," he instructed. "We move west. The Work begins."

They followed their Intuition past a bustling market square teeming with people, glittering with wares and fabrics, reeking of scents, and at last they found a young man floating in an alley. A boy entirely supine but airborne. He was luminous.

Belle shrieked. Beatrice moved in front of her, placing

herself in the spectre's line of sight, and she was the first to enter the alley. It wasn't that she wanted to see this abomination any more than Belle, but her instinct told her that this was her proving ground and she must rise to its challenge.

Ahmed held out his hand to Belle, a gesture not to worry, and he smiled. The French girl's shoulders immediately eased, as did everyone else's. Ahmed's joy was potent magic.

"You each have a gift," Beatrice instructed, using the sort of voice that made people turn and listen. Surprising her, they did. "And we each have an instinct. Use it. Now."

She whirled toward the floating boy and flung out her hands. In them, phoenix fire was instantly ready and eager to be wielded. It flowed from her hands, seemingly knowing what to do. The flame enveloped the youngster's hovering form like a bubble of water, and the boy's possessor became visible.

Ibrahim reached into the new and vast library of his mind. He chose scripture from the Quran and spoke it bravely, directing his words at the demon above. Clearly, the boy's inhabitant was displeased. The offending spirit strained and thrashed inside the youth's skin, tearing at the dusty linen of his long tunic and frayed vest, turning the boy's honey-brown skin a pallid grey, threatening to transform him into a ghost before their very eyes.

Verena gasped. From the look on her face, the entwined beings clearly horrified her, yet the living victim's obvious pain drew her forward and she reached out to touch him. His racked body went limp when she did. Her hand was soft light, and its application was mercy.

George reacted next. Taking charcoal from his pocket, in a few swift strokes he etched the outline of a great dove. Beatrice squinted before realizing his intent. The dove was not only a picture but script, the body of the bird curved down and continued into Arabic script that read *Peace*.

"Now that is brilliant," Ahmed breathed. George beamed, his fair skin pinking, his cheeks dimpled, making him somewhat the cherub.

None of them knew precisely what they were doing. Nonetheless, instinct proved true, and Beatrice was proud in a way she had never felt: of herself, and of these strangers who were suddenly family.

The possessed boy's gaze snapped to the dove, to *Peace,* and the sight kept his eyes from rolling and his mouth from foaming. She could tell they were making progress. As well, Beatrice noticed that if she moved her hands closer together, her binding blue fire constricted the creature within him. The spirit hated its shackles.

Belle came close and touched the boy's ankle, but she hissed in pain at what she felt. Her touch was giving her insight that was clearly unpleasant. Ahmed was swift at her side, bestowing joy. He reminded them each to breathe deep, and he demonstrated, giving a soft laugh to buffer their hearts. A possession infected the air and the mind with heavy negativity.

"What did you learn, Belle?" Beatrice asked.

"It cried out from the towers and saw dumb sheep below. A muezzin, he was. But at some point he turned and sang for evil. Sang not to lure men to prayer but to depravity. Humanity, dumb sheep . . . He wanted to scare them, to turn them all. It *wants.* It hungers for so much more than this life can give . . ." She shuddered, and Ahmed's attention was again needed.

"He sang from the towers calling others to prayer," Ibrahim murmured. "And yet the creature never learned how to pray for himself. Clearly. How sad." After a moment he cleared his throat and recited:

I desire fire from Your burning sorrow,
and I want to take cover under the dust of Your
   threshold.

I am in a death struggle with my ailments
and from Your presence, I ask
a moment of happiness.

Ahmed had tears in his eyes when Ibrahim finished. "Ah,
Rumi! Well chosen, friend!"

The other just bowed his head in reply.

Beatrice, gazing at Ibrahim and listening to his recitation
of the beloved Sufi poet, had let her fire slip. The beast within
the boy wrestled more violently, flailing against the sense and
beauty of the poetry. She scowled and squeezed her fists. Her
fire constricted in reaction. The boy gurgled in pain, suffering
with his possessor, but Verena placed a hand on his throat and
his choking eased.

Belle had moved to the mouth of the alley and was turning
away the denizens of Cairo. At first appalled to see a boy
floating in midair, now they would move on as if touched by
nothing unusual.

"Cantus," Beatrice said, her mind full of song. Her powers
commanded the conclusion of this rite.

"Which?" Ahmed asked, surprised by the question. It was
indeed surprising to find a new language upon your lips, a
songbook as well. Their work came replete with hymns, and
their fluid teamwork suggested they'd toiled together for
centuries. Whatever guided them had.

"Quietus," Beatrice replied, with no choice but to trust
her newfound instincts. This poor young man was not the
only one possessed. They all were. Of course, The Guard was
possessed by the powers of Light, and she far preferred those to
the glimpse the goddess had given them of the alternative.

Belle returned to the circle, Verena stepping forward as the
young boy's body seized up with pain; Beatrice was winding her
fire tighter around his limbs. They all began the cantus: a soft
melody with words formed from the root of the first human

language. They sang of a return to the simple raw materials of life, encouraged all things to abandon earthly trappings and return to the bosom of creation. Something older and wiser had formed these words. They felt eerily familiar, like a long-forgotten mother's lullaby.

It wasn't merely their voices that provided music, either; the very air was full of song. The fire was, too, and the wind that wrapped around their skirts and linens.

The muezzin's spirit exited the human body it had tried to wear, violently ripping free and causing the boy to fall to the ground. Verena and Ibrahim dove to catch his head so that it would not strike the stones. The malevolent spirit floated above, transparent and skeletal, having lost whatever humanity it might once have possessed, rags hanging from its bones.

The majority of the spirits Beatrice had seen coursing the streets were more like transparent people, appearing as they would in life, recognizable, not rotting or skeletal. Perhaps, she mused, the more intact a spirit, the less harmful. The more it wore a raw, rotting existence, the more cause for alarm.

She flung her arm forward, whipping cords of blue fire about the spectre's wrists and ankles, and it struggled like a puppet trying to free itself of strings. The creature's jaw sagged and snapped furiously, and Beatrice assumed it was speaking. She wondered if he was saying something important or just spewing vile, impotent threats. Why were they not gifted with the ability to hear as well as see the dead? She prayed the instigators of The Grand Work knew what they were about.

She tried to pull her fire tighter, unsure what should happen next. Would the spirit disappear, break apart? Turn to dust or mist? How would they know when they had won?

The ghost threw its head back as if to wail. Loose bricks in the alley trembled. The creature broke from its phoenix-fire bonds and spun upward, floating high to a turret, to a mosque's minaret where it played muezzin again to whatever would listen. Still they could hear nothing.

Ibrahim watched thoughtfully. "I shudder to think what sorts of calls to prayer it offers today for the dead."

"Damn," Beatrice muttered. "Quietus was not strong enough, perhaps."

"The boy is alive," Verena replied. "The cantus was good enough. But I need time with him. I feel that, with practice, I will become quicker, stronger, but—"

"None of us are experts yet," Belle said. "You did a brilliant job."

Verena smiled and glanced at Ahmed, who when he beamed back, had her practically glowing with pride.

"Wait with me a moment," the Healer bade them, "I'd like to make his skin seamless once more." She gave a slow and steady pass with her subtly lit hand over the boy's body. Her work was painstaking, for there were tiny fissures in his skin where the possessor had tried to crack him open like a shell. She had to pass her hand over him twice.

"I doubt we've seen the last of that one," Ibrahim stated, staring up where the spirit had finally disappeared.

"Why?"

Ibrahim shrugged. "Because my instinct says we haven't. And my instinct is yet to be proven wrong."

Beatrice laughed. "The Work is hardly a day old, there's plenty of time left for that." But, truth be told, she didn't mind his confidence in his powers. It more evenly distributed the massive weight of their destiny. She didn't want to have to act confident alone. She wasn't sure she could pull it off.

"What do other cities do without a Guard?" George asked as they sat around the boy waiting for Verena to finish.

"The Grand Work must move about the world, city to city, as the angel said," Ibrahim stated. "It is about balance, and the fabric of spirits is a blanket cast wide over the earth. I imagine that we are sent where the disturbances are worst."

Whether her second-in-command could respect her or not, Beatrice couldn't help but be glad he was around. He said eloquent, sensible things that made their strange new world more digestible. And he was exceedingly pleasant to look at. That would offset staring down ghostly skeletons and spectral horrors quite nicely.

"I wonder where The Guard were before us," Ahmed murmured. "I want to say in a war, but I may think that because of my vision."

No one had an answer for that.

"Well, my unlikely new friends," Beatrice said. "The lesson of the day seems most certainly 'Be careful what you wish for.' I'd been thinking I wanted more mystery and adventure in my life. I seem to have called down entirely more that I bargained for."

"And yet you led the charge. *Leader,*" Ahmed stated, and then he gestured to their recovering subject. "We saved a life and a fine young mind today. The first battle in The Grand Work is already won."

Beatrice was not the only one heartened. Ahmed opened his arms to them all; his smile was still pure contagion. Embattling that skeletal hatred, insanity that drives souls to suicide and madness had lingering effects, and mortals could not help but be rattled by it. But Ahmed's joy moved like a bright lamp among them, rallying his fellows to appreciate the wonders they had wrought.

The boy stirred. His eyes fluttered open. He stared at the dove that read *Peace.*

Belle moved close. "It was all a terrible dream," she murmured in French-accented Arabic. The boy's eyes clouded, as if the memory of the event were being removed. Then he sat up, blinked, stood and wandered off toward whatever business he had abandoned when first overtaken. The Guard watched him go, six silent companions atop the hard stones of an ancient alley.

"I'm starving," George stated suddenly. He grinned. "Belle, persuade some fine café to feed us, else we'll make sure they're haunted forever."

They all stood and brushed themselves off. As they did, Beatrice noticed a tiny excitement in her fellows' expressions, as if they were all thinking the same thing: without their families or any attachments, wasn't this great responsibility more of a great adventure?

Chapter Seven

Persephone sighed as the portal shut behind her. She was again bound to a world of shadow. This damnable purgatory that she was never meant to live inside would yet drive her mad, its wailings and whispers, those eternal regrets voiced in endless repetition. And its king. She heard his tread. Nearby. There was no avoiding him. A footstep, a scrape. A footstep, a scrape. Flesh, then bone. Tick . . . tock. Life. Death. Each in the blink of an eye.

But she was first accosted by the needy.

"My Lady," came the sad voice of a rotting female in clothing that may have been Puritan. Or perhaps she'd been a nun; it was austere and black and absorbed all of Persephone's shifting radiance. The spirit collapsed at her feet, kissing the pale posies that bloomed then rotted there as she walked, that tried to bloom again but failed. Persephone felt tears wash her feet and water the dead and fallen petals.

"What is your name, spirit?" she asked, bending to touch the wretch upon the cheek. In doing so, she lifted the ghost to its feet.

"Maria."

"Why do you weep?"

"I cannot quit the darkness, it will not quit me. There is blackness in my soul."

"Maria," Persephone commanded. "Look at me."

The grey, shuddering spirit did so. Her eyes were cataract-covered sockets.

"Maria. *Choose* to quit the darkness. The blackness only wins if you let it."

"Show me light, my Lady, show me light!"

The spirit's cries were hungry and desperate, and Persephone had to hush them. If the ghost went on like that, half of this purgatory would flock here and devour her whole with their misery and need. She closed her eyes and felt her bosom burn. Her light cost her nothing outside in the mortal world but here it caused great pain. This place had begun to slowly eat away at her insides; her divine form had been rotting for centuries, soured from within and corrupting her budding life and infinite youth. Yet, she opened her eyes to see the shifting rainbow of her life force clear the cataracts from Maria's eyes.

The spirit cried out in celebration. Thoughtless, she ran past Persephone singing, hurried down a corridor that brightened from a deep dark to a pale grey, a brightening path that occasionally sparked. Maria was being drawn toward the Liminal, and from there the Liminal would send her onward. To the Great Beyond, if the spirit was cured enough. If not, perhaps she would return to a haunting on earth, another round as an observer. Or maybe she would be recycled into another human life, given one more try to get it right. Persephone wasn't ever quite sure what happened to them, these freed souls, for she had never made those rounds herself. Her own cycle was more limited.

The use of her light made Persephone cough, a sickly sound that rattled more as the years went by. Now and then she brought up blood and seeds. She spat them upon the wet floor.

She heard noise. A fleshy clap, then the click of bones. The slap of palms, the click of bones. He was here. Clapping.

"They so adore the one who hates them," came his voice, as if from across a cavern.

Persephone turned and squinted down the long corridor behind her; the shadows were tall and regal, and the red eyes of the shadow king burned within. She sighed. This conversation was always the same. Darkness adored and abhorred when she did such deeds as this. He loved that his subjects welcomed her as queen and begged her attention. He loathed that she set so many to rest.

"I have never hated them. You always think you know my heart. And you always fail."

"I know one thing."

"And that is?"

"You hate me."

"I didn't used to. I pitied you, as it wasn't your fault mankind made you from its wastes," she stated, her voice flat, the script true yet spoken so much by rote it was absurd. "Then you killed my love. Made him a ghost so that his arms will never again hold me. I will forever hate you for that."

"Promenade with me."

Persephone knew if she didn't, he'd not allow her to wander without trailing her. When she humoured him, he allowed her freedoms.

"Shall you set more of my minions free?" he asked.

She coughed again; this time fewer seeds, more blood. "I wish I could."

"I'll tell them you are indisposed."

And so king and queen walked the corridors and caverns, along the riverbank lined with skulls and trellises made of bone that the Groundskeeper created with such care. All Darkness's subjects fell at their feet, and many cried out for Persephone's touch, for her time, for her nearness, for a glance. Darkness batted them away with great sweeps of his robe. Its fabric in the ghostly light was crimson. All light was ghostly in this place save hers.

She wept because she could not help those who begged her;

her constitution was too weak. Quicksilver tears fell from her face and rolled away in tiny metallic beads along the stone, disappearing into the crevasses and muck of mortal misery. Sometimes those tears made talismans and magic. Sometimes they fell useless to the ground. She tried to avoid looking at the floor of the Whisper-world. While her step birthed flowers that soon died, the tread of Darkness brought forth insects, scuttling into cracks and seams. The countless tiny movements never ceased to disturb her.

"I want to do so much more," Persephone murmured. "Every year I can do less and less. This place rots me."

"Mmm," Darkness replied. He'd heard this before and chose not to engage. He knew it to be true. And yet, setting her free was inconceivable.

She recalled a time when she'd been free. Or, somewhat free. She'd once used so much of her light trying to set souls to rest that her heart actually projected itself outside her sternum and the following seizure had almost destroyed her. The episode had been so frightening to the entire Whisper-world that Darkness made Luce the Gorgon magically ascertain where The Guard was, and he had hurled her body into their care. Shutting back up the Whisper-world, he had left her there to heal. It was in old Ireland, and she remembered her convalescence with some wistfulness. Darkness had of course eventually reclaimed her.

The man who healed her came here. All members of The Guard did, though they rarely knew it would eventually be their fate. This man had been given a certain amnesty when he arrived. His spirit knew the ways of the Whisper-world like few others. He kept well out of the way, and tried his best to have the Whisper-world forget him, lest Darkness change his mind and turn spiteful. Darkness had a limited memory, for good or ill. He rarely walked the full breadth of his domain, and there were ways to stay safe if you did not draw his wrath.

Persephone never would forget him. Good Aodhan, brave

Healer. He was one of her favourites. She always did what she could for him.

They passed the grand dais where the river became a moat surrounding vast stone pillars wound thickly with dead ivy, crumbling ruins that had always been ruins. As they circled back, Persephone withdrew her hand. One pass was plenty, and Darkness would not dare press his suit.

She could use her light to scald him if he did. She'd done so before. It was never enough, though. She simply was not powerful enough to overtake him in his domain. For that she would need help. She would need an army. Gaining freedom was not a task for a sole, faltering goddess.

She would need an army just to fight the minions who would flock to him. For as many of those that sought her help, there were many more spirits in the bowels of this place who would rather see her bleed. An army of the best of life might fight against the worst of it. There had been a discussion at one point that she might have just such a force, if she could just figure out the when and the how it might be deployed. But she was not a creature of war but of love and peace. Thusly, plans of battle were lost to her. She'd had visions. She'd yet to see one in which she was free, however. She had yet to envision her salvation.

"Good night," she murmured. "I continue my walk alone."

Darkness's Raphaelite face—and then his skull—scowled. He stalked to his throne, sat and whipped his robes up around him. Their layers peeled and settled in a pattern, the shape of a great crimson rose. It was the only colour, save for hers, in this dreary place: an enormous red rose frozen in the heart of darkness. Beneath the petals, mere bones. That was Darkness's tempting lie.

Persephone turned away and strolled as if wandering aimless, but she headed in the same direction Maria had run;

the Liminal always helped her find her way in this labyrinth. It would light a spark down a darkened path and she could follow. It would know whom she sought.

She took roundabout corridors, looking behind her to see if any of Darkness's minions followed. It was the Gorgon that worried her most. Their hatred ran mutually deep. Since her seizure, and after a separate traumatic episode earlier in the nineteenth century, one involving a great deal of blood and a lapse in Persephone's mental stability, Luce had been emboldened. Relations always worsened when she saw Persephone weak; the shark smelled blood in the great river of souls.

It was a dangerous game she played, hiding all The Guard spirits in one place. Her army . . . But this deception had sufficed for centuries now. Though, what was that span to eternity? She had to keep her secrets. Darkness would never let the spirits pass to the Great Beyond, to the place that even Persephone couldn't fathom but that was their just reward. Someday that sweet release might yet be earned, but her hour had not yet come.

Ducking into a cavelike crevasse in the dark, wet rock, she felt the damp of death press in upon her and fought its cloying tendrils. Sorrow stifled her nonetheless. Her mouth welled up with fluid. She spat pomegranate juice, red and sour, and addressed the land that laid claim over her. "Light, I say," she murmured.

She raised her hand before her face, bright white here, and ignored the taste of fruit in her mouth that rotted her mind and corroded her spirit; it was one of Darkness's many tricks to keep her here. If she didn't focus, if she didn't keep her mind on her mission, she'd start to drift, eat seeds, drink red juice and finally lose her core of light and mortal joy once and for all. Darkness desperately hoped for that, though neither of them knew what would happen next.

No. She'd made a promise to her beloved never to give in. Never.

Moving ahead, her ghost-white hand was a lantern in the gloom. To all else, and in her reflection, she was all colours at once, shifting, prismatic, iridescent. But to her own eye, when gazing down at her own flesh, she was entirely colourless: a bright, luminous white; an eerie, ghostly blank canvas.

Holding her breath, she plunged into dark, cold water. The murmurs of the dead roared in her ears like the crashing of ocean waves. She swam, feeling her thin garments float around her limbs. It wasn't far to the other side, but she hated this journey. It always felt like eternity, and she'd had a good taste of that already.

She pushed her head out of the black water and squeezed her eyes shut. The light on this chosen shore was bright and blinding. It was as close as she could imagine to heaven. Especially here.

Opening her eyes, she gazed upon the denizens of this fabricated Elysium, drank in the sight of a host of transparent forms from every human epoch and culture, staring down at her from the crest of a rise and holding out their hands for their great Lady. Here, she was reminded once more, was the beautiful, luminous army that she needed. But how and when she could best use them was uncertain; she didn't dare risk them if she couldn't be sure . . .

Thousands of Guards were there. Her white hands fumbled for the riverbank in her eagerness to get to them. Their welcome buoyed her to shore, and she placed her bare feet on solid, warm grass.

It was a miracle, this area, an expanse of open green on a perfect day. That had been The Guard's choice for their solace, an Elysian field where she did her best to keep them happy and protected. It sapped a degree of her remaining power. Still, here they all were, or nearly all of them. Some had chosen to remain on Earth, of course, to wander or watch over mortal loved ones, a few had managed to slip away uncounted, and the very first Guard had long gone on to peace. But there were thousands who remained.

"Dear Lady," she heard them murmur, in many different languages, bobbing, floating or kneeling before her.

"Hello, darlings," she said, and the echo of her voice splintered into countless different tongues.

"We've a new set," she stated. "Cairo this time. Did the others make it here all right?"

A broad, rugged-featured man in a plain tunic and sash, his long hair a mane down his back, stepped forward. "Yes, my Lady, they're just being shown around and made comfortable," he said in old Gaelic, gesturing down the field.

Down the slope, a group of six spirits in wide skirts and uniforms, mustaches and fine hats bent over a bubbling spring, dipped their hands in glistening water and smiled. Persephone overheard their American-accented voices say that this field was better than their proposed Central Park, if that ever would be complete. They agreed with a laugh that they'd have to haunt it.

"Hello, Aodhan. Thank you," she replied in Gaelic. "You know it always does my heart good to see you, my saviour." He'd been the one to literally put her heart back within her body. Her appearance had shaken his Guard for weeks.

"Of course, my Lady." His greyscale face darkened in a blush, and he gestured her to precede him.

"How long ago was that, when I nearly died in your arms?"

"You're immortal. You can't die."

"Well, it hurt. Terribly," she said. "But how long? You see, Aodhan, time is so different for me. When I'm with mortals I've this desperate sense of time, as if everything moves in a blur, vanishing like hourglass sand, but here . . . it's all hazy, odd, disjointed. I don't know if Darkness has had me here a hundred years or a thousand. Or more. I'm not faring well," she added, a cough encroaching. "Pardon me."

Her lungs rattled, a disgusting, alarming noise.

"That was mortal centuries ago, my Lady," Aodhan replied. He placed a hand over her throat. His healing powers had been long since passed along to a successor, but there were faint traces left, and he bestowed what little succor he could. Her seeming death rattle quieted slightly.

"Thank you," she murmured. A tremendous guilt washed over her, one that had been building and becoming unbearable.

"My darlings, I should let you go," she murmured to all those watching. "I should find a way to get you to your reward."

Their faces were a wash, bright white spirits one next to the other. Aodhan stepped forward and said with a gentle smile, "You say that every time."

"I am a too-fond parent, scared of the evils of the world," she mused. "If I'm made of sentiment and of hope, just as my husband is made of misery, then why do I falter?"

"Because you were never meant to be trapped. None of us were," Aodhan replied. "And you're not sure how to free yourself. Or us."

She looked at the grass blowing gently in a magical breeze. "So Hope must trap her children with her?"

"For our own safety," Aodhan said, but she could also tell he was tired. They all had to be. Very, very tired.

Aodhan understood. When he had taken pains to repair her heart, he'd been taken into her memories, shared her pain that no touch of his healing hand could cure. No magic in the world could undo what Darkness had taken from her, or the terrible cycle he had put into its place. Sometimes she just needed them to understand what they were fighting for. Sometimes she needed a reminder, too.

"One day it will change," she insisted.

The Guards were listening, intent. She opened her mouth to continue, to perhaps propose a plan, but stopped short at a warm caress. Looking down, a disembodied hand made of blue flame pressed her lips. Signaling.

"Go." Aodhan smiled. "Spend time at your true husband's grave."

She felt tears well in her eyes and she turned away. Far down a gentle slope there was a ring of birch trees, their bark white and elegant, their leaves rustling and their limbs bending as if reaching toward her. There was a ring of heather surrounding the tree and a faint haze of blue light. She felt his power humming around her and within her. What pieces she'd managed to recover of her lover lay beneath this soil. A part of his fire was ever tied to those remains, and to her. It was a modest portion of power separate from The Grand Work, with a will of its own.

She ran and nearly fell into the ring of flowers, pressed her body to the earth and ran her fingers through the heather as if it were her lover's hair. The leaves rustled and the flowers enlarged, filling her nostrils with a sweet and living smell, obliterating the long-ago stench of her lover's burned flesh that never entirely left her consciousness.

Persephone turned and lay on her back. Two tiny wisps of blue flame hovered just over her face, as if he were there atop her and the flames were the sparkling love in his eyes. She tried to imagine him, to see and recall exactly what he had looked like in his original form, every strong feature and tiny, gorgeous detail of wisdom, of that power and light made incarnate. But it had been so long. She felt her lungs grow heavy, and she turned her head with a helpless, ugly cough.

"We should be looking for a body *you* might take over," the fire murmured. "Perhaps you should join the next Guard. You sound worse by the day. No matter what you tell me."

"I'm scared," she whispered.

"I know."

The breeze caressed her intimately. Tendrils of air spread palms down her body, her diaphanous layers of clothing no barrier to his spirit. A pressure curled down along her flowing locks, over her arms, dragged up her thighs, thrilling her to her core. She gasped, the flowers the only witness to this passion as she writhed against their bed, welcoming his essence upon and within her.

"I need you," she whispered. "Now more than ever. What did you find out about that boy? The one I asked for? That Alexi?"

"His family is in London," Phoenix's ghost replied. He added, "London always was one of your favourite cities."

She giggled. Flowers bloomed beneath her shoulders at the sound. "I remember when you flew me over the Thames, before there were bridges . . ."

He purred in fond recollection. She gasped as a particularly brazen if ghostly caress silenced her further, and she gave herself over to acute sensation. It was some comfort, but not complete. This was hardly his body. It was only an echo of all they once knew.

Rising to her knees, she caressed the sturdy heather all around her, a flower she'd planted here because it reminded her that sometimes life could thrive and be beautiful in difficult climes; a purple glory amid a harsh and howling heath. But then she noticed that the white skin of her hand appeared less youthful than ever. Hope was withering.

Overwhelmed, she smoothed the layers of thin fabric that floated about her body. Kissing the ground, she bid farewell to her beloved's grave and fled up the slope, leaving this echo of what should have been her marriage bed. There the many incarnations of The Guard strolled along the green crest, arm in arm, group with group, beside tree and flower, appreciating the blue sky and one another's company. They seemed at peace, happy. If they weren't, she wondered whether any of them would say.

She approached the boundary waters again, dreading the cold black misery it contained. As if The Guards were already calling across a chasm, she heard them say good-bye in their many languages. She was praised using her many different names, words as diverse as the varied beliefs of the world.

Blowing kisses, she fell backward into the water and shot herself across to the other bank in a graceful few strokes, jumping up and into the grey shadow, shaking off the river that clung to her and made her garments heavy with sorrow. Only later would she recall that, as she moved along into the crevasse that would take her back into the Whisper-world's unmitigated clutches, there had come the sound of hissing. She was faltering indeed to have been so careless, to not more carefully hide where she had been. It was foolish to not have more zealously guarded her treasure, for it was all that she had left to live for.

Chapter Eight

Ibrahim settled in at Ahmed's home, and the two young men marveled at the ease with which they now floated in and out of the consciousness of the Basri family. Ahmed was the only child, clearly adored; but now, since the magic of The Guard claimed them, he was adored at a distance, quietly, as if through a veil. A meal was prepared at a long wooden table, the finest piece of furniture in the modest flat. There was pleasant discussion, but only about things of no substance. Like they were all having a lovely, carefree daydream.

The shift clearly saddened Ahmed. That joyous, expressive face was so easy to read. When even a hint of The Grand Work passed between them, the glow of the Heart would obliterate all else, and it seemed the whole house lit with him, even after the sun set. In general, things seemed to be going well. Thus Ibrahim was surprised to be awoken by his friend in the middle of the night.

"The war in the ground!" Ahmed cried, launching up from his cot, moisture dotting his brow.

"What?" Ibrahim sat up across the room, rubbing his eyes. His sleep had been heavy, his body still adjusting to its new powers and sensibilities. The Grand Work was more than mere mortals could digest in one fell swoop. And yet, here they were all alive. Reeling but alive.

"A vision," Ahmed murmured, shaking his head and walking out into the main room. Ibrahim followed. Ahmed lit a tin lamp whose mirror brightened the candle flame and cast its ornate metal pattern onto the richly coloured rug. He sat at a carved wooden chair positioned below a bookshelf filled with tracts and other Sufi literature.

"Would you like to speak about it?"

"I see a war. A strange war with metal dragons and guns like I've never known, horrible guns dispensing death like falling rain."

"Why do you say it is a vision rather than a fancy, a simple nightmare? What have we to do with such sights?"

"Because it's about the dead. They've nowhere to go. There are simply too many. It's terrible. I should tell the angel when next she descends."

Ibrahim nodded, then suddenly clutched his heart. A seizure took him, a flash of pain unlike any other save one. This was his Intuition at work. This was the Pull. The sensation was raw, as if something were spreading across his nerves; his circulatory system shifted to match the haphazard streets of Cairo, and all he could think was: Giza.

He knew, too, the location of each of his compatriots. Most strongly he felt Beatrice. He felt them all rise from chairs or beds and pinpoint the same location his own senses decreed. He scowled.

"What is it?" asked Ahmed, rising.

"Of course," Ibrahim replied, grabbing a long coat near the door and tossing another to his friend. He then strode out into the courtyard, Ahmed dogging his heels.

They both wore simple linen tunics, and Ibrahim felt the night air bite his skin as his brow knit further. They threw on their coats as Ahmed prompted, "Of course?"

"Of course there's trouble at the pyramids."

"Wherever great spiritual energy has amassed, there shall we be," Ahmed stated. Ibrahim glanced at him, as if awaiting some further explanation or theory. His friend shrugged, adding, "Full understanding of our duty will come in time."

Ibrahim pursed his lips. "Lovely. My new companion, with

whom I'll be forced insufferably close, will counter every concern with mystical platitudes."

"I'll try," Ahmed agreed.

Ibrahim couldn't help but laugh. A new thought made him scowl. "I say, it's the foreigners meddling with our dead that's causing the trouble."

"Believe in curses, then, do you?" Ahmed asked.

"No, I believe in human stupidity, disrespect, greed and obsession with conquest. Things that never fail to cause harm."

Ahmed put a hand on his friend's shoulder. "All fair and understood. However, I suggest you add something of joy to your list of beliefs, brother. It is necessary for a life well-lived." He then added the lacking component through use of his gift.

As they traveled southwest through Cairo from their position near the citadel, a wind at their feet gave them an uncanny speed, as if they'd been given Mercury's shoes.

"I suppose the angel could have stirred and rousted the dead," Ibrahim muttered after a long silence. "She was keen to see our 'mortal wonders.' I wouldn't have expected tourism out of a divinity."

"She's a creature for peace, not unrest. Surely her intentions were solely to admire," Ahmed countered. "If anything her presence might have inadvertently stirred a yearning for life again. She does have a way about her, does she not?"

Ibrahim shrugged. It didn't seem proper to be moved by a being he could hardly comprehend. But it was true; she was a raw and captivating force of nature that could not be dismissed.

Their augmented movement had them, some half hour later, coming to the Cairo outskirts, the vast sands of Giza beyond; the Pull had drawn them to a café and shop that catered to foreign tourists seeking the pyramids. It was such an abrupt shift from streets to unruly, ever-shifting sands.

The nearby stables were wide-open. Belle stood with the reins of six docile camels in her hand, the wide-eyed creatures easily twice her size. George rounded the corner at a run, his half cloak, vest and undone shirtsleeves flapping against his gangly form. The sight of the young French girl in a fashionable pink dress with six camels at her back made him howl with delight.

"Bloody genius!" George exclaimed. "How did you—?"

Belle tapped her temple and smiled sheepishly. "I've learned I can get my way in absolutely anything. Terribly dangerous, this gift of mine." Her French accent was heavy, but she was all the more charming for it.

Everyone glanced around at one another but Beatrice, who was standing a few paces off toward where the road widened. Her simple black riding outfit was suited for travel but elegant on her tall frame, and her dark blonde hair was pinned beneath a sensible hat.

Verena was the first to move forward and collect the reins of a beast, her dark robes rustling in the night breeze. Ahmed offered his help to ease her up to the fabric saddle, which she gracefully accepted. George ducked and narrowly avoided a veritable grenade of camel spittle, then giggled, standing on his tiptoes to scratch the beast's golden muzzle.

Ibrahim turned to Beatrice. She was staring ahead of her, mouth agape. He moved to ascertain her line of sight and gasped, seeing what she saw. "Allah, God, Yahweh and Osiris have mercy," he muttered. The rest of The Guard shifted, their camels in tow, and one by one they gasped.

The sight surpassed the wildest, most morbid of imaginations. At the edge of Giza, the shops ended and the desert began. Many kilometers ahead stood the necropolis, the great pyramid and its family *erupting* with ghosts. The pyramids had become volcanoes of the spirit world, the restless dead like luminous silver lava that coursed down their perfect slopes. What the half-moon did not illuminate, these spirits made bright.

"Do we have to deal with *all* that?" Verena breathed.

"I hope not," Beatrice replied. She set her jaw, turned and was up on a camel with ease.

Ibrahim furrowed his brow, impressed. He followed suit, grumbling as he had a bit more difficulty swinging his leg to situate himself against the hump. The camel turned its head and glanced back in irritation.

The group plodded to the edge of the desert and were a few paces in when Belle's voice made them turn.

"Mon Dieu!" she murmured, tears glistening in her eyes. "One spirit is fine. But that . . . *that's* a bit much. That is absolutely terrifying." She added the word meaning frightened in Arabic, just in case anyone failed to catch her faltering English. A chorus of assent followed from the others.

Neither Beatrice nor Ibrahim joined in. She looked over at him, and seeing his reflection in her pale eyes he felt suddenly older. They faced the absurd terror of floating haunts and the biddings of angels. She didn't seem any more elated about it than he was, but she didn't seem frightened, either. Instead she appeared sturdy, elegant and composed. She, too, had faced recent, cataclysmic loss, he reminded himself.

She stared at him as if he were a peer, which was unsettling because she was Western and a woman. Then again, they were in uncommon circumstances. He'd never again be able to evaluate life in the ways to which he'd been accustomed. He sat straighter in his saddle.

Beatrice asked, "Well, now that we know everyone's petrified, what are we to do about this little circus?" She held up her hand. Blue fire hovered in a ball. "I've been practicing," she added, staring at the flame, which she cast out, then brought back close again like a toy. "Bloody fascinating. I keep thinking I've lost my mind, but if I have, then so have all of you. I hope you've all been thinking? Practicing? Or have you just been answering life's suddenly inexplicable questions?"

She looked at every one of them in turn and spoke, Ibrahim had to admit, with the stern and unaffected air of capable command; it was critical that she not be frightened, for that would not do in a leader.

She chuckled when they all nodded or shrugged. "Lovely. Like lambs to the spiritual slaughter." Then she spurred her camel on. "It's all right," she said to the beast. "I'm still not convinced I believe in ghosts. Perhaps that is a healthy separation. Psychological detachment may equal greater efficiency."

"Will we have to go *in?*" Belle breathed, her fear mounting. She stared at the enormous monuments and their attendant clouds of spirits.

"No," Ahmed replied. "Look. We won't have to go far at all. They're coming to us."

It was true. While the bulk of spiritual activity clustered in bright grey light around the great pyramid, those ghosts seemed unconcerned with anything outside the necropolis perimeter. But there was a platoon of spirits marching directly toward their small band. They were floating above the sand a metre off the ground, in neat rows, bare-chested and clad in pale loincloths.

"Servants. Buried with the royals—some say alive," Ahmed remarked quietly. "I can't imagine they were happy about it."

"Who would be?" George murmured. "I mean God save the Queen and all, but I'd rather not be buried with her when the dear lady goes."

Beatrice smirked and Belle giggled. The sound of laughter was welcome against such a spectral host.

Ibrahim closed his eyes. Information was at hand. He owned a sensibility that was foreign to the way he was used to his mind working, but the knowledge felt clarion and true and he wished to the heavens he could explain it. "No. These aren't servants, these are those who *built* the great pyramids. It's the engineers who are angry. Their nobles' remains were disturbed. They're looking to settle a score, recover goods, or perhaps the body—or visit a haunting upon the offenders," he said. He'd spoken in Arabic, then translated a few words to English, but Beatrice was nodding, understanding him from the first. He added, purely for her, "There are many offenders when it comes to the ancient dead here."

Beatrice held up her hands. "Not my father. I know the sites well. He's lauded by all Egyptian colleagues at the university and within Antiquities for his reverence and respect."

"Tell that to these gents," George murmured.

The platoon of restless dead were upon the company quickly, a wave of ice-cold air preceding them. A sound flew from Beatrice's lips, a command spoken in The Guard tongue now native to each.

One by one the six slipped off their camels, jumping into the sand. Belle went to each of the creatures, appearing shocked by her sudden facility with them and surprised when they listened, but she guided them a few paces back. Thankfully, camels seemed unconcerned by the dead.

The Guard formed a circle in the sand, their young faces illuminated by the moon, the light of the spirits, and by a great blue fire that coursed around them and rose like a waterspout. Their distinct, powerful wind whipped up, too. Sand tumbled over the hems of their dresses, robes and boots. Notes of music caressed the air, an angelic choir tuneful and vibrant. Clouds cleared from the sky above them, and the stars seemed to burn brighter in affirmation. A few slow tears rolled down Ahmed's smooth face, bright with serenity. Ibrahim wished that he felt so at peace.

With a deep breath and a forceful exhalation, Beatrice

opened her hands. A net of blue fire leaped up, surrounding the spirits that had formed a separate and opposing circle above them, back to back, leering down at The Guard with transparent, hollow faces. The skeletal spirits were speaking, their loosely attached jaws flapping rapidly and angrily, but The Guard heard nothing.

Ibrahim felt only the oppressive weight of death and the surety of his own mortality. A dread flooded his veins, and in staring up at one of the ghosts, those empty eyes drew him forward a step, the icy chill of them seeping right into his bones. His mind was flooded with images. Every moment that he had said something hurtful, done something hateful, flashed before his eyes, and he knew he was a wretched being, meant only for decay.

Then his mind washed clean; the oppressive fog lifted from his brain. Belle had come near without his notice and brushed his temple with her finger. He turned to her and nodded, and she smiled demurely, her round cheeks dimpling.

The Guard's separate gifts worked increasingly in concert. George pulled out a walking stick, darting about in the sand. Ibrahim wanted to watch him—there was something compelling about what George was doing—but he could sense Beatrice's energy straining as she worked the fire to keep the spirits contained. A surprising text upon his lips, he recited the Book of the Dead, though the ancient Egyptian vernacular was previously unfamiliar. Some of the spirits became captivated, nodding, suddenly rethinking their mission. It seemed that while The Guard could not hear the wails of spirits, the spirits could hear the living quite clearly.

Others strained against their confining fire, thus straining against Beatrice. Ibrahim could feel her energy falter, and he was alarmed that he felt so attuned to her, in a way that science could never explain. The metaphysical bond was both intimate and unsettling. Seductive.

Beatrice growled in frustration. A few of the spirits broke free and lunged at her, their incorporeal hands around her throat. Another manipulated the sand and sent a rock hurtling forward, and her cheek wept blood in a thin scarlet line.

She cried a command. The spirits reluctantly unhanded her as if scalded. They backed away, toward their fellows who were still contained.

Verena glided near. Her glowing hand touched Beatrice's cheekbone, and the blood vanished. Ahmed countered the black clouds of misery that the spirits shed. Ibrahim offered a new Book of the Dead text to keep the ghosts engaged rather than violent.

Beatrice gritted her teeth. "Now for a cantus to quiet them into submission."

"I've got something I'd like to share," George exclaimed, running forward. "Excuse me," he called jauntily to the spirits floating above. "Oh, ghosties of the great monuments, do come and look at my exhibition, it may move you," he declared.

A few of the spirits turned, hovering over the elaborate grooves in the sand that he'd wrought. They placed hands over their mouths and reached for the others; then, in a rushing burst of grey light, they were scurrying back toward the pyramids. They vanished there into the sand, one by one, beneath the smallest apex.

The Guard stared after them, catching their breath. They turned to George, who was looking rather pleased. Beatrice cast blue light over George's creation, illuminating the source of the spirits' defeat. Into the sand, with his walking stick and some creative footwork, he'd drawn a large outline, beautifully rendered, of a great bird of grand myth with outstretched wings, flame wreathing up from its claws and tail feathers.

"I haven't a bloody clue what I meant while doing it, but looking at it now I think it's quite nice—don't you?" he asked with a grin, running a hand through his hair.

"A phoenix," Beatrice murmured. "Why, that's lovely, George."

The English youth blushed, staring down at his work.

"And quite meaningful to them," Ahmed added thoughtfully. "Transformative power. Rebirth. The Egyptians worshipped Phoenix; he was a god to them. They must have thought we were his votaries and dared not test us further."

"We *are* his votaries," Beatrice reminded them all, blue fire shimmering along her fingers like liquid jewelry.

"The air!" Belle exclaimed with satisfaction. They'd begun to feel the Balance as if it were temperature. She went to her camel and hopped up with a facility that defied the restrictions usually caused by her garments.

"And yet . . ." Beatrice scowled, gesturing to the still-active overflow of spirits.

"No, I understand," Verena said quietly. She turned to stare at the monuments still erupting with bright grey light. "We're here to protect mortals, not to police every ghost. We'll never be able to look at these again without seeing the tumult, but we're not called forth into that melee. Not yet. Not unless it comes for humanity. Tonight troops came charging toward the Giza populace, so we had to stand in the way. A mortal barricade for mortal hearts."

"Well said," Beatrice realized.

Everyone nodded slowly. Ahmed reached out toward Verena as if he wanted to take her hand. She stared at his hand, then him, and smiled. Beatrice's expression became a scowl. She must have felt Ibrahim watching her, however, and turned away.

The feast of unrest here saddened Ibrahim. He wondered if the Book of the Dead had helped any of the pyramids' souls to peace or if it had only served to confuse them. He was certain the unrest had more to do with mortal meddling than any flaws of faith. He was so lost in thought that when he turned back to Beatrice, she and her camel were already many paces ahead. So were the others.

They hadn't gone far, and so the return from the sands into the streets of Giza was not long. Beatrice was the first to arrive back at the tourist depot. After a limber dismount, she tied the animal to the stable post from whence they had come and turned to her fellows.

"Well, my troops. Good work, it would seem. Until we next feel the call to arms."

The rest stared after her, blinking as she walked away, still unsure what sort of protocol they should follow at the end of meetings such as this. Eventually they took her action as dismissal. There was little else to do at this time of night but return to the central city.

Ibrahim watched his fellows sort themselves into couples in a way that seemed natural and understandable, Ahmed asking Verena in which part of the Coptic *hara* she resided, Belle and George exchanging halting French and English sentences and smiles. A few Giza residents stumbled past and stared, surprised at the seemingly upstanding and well-kept youths, odd acquaintances that most certainly shouldn't be wandering the streets at such an hour. But before they could question, Belle waved a hand and they turned, dazed, and wandered away.

Beatrice vanished around a corner, and Ibrahim practically ran to catch up.

"Do not misinterpret this," he called after her in smooth English. "It isn't that I require your company, it simply isn't the wisest idea for a young woman to walk alone at such an hour." He watched her tall form, her black traveling skirts swishing about her as she strode forward and then bouncing to a halt. She turned, her eyebrow raised.

"While in any other circumstance I would entirely agree," she began, "I somehow think I'll be all right." She gazed down at her palm, in which she held a ball of blue fire.

"I'd suggest you not entertain any unrealistic sense of security," he cautioned. "Don't tempt fate. Your fire works on ghosts, not human criminals. Don't think you're a god."

Beatrice made a face. "I know I'm not a god. But I would like to be left alone. This Grand Work—madness came at a most unwelcome time. I must remember that I'm in mourning."

"As am I. And I respect that. But as your"—he swallowed—"second-in-command, I should see to it that you are escorted home. I can walk several paces behind you if you'd rather."

Beatrice's face softened. "Thank you, Ibrahim," she said after a quiet moment. In Arabic. "You are a gentleman. Walk with me, then. But please forgive my silence. While I know I ought to be asking all the things new friends should, I've no stomach for niceties at present. We'll have all the time in the world for cordiality—or so it would seem."

Ibrahim nodded and caught up to her, intrigued by her sharp tone. Intuition told him that her coldness hid something. She was forcing herself to be distant.

They kept to shadows and silence as the city thickened around them, veering toward the Citadel. Glancing at the passing ghosts, seeing that they seemed uninterested in him, Ibrahim wondered if he and she really were allowed to speak freely, like peers and comrades. If so, what on earth should they say? Where would they begin? The Grand Work was redefining their identities, and he could hardly remember how the world looked and felt before, though he knew that at the core they each had been chosen for who they were. They were not changed but . . . heightened.

Despite that, they were no less alone.

★ ★ ★

The Whisper-world echoed with the Gorgon's triumphant cry. "I've found where she keeps them all!" Luce crowed as she ran to tell her master, dancing around those shadows lit by red eyes at their centre.

Darkness launched to his feet. Down from the massive stone throne he stepped, casting open the veil of darkness and standing, a luminous white skeleton. "Where? Where is she? Is she there?"

He was suddenly a beautiful man. In the next moment a skeleton.

"No, she's cavorting with mortals, as usual," Luce sneered, daring to slide her black-robed arm into his, which was flesh, then bone. "While she's out, you ought to make your move. Gather your most miserable minions, the ones without hope, the ones who have refused redemption. Bring them. We've a field to burn."

Chapter Nine

Putting the gaping maws of the restless Giza ghosts behind her, Beatrice unlocked the front door of her father's apartments and went directly to the study, where she assumed a lamp would be lit. It was. She kissed her father on the head without a word—he who was always up until all hours poring over glyphs and pieces of pottery—then glided silently to her room. Rest was imperative.

She tried to ignore the pain of her dear father having hardly noticed her. But that was the way of things now. It wasn't for mere parents to ask questions of The Guard, nor to even acknowledge their children anymore. Her cohorts across the city were surely feeling the same, passing phantoms in their own home.

Alone in her room, Beatrice stared at the ceiling as a vague horror crept over her. She should be in mourning, as she'd stated. She should be helping her father make discoveries, should be creating a name for herself in Egyptology, not chasing ghosts. This was not what she'd been born for. And yet, here she was, knowing that her purpose in academia was supplanted by something she couldn't accurately describe, even to herself. Her family had been replaced by five strangers and an odd goddess or angel.

Ibrahim. He was nothing like what she wanted. Yet here she was, and instead of Jean's image on her eyelids as she closed them was the disturbingly handsome face of her second-in-command. As if it was meant to be. As if *they* were meant to be. But how could such different people be fated to unite? It was absurd! He was a stranger. Where was this odd sensibility coming from?

She knew she'd been sharp when she spoke to him. A defense. That was all she could do to keep boundaries. Everything had been broken down, and she couldn't let a stranger so cool and detached toward her know that she found herself so drawn to him. He was, after all, just as sharp in return. He was her second-in-command, and he likely resented her for it. Men always did.

"I couldn't help that I was chosen as Leader," she murmured. Then she was overwhelmed by contrition. "Surely he doesn't feel this stupid, weak, womanly contrivance of emotion. He can't feel any of what I do. I'm grieving. Even though life with Jean may not wholly have been what I wanted, still the shocking events are taking a toll. I'm projecting my grief onto him, feeling a strange attraction . . . No, the man hates me. This is absurd."

"It isn't," came a voice at her bedside. The light of the room shifted colours.

"Good Lord! Couldn't you knock or offer a bit of warning?"

The goddess sat at the end of her bed and smirked. "I thought you didn't believe in the Lord."

"I don't know what I believe. But recent events have renewed my faith in cursing," Beatrice replied.

Persephone chuckled. "It isn't absurd to find yourself drawn to your second-in-command. It's only natural. Leaders and seconds have loved one another for ages. Not always, of course; it isn't a mandate. But it's common." She leaned close. "He's dreadfully handsome, isn't he?"

"You were eavesdropping," Beatrice hissed, blushing. That would teach her to sort through her emotions aloud when this odd divinity might drop in at any moment.

"No," Persephone argued. "I just wanted to come and say

good-bye before I go back to the Whisper-world again, as is my doom. I never know how long it is that I'll be gone in terms of your time. It may be a month or a day to you, I've no idea. Being away from the living always feels like an eternity to me. When I feel a pull to my Guard I try to make my rounds to those most influential. You've done well. Take care. Keep faith."

And with that the goddess vanished, leaving Beatrice still blushing and awkward. But, at least she had some sense of why she was feeling such a pull toward Ibrahim. There was a Guard precedent.

She couldn't be blamed, then. And, of course she wouldn't act on it, considering his indifference. She did have her pride, after all. A whole hell of a lot of it.

★ ★ ★

Several streets away, Ahmed woke with another cry. Ibrahim stirred groggily, rubbing at his eyes and fighting a sense of déjà vu as he sat up.

"The nightmare again?"

At the foot of his friend's bed sat the angel, Persephone. Ibrahim found that calling her an angel still felt more natural to him than calling her a goddess. Not everything he believed had to be overturned at once.

Ahmed breathed heavily. He saw Persephone, turned to Ibrahim and offered a valiant smile.

"What is it?" the divinity asked.

Ahmed addressed her. "Visions came at the same time as The Grand Work. They showed a war in the ground, where the dead have no place to go. Why do I keep seeing it unless it's a warning? I tell you, this is important. The dead have nowhere to go . . . Surely that means something to you, my Lady."

She considered before shaking her shifting-coloured head. "Alas," she admitted, "such a vision is unfamiliar to me."

"It is of a time I cannot yet fathom. There are machines, terrible constructions of metal. It all seems fantastical and impossible. The dead, oh, so many dead! They speak to me. They tell me not to close every door. Do you know what door?"

"I recall that the Heart was desperate to go to you, was so very eager to choose you, Ahmed. Perhaps this was why. It knew it gained both a joyous heart and a visionary. It sensed that you could help our cause; suggesting something to that effect."

"Perhaps," Ahmed said, shaking off the nightmare and regaining hope.

"Or it is all-too-human madness," Ibrahim muttered.

The angel turned as if to admonish him but instead replied, "Visionaries or madmen. There seems a hairsbreadth distinction at times."

"But you'll be alert, should this suddenly mean something?" Ahmed begged. "If this torture was for no good purpose . . ."

"Of course I'll take your vision to heart!"

The Sufi nodded, satisfied. Ibrahim noticed that his eyes had dark circles underneath. How long had Ahmed been suffering these dreams?

Persephone bit her lip. "May I offer you something?" she asked. "I wish to counter your pain with something beautiful."

Ahmed nodded, eager. Ibrahim watched her a bit more closely.

"While I'm hardly omnipotent, I can deeply feel the human heart—of my Guards in particular. I can affect a journey of release should you choose to accept it. A living daydream of something beautiful. A journey into a favourite, perfect place, if only for a moment. Think on that and we'll travel there. Close your eyes and think of something heavenly."

Ahmed did. Persephone touched his temple with her fingertip. He shivered—in delight, Ibrahim hoped.

She turned. "Would you like to come?" she asked.

He stared at her a moment. She cycled through a few different shades. Finally he moved toward her. She gestured him closer. Reaching out a fingertip, she touched his temple . . .

The world changed. They were all three on a wide rooftop, a vast stone courtyard up in the air. The Nile delta stretched out below, lush, verdant, the source of all life. There was music, incredible music, as if a thousand muezzins stood calling out in pure, powerful, all-encompassing tones from a hundred unseen towers.

Ahmed was transformed. His long, layered tunic was all white, a tall camel-hair cap upon his head. The Sufi's eyes were closed in rapture to the music, a huge smile upon his face. The sung prayers were in Arabic.

Persephone stood at a respectful distance, eyeing Ahmed with unquestionable love. In this moment she did not shift. She was entirely without colour, her hair and skin from head to toe, her diaphanous robes; all was solid white as if to match Ahmed.

The Sufi began to turn, his left foot the pivot, his arms up as if welcoming the world; one hand was turned toward heaven, the other to Earth. His white skirt spun out around him, low at first, higher as his spinning grew and the hymn swelled. From what Ahmed had described to Ibrahim about his faith, Ibrahim recognized this as part of a worship ceremony. This was Ahmed's personal, private joy; Sufi whirling. And the beauty of it, of the singing and of the simple meditative movement and worship of a mysterious divinity, brought Ibrahim close to tears.

Ahmed opened his eyes to fix his friend and their mysterious angel with a meaningful gaze. In one gesture, he encouraged them both to imitate his form. To join in his affirmation. Which they did. How could they not?

It did not matter how much time passed. Eventually, the music quieted. The bright expanse of the perfect day darkened, Ahmed turned to Persephone and suddenly they were all back in his small Cairo room.

"Thank you for that," the Sufi said, his voice thick with emotion. He turned to Ibrahim and added, "Such as that was a glimpse of the unseen world, as close as we'll get to the afterlife while we yet live."

Persephone smiled, her colours bright, refreshed.

Ibrahim chuckled, enjoying the memory. "You may convert me yet."

Ahmed shrugged. "I don't worry for your soul."

Such a pronouncement was good to hear. Ibrahim smiled.

Persephone's colours darkened. "I must go back."

Ahmed frowned. "Again? It is not yet the season, is it?"

The goddess's smile was fond. "There are many different seasons across this planet. We abandoned the old schedule long ago. It's better that way. I am leashed but come and go as I please, and if I return regularly, he tends not to watch so close. But I'm sensing things are about to change. We're on the cusp of a new dawn, and I want to be both places as much as I can— so I can react quickly." She blew both Ibrahim and Ahmed kisses and her eyes were sad. "You be sure to enjoy this world. The next one comes soon enough."

Ahmed nodded. "Be sure to think on my vision, my Lady, should you find it useful."

Persephone sighed. "I never take what a Guard says for granted. And if there comes a time to use your wisdom, I shan't forget. But as for now, I see nothing."

She cast her arm forward and a black portal ripped into the room. Ibrahim and Ahmed watched in awkward silence as the beautiful creature steeled herself and straightened her shoulders. Did her hands tremble? She drew a deep breath and stepped inside. With a snapping sound the portal closed. They were again alone in the room.

"It is terrible to see a divine being of such gentle, kind beauty move frightened into a dark night," Ahmed stated.

Ibrahim nodded. The sight was indeed deeply distressing, and Instinct rustled his blood, shuddered against his bones. There were many dark nights ahead for all of them, not just Ahmed. If these mounting shadows were hard for a divinity, what would they be like for mortals?

Chapter Ten

It was true what Persephone had said to Ibrahim and Ahmed, that she had some freedom but that it was best if her feet often touched the ground of both worlds. And if she didn't go back voluntarily, the maw would eventually open, she'd feel the wrenching pain in her blood and she'd be dragged back by shadowy claws.

She glided through the darkened corridors. He was not at his throne. Relieved, she turned toward her resting place, a platform a few paces off, nearer to the river, But as she did, a pair of red eyes blinked back at her from the floor. The dog.

It wasn't a dog, exactly, but what else could one call this gruesome guardian? It had elements that were fashioned like a dog, save that there were too many heads and tongues salivating for violence. Persephone had a fondness for animals, but this was not an animal. It was a swarm of shadow and teeth. And it, like its master, liked her to know when it was watching.

She was not without recourse, and she was unafraid to strike back. She wielded her light skillfully, and in one swift move, she struck the air with her delicate hand. A cracking sound reverberated through surrounding corridors, a burst of dazzling white light snapping out from her body like a whip. The creature turned its hundred tails. Uttering vague, canine noises it ran, shadows breaking apart like rats scurrying away.

Wielding her light here always had consequences, and Persephone's bosom seared with pain. She choked a bit, pomegranate juice upon her lips, that eternal bile that had bound her here so long ago. She spat, and the stones sizzled with the heat of her blood and residual light.

Gasping, she sank down upon the bed Darkness provided her. He'd grown accustomed to hardly speaking to her, as she would hardly speak to him, but it seemed to keep him satisfied when she lay upon a bier near to the throne. It pleased him and kept him from hurting her, like when she took his hand for a promenade through his kingdom. But now she felt something rip open within her, an old wound, something far worse than the usual repercussions from her powers.

She shot up from the bier where she lay and whirled to the throne, assuming Darkness had returned and was torturing her with another of his nightmares. But the chair remained empty.

Persephone picked her battles, always had. Now a battle was picking her. Something was happening in the field. She had an inkling that, in one eternal night, everything would be different, like the day he'd killed Phoenix and the vendetta had begun. Somewhere Darkness was stoking the fire of eternal anger.

She ran, but the stone corridors confounded her. He'd changed them again, a maddening habit where he enforced his will on the whole of his world. While she had power to create rooms, paths, sanctuaries and routes—all the ways in the Whisper-World belonged in part to her—she had neither the time nor the energy to change them back. Theirs was an ever-shifting pendulum of power and stubborn resistance.

Her hand was raised in front of her face, and she narrowed her eyes as she ran. Her light burned out to illuminate the darkness. The haggard spirits in her way ducked clear, knowing not to trifle with this luminous fury.

Was Darkness moving against her Guard? It was time for a fight. It had long been time for a fight. Darkness hadn't bargained for a fiery bride when he'd kidnapped youth, beauty, love and hope; all elemental aspects of one prismatic being. He'd thought these meek mortal properties were easily controlled. He was mistaken. But she'd been losing all sense of time. And in part she was a coward, too scared to see anyone hurt.

She could feel the field burning even before she saw the flames. They rose high, the fog of misery thick, her created sky unnaturally dark. An unearthly sound tore from her body, and her rage lifted her into the air, great gusts of wind whipping all around. The smoke flashed shifting colours as she floated forward. Age-old anger burst open deep wounds and her ancient terror again made the rain come and douse the flames, but it was too late; her gorgeous field was blackened.

A battle raged by the birch trees, and The Guard's many spirits fought an equal number of infernal dead. Blue fire trickled between them but was spread thin. What remained of the Power and Light had always done best when channeled by human flesh, and the bulk of him was in Cairo, in Beatrice Smith. However, a portion would always be tied to his remains, and that portion fought fearlessly.

There was a hole in her paradise, a cracked archway in what looked like an expanse of rolling hill but what was in fact an illusion, a mirage ripped apart by jealous Darkness. Through that hole, his realm, now visible, was horror. Her Guard were being tormented by the most vile of his minions, and they did not have the advantage of their old powers. They were surrounded, being driven in clusters, picked at, brawling. Screams were deafening.

Darkness was nowhere to be seen. This place, even with its once blue sky now made a charred purple twilight, was too bright for him.

"Halt!" Persephone cried in that language known only to

The Guard and the dead. The battle paused as if the combative arms were uniformly lifted by strings.

The Guard stared at her and nodded, but the infernals just grinned. A battle cry from somewhere deep below rumbled the blackened earth beneath her feet, an ugly cry from Darkness's hollow throat. It sounded louder from the water, from that rising tide toward which her friends were being pushed. Darkness wanted to flood out his foes, to suck them down into the whirling depths. He was sending the river.

The battle resumed. The screams of her Guard had Persephone tearing out her hair.

It was her favoured Aodhan who broke from the battle, drawing her away from the breach. "Take the remains of your beloved and go. Leave this place. Don't let what's left of him fall into Darkness's hands, he'll just scatter the ashes in the river, or worse," the spirit of the Irishman told her. "You're going to have to use all your energy, all your heart, to get yourself and him away from here. You can fight a battle for us another day."

"Where is he taking you?" Persephone sobbed.

"A tower. Far behind his throne, in the niches and the shadows of the shadows. He's imprisoning the others there. Gather your lover and make a plan for tomorrow, for today is already lost."

Persephone batted at her eyes, her tears having made tiny, sharp tacks that she threw at the ground near her foes. The dog had come, leaping and yelping, its one then a hundred forms nipping at Guard flesh, and it squealed as its dread pads were pierced by these quicksilver thorns.

As much as rage bade her fight, she knew Aodhan was correct. Persephone blazed her light forth and tore ahead, casting back restless spirits as she ran to the circle of heather, to the tree that grew from his resting place. His fire was there, lashing out at offending spirits, but soon it sensed and flowed around her, sustaining her light.

She fell to her knees and tore into the soft earth, desperation giving her fingers strength. She could hear Darkness screaming, but he could not come within paces of her here. Especially not lit like she was. Her breath was ragged in her throat, her bosom burned and she knew she had only moments to maintain such an impenetrable aura.

She unearthed a vessel carved with a feather and lit by blue light. Phoenix's physical remains. His remaining essence not confined to that bone and ash wreathed upward and urged her on.

"My Lady," Aodhan breathed, suddenly at her side. "We have safe passage for you, *there*. Come quickly while the bulwark holds."

She glanced up to see The Guard spirits again fighting back those grey, sagging, miserable wretches from the bowels of the Whisper-world, creatures that hardly had human form. One opening through a grey stone arch was clearly awaiting her.

"Aodhan, tell them I'll come for them. Please. Tell them I'll come."

"They know, my Lady."

"But you must remind them, they'll forget. Rally them. They'll despair in this place with no—"

Aodhan held up a hand. "Just don't be long."

Persephone nodded. "And you, stay clear of him. Do not be captured, no matter what. Follow behind me. Haunt the Earth, bide your time. And, come to the Liminal with me, I have no choice but to beg its help."

Aodhan cocked his head as if suddenly hearing a noise. "Something's coming, my Lady." He smiled, his eyes faraway. "And it isn't bad. Not entirely. Some strange and beautiful things are coming, my Lady. But you must make them happen."

Persephone nodded, clutched the vessel of her lover's remains tightly to her and ran. Aodhan followed, pausing at the burning edge of the field, torn open like a wound, grey shadows beyond, and aided a comrade at the jagged threshold, a woman from a Chinese Guard centuries prior, who screamed rallying cries for their *Fenghuang.*

Where to go? The Liminal would tell her. Persephone concentrated all her remaining energy, nearly broken by burning pain, her breathing laboured. Her light flew out in an arc, shifted stone and cleared a path directly to that magical place whence angels were appointed. She quickly made her way to it, being sure to close the pathways behind her. She would not be followed.

"Dear Liminal," she gasped at the vast frame most like a proscenium, but with all the power to enact any play and every player. Its glassy surface bore no picture, no future, but it crackled and sparked, sensing what was happening in the field. And if Persephone wasn't mistaken, murky traces of blue passed over its surface like roiling clouds. A loyalty to Phoenix fire.

"I beg your help," she continued. "I know you've allegiance not to our kind but to the mortal world, but The Grand Work is for mortal good, as well you know. Darkness has taken the field; surely you feel that suffering. I dare not leave our great source of power within these walls. Though his spirit lives beyond, I fear Darkness would pervert his remains, destroy what little I have left of my beloved in this vessel. Please. Show me where to go, where to take him. Everything is changing, and I'm not even half as strong as I once was. Help me set a new course."

She reached out her hand, begging powers that were stronger than she, begging the universe and all that she couldn't fathom for a place of succor. She glanced around for Aodhan, hoping he'd found his way here somehow and that the Liminal might at least offer him passage. But she couldn't wait. If she faltered, if her light ran its course and Darkness caught up with her here, he would choke her, bind her, and she'd not see sunlight for months, years, epochs, and never again see the remains of her love.

The Liminal sparkled. It whirled, it shifted, and Persephone found herself lurching forward and through. Her bare feet touched smooth marble.

She had landed in a grand, dim, open foyer. It was unfinished. Moonlight filtered through dusty, pale curtains and gave the vast room an eerie glow.

The perimeter of the foyer was lined with pillars; a hall continued out from under an arch on either side. There was paint on one wall but not on another. There was a seal, a mosaic at her feet, but it, too, was unfinished. The part of the seal that was complete declared the word FRIENDS and sported a dove of peace.

"Friends," Persephone echoed. "I could not have asked for a better word of comfort."

What was this place? She licked her finger and put it up to the air, testing the winds of time.

"I'm in your day, my dear Guard. This is 1867. But where, then, are you?"

She moved across the great foyer, her feet padding across the silent, empty space, and she stared out the window at gaslit carriages and paupers upon cobblestone streets.

"Oh. Why, it's London."

Her heart quickened. Somewhere in this great city was a young man who had inexplicably captured her interest, a boy who her instincts said would be important. Who could mean *everything.*

But, none of that now. She had her Guard spirits and the

remains of Phoenix to think about, so she returned to the place she had first planted her feet, to the incomplete mosaic. In her arms, the vessel glowed.

"Bury me here. This feels right," Phoenix whispered.

"But you're so far away from Beatrice, from your Guard."

"Beatrice owns part of my fire, not all; you know that."

"Still, won't you be spread too thin? You're not used to resting in mortal soil. The Whisper-world has access to all places, it sits beside all cities, lands, fields—"

"We have to test this. Darkness did not offer us much choice. Wander. Tell me about this place."

Persephone took to the halls, the rooms marked with numbers and stocked with an inordinate amount of boxes, filled with books. Schoolbooks. "Of course a god of wisdom should rest in a school," she murmured, feeling it fitting. She held her beloved's vessel as if it were a fragile baby. "But, what happened to this one? Why so empty and abandoned?"

The school was beautifully appointed on every floor, stately, Romanesque in style with a courtyard and four halls that joined into a fortresslike square. Gazing out the windows she saw that it appeared tucked against alleys. No grand lane showcased its entrance. It must be unassuming to London as a whole, but was clearly grand to those within.

Persephone glided across the floors, descending to the wide entrance foyer and passing below a space in the vaulted ceiling she assumed was supposed to hold a chandelier. It was entirely dark here, the windows on the first level having been boarded up. Her shifting colour provided the light she needed, however, and across the room the word HEADMASTER on an office door caught her eye. "Perhaps *you'll* tell me your secrets," she murmured, opening the door.

A small office sat beyond, stacked with books and strewn with papers. Persephone set her urn upon the desk and sat at the high-backed chair, glanced at letters and ledgers, all of which dealt with curricula for men and women, supplies, details, orders and employment referrals. All were quite friendly. Truly. The word "friend" was everywhere.

It dawned on her.

"Of course. *Friends.* You're a Quaker institution, aren't you? I've always liked them; they've the right idea about things."

And then her eye fell upon the edicts, a stack of papers crumpled on one side, as if held in a hand that had closed into a fist. Foreclosure? The bankers had withdrawn funds. A parliamentary outcry. Boycotts. Finally, a government move to close the institution before it even opened.

"Ah, yes," Persephone murmured sadly. "The Friends have long been persecuted. Well, we'll see about that."

She returned to the foyer where she first landed, to the loose tiles of the incomplete mosaic. She brushed them aside and lifted a loose plate of plaster, revealing floorboards beneath.

"Here, my love?"

A tendril of fire kissed her cheek, offering assent, so she placed the vessel within, nestled it between two floorboards and laid the plaster atop, smoothing the loose tiles down once more to make an even surface.

A crackling noise from behind made her turn. She gasped. The wide, stagelike portal of the Liminal edge had opened again, even without her bidding, lightning threading across its glassy surface. The Whisper-world was grey and hazily visible on the other side, a great wind emanating from its frame. Aodhan stood on the other side, his eyes distant, though he was smiling. She rejoiced that he was safe, if only for the moment. She thanked the Liminal for letting her know.

When she turned back to the transplanted grave of her beloved, she gasped again. The mosaic was entirely transformed. Now it was complete, and cerulean fire coursed along its outer edge. The dove had become an eagle, a fiery torch in its great, glittering golden claws. And a new message was a shouted proclamation in that seal:

AS THE PROMETHEAN FIRE WHICH BANISHED DARKNESS,
SO KNOWLEDGE BEARS THE POWER AND THE LIGHT

Phoenix fire had a new home. He, and the power of The Guard, was safe in this abandoned place. A place she would make vibrant with life and opportunity.

But it was a long, long way from Cairo.

Chapter Eleven

In a matter of weeks The Grand Work was becoming habit, uncomfortable as some aspects were. Its six practitioners had begun to develop routines; they were growing accustomed to their powers and to one another.

The gentlemen had begun congregating at the edge of a small café in central Cairo, in the heart of the old city. The hookah smoke was powerful there and made them feel as if they were somehow shielded from the outside world by that screen of scented cloud. There it could be keenly felt that epochs had come and gone, with the old streets encumbered with mosques and other great buildings, countless paths and squares no less grand for the massive asymmetry, all filled with a great antiquity. A modernization—or as some might call it, a "Westernization"—had begun around great al-Qahira, but here, surrounded by buildings centuries older than they, The Grand Work felt itself in good, ancient company.

It was only a matter of time before all the men began talking more pointedly about all the women. On this night, when the stars were bright and the smoke particularly sweet, Ahmed sat across from Ibrahim and went so far as to recite a poem written about Verena:

Your hand is that which bestows life.
Your face is worthy of a jewel mine.
Great forces brought People of the Book
Together in ways that sing glory

And I shall sing your glory always.
Your heart is a dove of peace.
Your whole being enslaves me.

Ahmed's kind, affable face was hopeful as he finished. "Well?"

"It's not Rumi," Ibrahim replied, knowing the beloved Sufi poet was Ahmed's favourite. Ahmed's face fell. "But I think she'll love it," Ibrahim added and chuckled when Ahmed's face again beamed. "If we encounter a lovelorn spirit, perhaps I'll recite it."

Ahmed slapped his hand on the table in delight. A moment later he gave a thoughtful sigh. "Since The Grand Work has disrupted my ability to study with my father and our teacher, I find that writing helps alleviate my guilt—and reading, of course. I may have gone to *khanqa* like Sufi before me, but well, I've a different commission now. Still, I sometimes feel I should be farther along on the path of faith than I am."

"If it's any consolation, I think you're the closest thing we have to godly," Ibrahim offered.

His friend chuckled, then shook his head in modest denial. Then Ahmed launched into a new recitation, again of his own creation:

O Grand Work, we wield you with our minds and
    hands,
You chose we special few as servants of your Peace
When those who do not know you would yearn for you
Bound to earth, you tether us to Heaven

It was in the midst of this rapturous ode that George joined them. He absorbed the reverie Ahmed had put himself in, and the one raised eyebrow of Ibrahim. He said nothing.

When the Sufi finished, the English youth applauded. Ahmed bowed his head. Ibrahim's cocked eyebrow remained.

"You know, Ibrahim," George said, pulling up a chair next to him. "Your name 'Wasil' is like the English word 'wassail,' which means to drink heartily in good company. To be merry, festive and hospitable. I think there's a secret, jolly, festive, drunken Englishman inside you somewhere."

Ibrahim blinked. "If so, please gather our friends and exorcise him."

George paused, frowning. But once Ibrahim's blank face gained a smirk, he pointed, registering the shift and laughed heartily, clapping Ibrahim too hard on the back and nearly spilling his Turkish tea. "That, my friend, is dry English wit."

Ibrahim replied, "While I did learn much from the man who raised me, please don't think you English invented everything."

"Fair enough!" George held up his hands.

"You Westerners, in all your conquering and claiming, think you created civilization. It began here, you know," Ibrahim added.

"And I love this land for that. Truly, I do." George then turned to Ahmed and grinned, changing the subject. "I've filled my brother's room entirely with art. He hates art, but Belle has him praising it and asking for more. It's wonderful!"

Ahmed returned his smile. Ibrahim enjoyed a quiet chuckle.

George continued, brimming alongside Ahmed, a picture of rapturous youth. The two were almost unfailingly cheerful. "Here I am, doing the one thing, the only thing in the world I've ever wanted to do—paint—and I suddenly have my family's blessing. They're merchants. All they know is trade on the pound, franc and the para; they know nothing of spirit. They were going to disown me! I tell you, The Grand Work hasn't just saved other souls but mine, too."

"But has it saved your heart?" Ahmed asked. "It has mine. I just read Ibrahim a verse I composed for Verena."

George's fair skin flushed. "Belle? Well . . . she's marvelous. Her parents couldn't have chosen a better name. The French word for 'beautiful.'" He said no more, but they could read his face.

Ahmed turned to Ibrahim, a mischievous sparkle in his wide, dark eyes and his smile radiant. "And so that leaves you our auspicious leader. Unless you'd like to duel me for the fair Verena and compete in composing Rubaiyat verses? George's heart is wide-open to me. Yours? Inscrutable."

Ibrahim did not answer. Instead, he stood. "I feel the Pull," he hissed. It had hit him like a wave of heat from a fire. "A disturbance in the Copt *hara,* not far from the Smith and the Gayed households."

George raised an eyebrow. "Did we make him so uncomfortable that he uses our Grand Work to change the subject?" He gave Ahmed a coy grin, but a moment later the two both groaned, thrown forward by the pain of the Pull themselves. Ahmed rose, tossing coins on the table as the English youth muttered, "That was too convenient."

Already headed out into the dark city street, Ibrahim cast a glare at his friends over his shoulder. "You were being worse than matchmaker women. Come. We've work to do."

Their walk was hurried, and it wasn't long before they turned a corner to find fabric, litters, chariots and palm fans floating everywhere down the avenue. Mortals in the employ of a European tour company, likely Cook's, were twirling and squealing, horrified, for everything they'd gathered for a paid reenactment of an ancient parade was being lifted away by unseen hands. The ghosts of those who would have actually participated in such a rite—or a ritual somewhat similar; one could not count on Cook for historical authenticity so much as providing what Westerners assumed and wanted to see—fussed over them like locusts. The avenue was a mess of floating props and a chorus of mortal screams.

George opened his pack to pull out a small, paper-wrapped rectangle. "Well, this is a right bloody mess," he grunted, ripping the paper to reveal a small canvas in a wooden frame.

Beatrice was already present. She had her hands full, literally. Cords of blue fire were attached to the legs of litters and to the wheels of chariots in an attempt to rein in the items and those spirits running about with them. It looked as if she were holding handfuls of absurd kites. Ibrahim almost wanted to laugh along with Ahmed, who was doing so freely, but watching Beatrice he was stilled. Struck.

She was dressed in an elegant taffeta evening gown, likely having come from some sort of university function with her father. The plunging neckline of the rich plum-coloured dress showed far too much skin. Western fashion. In the struggle, her hairpins had come undone and a few dark blonde waves fell down past her shoulders. Her piercing blue eyes, which sparkled in any light, were ferocious sapphires here, reflecting blue fire. Ibrahim felt the button at his collar poke into his throat.

"Could you enlighten us, please, sir Intuition? Or do you plan to stand there staring?" Beatrice called, trying to catch her breath.

Ibrahim cleared his throat, moved to loosen his collar and touched his temple, suddenly spouting a set of old city rules about where public assembly was appropriate and when. A few cowed spirits vanished, even in death terrified by the prospect of law enforcement.

Belle was busy directing traffic, removing the considerable crowd of gawking bystanders. Verena was attending the bruises and scrapes caused by the melee. George shrugged and hung his picture, a winged and glorious form that compelled the viewer to dream of angels, atop a plaque commemorating some military victory no one remembered.

"Lookie!" he cried. The spirits slowly did, one by one lowering their resistance enough for Beatrice to give them a swat of blue fire that caused their flight. At last they had all relinquished the purloined goods and fled.

George gathered up the wreckage. Ibrahim helped with the heavier items, so that the street was soon passable. Slowly but surely the lane was emptied.

Beatrice stepped up onto the walk, off the cobblestones, and leaned against a stone archway intricately carved with geometric arabesques. She breathed heavily, patting the sweat on her brow with a handkerchief embroidered with butterflies, a truly delicate item. But Ibrahim was reminded that she had been chosen as a warrior, young, female and all. It increased his interest to see she had not discarded what she'd been before. He found such antitheses fascinating. They had even factored into several recent reveries.

Ahmed moved close to Beatrice and bestowed his gift by staring into her eyes. The smile she returned him was wide, genuine and heartfelt. It made her face, that sometimes fierce visage, into something more appropriate to her undone tresses and glimmering eyes, and the effect was as beautiful as the painting of Athena that Ibrahim's father so treasured, that woman in armour whose expression was soft while she considered a bouquet of flowers. Ibrahim, to his surprise, found himself wanting Beatrice to turn that gentle smile upon him.

But she was always sharp, curt, full of business when interacting with him. Exactly as he was to her. It was best that way, of course. He had neither the heart nor the effusive power of Ahmed. He could not summon such a smile from a creature like this; it wouldn't be proper for either of them.

Why did that thought cause a sudden sorrow?

★ ★ ★

There was a particular weight to Ibrahim's gaze that Beatrice had never experienced. The way it touched her, as if his gaze were a lasso, gently but firmly capturing and reeling her in— she could not ignore it.

She tried. "Good work, friends," she said. Everyone nodded, wiping their brows and shuffling their feet.

New feeling coursed through her. The thought of them going their separate ways, six separate heartbeats settling out at paces throughout the great city, brought Beatrice a sudden pang. Life no longer made sense without the company of these friends. While at first she'd needed solitude and distance to think, she now needed their company to survive. Whether or not it was a natural progression, it was the truth.

"Come," she said, "the night is cool, refreshing and finally peaceful. Take some tea or coffee with me. My home lies just up the street."

"Tell me you've liquor," George said.

"I'm sure my father has a cabinet full." Beatrice smirked. "Whatever poison suits you."

"Huzzah!" the English youth cried. He held out his arm for Belle, who took it without hesitation. Ahmed gestured for Verena to walk beside him at a respectful distance, but not far. Beatrice charged toward home awaiting no man's arm.

Mr. Smith was asleep in the tall chair of his study, and Belle made a shushing sound in his direction to make sure that remained the case; their company left undisturbed. They took to the main room, making themselves comfortable on poufs and a divan, or, in the case of George, after one sip of the brandy Beatrice handed him, on the floor. Lying flat upon it he groaned.

"So. Tired."

"I daresay our leader did most of the work tonight," Ibrahim spoke up.

Beatrice stiffened at hearing this, preparing tea at a standing tray, but her lips curved into a small smile and a sensation of pride and pleasure gripped her stomach.

"Art is exhausting!" George insisted, splaying his body further upon the floor.

Belle and Verena chatted in hushed tones. Beatrice couldn't determine the subject matter, but the French girl blushed and her eyes flickered to George, the contours of whom were evident in formfitting breeches and with undone shirtsleeves, his body prone, facedown now upon a pillow.

Ibrahim went to the bookshelves that took up the entire north wall, his impassive face as engaged as she'd ever seen. He drank in the spines one after another. Beatrice moved first to his side, offering him a cup of tea.

He took it with a polite nod and pointed to a shelf containing Jane Austen volumes. "I assume those are yours?"

Beatrice blushed. "Well . . ."

"They're not bad. But I like Dickens better."

She was about to express her surprise that he should have read popular English writers, but then she remembered the English name he honoured. Also, surprise that any intelligent person had read something not native to them was rather limiting and condescending. Instead she offered, "Most men do."

"I'll look at his *Carol* quite differently now, I suppose, working with ghosts and all."

"I look at everything differently now."

Ibrahim nodded. "*Pride and Prejudice?*"

"What?"

"Your favourite?"

Beatrice shrugged. Then she nodded. "I suppose I'd say so."

"Most women do."

Beatrice raised an eyebrow. "You've asked them, have you?"

Ibrahim smirked. "No, not a one. It's simply the best known, so one assumes." He gazed at the wall. "James had countless books and papers, cycling between our home and the university. Hundreds. Of all kinds. All cultures. They were my best friends. All of them. Counting the characters, I had thousands of friends. It isn't often a man can say he has thousands of friends, can he?" His eyes were warm despite the melancholy in his tone. "All those friends died in a fire."

Beatrice bit her lip, her sympathies going out to him as he turned, took his tea and exited onto the arched, pillared balcony decorated with intricate arabesques of birds. She keenly understood loss, though she felt guilty that she did not miss Jean more. He seemed a lifetime away. If it had been her father, things would be different. And even Jean, if her heart hadn't already begun to—

She clamped down on the thought, though a blush remained upon her cheeks.

His dearest friends were in books. Oh, how she, a precocious and lonely child deemed too intelligent for her own good, understood. Oh, how she understood being raised by a father, no maternal warmth in the home. She wanted to extend more than courtesy to Ibrahim, and staring at the vast bookshelf she knew something she could give.

Moving to join him on the balcony, she said, "Please, take some of these volumes with you, whichever you like. Old friends, perhaps . . . or make new ones."

She hated how her voice sounded more like that lonely child

she once was than the woman she wished to be. But the fact remained she *was* young, despite how The Grand Work had aged them. Yes. Still young. And lonely.

Ibrahim stared at her a moment, his dark eyes like gleaming onyx, entrancing in the moonlight. "Thank you," he said. "I would enjoy that."

He turned back to stare out at the city and narrowed his eyes at a fixed point in the distance. "My house was there," he stated, nodding east, pointing a finger. He then swept his gaze across the asymmetrical sprawl of streets, squares, cupolas and towers. "I would like to think the whole of the city my home. Alas, our thoughts like ghosts haunt one mere building, unimportant in the grand scheme . . . and yet, everything to that person."

Beatrice wanted desperately to say something clever, something as effortlessly poetic as he. But instead her throat was dry.

He sipped his tea, then grimaced. "But I wax melancholy, unfit for company."

She shrugged. "I lost my sweetheart. You lost your home and your guardian. We were both thrust into the strangest of fates, have the weight of the city's very sanity on our shoulders. Do you think I have no capability to empathize? We're quite the pair."

"We are not a pair," Ibrahim replied.

Beatrice blinked. Goodness. Did he have any idea how cold he sounded? "Of course we aren't," she replied. Her sharp tone made her seem too defensive. "I didn't mean it in a . . . in a coupled sense. Wouldn't dream of it."

Ibrahim exhaled. After a moment he said, "It would seem fate has placed my life entirely in the company of the English. I'm in no way objecting to that circumstance; however, it does leave an Arab child at a loss, at times, as to touchstones for his soul. I beg you to try to understand," he added quietly, turning away. "Thank you for the tea. And very much for the books."

He moved back in toward the bookshelf. Beatrice was left to stare up at the stars and then back down at the place in the distance where James Tipton had died.

Chapter Twelve

Persephone paced the third floor of what she had decided to boldly name Athens Academy and tried to calm her desperate, careening thoughts. How could she free her Guard spirits? She'd have to unlock the prison gates Darkness had fashioned, then find some way to give them the advantage once they were unchained. She would need an army.

An army she had, she reminded herself. As soon as they were free, and if they could be reminded of what they once were. As long as they could access the Phoenix fire, they could work together as echoes of their greatness. They could win a great victory over Darkness. Perhaps they could do so here in Athens.

"Could that be so, love?" she asked, gazing down at the seal in the floor. "Shall these bricks prove the conduit?"

"Bring the precipice here," the Power and the Light murmured in her ear. "Bring the depths of the Whisper-world to me and let me bathe it in fire. It's time for a war. On our terms. With the army we have gathered. There are enough Guard spirits to best him and his agents of misery. Begin a merge."

"But, my love, the danger! The whole point was always to keep the Whisper-world safely shut away." Persephone's heart pounded wildly. "To bring it *upon* the mortals . . . It undoes the very purpose of The Guard, does it not?"

"Limit the fight to Athens alone, contain it. I shall bless these bricks with fire, and from here we'll end the vendetta. Darkness can't help but be drawn in when worlds collide."

"Knitting the worlds," Persephone mused. "Do I dare?"

"Reckless as you were, you must remember how it was done," Phoenix said. "I hope this time you will be more careful."

Persephone looked down, and a silver tear splashed onto the brass seal. It rolled away.

"Not that you have to relive it, darling," her beloved cautioned, but it was too late. She was lost to the memory of a painful, vital revelation earlier this mortal century.

★ ★ ★

It was a time when the dread press of the Whisper-world so choked her soul of light that ending her existence seemed the only choice. Her form was not human, nor did her body operate on human principles, and so she doubted she could throw herself on some funeral bier like Juliet did over her Romeo. Dearly fond of Shakespeare, she'd been desperate for some extreme show of despair.

She had plucked a hearty rose briar that was born and died at her feet, the thorn strong and sharp. She dug it into her, winced, wept and bled. Bled and bled. That blood had poured onto the dank Whisper-world stones. It had a life of its own, and it gathered in eddies, surged in rivulets toward all the Whisper-world barriers and there began to dissolve the stones. Her blood wanted out. It wanted free of this place. She herself collapsed.

Her beloved had felt the shift in her, caught the scent of her draining life force. The part of his fire in the Leader of The Guard had immediately reacted, abandoning its human host to rush to her, streaks of blue fire flashing through the Whisper-world darkness. Phoenix flew to Persephone, his flame meeting the pools of her blood that in the grey light appeared thick and dark like tar. When the two mixed, the reaction only increased. Light began to shine through from beyond. The two of them were creating tiny windows, merging the two worlds.

There were those who gathered at those holes: the restless dead both inside the Whisper-world and the ghosts on Earth, those caught in shadow and those on the mortal side. They stared into one another's worlds, stared down upon the struggling body of that goddess of shifting colours. Small flowers grew and died at her feet and fingertips; she evoked a thousand tiny cycles as she wept for a life she could never regain.

The dead began to beg and rally her. Even those she'd have deemed hopeless cupped their hands and gathered her blood, trying to return it to her, not sure what else to do. They gathered around her and lifted her body, cradled her, stroked her face. Even the spirits of murderers and fiends lent aid; even these were struck by the plight of a falling angel.

"We need and love you," crooned the spirits on the mortal side, staring in from flowering fields or busy streets. Those standing in dank black corners within the Whisper-world mourned, "Don't fall. Don't give up. Not like this . . ."

Traces of Phoenix fire raced over her body, his ghost doing what he could to rouse her. "My love," he whispered. "Why this? Isn't there another way for release? Why this instead of becoming mortal? Why this instead of attempting a new form?"

Persephone's eyelids drooped and she fumbled for words. "I . . . I'm scared. Being divine has been . . . hard. I doubt mortality is any easier. And I'm tired." She gave a slow shake of her head, then noticed the shadows around her faltering form had lengthened. *Him.*

"Go," she begged Phoenix. "He's coming, hide."

The ghost of her beloved knew to pick his battles. His cerulean fire retreated and dimmed, but he watched from a distance as the assembled crowd of spirits whirled to face the tall, regal shadows and bowed to their master.

"She wants out," they said.

Darkness stood like an ebon tower, red eyes in a black silhouette. Sometimes he was beautiful. At that moment he was not. He growled. His shadows bent like a huge claw, clutched Persephone's wilting body and threw her toward one of the windows her blood had opened. Phoenix's ghost encased her in an embrace of fire as she spilled into the space.

She would have been cast out onto some deserted space, but a familiar dark maw opened at the last moment and caught her instead: the portal used by The Guard. The dark rectangular door led to The Guard's sacred space, and Persephone landed in its centre, Phoenix's ghost slowing her fall with an embrace of fire.

She heard Darkness grunt. "I'll drag her back once she's recovered." But she knew he was already working furiously to seal the shadows behind her, hissing at the light that discomfited him as much as the flowers that grew in her wake. All life was extinguished in his realm, life and light. Only decay remained.

She was scooped into the strong arms of Dmitri Sergeyevna. At the time, the beginning of the nineteenth century, The Grand Work had been operative in Russia.

The Guard gasped at their herald, their Lady, so humbled. She looked up with tears in her eyes, blood dribbling from her arms, robes splayed around her, at a tall, black-haired stable boy-turned-demigod. Dmitri. Leader.

"I don't know how much longer I can hold on," she murmured to him, leaning forward and allowing him to hold her, to rock her, to say everything would be all right. Their Healer was soon at her side, his glowing hands offering a tingling release as her flesh was once again made whole.

Dmitri and his Guard, like every Guard before, were aware of the vendetta for which they fought. They believed it, and each Guard had seen how much their Lady struggled to maintain Light. And, Russians, they of all people embraced the firebird. They'd easily made him their own.

"My Lady," Dmitri murmured, his voice rich and low against her ear, very much like the voice of Phoenix himself. "Don't let the shadows take you. We wish we could shelter you here with us always. Could you not take pains to join us?"

"It is good to be with friends," Persephone replied, not answering that valid question but instead relaxing further into his embrace. He stroked her hair and held her tight, and for a moment she almost believed that she was again with her beloved. In the light of the Russian Guard's sacred space she was healed. More important, she'd inadvertently gained knowledge that altered the game.

★ ★ ★

"I'll bleed the worlds together!" she declared, dragging her mind again to the present, her feet bare and cool upon the marble floor of the Athens foyer. It occurred to her that the scene she'd relived hadn't been very long ago in mortal time. She wasn't terribly adept at tracking mortal years, but she believed her mounting desperation and volatility had been entirely contained within their nineteenth century. She had apparently reached a breaking point in this age. They all had.

Padding slowly about the grand foyer, gazing out through windows over chimneys and the darkening London sky, she felt her determination grow. Speaking to the seal, this time she stated it more firmly: "I'll knit the worlds with my blood."

A sparking tendril of blue fire offered agreement, and her words became a vow.

She heard a tearing sound. Behind her was the Liminal edge, open and lit, as if it were the thing projecting forth reality. But the reality it projected was not hers. The vast metal hands of its overhead clock shook and shuddered, meaning the vision it projected was not certain; this future was not set in stone.

The vision took place on a dark night in the very foyer in which she stood. A tall, striking man dressed all in black swept a young woman across the floor in a delicate waltz. The pair was alone, and the moonlight magical.

Persephone gasped. The woman . . .

"It's *me*."

It wasn't her, exactly; she was watching a young mortal. But the woman looked very much like her. Not how others saw her, but what she saw when she looked at her own hand. Flesh *entirely* devoid of colour. Pearly hair, blanched skin, eerie, ice-cap eyes with faint slivers of blue—it was as if she was watching a younger self in a mirror, her hand upon the shoulder of a magnetically beautiful man who looked so very familiar.

"And it's *him!*" Persephone breathed. "That boy. Grown. It's Alexi."

The vision was silent. Its subjects did not speak; the two only stared at each other, enraptured. Then the young woman's lips parted in a silent sigh, a small gasp. Her ice-blue eyes drank in her dance partner, her gaze a glorious surrender.

If Persephone was not mistaken, the man was equally smitten. His stoic expression was betrayed by the way his dark eyes glittered; his sculpted lips curved slightly whenever she sighed. This was the start of something wonderful.

Persephone whispered in delight, "An unchaperoned waltz by moonlight? Scandalous for the mores of your age!"

Yet, who could have denied them this simple dance, this pair holding each other at a decorous if fond distance, this luminous girl lit by moonlight, this ghostly, eerie goddess—

"I'll be *you*," Persephone cried.

The vision bled into another, where the two dancers waltzed

once more. Alexi was again in all black, the same as when she'd first glimpsed him, as a young man. This time, however, the strangely beautiful girl wore a finer dress. Something else about her was older, too; not years but experience.

Their waltzing bodies stood close. No longer decorous, this was the dance of two lovers. A silver ring glimmered on the girl's finger, a silver band on his, too.

"Oh, Alexi, how your wife will stare at you," Persephone breathed.

His face was transformed by adoration. Yet, there remained a hint of wild desperation along with the new softness. Why? She wondered. He had her, so what was to fear?

A third vision appeared, a blaze of blue fire. The two were now bent over the Athens seal, there was a key and an explosion. The foyer was suddenly awash with ghosts. Not just any ghosts, either. Ghosts of The Guard. Persephone recognized them all. Here were all The Guard that had ever been, from every city, every age. All were taking up arms at this academy and—

Persephone gasped. "My army! It's true, we must bring the army here."

But, why was the Liminal showing her this? Seeing the way the hands of its clock trembled, this future couldn't be certain. If Persephone knew the Liminal, it was showing her a future it wanted—for these two mortals, for her, for what she would become . . . But this was no fait accompli.

She saw the girl again, a mirror of herself, and for the first time in eons Persephone saw herself reflected in another's eyes and beloved.

Alexi held the girl. Blue fire erupted around and through him, cascaded over the bricks and left Athens awash. So, he was the Leader of The Guard after all in this vision, despite Phoenix's earlier concern. What would happen to Beatrice? Alexi was a glorious conduit, Persephone admitted. This was where the battle would come to pass, and he looked ready. Where else should they fight but at the source of their power, where she had buried her Phoenix?

Persephone glanced around. The Liminal proscenium had not snapped shut; it gaped, a glorious stage sparking with hopes and dreams. But still, this fate was uncertain. All things, mortal and divine, had free will. And there were plenty of those who would stand in the way of this mortal partnership.

"I'll pledge my fading light to this future," she vowed.

Her declaration made the Liminal crackle. Persephone felt a wind sucking inward, into the Whisper-world, beckoning her to return. To begin. The visions had faded.

Indeed, there was no time to waste. She had work to do. Painful work. But rather than bleeding herself recklessly, as she had the first time, she would wield her magic carefully, methodically. And to keep herself from despair she would think of people who made her smile. She would remember the comfort she'd felt in Dmitri's embrace, would recall the vision of a grown boy whom she only knew as Alexi, twirling her embodiment around this very foyer. If she could hold on to these signs of hope, all would fall into place. Finally, she had something worth fighting for.

But, could she do what the vision wanted? Could she take the form of a colourless mortal girl with the mind and heart of a goddess? Yes, she would come into that black-haired boy's life with all her power and glory, with all her collected knowledge and wisdom, and she would have to make things right. Gloriously right.

"Hold on to Light, my love," Phoenix's ghost called out, a trail of fire coursing out from the seal, out and around her body. It was warm and tender. "Face the shadows knowing the house of Darkness will come crashing down. As long as you hope, Darkness cannot overtake you. You must now plant seeds that will sprout and flower."

"I'll begin anon," Persephone murmured, moving to the Liminal edge. She paused only a moment before she stepped through to her next destination.

Chapter Thirteen

Beatrice had been in pain for days. It was not the Pull; it was not instinct. It was not the increasingly exquisite agony of being so near and yet so far from Ibrahim. This was something else. It was good that she generally wore gloves as a lady must, for they lessened the sting. It was as if patches of her skin were peeling away.

She was startled by a luminous and colourful appearance in her boudoir. The newcomer appeared worried. Maybe this pain was related.

The goddess was awful at hiding emotion. Beatrice imagined it was something her ancient lover found attractive, such artlessness, but she found it troubling. It didn't seem proper, to so blatantly wear one's heart on one's sleeve. That was something one trained out of a child.

"What is it?" Beatrice asked.

"The game has altered."

"Game?" Beatrice repeated. "Please don't say our lives are a game to you. We, your mortal pawns? I don't suppose you could tell me why parts of me feel on fire. It tests my ability to be polite."

"By 'game' I mean the struggle in which we are *all* caught up," the goddess exclaimed. "The king of the Whisper-world has captured every Guard spirit that ever was, save for the original set. They were so long ago, before we thought to build the field . . ."

Beatrice blinked.

"There's a field," Persephone explained, clearly wistful.

"Gorgeous, built by consensus. You can't spend eternity surrounded by gloom. But it's gone, washed away by Darkness. I was forced to move the remains of Phoenix from their rightful resting place to untried ground. This is an unprecedented action for an unprecedented time. Unless we take a stand, you'll never be free of hell. Something new must be undertaken for your eternal safety—yours, and for every Guard."

"Hell." Beatrice set her jaw. "That's lovely."

The goddess gestured. "Pack your bags. You're leaving for London."

"Excuse me?"

"Operations are moving to London," Persephone repeated.

"Why?"

"Because it's where the remains of Phoenix burn on. From inside the Whisper-world, he has been transferred to mortal soil. It's likely why you're in pain. I'm sorry to hear it, but a Leader's never been so far from the very hearth of his or her fire."

Beatrice shook her head. "Why London?"

"Why not?"

"Why not *here,* where we, your chosen Guard, were planted?"

"Because in the coming years the Power must be in London. That simply is so. The source of The Grand Work now lies near the banks of the Thames, and you must go to it."

Beatrice fought a wave of anger. She was tired of the pain, tired of having her life uprooted by the whims of the eternal. Tired of the pendulum of yearning when it came to her second-in-command. "By whose omnipotent authority has it been supplanted?"

Persephone lifted prismatic hands. "I never said I was omnipotent. I simply moved my beloved to a safer location. I've no precedent here, I'm sorry. As for why London? Because I was told that's the place to bring the war!" Her hands began to shake, and she wrung them. "The Fates decide. The Liminal decided. And it is because someone is already there, someone who will prove critical."

Beatrice tried to sort through this mess of new information. "Persephone, you cannot expect to overturn mortal lives whenever you wish. For us to simply pack bags, leave home, blindly follow danger . . . All without answers! We live in a gilding age of *science*. 'The Fates decide' is naught but an incitement to riot."

Persephone gave her the first hard and unflinching look Beatrice had ever seen from her. "All creatures must adapt to existence, inhospitable clime though it must be. Even I know that. Shall you tell your fellows or shall I?"

Beatrice sighed. It wasn't that she didn't want to help the goddess, to do her duty, but how could she fight when she'd give goodly years of her life just to stop her pains? "I'll call the meeting, but this is your doing. You must tell them. And what the hell is the Liminal?"

Persephone glanced at her. "The place from which all blessings flow. And curses, I suppose. It depends on the soul doing the asking." She took a deep breath. "I'll make the announcement, not to worry."

The prismatic creature vanished then, leaving Beatrice to mounting anxiety. Suddenly, interpersonal dynamics and itchy skin paled in comparison to moving six unlikely companions across the world. She doused her irritated hands in cool water for the thousandth time and cursed supernatural whim.

★ ★ ★

It was not pleasant for her, but Persephone returned to shadow. She had to. There were cycles, of course, and he wouldn't have noticed yet that she hadn't come back. Time was indeed different here. But Darkness would eventually require her presence. She would have to act as if he had won, as if he had cowed her at last. And he would believe it.

He would be unbearable, lording over her in his perceived triumph. Not until she discovered how and dared take that colourless mortal body of her visions could she maintain a prolonged absence. She would do so someday. Someday soon. But first, blood. She would begin her task immediately.

Persephone knew vaguely where the seals were, the pins that held the worlds apart. Those seals were formed of stone and spirit, and they had existed since the Whisper-world separated from the mortal back when civilizations were new. She knew that to proceed with this task required forethought. The torn-open Whisper-world needed to pour down in one precise location, and thusly she needed to route the seals. All to London. All to Athens Academy. All roads must lead there.

The seals were set deep in the Whisper-world's murk, but those attuned to the mortal world could sense warmer, fresher air in their presence. The flowers she created always told her. It took her bouquets longer to die near the seals; they struggled and fought before curling and giving way to putrefaction. Seeing that change was always a dagger in her heart, but soon there would be no need for such. Not for her. Not anymore.

Deep into this darkness where the promise of life and love hung in the air, so did the acrid vapours of suicide and slaughter. They burned Persephone's nostrils. In case anyone might gain hope at this crossroads of the seals, Darkness had made sure to deter them with a font of despair, rerouting the more horrid underground currents of the Whisper-world to these fixtures.

She stepped into the shallow water, felt it nip at her toes with tiny teeth and allowed just enough of her light to illuminate the alcove of grey stone before her. A thin golden ring was visible glimmering against the wall, its circumference a few feet wide.

As always, at her feet grew flowers. Persephone plucked a

particularly sharp rose briar and watched it harden and grey. Using it to prick her thumb, she hissed as her blood, thinner in these dark depths, flowed free. She then placed droplets upon each of the stones, ran it in a circle around the golden band where it must wait. Only when met by Phoenix fire would it open the world. Through blood and fire her army would be free. In time.

In the distance came the sound of hissing. Persephone hurried on. The last thing she wanted was to be seen by a spy. Sour pomegranate juice was always at the back of her throat in these dread corridors, so to mask her pastime Persephone spat. The Gorgon would assume she'd had one of her frequent ailing spells in the shadows and be none the wiser.

She glided back to the great stone dais, wincing as she ignored the weeping pleas of the Whisper-world's denizens, today unable to spare any light. Her power must be saved for a ghostly girl and the man she loved. Those ice-pale eyes confirmed that Alexi was the one she'd been waiting for. Suddenly she was no longer afraid of becoming mortal. Not if her beloved could be there in that magnificent form.

Stopping at the moat edge, she scowled at the bold bulb of crimson in his world of dreary grey. It was always jarring, to see that distressingly beautiful great red rose at the dais, Darkness's immense crimson robes arranged artfully into the vast bloom. Persephone assumed he rested in such a manner to mock all the dead flowers at her feet.

The petals peeled back one by one to reveal a naked man. He was beautiful; then he was a skeleton. Then again a man. He stood, and those crimson robes hovered around him in glorious folds, as if he were imitating a painting of Christ; the colour scarlet representing a certain carnality, reminding the viewer that the depicted was a *mortal* saviour. But Christ had been a child of light. Darkness ticked away life and light, second by second, flesh into bone and back again.

"Back. So. Soon? I thought you'd run off and punish me."
His voice was like wet gravel.

"I came to check on my beloveds."

"Wasting away, as should all who exist here. Exceptions are
not fair."

There had always been an unseen, unlit stone tower behind
the dais, a column of moist slate growing like a vast tree trunk
with no leaves or life. Persephone hadn't thought much of
it, never dreamed it would become a prison. But Darkness
gestured to it, and Persephone moved closer, around the moat,
toward a door with a long hanging chain and a lock. A hefty,
dull silver key with a slender ring hung in the lock. Persephone
moved to snatch it.

Darkness batted her away. "Ah, ah, ah."

He alternately clucked his tongue, then clicked his jaw.
Removing the key, he glanced down at his breastbone. When
it was bone, he slid the ring about his sternum. It was visible
when he was bone, then hidden under flesh when he was
man.

"It's fitting, you know, this." He gestured to the key as it
flashed into sight. "You cry your silver tears here on my stones.
Sometimes I collect them. They can make useful things. You
have imprisoned your friends yourself. This very key, made
from your tears."

Persephone balled her fists. It took every ounce of her control
not to slap him with a burst of light, to level declamations and
threats, to use every last bit of her power to crack open the
prison gates and flee with them. But such an act would be
fruitless. If she did that, she'd tear herself in two, and Darkness
would simply round The Guard up again. There was no escape.
Not this way.

Instead she turned to Darkness and shook her head. "Pity
and hatred. It's all you'll ever know from me. It's a shame. You
could know love."

"I have others who bow to me, who love me," Darkness countered.

"But do you love them in return? What do you know of love's equality?"

"I love you."

Persephone laughed. It was a hollow sound. "Hardly. You seek to *possess* me. You act as a child. You act as a prison guard and torturer, nothing more. What you are made of does not include love in its ingredients. And that deficit will one day destroy you."

She took that moment to flee, hearing Darkness grind his teeth behind her. Standing in shadow, she waited in a side corridor to see if he would follow. He didn't. A small light flickered like a firefly a small distance ahead. She followed it to the end of the corridor, and there she found the Liminal edge. Apparently it was ready to assist her once again.

Allowing her face to fall, her light changing slowly, she gave herself a moment of despair. "Don't let him have any more of my tears—please," she begged the shimmering portal. "He even uses those against me."

The mercury beads that fell from her cheeks were sucked into the Liminal, where they would be put to better use, there at the portal where a bright dawn could break.

★ ★ ★

A Guard meeting was called, and as Beatrice and her fellows descended to their sacred space, the goddess awaited them.

"I've a mission for you, friends," she said.

The Guard stared blankly at their angel. Her eternally youthful voice was anxious.

She looked at Beatrice, then at George. "On a distant shore. For some of you it is a homecoming of sorts. For the rest of you, an adventure. But I need you. The source of your power has been relocated due to . . . an emergency."

"You're asking us to abandon our homes?" Ibrahim asked. "To leave Cairo?"

Persephone sighed. "You understand the basic principle of The Grand Work, do you not?" she asked. "That Darkness feeds upon mortal misery, and he sends his restless dead to collect it. You—The Guard—have been starving him for ages. Eventually, however, you all must pass. You six must all die. You are mortal, if what you host is not. So this is now your war more than ever. Darkness has taken the spirits of every Guard that ever was and locked them away.

"Look. Look at what he has done to your kin!" She opened her arms, lifting a window onto endless, miserable shadow. At the centre of this lifeless purgatory sat a vast, huge tower. Inside it could be heard crying. "All The Guard that has ever been, they're trapped in that prison," the goddess cried. "And so will you be if you do not join the fight."

She whirled on them, an exhilarated but mad look in her eyes. "And you fight for *love.* You fight for me and my beloved. Oh, my darlings, this age of yours! Such books will be written, such love stories, such letters and poetry . . . But while some art may evoke me, no one will truly *know* me, and mine is a tale for the ages. I need you to make it beautiful. Tell not only my trials but my triumph! For I will triumph over Darkness at last. I've begun my tasks. We shall prevail."

The Guard stared at her, frightened both by Persephone's sudden madness and the fate that awaited their failure.

The goddess spoke again, more evenly. "You'll go to London by sea. No one will question you, not when Belle casts her magic. Pack your things, there's a ship in the morning. I'll see you soon."

The reply she received was silence.

Persephone turned and gestured to Beatrice. "If nothing else, do it for your Leader. While she has not complained, I know that she is in pain. The remains of Phoenix have, for the first time, been moved into the mortal world. Into safety far away. The separation wounds her. To *London,* my loves. To London. That will solve all." And then she was gone.

The Guard stood staring after the goddess long after her shifting colours vanished into the shadows. They then turned to Beatrice, concerned, and she grimaced. She was sure they were all left with the same thought.

"An adventure!" George cried, surprising her.

Ibrahim turned to Ahmed and Verena, then turned and addressed the Europeans. "We're not posing as your help."

"I wouldn't dream of asking," Beatrice snapped. Were their worlds truly so impossible to bridge?

Verena moved close. "I'm sorry for your pain," she whispered, placing a glowing hand upon Beatrice's closed fist.

"Thank you." The physical pain eased slightly. The rest would remain.

★ ★ ★

The oddest part of what followed was watching Belle go to each of their families and tell them simply that their children were going away. To school, it was explained. The families seemed heedless; they nodded and wandered off, indifferent. The only emotion provided was by The Guard themselves in support of one another. They stepped up, pressing a shoulder or offering a nod of encouragement.

Ibrahim was the only one who didn't go with the group. He quietly excused himself as each child said good-bye to a dazed parent. Beatrice wanted to know where he went wandering instead, what his lonely soul might be feeling, but they were not linked in a way to share such things.

Late that evening, Mr. Smith called to Beatrice in the sitting room. "Bea, a nice boy is here to see you!"

Beatrice rose from the divan, smoothed her skirts and wondered who had come to call. It had to be a Guard, but which? Weren't they all spending last moments with their families? She glanced at the trunk she'd just spent hours packing. It sat like a millstone in the centre of the room, a weighty crate representing the terrifying unknown.

A "nice boy"? Surely it was George. Her father hadn't been too terribly fond of Jean, and Beatrice had assumed he'd rather she be courted by an Englishman. She wondered what on earth he'd say if he ever actually noticed she spent time with two Egyptian men. Her father worked with the locals, respected their artifacts and had done a great deal to learn both Arabic and the meanings of their ancient symbols, but his daughter keeping company with their boys? Her study of society had led her to believe that the British were oft masters of hypocrisy.

She made her way to the door of the sitting room. "Oh!" she blurted when she discovered her visitor.

"Disappointed?" Ibrahim asked, sounding almost amused.

"No. Just surprised," she replied. Her womanly sense of hospitality, a quality ingrained despite her mother's early passing due to cholera, bade Beatrice gesture across the room. "I could make some tea?"

Ibrahim looked at the tea service and shook his head. "No, thank you."

"Please, sit." Beatrice gestured to the fine divan, taking a wooden chair opposite.

Ibrahim sat but did not relax into the furniture. His back remained straight, his movements showing simple grace, uncluttered, efficient. To the point and full of purpose. It was a quality Beatrice admired and wished she had, but she fussed and fidgeted too much. To her chagrin, she now found herself fluffing the lace at the edge of her blouse sleeves.

He studied her briefly and spoke. "While my gifts are still young within me and I cannot credit myself with an expert conclusion regarding their meaning, my Instinct is that this trip to London is dangerous. I feel it in my bones. I cannot in good faith allow it to go forward without voicing concern. And while I deeply regret hearing that you may be in pain, our Leader and the whole of The Guard should know of my concern."

Beatrice took a moment to register his words but soon found herself arguing. "My discomfort aside, all travel has its dangers. We've a mandate from a higher power that expects us elsewhere. Our power has been relocated. I'm as leery of the journey as you, but do we have a choice?"

"Of course we have a choice," Ibrahim said. "Let The Grand Work choose other youths to take up our mantle. Others in England. Why us? There are plenty of people in the world to create an odd, ragtag band. They only need six."

A smirk played at Beatrice's mouth. "But we were already chosen. Truly, Ibrahim, I question The Grand Work every minute of every day myself. Yet I can't deny that it has changed me. If the power that grants it is elsewhere, do I have any choice but to follow? Do I brook further pain, further risk to the world, by staying apart from it?"

"But it won't be safe. I feel it. I feel some tragedy will come to one of our number, that the goddess, well meaning as she may be—"

"Infuriating as she may be," Beatrice added.

"She may be playing loosely with our safety, her eyes on some larger future goal. Did you notice that she told us of our fate after we die?"

Beatrice sighed. "While I agree with you about this, what do you suggest?"

"For us not to go. I'll be more than happy to state my reasons.

I was granted a gift. It is warning me. I am only honouring The Grand Work by stating my concerns to you."

"I don't doubt it."

"Good. Then you'll understand why I won't be on that ship in the morning."

"The goddess may have something to say about that."

"Should she, I'll tell her exactly what I've told you. As Leader, if you're interested in protecting your comrades, we should not board that ship."

Beatrice shook her head. "We'll talk about it at the docks tomorrow. I'm happy to relay your concerns, or you're welcome to speak your mind yourself, declare what you think should be done. I've no taste for a dictatorship. However, while I respect your gifts, other reasons lead me to board that boat. I am weak, drained. I believe that is because the tether to my power now stretches an ocean away."

"Could it be a psychological reaction?"

Beatrice set her jaw, fists clenching. "What are you saying? I'm a credit to my sex. My father and every one of his colleagues at the university would attest to that. I'm not sure what—"

"I'm not calling into question the quality of your mind. Or your father and his colleagues at the university . . ." Ibrahim swallowed hard and looked away.

Beatrice recalled Mr. Tipton. He'd worked at that university. She hadn't meant to bring that up.

Ibrahim's sentiment was fleeting. "Our lives no longer operate on the principles by which they operated a mere month ago."

"True," Beatrice acknowledged. "But what makes your gift any more trustworthy than mine?" Her second-in-command wasn't arbitrarily trying to be difficult, she recognized, and truthfully she didn't want to go any more than he did, but her body felt pulled, magnetized toward the West, and she couldn't ignore the sinking sense that failing to take the steamer wasn't an option.

"I suppose trust is entirely subjective, and a personal choice. My preference is not to board that ship. And because my Instinct has labeled Verena as particularly vulnerable, I will share my thoughts with her—which may influence the outcome of her willingness to travel."

Beatrice sighed. "You're welcome to your thoughts and actions. I'll inform the group of them, but you'd best be prepared to tell the goddess if she shows up wondering."

"Indeed," Ibrahim said. Rising he added, "I know my way. We need not stand on ceremony."

Beatrice sat stunned as he departed the room. Nothing in her life could have prepared her for this circumstance. She commended herself for dealing fairly, calmly and evenly with her second-in-command, having made the appropriate decision in letting him go his own way. And while she credited him with being respectful despite disagreement, she still had to calm her racing heart. Her discomfiture had nothing to do with the politics of the situation. It was infinitely more personal. Which made it infinitely less agreeable.

Chapter Fourteen

The next morning Beatrice awoke at first light. She dressed in a sturdy skirt and blouse designed for traveling. While there was mutiny afoot, she wanted to be prepared for any eventuality, and if boarding that ship meant her hands would stop burning, she'd take the trip alone if she had to.

With a cool detachment that should seem deranged, Beatrice went into her father's room, kissed his forehead as he slept and went out to the street. She stood looking up at the fine building that housed several English families in relative space and luxury for so dense a city, at the arches and ornate finery so unique to Arabian aesthetic, and she wondered if she'd ever see it again.

Something about The Grand Work, Beatrice surmised, dulled the human heart. It rearranged priorities and kept emotions distant like storm clouds on the horizon. She could sense the pain and uncertainty in herself of having to leave behind people and places she loved, and yet she stared at this with an odd, objective eye. Perhaps that was what Leaders did, looked at everyone's pain from afar. Especially their own.

The task seemed unwomanly the more she thought of it. Odd. Dangerous. At some point, all that sentiment would come crashing in, and she hoped it would not prove stronger for having been put off.

She flagged down a young man she knew to be a neighbourhood errand runner. In moments her trunk was collected and packed into a rickshaw, and she was jostling onward to her destination, unsure what fate awaited her.

Other rickshaws with familiar passengers converged at the docks of Alexandria at a similar time as hers, as if a great hand were bringing them all together. George was assisting Belle out of one rig, and Ahmed was already standing at the dock, contemplating the vessel used to transport curious Westerners here to the seat of civilization. It was upon this, it seemed, that they would voyage to England.

At least, Beatrice hoped they would. She needed to be there long enough to rub Phoenix's ashes over her skin as a salve, or whatever the hell she was supposed to do. She didn't remember much of London from her childhood but that it was grey and crowded. She felt a pang in her heart. Cairo was golden.

Glancing about as her hired help carried her luggage onto the platform, Beatrice saw that Ibrahim and Verena were nowhere to be found. She gave the young man a larger bill than was necessary, feeling nostalgic already for her old neighbourhood. He beamed, bobbed his head and disappeared.

Belle stood squinting up at the ship. At the head of the dock was a man in a fine suit who was clearly there to assist English and French tourists, and it was directly to him that Belle strode, George at her side. Beatrice watched the man's eyes cloud; then she overheard assurances about first-class luxury and such. After George elbowed her, Belle pressed for champagne. Success was soon confirmed by George's ridiculously large grin.

George and Belle were just about to direct ferrymen to take their trunks into cargo, so Beatrice halted them with a call, a word in Guard language that beckoned them over. She was soon encircled by comrades. The three who were present.

"Friends, we've dissention in the ranks. But it's not without its just cause. I would let Ibrahim tell you himself, but—"

"And so I shall."

Beatrice turned. Ibrahim came striding forward in a finely embroidered tunic and linen coat, his dark eyes confident if hard. Paces behind him stood Verena, shifting on her feet like a frightened little girl and not a woman of eighteen. Perhaps Ibrahim had told her she was destined for danger.

"Friends . . ."

He spoke the word as if he were still getting used to the idea, even after the weeks they'd spent, which rode Beatrice a bit roughly. There was no other word appropriate for people thrust into such strange affiliation, even if they were not those you would choose for yourself. She took a moment to wonder: if George or Ahmed had spoken thusly, would she have thought twice? Perhaps she expected more courtesy, cooperation and camaraderie out of her second. Again she considered that the Muses might have made a mistake.

"I'll not be taking this vessel with you. Neither will Verena. My gift of Intuition has warned me that there is danger ahead for the most vulnerable among us. Thus, for safety's sake, I cannot condone this journey. My foremost commitment is to the protection of our comrade."

Ahmed stared at Verena, his joyful expression becoming anxious. Beatrice could feel a wave of discord wash through her fellows like strains of music gone terribly off-key.

"But . . . but the Work will always have its dangers. Is this any different than before?" George asked the question while Belle nodded.

"I fear the danger shall worsen. Cairo is our home soil, the place we were chosen. To uproot ourselves is to run the risk of being tossed to the wind, of becoming groundless, no better than those spirits out there."

Ibrahim gestured to the sea. It was true; there they were, like sails without a boat, rigs with no tethers, white bodies billowing in the breeze, buffeted and hapless, not knowing their purpose, from whence they had come or where they were going. It was a sobering image. And then came the unsettling notion that there were many more spirits here than when she first arrived. As if they were gathering.

Was it a farewell committee of the dead? Or was it a ripple of conflict that Beatrice felt very truly in her blood, a distinct, uncomfortable sensation that this was not right? A good-bye and a separation was not an option; the tethers that bound them in this fantastical fate could not be severed, not by choice nor by any surgery known to mankind. So, was this all having an effect on the very fabric of the air, on the Balance they were bidden to maintain?

There came a separate ripple in the air and a burst of light.

"What's this?" the goddess said, her feet touching down on the dock. Where they did, Beatrice marveled, delicate ferns sprouted up. "Why are you here when you ought to be on that boat? Isn't it nearing departure?"

Sure enough, there came a clanging bell that made them all jump. Beatrice glanced around to see that their luggage had been stowed; Belle's lingering magic must have influenced all around her with its subtle magnificence.

Ibrahim and Verena hung back. The Egyptian girl's face was pinched in a grimace; it was clear that she was torn. If Ibrahim felt the same conflict, it did not show. The pair had brought no luggage.

Because the goddess had made herself visible, Belle had to make sure the busy docks were dealt with, and so she found herself circling the group like an officer on patrol, waving her hand at any that gaped, paralyzed by this prismatic creature of unparalleled beauty and magic. Belle's gift sent the dock workers, ferrymen and passengers drifting dazed to other destinations.

"My Lady." Ibrahim turned to the goddess. "My Instinct warns me there is great danger for us in London. It is my duty to inform the group if we are walking into a trap. While I'd not dare accuse you of duplicity, I fear there are perhaps unintended consequences to this sudden journey that even you may not be able to foresee."

He spoke with such cool intelligence that it seemed a crime to disagree, thought Beatrice.

The goddess managed. "There is always danger courted by The Grand Work."

"See?" George said.

"But what sort of man would I be if I, sensing danger, sent my comrades directly into it?"

"I commend you for your caution, Ibrahim, I truly do, but the danger is in staying behind when the pendulum of power has so radically swung elsewhere. When the balance is so terribly skewed against you, the danger here outweighs whatever you feel awaits you."

"How can you so easily override what is felt in my veins?" Ibrahim asked. "Am I not afforded more proof than words?"

"I'm sorry," the goddess murmured, her tone sad. Waves too tall for the weather rose to slap the docked ship. "I showed you the dread of the Whisper-world only. When you asked me why, before, I should have shown you the *whole* of the picture. I forget that we ask so much while offering so little." She closed her eyes, and a wave of pain crossed her. Flinging an arm forward as if in a punch or a cutting blow, she cut a vast rectangle in the air.

Something caught Beatrice's eye. At the distressing sight of what she could only assume were a few drops of the goddess's blood dripping down her arm, Verena darted forward, her hand glowing. Persephone opened her eyes and held out a hand, halting Verena but offering a soft, gracious look of thanks for a healing attempt. But it would appear this blood was not meant to dry or fade. She turned to the rest of them, the look replaced by one of bitterness.

Behind her, a grey rectangle had appeared, as if a gaping wound had been cut into the fabric of their reality. On the other side was that wet, grey world, the one they'd glimpsed from their sacred space on that first day. It was that same world of corridors, of rushing water and countless restless dead, walking, tethered to those stones rather than floating free upon Earth or having gone on to some greater reward. They wandered, devoid of any colour, existing in monochromatic misery.

Beatrice felt the warm Cairo sun through the muslin of her blouse, and yet her heart felt the terrible cold of this other world. Two temperatures she endured, one that was warm upon her skin and another that was internal and yet no less real. The Guard could only gape.

"Again, the Whisper-world," Persephone said. "It is not down but sideways. It is always just to the left or right of your soul. It was made and fed by mortal misery. If you six should part, it will tear a small hole in the mortal world and just a bit of hell will break loose. The longer you are separated, the greater the hole. When The Guard was formed, the Whisper-world reacted. You and it are inextricably tied."

One by one, some of the ghosts turned. Looking into their hollow-eyed, harrowed faces was like staring at assured doom; it was a contagion of the soul, a festering wound for which there was no cure. Just looking at the Whisper-world was suffocating, let alone stepping across into it or letting it pour out unchecked into . . .

Ahmed moved among his comrades, bestowing his gift with a slight touch upon the temple. A jolt of fresh air into struggling lungs, and each of them revived.

The grey dead approached the threshold opened by Persephone. Beatrice wondered with alarm if they could step across, so many of them that The Grand Work would be entirely overrun and outmatched. The spirits on the living side approached it, too, blanched white and floating like vertical clouds above the water, and soon there were dead looking at dead, all of them in some hazy state of remembrance. The spirits on the mortal side were harmless wisps. Not so on the other.

"The unseen Balance," the goddess declared.

The water began to slap against the dock. Belle was standing closest, trying to deter foot traffic and muttering that if they'd had any sense in their heads, they'd all have had this conference in private. Looking down, she squealed. The whitecaps on the water were horse heads, but with sharp teeth. The thrown-open Whisper-world was turning nature sour and vicious. The delicate ferns at the goddess's feet were rotten and moldy.

George dragged Belle toward him. Verena rushed to Ibrahim's side, completing the circle of friends. This small gesture caused a ripple through Beatrice—and, she assumed, through the rest of them—a feeling of affirmation that the circle was not meant to break. Ever.

"My friend," Verena murmured, staring at Ibrahim. There were tears in her eyes. "Do not endanger everything for my sake. You yourself said there's nothing about your gift that makes this certain. I'll take my chances . . . if you'll help protect me." She turned to the others. "I don't mean to be trouble."

"I'm not going to let you end up a sacrifice," Ibrahim hissed. "While I comprehend the value of The Grand Work, I am not convinced being at the whim of gods remains in our best interest . . ."

Beatrice stared at the two and was alarmed by how keenly she felt her heart. Something about the way the two of them stared at each other . . . Surely Ibrahim fought for Verena out of love. She was unquestionably beautiful, as the men could not help but see.

Verena turned helplessly to Ahmed. She did not wield her loveliness like a weapon, but it invited protection nonetheless. Beatrice wondered which man the Arab girl cared for more. Then she chided herself for indulging in personal drama when the world of the dead was gaping open and oozing mortal despair into a perfectly nice Cairo morning. A love triangle should hardly take precedent.

"It's your choice—to weaken the barrier between these parallel places or to fight the good fight as commissioned," Persephone called out, her eyes no longer shifting colour; they were the same grey as the terrible place behind her, that place where such colour as hers was not welcome but that had so long ago laid claim to her. Beatrice wondered anxiously if the Whisper-world's pull was affecting the goddess and if she'd be able to close the gate she'd opened for emphasis.

"I'm not refusing to fight, I'm refusing to place my comrades in harm's way," Ibrahim insisted.

"You're mortal. You'll always be in harm's way," the goddess breathed. "It is not the fault of The Grand Work, Ibrahim Wasil-Tipton, and you know that better than anyone."

The goddess and Ibrahim shared a sad, knowing look that made Beatrice wonder. What did Persephone know about him and his fate that she did not?

The goddess continued, wringing her hands as the boarding bell tolled again. "Don't you understand that The Grand Work has reached a new height? There lies a worthy army to put back in its place this growing cancer that is the Whisper-world. I'm fighting for a way to make things right, but you must trust me. You cannot stay here, and you cannot be divided."

Beatrice noticed that the people nearby were slowing, that the mortals all around them, Egyptians and tourists alike, workers and the leisure class, were holding their hands over their hearts and glancing around as if trying to find the source of a sudden and eviscerating pain. Belle was doing her best to remove their memories, but if they weren't careful, these mortals might drop dead right here, feeding the Whisper-world precious food and flooding the monstrosity-capped waves with yet more souls, creating a thick nimbus that might obscure the shore with death.

"All aboard!" the ship captain cried.

"Ibrahim," Beatrice pleaded. Verena bit her lip, tears in her eyes.

The goddess moved forward, her step still creating life, but it was sparse. Thorny green, budding sprouts bled her feet while struggling to bloom. Their flowers faded behind her as if mirages. Reaching out, she took Verena's hand and kissed it. "That is a kiss of life," she breathed. "I do not give it lightly, as it requires strength I ought to conserve. I cannot promise danger will not come, that would be lying to you. But you'll not die on my watch. That I vow."

Ibrahim gave a shuddering sigh. "I suppose it is the best offer we have," he said. He turned and waited for Verena to meet his gaze and give consent. Beatrice doubted, with a jealousy that shamed her, that he would ever offer her the same gentle patience.

Verena nodded and addressed the goddess. "Please close up that terrible world. The example was not lost on us." Even Ahmed was visibly rattled.

Ibrahim's concern made way for the greater cause. He nodded, his face impassive, his expression unapologetic. As well it should be, Beatrice thought; he had nothing to be sorry for in trying to assure his fellows' safety. But he gestured to the ship. They would leave their homes.

"Don't worry," Belle assured Ibrahim and Verena. "Luggage or no, I'll make sure you've everything you need."

After the group shared one communal breath, Beatrice strode forward and was the first to step onto the gangway. She was not eager for the journey, but she was Leader, and the discomfiting pull toward England was undeniable. She would set an example. While her compatriots, especially Ibrahim, did an impressive job of hiding their fear, she wanted to show them no hesitation.

On the ship, Beatrice wandered to the railing. Her compatriots followed, staring down at the water. The goddess boarded, too, and joined them at the rail.

Beatrice felt a sudden chill at her back and turned. The chill worsened, and she saw a skeletal spirit in torn robes, its jaw hanging open like that of a gruesome puppet. It bobbed before her, having walked behind as one of their party. The thing looked familiar, much like the ghost they'd first fought, that muezzin of malevolence.

The goddess batted at it. "Shh," she hissed, and Beatrice wondered what it was saying to make the goddess grimace so.

The spirit hung its head, chastened, but instead of sinking or slithering away it moved to the boat's prow and hung there suspended in midair. Beatrice would swear that it was smiling. But, it was a skull. It couldn't smile. And yet, there was something about the ghost that filled Beatrice with unusual dread, like it had been waiting for them or perhaps for a new world to terrorize. It turned to the sea and opened its bony arms.

Her cohorts all were watching, too.

"It seems we have brought some stowaways," Belle muttered.

"That's bound to happen," Persephone remarked. "The Grand Work is a magnet for spiritual forces. It's inevitable that you trail the dead, and they you."

"What a joyful life we've earned," Beatrice muttered.

"It *is,* isn't it?" Ahmed exclaimed, inverting her sarcasm into truth. He put hands on Beatrice's and Belle's shoulders at once, and they felt a breeze in their veins as if he had loosed a dove in their hearts, the flapping of its wings a flurry of peace. His eyes were on Verena, and she grinned. No matter what lay ahead, no one could refuse the Heart.

★ ★ ★

The vessel pitched. So did Beatrice's stomach. She hadn't had the opportunity before to know whether she was good on the water, but now she knew and she prayed for swift currents to bring the trip to completion. The sea was rougher than usual, she heard crewmen say in inelegant tones as they clomped past her door. She wondered if that was because the ship carried an entourage of death and restlessness to London.

Every rocking motion of the vessel brought another curse, and bile, to her lips. The burning itch of her hands had been one thing, this quite another. She clutched the sides of her narrow bed with white knuckles, unaware of where the rest of her company was aboard the vessel, too queasy to take note of the multiple pulses tied to her own. Frankly, she didn't care; she was unfit for company and too embarrassed to ask for help.

They'd settled in without incident. Belle's powers were so frightfully useful. It was true that they were an unlikely traveling set, the six of them, and they'd raised more than a few eyebrows when seen together above deck. But one little smile and wave from the French girl and they were making themselves at home in first class. Beatrice was surprised by the luxury. Cairo had become quite the destination, she supposed. This brought thought of her father with a small pang, and she wondered if more traveling English would help or hinder his work.

There was a dark porthole above her bed that Beatrice fixed her eyes upon and tried not to move; the stiller she could be, the less disruption to her reeling body. "Let's go to London. It will be an adventure," she muttered. She missed Jean. Suddenly she missed the entire life she could have lived, a haunted life that never again could be. In times of discomfort, one always wishes for alternatives.

She wondered if her mother had been this ill when traveling

to Cairo. Beatrice didn't remember the journey, as she'd been four. She remembered her mother, though, and she missed her. Was her mother a ghost somewhere?

When the new life of Leader had first begun, Beatrice had looked for her mother everywhere. Now, realizing that only the restless remained, she was grateful for never having seen her. It gave her a small amount of comfort to think her mother had somehow found peace. From what her father mentioned, in murmurs, usually after he'd had a drink, she hadn't much liked Cairo. So, perhaps she was better off. But Beatrice would have loved a mother's touch upon her forehead at that moment, gently telling her to hold on and have faith.

She felt something, a tweaking at her temple. Oh, yes. There were ghostly happenings afoot, perhaps the work of those who had followed their coterie aboard. They were likely causing trouble, damn them. There was Work to be done and she couldn't possibly sit up straight.

There came a knock at her cabin door.

"I am indisposed!" Beatrice called. She snapped her mouth shut and willed back a wave of nausea.

"Leader, your services are required aft. There is some sort of . . . siren," came a deep and concerned voice.

"You'll have to fight her without me, Ibrahim."

The door swung wide. "I thought I locked that," Beatrice muttered, turning away from Ibrahim, who stood in the doorway like an elegant statue; a stern yet beautiful work of sculpted art guarding ancient treasures. She didn't want him to see her like this, so helpless. It would only feed his disdain.

"The sea does not agree with you," he said.

"And what, you and it are old friends?"

"I'll call for Verena."

"This is no work of a phantasm," Beatrice said, and hissed as she felt another wave of nausea attack. She hoisted herself over the nearby basin. "She will be of no help. Please leave."

"I'll call for Verena," Ibrahim said again. Then he exited.

Had he not heard, or did he consistently refuse to accept the words out of her mouth? She just wanted to be left alone. At the very least she wanted to avoid being seen by him when she was so weak. Damn her pride, but it undermined her position, and if there was anyone with whom she didn't wish to be undermined, it was he.

Cursing, Beatrice determined through gritted teeth, did indeed help. No wonder sailors did so with such gusto.

Verena appeared a moment later, lifting her hands and giving a friendly smile. "You're quite green," she stated.

Beatrice moaned. When the Healer placed a glowing hand on her stomach, she shuddered once, then seized up. Verena's glowing fingertips traced a line up her arm toward her neck and then her temple, as if gauging her pulse. After a moment, Beatrice heaved a long sigh and sat up.

"Better. Why, that's better! Thank you, Verena," she stated. Ibrahim had been right to fetch her. "What did I hear we have out there? A siren?" She made a face and stood up. "Honestly."

But, going aft, seeing the glowing spectre, she couldn't help but come to the same conclusion. The ghostly woman's form was lithe and long; she trailed phantom fabric a metre above the deck, and her hair whipped behind her in a snaky halo. Her mouth was a wide O, and while The Guard could hear no sound, the panes of glass in the door to the captain's cabin began to fissure and splinter.

The Guard circled up below. The floating form was even more luminous against the moonlit mist. Beatrice glanced around. Belle must have cleared the deck of all persons, for it was just them, the rough sea, an encroaching storm and this unhappy wraith.

"Bind," Beatrice commanded. A trickle of blue fire leaped from her hands and lit a ring of light around the group like a match dropped upon a line of oil. The spirit snapped her face down to stare at them.

"She's shrieking. So sad," Belle said. "Drowned, drowned she was. Taken by the sea."

"Can you hear her?" George asked, always in awe of her talent.

"No, no. It's just what I sense. My powers could gather more sense of her if I had something to touch. Ibrahim, what do *you* feel?"

Ibrahim closed his eyes and concentrated. "I don't believe she is malevolent," he admitted, "she is merely displaced, having drowned as Belle said. Perhaps she is warning us. Perhaps she doesn't want us to perish in a storm as she did."

"Or she wants us to follow her to those yonder rocks," George muttered.

"Perhaps," Beatrice replied, gritting her teeth against the nausea that threatened to overtake her body once more. "And so we ought to try and quiet her."

Ibrahim opened his mouth, prepared to give a benediction and begin the process of importuning the ghost to peace when his brow furrowed and he stared at Beatrice's hands. She lifted them, showing everyone the flickering, faltering flame. "Yes. The fire is hard to muster for long, given the new distance." She hissed. "And it's uncomfortable."

Ibrahim looked around him, paced the prow and leaned over the rail with an ease that made Beatrice's knees weak. If she went to the railing, she might faint.

"Where's our goddess when we need her?" he asked grumpily. "Wasn't she just with us?"

"Our Lady comes and goes when and how she will," Ahmed said. "She's likely resting. Didn't you see how the Whisper-world affected her?"

Beatrice felt similar to Ibrahim, but she didn't offer any comment.

There was a sudden great light as Persephone appeared. Her bare feet balanced on the ship's masthead, the shifting-coloured beauty glanced down over her shoulder and smiled at them. "Sometimes you need only ask," she said, and turned her attention to the sea.

"Thank you for the help," Beatrice murmured, glancing to her dim hands, which held hardly the light she would need for a fight.

"I only wish I could do more. I wish I could fight at your side each and every time," the goddess said.

It only took a moment. The air around her calmed, the clouds cleared above, and while the sea did not grow immediately still, the boat ceased its frightful rocking and adopted a more gentle sway.

"How the spirits obey you," Ahmed wondered. "Would that we had such swift facility."

"Oh, but I need you as my warriors—to remind me of my duty, to bring out the best in me, to rally me to my own cause. And I cannot always be in this mortal world," Persephone said before turning again to the troubled soul. "Peace, friend. Peace."

As the once wailing spirit ascended like a star rising into the sky, calmed by the goddess's gentle powers, Beatrice ran to the rail and vomited over the side.

Verena went to her, placed a hand on her shoulder. "Come on, dear, let's get you back below. I wish my cure were constant, or that my hand could utterly smooth the sea."

As she took Beatrice's hand, a few crewmen passed, scrambling up to the prow and gasping. A few crossed themselves, others murmured how they were being watched over by angels. Belle and George remained on deck, Belle doing her best to keep the damage to a minimum.

"Angels and devils both," Ibrahim muttered.

Beatrice longed to ask him how he was feeling, what he was

feeling, if his Instinct was roiling here like her stomach did. But he was her business associate and not her friend. He would tell her only if it became necessary. She let herself be led below, steeling herself for the rest of the two-week voyage.

Chapter Fifteen

The following day brought a knock at Beatrice's door, and the loud rap made her aching head reel. From the other side came Ibrahim's smooth voice, "Miss Smith, I have come to pay you a visit, if you are of a mind to admit me."

Thankfully she had thought to dress, and had decided to dress nicely. But looking in the mirror she scowled. Why should she care what Ibrahim thought of her appearance? She did regret the dark circles under her eyes that ongoing seasickness brought about.

"Yes, Mr. Wasil-Tipton, how may I help you?" she asked, moving carefully to the door and bracing her hand hard upon the frame so it would mask the shaking of her limbs. They trembled yet from the voyage.

"As second-in-command, I thought I should confer with you."

"About what? Is there a decision at hand? We're trapped on a boat. Have you had another inkling? Do you bring another doomsday account?"

"No," he said simply as she opened the door.

"Then why are you here?" Her tone was sharper than she intended.

Ibrahim blinked. "I . . . I came to tell you that I appreciate the way in which you allowed my viewpoint to be presented to our fellows, and to our Lady."

"Noted. You are welcome," she replied and moved to sit upon her bed, her head swimming. Fainting in front of him would be beyond humiliating. He'd have to catch her in his arms . . . Not to mention it was terribly improper for him even to be in her room.

He peered at her. She was sure it was just her miserable imagination, but it seemed he was masking a laugh.

"Please go," she growled. "Stop enjoying my humiliation."

Ibrahim came close. "Lay back," he said.

Beatrice felt a shiver rush down her spine, this one not originating in her quivering stomach.

Ibrahim reached over to the basin on the bed stand, dipped the cloth beside it into the cool water and placed it on her forehead. It was the first time there had been any contact between them. Granted there was a cool cloth between, but Beatrice felt the exchange nonetheless. She tried not to have her pleasure register as he stared down at her, his face impossibly noble. He looked too much a sultan, a prince, to have been left on a doorstep. How could anyone abandon such beauty?

Perhaps it was the gentleness in her gaze that allowed his hard lines to soften, his dark eyes to warm. The two of them said nothing, but Ibrahim kept his hand on her forehead and the compress. For a few more moments there was just the rocking of the boat.

Beatrice closed her eyes as she felt her cold sweat return. "I want to go home," she groaned.

"That's something we can agree on," Ibrahim replied. "Breathe deep. Try to rest."

He rose and was about to leave the room when he paused and turned. "I cannot presume to understand your recent physical state, as your powers differ from ours, but I was quite overtaken by the physical effects of The Grand Work, and if the force you've been cloven to has been ripped away, I cannot imagine the discomfort. I cannot imagine it helps seasickness, either. You are somewhat composed, considering."

Beatrice eyed him. "Are you attempting to give me a

compliment, Mr. Wasil-Tipton? You might practice a bit more."

The corners of his lips twitched and his dark eyes sparked. Then he shrugged. "It isn't my fault if you women have a need for praise but no appreciation of subtlety. Good evening."

"Good evening," Beatrice replied.

She stared, giving a bemused chuckle as the door closed behind him, and she told herself that it was only because she hadn't been touched in so very long that his small gesture had been so pleasant. Had the seasickness upended more than her stomach? She gave a moment's pause to considering Ibrahim's hand and what it might feel like were there no cloth between it and her skin. A shiver coursed her spine. This one not from seasickness.

Beatrice cut the thought from her mind. Touches were meaningless, and she could do fine without them. She was a woman self-assured, set apart from such romantic nonsense.

★ ★ ★

When she went aloft, she found the ladies of The Guard appreciating the bright sun from deck chairs, soaking up as much as they could before the clouds of the British Isles were drawn. Thankfully the sea was calm and her battered nerves were in better cooperation.

They were chatting happily, shifting between languages with a fluidity that went without comment, facilitated by occasional words in The Guard's communal language and the uncanny aid of Belle's mental tricks. But into their second pot of tea they noticed a bright light had appeared in a wicker chair beside them.

"May I sit with you? The company of bosom friends is something I've always craved," murmured Persephone, and the goddess smiled shyly. As powerful as she might be, she often sounded young and preciously awkward.

Belle and Verena turned to Beatrice, who shrugged and rose to play hostess. The teapot was suddenly fresh and full, when no help had been by to refresh it. And there was a fourth cup waiting at the ready. Such, apparently, was the benefit of taking tea with a divinity.

"You were talking of love?" Despite her shifting colours, it was clear Persephone blushed.

"Are you certain you're not Aphrodite?" Beatrice asked, handing her a cup and saucer.

The goddess chuckled. "Would that I were."

This brought up another question, and Belle voiced it. There seemed like there would never be a better time. "Do you know them, other deities of old? Is everything we've come to believe in our respective faiths a lie? Were Greek myths right all along?"

Persephone gave an odd laugh. "Is there a conflict between what I knew and what you might believe? I know . . . *forces*. I do not call them the names you do. We've our own titles, if ever such words are spoken. I took this name because it came from mortals, whom I adore. Of all my names I like this best. I drift in my sphere and other forces drift in theirs. Sometimes paths cross because they are destined. Something far greater than I turns the prism that changes my colours, and it alone knows every mystery."

"When did you meet, you and Phoenix?" Verena asked, her face aglow. Beatrice guessed she was the true romantic among them. The quiet ones always were.

Persephone blinked. Then she smiled. "I first spied him in a field full of sunflowers. He was touching the seeds and arranging them into iterations. A divine mathematician."

"When?" Belle pressed.

"My sense of time and yours differ. I know it was a simpler

age, back when we were made new from you beautiful mortals, congealed of all your hopes and dreams, sprung from your needs, desires and all your energy. Beautiful beings were birthed from your souls—and terrible beings, too. But he . . . Oh, he was *always* beautiful."

"Show me, please," Verena breathed, adding passionately in Arabic, "I seek windows into souls. That is how I can see my own more clearly and heal more precisely. Give me a window. Do you think or live in any way like us?"

Persephone sighed. "I'm filled with mortal emotions. In fact, I am able to hold more within me than your mortal bodies ever could. But I imagine falling in love is just the same for us both."

The goddess grinned. Verena looked at the ground as if blissfully guilty. Then she glanced up and looked hopeful.

Persephone laughed. "If you wish to indulge me, who am I to decline?"

It was as before in the sacred space; her vision overtook them. Suddenly they were in that very field of sunflowers, blooms of a brighter yellow than they'd ever known existed. In the distance was the sea, vast and sapphire, the sound of its waves an intoxicating lull.

Phoenix surpassed beauty. The women collectively gasped. He towered above the flowers, yet he bent to them with grace and fascination, a vision wholly angelic. His great wings were pure energy, incorporeal and delicate, transparent feathers made of light. His long black hair made a striking contrast to the rest. He was without clothes; his luminescent body was lean and powerful.

His wings artfully hid his nether regions from view, which was just as well for the ladies watching lest they blush or faint. But Beatrice was sure they were each as curious as she. Verena in her robes, Beatrice and Belle in their European traveling fashions, they stood invisible amid the flowers of this ancient field and watched Persephone approach. Her shifting colours infused his lit wings, like beams through a stained-glass window.

His dark eyes drank her in.

"Patterns," he said, his voice distinct, low and rich. He held up a sunflower and pointed to its dark centre. His finger traced the ridges, and the seeds ordered themselves at his command. "Everything can be arranged into one. Perfected. Life—one beautiful equation."

The goddess gasped, delighted, and the sunflowers grew taller. Their petals opened wider. "Can I be arranged into a pattern?"

"I know nothing of your properties," he replied. "Not yet." He took a step closer. "Would you give me leave to ascertain?"

"I give you leave," she whispered.

He took a moment to devour her with his eyes. Finally he said, "Your heart is constant, for it is your heart that so illuminates you. Your colours are ever-changing, painting the world with every emotion. You would never bore me. I find that . . . of wondrous value."

She took a step closer. "My palette is vast but my heart unchanging. None yet has won it."

"Ah," he said. "My equation was missing a variable. You could be that variable, should you desire such a place. I am a constant." A light danced in his eyes as he reached out and touched her cheek. Wildflowers of every kind grew up at her feet, rising amid the sunflowers. The field was thus awash in every colour the cosmos ever saw. Phoenix looked around, greatly pleased. "Action, reaction. Good."

"Action," she breathed, and turned her face into his hand to kiss his palm.

"Reaction," he countered, and his wings enfolded her.

The field was suddenly filled with music. The rhythms of

their pulses were perfectly complementary. In the distance, shimmering, glimmering forms of indescribable beauty danced upon a hilltop.

"The Muses approve," Phoenix stated. "They sing for us."

He put his palm in the air, and Persephone pressed her hand to it. "You are a being of light," she said, "so why hair of onyx hue? Your eyes, too. Such contrast. You are light but not *all* light. Tell me what you're made of."

His voice was rich thunder, a promised storm. "I am tethered to this world, to its mortals and the birth pangs of their civilizations. They begin to understand darkness. As day must pass into night, so we must learn to love darkness, to own it and still remain true to the light. I am Balance. I am the between, with feet for the ground, wings for the air. And you, you are all the colours I've awaited. Together, we are comprehensive. May I hold you?"

"For empirical evidence or for pleasure?" she countered.

"Both."

"Please do."

He seized her in powerful arms and suddenly she was airborne, lifted up by his great wings, the music of the Muses swelling in response. Her shimmering robes buffeted him as he coursed over the field with her, slowly, a flight of both leisure and delight. It was revealed that the flowering field grew atop a sheer cliff and out they flew out over that crystal sea that arched its waves toward them, magnetized by their pull. The drama of the vista was as breathtaking as their airborne, graceful forms.

He watched her intently as they soared, her shifting hues, and he ascribed meanings to every one. Midair, he held her tight with one arm and traced the outline of her face with his fingertips.

"Of your colours I am most drawn to the blue—your willingness to see solutions to everything." He touched the hollow of her throat. "You render the mathematician an alchemist. You have wrought change in me."

She placed her hand on his cheek, examining it. Their caresses were each an exquisite experiment. "The colours you see in me. I do not see them. I see none on my skin."

"The white of light contains *every* colour."

She wrapped her limbs more fully around him. "You are the solution to everything. Your white wings hold constant all my variables."

"While you light the world with your rainbow. Do you declare constancy?" he asked, a rumbling, hopeful murmur.

"Give me your vow and I will."

He planted a firm and claiming kiss upon her, and the gods sunk from the sky and again touched the sunflowers. They fell to their knees. A ring of birch trees sprouted up from the ground. The trees towered over them, sheltering their pressing, impassioned embrace, and the field became a verdant space of leaf and blossom, sun and shade. The whole of the land shimmered as the flowers continued to grow, diversify and magnify. It was a celebration of a glorious union.

The Muses danced, the music swelled—and suddenly the women were on a ship deck again, all of them blushing. The vision had been inescapable and all-consuming. Two such powerful forces of nature coming together had created a wave of heat and emotion beyond any mortal experience, and Beatrice thought poor sensitive Verena might faint. She herself was feeling a bit woozy.

The goddess had vanished. Perhaps she was living in her memories. Beatrice could not blame her; that was a memory to relive. Unlike his death.

Belle sighed. "How poetic and beautiful!"

Beatrice raised an eyebrow, reluctant to give over to the emotions within her. "Well, yes. But, truly, the gods are such shameless flirts."

Verena giggled into her teacup.

Beatrice remained privately overcome, hoping there was some pairing for her in the world that was just as meant to be. At the thought of such a partner, her stomach tightened. She recalled a cool cloth upon her forehead, the gentle press of a golden-skinned hand.

Her sigh became a scowl. The gods had been scandalous and artless. Phoenix's claim had been sudden and bold. Gods, she supposed, might act thus without censure. Mortals could never speak with such freedom, certainly not if they valued propriety. Mortals must dance, play games and say fine words, all within the rigours of societal constraint. Gaining such a partner was never so simple a path. For most mortals, love was as much misery as it was joy. She wondered if the goddess understood that. It might hurt them all if she didn't.

★ ★ ★

Time aboard the ship continued to pass. Numerous teas were prepared and drunk, George had a good deal of champagne and The Guard listened in on the frivolous conversations of wealthy travelers. Beatrice caught Ibrahim rolling his eyes at ignorant comments made about Egyptians, as if one trip to a foreign country afforded the English all the evidence they needed to concoct theories and assess values of those cultures not their own.

"I promise we're not all like that. My father doesn't say such things, nor would I," she found herself saying.

Ibrahim nodded. "I am well aware that not all Englishmen are insufferable prigs. Just a great number of the ones who travel."

Prigs? Beatrice snickered, caught off guard by a word she wouldn't have expected him to use. But then again, he was raised by an Englishman. That was a man and a relationship about which Beatrice wanted deeply to know more. Frankly, Ibrahim spoke with such simple grace she found she liked to hear him talk about anything at all. But there was no further conversation between them that day.

George had taken to drawing caricatures of everyone on board, and he came away with a healthy roll of bills in his pockets. When he kept offering to pay for the most expensive wine for them, Belle was quick to insist that it was money honestly earned and that The Guard should not judge him for his indulgences.

Beatrice could hardly eat more than biscuits, even fortified by Verena's healing hand. She tried to pretend to her coterie that she was the picture of health and hadn't a care in the world. She was sure her pallor betrayed her, but she attempted to be valiant. Thankfully, no one offered her pity or special consideration.

Ahmed had found someone who had bought a *kissar,* an instrument in the lyre family, and with great cheer he admonished that it should not go on a wall as the Englishman intended but instead be loved and played. And so he did, singing and entertaining the entire vessel.

His gift was transcendent. Power flowed from his voice, his eyes; the poetry of Turks and Arabs and great Sufi leaders washed over all the travelers and made their hearts soar. It was heavenly. Aside from Verena's occasional helping hand, it was the only thing that made Beatrice able to forget her seasick nerves. It made Belle and George take hands, and Beatrice realized with a surety she didn't question that their touch was a vow. The music made Verena drunk with awe. She stared at Ahmed, and with the same surety Beatrice realized another choice had been made. It all seemed so natural, this pairing off. And yet, Beatrice and Ibrahim were utterly unable to look at each other.

At least, Beatrice didn't feel she could look at him. Not

without betraying something. Her heart was lonely. The pulse of her friends beating in her own blood made it all the more evident. She did wish to love again; she was young, so it was a crime not to. And yet, in every sentence, movement or glance, she was reminded that she and Ibrahim were stoic, stubborn creatures of different worlds floating on an ocean as vast as the gulf between them.

When the music ended there were the dead. Always the dead. Beatrice felt her coterie's hearts plummet as dread of their tasks crept in, like waking from blissful dreams to find a world less beautiful than they'd imagined.

Ghosts were seen on the water in vague clusters, likely hovering over sunken ships that lay on the ocean floor. It was the ones that followed them that required attention, however, the ghosts of Cairo. Were they so eager in life to get to England? It defied the laws of spirits, she believed. Spirits were tied to people, land, hearths and homes. The dead weren't adventurers that she knew of. Of course, as the goddess intimated, perhaps things were changing.

For the remainder of the journey Persephone was absent. Beatrice imagined her wandering those terrible grey corridors of the Whisper-world, a prisoner remembering love in a time of flowers. That saddened her. The creature did deserve a verdant field and an angel to hold her close. But it would seem that life, for divinities as well as mortals, did not always afford one what they wanted.

When George alerted them that their journey was nearly over, her body rejoiced at the idea of solid ground.

"Home."

The English youth's voice was not exactly certain. Beatrice doubted her own homecoming, but at least the pain in her hands eased. She could finally remove her gloves a moment and flex her aching fingertips.

The cityscape grew in their vision in sporadic clusters, and then suddenly became an undeniable leviathan. The bosom of the great empire was beautiful and terrifying, a large and sprawling, huge, sooty creature. It loomed, a mammoth collection of interlocked beasts; sporadic fires of industry spouting from the smokestack noses of countless sleeping dragons. The waterways were covered with a crouched horde, any of which could wake at any moment and in one lick swallow their large boat whole.

Beatrice studied the light in the sky, how it changed, how it thickened and greyed. Perhaps the walls between the Whisper-world and the mortal world were thinner in London. There certainly were plenty of spirits.

The pit of her stomach that had been reserved for pains regarding seasickness and the occasional horror at being so agonizingly near to Ibrahim with nothing to be said or done about it was now overtaken by a dread of the numerous spirits. While she hadn't ever taken a census, she could say there were more spirits here than in Cairo; she was sure of it. Clearly they had their work cut out for them.

A welcoming committee indeed. The Guard could all see for themselves, so there was no need to exacerbate the situation with pointless commentary, but the dead were waiting.

Chapter Sixteen

A few of the many barrier pins keeping the worlds separate were now spattered with blood—and with tears for good measure. The pain seared deeper the more Persephone cut. The flesh of her arms and thighs were scarred for it and not healing as quickly as she wished. But she hid the traces, wound her robes tight and acted like nothing was out of the ordinary.

"You do realize I'll do anything for you," Darkness blurted amid another of their obligatory promenades. His jaw chattered, making his earnest tone something absurd.

"You mean *to* me. You'd do anything *to* me."

"I'd rip the worlds apart if you abandoned this place entirely."

Persephone felt her pulse quicken. Was he sensing something worrisome about her mood that he dared such a threat? She had to play the game as much as she could bear. She couldn't have him tightening the leash now, increasing the illness in her blood to the point where she'd be bedridden with the rot of the Whisper-world. He always seemed satisfied to see her weakening. She had to seem too dispirited to be inventive.

"I can't escape," she stated. "I've tried to die. I've tried everything possible. The Whisper-world infects me, and I remain bound to return. You've won."

Darkness made a sound, a delighted child's noise. Persephone quit his dais, not waiting for him to make her repeat the lie. She left him to his glee. He seemed happy to stay in that misguided state.

Following paths to the Liminal, she slipped through the gate to the mortal world. There she found herself, as she often did, in the sacred space. The Guard were absent.

Bitterness, bile and anger surfaced and began to flow, and she allowed it. If she'd done so in the Whisper-world it would have magnified into veritable shackles, but now she echoed Darkness's words. "He'd rip the worlds apart. Dear God, he'll undo the barrier pins himself in order to find me."

Yet, wasn't that the point—to in fact rip, *collide* the worlds? But they needed to do so to The Guard's mortal advantage. Wasn't that what she'd glimpsed on the seal above, a veritable army of spirits crashing down on Athens? That indicated the worlds were merged. But glimpses weren't a plan, and one did not just flirt with opening such barriers. It would be the end of mortal life as they knew it if things were not controlled.

Hopelessness accosted her, fear for the vagaries of what she was attempting, and she let tears come as they would. It was safer for her to shed them here, lest the shadows lap them up to use them cruelly against her and those she loved, like Darkness had done by making the key to The Guard's prison.

Falling to the stone floor, her tears rolled into a peculiar, particular pattern. Lines and curves shaped themselves, her sorrow calling out for soothing. It drew Phoenix fire, a portion of his flame coursing through the room in immediate empathic response, rising above and engulfing the tear-drawn symbols.

Persephone watched, fascinated. All the tears drew together, hundreds of tiny beads running toward one another into the centre of the mosaic tile to find a small hole. The mercurylike tears filled that hole, and they began to stack upon themselves, into something rounded at the top, oddly notched and gleaming silver.

A key? It was another key. But what was it to?

This sacred space ever magnified Phoenix's force, and now the pattern being formed was distinct. As they continued to shift, Persephone realized the lines, curves, boxes and grid on the floor were a map. A map of a space that looked familiar . . . Yes, the floor plan of Athens! And then she saw a map of sloping curves and meandering paths besides the Athens halls, rooms, courtyard and foyers. These were familiar, too; they were the paths of the Whisper-world.

At some point, these places would join. Here was a way for The Guard to prepare; this was a map of the merge. Phoenix was lighting their way.

"Oh, beloved," she murmured. "Isn't it beautiful how magic can still be new to us? That there are gifts around every corner, despite our suffering? Isn't it wonderful that I can still be amazed?"

Only two places remained to her a complete enigma: the Great Beyond, as she'd never seen it, and the mysterious Liminal edge. She wondered if the sacred space of The Guard was in fact an extension of the Liminal, sharing its mysterious properties to shape lives or destroy them. Persephone shuddered with chill.

She pressed her hands to the stones of the floor, bending to kiss them. The sacred space had been created when The Guard itself was born. Much like how the Whisper-world had separated from the mortal at the dawn of civilization, so had the sacred space split at the inception of The Guard, separating itself from both worlds. Thusly it had its own properties, could sometimes fashion the unexpected to serve the Power and the Light. Or she supposed it could serve another power. She wondered if a future Guard would inadvertently call upon the wrong side of the light.

"You may choose the wrong path, beloveds, but I cannot hold your hands," she admitted ruefully. "You must make the right choices yourselves."

Beyond the stone pillars lay shimmering darkness, a place between space and time that was unfriendly for mortal and divinity alike. She knew that every Guard who put a hand into that darkness came away scarred. Many had shown her the scars, and she prayed that those shadows would ever stay static, that nothing came from the other side to infiltrate. She hoped that the dog would stay at heel, the Gorgon would never grow curious, and that Darkness would only fight when provoked. The time of their final battle was the advantage she sought.

Thinking of her vision, of Alexi and the girl bent over the Athens seal to free Guard spirits, Persephone took the key made of her tears from the floor. The map vanished when she did. Keeping her robes about her, she ascended to that upper seal and examined its fine tiles. There indeed was another keyhole. But when she tried the key, it did not fit. A different lock for a different key.

She thought again about her vision, seeking details. Her heart sank. *That* necessary key was the one Darkness had imprisoned within him. It would have to be stolen. She, whomever she would become, would have to obtain it. She would have to become a seventh member in a Guard of six, a mortal and the final piece of an age-old puzzle.

But how was this all to take place?

"Ah, Beatrice." Suddenly, an unprecedented idea filled her head. Two Guards. Was that possible? She would need the help.

Persephone blinked. She felt something shift within her heart, and she clapped her hands. "Oh! They're here!"

★ ★ ★

The city sprawled, brimming with life and sound. Beatrice and her Guard stood on the rails as the steamer docked, taking in the myriad sights. London was more populous than Cairo, but there was a similar bustle and old-world chaos.

A ripping sound and a burst of coloured light heralded the

goddess. Lovely as ever she appeared, her face visibly excited, though there were disturbing dark circles under her eyes. Her layered gown was spattered with what appeared at first to be blood but then shimmered like red silk when she stepped into their world. The Guard looked nervously at one another.

"Welcome to London!" Persephone cried, beckoning them like an eager child as the gangplank lowered. She tapped the temples of two cargo hands. "Your things are taken care of. Come! Let's see the city!"

The goddess was a wide-eyed child as she led them down a multitude of lanes and avenues. Beatrice and her fellows took in London with both wariness and vague excitement, but none could deny the joy of adventure once they were in the thick of it. Clattering sounds, chattering vendors, carriages clogging the fine lanes and refuse cluttering the dreary ones; discovery continued.

A divinity led them through it, too, through the most powerful city in the world. Each of them enjoyed a moment of awe. They were the votaries of gods. This city was in some part theirs, if its citizens would never know. The sentiment bolstered Beatrice as she tried not to be overwhelmed by its size, density, extreme wealth and staggering poverty.

Like every ancient city, it was host to many different architectures. England having borrowed from every culture it had pierced with its flag, it also held a host of different residents. Ibrahim and Ahmed glanced at each other. Beatrice noticed their shoulders ease a bit when they saw they were not the only persons of colour. Still, while Ibrahim looked heartened by the eclectic nature of the city, his striking face sported a furrowed brow.

Perhaps he felt a burst of homesickness. She couldn't blame him. London was a vast stage with countless sets and an infinite cast, asymmetrical and busy like Cairo, but the faces of its players were blackened. Where Cairo's rouge was vermillion dust, London's was soot. This place was grey where home had been gold. It would take some getting used to.

A great, weighty pain burned in her bosom, and the Pull—or something vaguely like it—dragged her in the direction the goddess was heading. Was the great soul inhabiting her so magnetized to its missing half?

"Separation from the fire has quite taken a toll on me, but it being close, my body yearns more than ever." Beatrice whispered this to Verena, who put a slightly glowing hand upon her back. It felt lovely. She tried not to show that she hurt, felt hollow inside and that there remained an irritant across her skin. While Phoenix's fire could apparently be in many places at once, it didn't seem to like being spread too thin.

In the Bloomsbury district they turned down a street that was more like an alley and came upon an oddly grand portico entrance to a Romanesque fortress of red sandstone. The lintel read FRIENDS.

"That's nice!" Ahmed exclaimed. "Friends!"

Everyone smiled despite themselves.

"What is this place?" George asked.

Persephone grinned, obviously pleased with herself. "We are going to open this school. It shall be full of friends, indeed, and it shall be called Athens Academy!"

"Why not the School of Friends?" Ahmed frowned.

"Because England is not terribly tolerant of the Society of Friends, or as some would call them—"

"Quakers," Ibrahim finished. "James. My . . . father spoke highly of his Quaker colleagues in America."

"Indeed. This school was closed because it sought to educate both men and women, employ teachers both male and female and from diverse backgrounds, and to allow students access to all subjects," Persephone stated.

"That it should be any other way is appalling," Beatrice agreed.

The goddess nodded. "So I assume I'll have your unconditional support in seeing it open once more under a title that shall draw less scrutiny. The classicists of this age won't mind a bit of Greek homage, for its students will never know that the Phoenix of their myths lives beneath its very eaves."

"Ah," Beatrice breathed. "That's why my body, standing here, at last doesn't feel so broken."

"Yes. My apologies," Persephone said. "A lesser person would have broken under the strain. You are Leader indeed, Beatrice Smith." She touched Beatrice's cheek with a sisterly fondness, then turned to the rest of the company.

"Unless you wish to settle elsewhere, you can take to the upstairs rooms here or to the unfinished parts of the hall that will be used as dormitories. Do wander this rapturous city. But first, before we settle in, we need to locate some friends to make good on this building's valiant mission. Ibrahim, my Instinct, would you be so kind as to show me to some Quakers?"

Chapter Seventeen

The wind had picked up, and there was something upon it. Something strange.

Alexi Rychman was a practical young man; his parents encouraged the quality. His grandmother, however, was not a practical woman. Not entirely. He knew that of his whole family she cherished him most. His sister loved him dearly, but his grandmother gave him the sense that he was the most important person in the world. It was a practice his parents found appalling but an honour young Alexi took very seriously. She encouraged hard work but also his fascination with alchemy, was an ardent spiritualist and oft spoke with otherworldly airs. If he believed in such things—he didn't—he would have thought his grandmother a witch.

Now, echoes of her spiritualism and mysticism had Alexi staring out from the flat where he was secretly apprenticed to a brilliant alchemist, even at the tender age of fourteen. He was very nearly fifteen, he consoled himself, childhood being such an inconvenience. Gazing down onto London he felt the winds of fate were blowing. There was something in the air. A chill. A frisson of possibility.

"Oh don't be silly," he scoffed, and returned to mixing his powders.

Chapter Eighteen

An unlikely set of seven companions threw open the doors of an unmarked building. Inside, a group of twenty middle-aged persons sat in silence, plenty of children scattered about them, all with heads bent. They were dressed in modest fashions of the day: wide skirts, full-sleeved blouses cinched to slender waists, fine coats and well-kept waistcoats. Nothing ostentatious. The children were the same, well-presented and not out-of-fashion but uniformly utilitarian. One woman was on her feet but not speaking.

At the sound of the doors thrown wide, everyone turned.

"Hello, friends!" cried Persephone. She was a prismatic, shifting, indescribable creature like nothing their mortal eyes had ever seen. The entire room gaped.

"Never mind her," Belle stated, her French accent more pronounced when she spoke loudly, holding out her hands, bestowing her magic. "She's a member of parliament, here to make a decree."

"I'd vote for her," George added with a grin.

"You'll henceforth remember her as one of . . ." Belle turned to the goddess. "My Lady, whom would you like to be associated with in their minds?"

"Oh." The goddess thought a moment. "I've been reading the papers. The papers! I *do* like saying that! I rather like that reform bill, too. Not perfect, but more egalitarian, more votes. Say I'm one of Disraeli's set. He's making history. Can't be certain I'll like all of it, but history nonetheless."

Belle turned back to the open-mouthed crowd. "You'll henceforth remember her—and all of us—as belonging to Disraeli's . . ." She turned to George. "What do you call it?"

"A cabinet," George said.

"Cabernet," Belle repeated.

"Not wine, Belle. Cab*inet*." Beatrice rolled her eyes. "This is absurd."

"Cab-*i*-net." Belle blushed.

The goddess continued with her proclamation. "I am here to tell you that your academy shall live once more. The building in Bloomsbury abandoned due to injustices and prejudices shall reopen as Athens. I demand this. And I will need you all to staff it."

There were murmurs among the crowd of excitement and joy, like a dream was coming true.

"But, we must keep quiet about our ventures, friends. We live in intolerant times. I know this as well as any, working alongside a Jew," the goddess proclaimed, turning to her newly arrived Guard in an utterly matter-of-fact aside. "You see, he is. *Disraeli* is, and his presence sends a tremor through the empire." The goddess turned again to the Quakers. "But you, fair ones, are not threaded with the intolerance of the small-minded, and you shall be rewarded. Who led the Friends Academy?"

A man stood, tall, sharp-featured, with blue eyes and a regal appearance. "I did, your honour. My name is Richard Thompson, and I wanted my niece to have the same chance that fellows at Oxford have." He gestured beside him to a young girl in her early teens. Tall and spindly in a sensible dress, she stood and blushed, locks of brown hair falling stubbornly from their coif and into her wide blue eyes. "Rebecca here is absolutely brilliant, and I wanted her to have every opportunity."

"And so she shall! You are henceforth employed, and you shall see these fine fellow ministers of mine around the institution as you work to open it. But for now this school must be London's best-kept secret. I daresay the rest of the Right Honourable Gentlemen back at parliament will shut it down again if they hear. So, carry on! Truth, equality, simplicity and peace be with you all!"

The goddess whirled toward the door with a flourish and exited, leaving the thunderstruck congregants behind. Her Guard trailed in her wake, not wanting to be caught answering any questions they'd be hard-pressed to answer.

"Don't worry about the practicalities," the goddess exclaimed, measuring their worried expressions. "*They'll* run the school, as they were quite ready to do before. As for the bankers' loans, well, let me take care of that. That whole world is delightfully intricate, but I can be *very* persuasive when I want to be!" Her prismatic eyes glittered with the delight of purpose and action.

As they darted again in the direction of Bloomsbury, Ibrahim caught up to the goddess and pointed back toward the simple brick building from whence they had come. "That girl. That Thompson girl."

The goddess nodded. "An Intuition if I ever saw one. See? You can spot your own, can't you?"

"But . . ." Ibrahim furrowed his brow. "Are my powers split in two?"

"No, not yet, two Guards at one time? Certainly not in one city. That cannot be. Yet . . . we're at a new dawning, so who knows what's eventually possible," the goddess cried. "Thrilling!"

They'd never seen her so invigorated. She seemed a bit feverish, in fact. But when one's heart is exuberant they become more compelling, and the goddess even more so, her luminous beauty something none of them could deny. Particularly not the men of the group. They stared, dazed and drinking her in. Beatrice set her jaw.

They traveled to the school. Ascending the steps below the

bold FRIENDS—a sight that again made Ahmed smile, though that took very little—the goddess moved through the foyer as if leading a tour.

She pointed to the left, down a colonnaded hall. "Sacred space, accessible there through the chapel." She pointed toward an upper floor. "Up there you'll find the grave of Phoenix. Make yourselves at home." Then she flung her hand wide, a portal opened up, and she disappeared without another word.

★ ★ ★

As The Guard chose their rooms within Athens, George and Belle decided to pair up to wander the city, as they had been wont to do all through the last days in Cairo and during their voyage. They found themselves turning down what appeared to be a twisting set of winding alleys and stumbled at last upon a cozy bit of treasure: a garden-level pub that was thoroughly warm and inviting save an unfortunate placard out front declaring THE BEAST and decorated with a hellish-looking dog whose dark paint was flecking. With naught but a nod, George and Belle descended the stairs and took a bay window seat that looked out upon the winding cobbles and wrought-iron rails of the narrow street beyond.

The place was nearly deserted and likely had been for some time, they determined, for the help waited upon them as if they were royalty. While the pair had dressed smartly, their trappings did not warrant such fawning attention alone. Their hostess muttered something about hard times and wishing someone would come along and take the place. This seemed to strike the both of them.

"I'm . . . getting a funny feeling," Belle said, rubbing her temple.

"Me, too. I think I've found home," George stated. "Sorry,

Belle, but I can't live in a *school*. A pub, on the other hand? Brilliant." Ever the artist, he was already measuring wall space and redecorating.

The hostess's husband came out to greet them, and it wasn't long before it was suggested that George—and his fiancée, they improperly assumed—buy the property, which consisted of the downstairs pub and a few upstairs rooms. Belle's family had long maintained comfortable wealth and a precedent of spending it lavishly on their daughter's random desires, so it wasn't long before a deal was made for an exceedingly reasonable price. Belle's powers of persuasion were a boon, working as they did despite her deepening blush.

"The first thing we must do," she insisted, leaning toward George over the table and its decorative if wilting violet, "is change that horrid sign." Her eyes lit up. "I've got it! I've got the name!"

When she leaned over and whispered it, George gave a great laugh. "*La Belle et La Bête*? Beauty and the Beast. We'll tame the beast indeed, and this shall be a place of respite for all our friends."

It was a wholly agreeable thought, and they passed several more pleasant hours dining and drinking and daring to hold hands, not realizing the sun was going down. It had gone completely dark before they stopped staring into each other's eyes. They had begun a new life, together, just they two, and the realization was glorious.

They were hardly thinking about how or when their group would come together again. But that was the job of the Pull.

★ ★ ★

It was an odd feeling here in London, foreign, not like the Pull had felt in Cairo. It wrenched Beatrice's heart as she descended the school stairs, and she dreaded to think this would be how it always felt here. Tears stung the corner of her eyes as her body all but dragged her toward the river.

The change troubled the whole of The Guard; it was clear from the looks on everyone's faces. They gathered on the embankment and stared at the mass of spirits that rolled across the Thames like whitecaps upon the ocean. London, it would seem, had more restless dead even than ancient tombs.

Beatrice noticed that Ibrahim's face was grimmest of all. She'd never seen him smile, and it was a look she couldn't imagine. She wanted to.

Surely he sensed her staring at him, for he snapped his head around to look at her. Glancing back at the spirits, his eyes darkened. "And so, which of that undulating mass are we meant to corral?"

"All?" Verena gulped.

There was an army, suddenly. Troop after troop, a wafting battalion in greyscale lines, a sea of floating forms that stared down from great height. It was a ghastly welcoming committee that didn't seem very welcoming, and they dove down upon The Guard at once. There was no time to take hands, bind them or gather their great fire.

"Why, that's the most coordinated effort I've seen yet," Beatrice said, dodging the spirits that flew at her. The others did, too. Righting herself and smoothing her skirts, Beatrice lifted her hands and blue fire leaped indignantly forth. It was as strong as it had once been in Cairo.

"Perhaps they've begun to unionize," said George.

Ahmed giggled. Beatrice could have blessed him for that sound, which reminded them all that they could choose to feel the freezing weight of death or instead find their position somewhat absurd. That simple point of view made it easier to fight.

What followed was a haphazard battle, unfocused and

unsatisfying. Belle was exhausted, and so it was more difficult to round up and send off the passersby. Beatrice didn't know which of the many spirits should be first upon which to turn her fire, so there was chaos for a time. Ibrahim read verses loudly, as if addressing the parliament, whose new houses were being built just down the riverbank. Ahmed and the rest kept up as best they could, but all of them flagged. In the end, the crowd of spectres was dispersed and attended, but there was still unrest on the London streets.

There was a reward, however. Belle and George had an announcement. They suggested all their friends come to the new café they'd just overtaken, and so the group agreed to the requisite journey. During the slow walk, Beatrice mused on the state of spectral affairs.

"We made a bit of a difference today, but we'll never put to rest *all* of London. The city is simply too haunted, and we but scratch the surface. Maintain balance? It feels more of a struggle here than ever."

"It's all this *grey*," Ibrahim murmured. "Are you sure this is England? Perhaps it is an extension of our goddess's prison, an extension of the Whisper-world itself!" He raised an eyebrow at George.

"There's sun!" George countered unconvincingly. "Sometimes."

"We'll address it when next we see our Lady," Beatrice said. "Perhaps the Balance has indeed changed."

"I suggest that a Guard may be less powerful when supplanted from their homes," said Ibrahim. "If, historically, we are tied to great cities and their residents, I can't imagine there's ever been an *emigrant* Guard."

"That may very well be true," Beatrice allowed. "Alas, we are thrown into an 'unprecedented time.' I'm sure that will have its consequences."

★ ★ ★

They had to wait a week to get any satisfaction. It was in the midst of a meeting in the sacred space via its new entrance, just as Beatrice called upon the Power and the Light. But their answer was not what they hoped. Instead, Persephone staggered out from a yawning portal, a gaping wound in her upper arm.

Everyone gasped. George, closest to her, dove and caught her falling body. He eased her to the floor, and Verena was immediately at her side.

"Hello, friends," the divinity breathed. There came a rattle from her lungs.

"What on earth?" Beatrice knelt beside her.

"Knitting the worlds," Persephone mumbled, her eyelids fluttering. "Preparing for a fight. It'll take time, surely, but once everything is ready I can take *her* body. We'll start anew. We'll wipe the vendetta clean."

The Guard all looked at one another. They had no idea what she was talking about.

"But you're bleeding," Belle said.

"Yes, it's part of the process," the divinity replied. "What to do . . . ? I came here to do something. Ah, yes." She stared sadly at all of them. "My memory is going. It comes and goes so much this century. Can you help me up?"

George and Verena did so, Verena steadying her with a glowing hand. None of the others said a word.

"Part of the preparation is in maintaining this building," Persephone remarked. "A shield for safekeeping. Beatrice, will you come with me? I need to kindle a bit of fire and could use your help. The rest of you can stay where you are."

Up several flights of stairs they ascended, the goddess, gliding otherworldly, her step birthing flowers as she moved, scented and lovely that faded into ghostly traces of perfume, Beatrice feeling each heavy tread of her own inelegant boot. While her carriage could never compare, she straightened herself and felt the rejuvenating rush of Phoenix fire in her veins; she'd never prove a goddess, but she would prove herself a wise choice for power.

In a third-floor foyer, atop a seal of Athens and a great golden eagle, the goddess placed her hand upon Beatrice's shoulder, drawing out the fire in her. "I give my breath and my light to these stones," she vowed. "I declare these stones safe haven."

There was a reaction in the air, sparkling and shimmering, a gauzy layer of light ascending like thin fabric cast high in a wind. The goddess looked up, pleased, and then her lovely face shifted with pain. She turned her head and coughed, and it was an ugly, terrible sound. A deep crimson fluid was dislodged, but this blood, which smelled of copper, dried flowers and distinctly of soured pomegranate, suddenly faded into the flowing, diaphanous sleeve of her robe and turned that patch into a smooth, gorgeous crimson silk.

Beatrice stared with horrified fascination. "Wondrous, how terrible things can be made lovely," she murmured.

The goddess smiled and was suddenly radiant, the sunken circles under her eyes lessened. "I do believe that's what I'm here to do. A certain alchemy—strange into beautiful. This world heals me. But, it can't heal me entirely. I don't suppose it would shock you to learn I'm falling apart, Beatrice. It seems I need to, like the Muses, take a body and live as The Guard lives. This will indeed come to pass, and here in London. But I don't know when. The timing is off, I'm *off* . . . We need to bring things together. Have patience with me, will you?"

Beatrice considered the goddess a moment, considering the vulnerability of this great, unpredictable force and trying to summon the right response. "I'll try. But patience is not my strong point."

"It never is, for Leaders," Persephone mused.

"I thought you said we were all individuals."

"You are. Leaders are chosen, though, with certain distinct qualities. You are of a kind, and all would love or hate one another if you were trapped in the same room. Every one of you— Oh!" Her face fell. "You *are* all in a room together. A terrible room. All The Guard that ever were, now in prison. Darkness made a key for his dungeon. It was a key made of my tears. Terrible, terrible. Would you fancy a drink? I would! But first, come. Let's take a look at the new sky we just fashioned! I've never done this before, let's see how it turned out!"

Beatrice shook her head, without a clue as to what she meant and reeling from the shifts of the goddess's mood. The only thing consistent in Persephone's chimerical nature was that her every action was underpinned with a sense of love.

Outside, looking up, they found the sky changed indeed. It had a layered, shimmering quality, and Beatrice blinked a few times. The thick clouds were quick to cover the changes, blanketing all London in grey.

The goddess seemed satisfied, however. "My spell took! I'm rather pleased with myself if I do say so. Come! Where do you and your friends take refreshment?" she asked.

"Our café," Belle replied. "La Belle et La Bête. We bought it."

"That sounds lovely," Persephone said. "Take me to it."

Chapter Nineteen

There was no longer any question; The Grand Work was more difficult away from home. This was doubly frustrating for Beatrice, who had felt such pain in Cairo when the Phoenix fire was ripped from the Whisper-world and transplanted. She'd assumed when she got to London she'd be twice the Leader for being near its source. Would that were so.

The work continued. Exorcisms in squalid rooms, chasing poltergeists down narrow streets, battling veritable gangs of spirit hoodlums that clogged alleys and arteries of the city alike, all of it took more time, energy, repetition and brute force than it had in Cairo. Weeks felt like years. Beatrice hardly saw the city for anything but work; then she made her way swiftly back to her cozy Athens Academy apartments.

There was a certain comfort in having most of her Guard at the ready there in the newly renamed Promethe Hall, named so to fittingly honour that purloiner of fire, in the upstairs sets of fine redwood apartments. Never mind that Ibrahim had his quarters just down the hall opposite her or that they all parted like water around a rock whenever the work was through.

The academy was a bustling place, workers finishing up and putting spare elegant touches around the entire affair. Now and then Beatrice would spy the Quaker headmaster Richard Thompson, the driving force behind the whole operation, his niece Rebecca with him. The two would stride about the place with pride, joy and admirable efficiency.

There was one thing. Whenever Beatrice found herself in

their path, Rebecca turned and stared at her, narrowing her eyes as if struggling to place her. A powerful mind churned behind those young blue-grey eyes, and Beatrice wondered about what the goddess and Ibrahim had said. Did Intuitions know their own? Would there be a changing of The Guard here in London? What did that mean for them?

With the Pull almost always in play, at times Beatrice would go out alone to do The Grand Work. She did so only when the disturbance was faint and she assumed the correction would be simple, the admonishment of a spirit with a smack of blue fire.

Tonight was a night like that. Something wasn't right and Beatrice knew it. But so did Ibrahim, apparently, for he appeared at her side in the upstairs foyer. Without a second glance or a word they had a cab brought round, and the pair traveled out of the corporation in pursuit of the Pull.

"Highgate," Beatrice said, though Ibrahim knew their destination. "Shall I call the others? It isn't much."

Ibrahim blinked. "It may not be much, but we're not very good."

"Not here we aren't. You're right, we need all the help we can muster."

She closed her eyes and trusted that Ibrahim was doing the same, reaching out. She allowed for the Pull to take over her body and felt it ripple, a sensation unifying all six who were connected. The others would follow the call if her message could find its way through the thick London fog that kept confounding them.

"How long can we—?"

Ibrahim finished her thought. "I daresay, if it's this difficult on this shore, The Grand Work will kill us."

It was uncanny. For one who seemed so indifferent, he had an odd way of knowing her thoughts to answer her questions.

Swiftly, thoughts of personal danger were overshadowed by questions of intimacy. She pretended to stare out the window, hiding her agitation. Suddenly she wasn't worried about how long their little coterie could withstand the forces of the Whisper-World, she wondered with sudden fright if there were psychic abilities he'd been granted that he hadn't told her about. He was so quick to finish her sentences; was he as quick to know her secrets? That she'd thought of him in quiet, private hours when she lay in lacy robes mere metres away from his rooms?

She was a fool. Unknown horrors were afoot, and she was worried that a man indifferent to her might have some preternatural sense that she wasn't indifferent toward him? Absurd.

"That's grim of you." Straightening her posture, Beatrice recalled herself to the conversation. "The Work will kill us, you say? We're not in tip-top form here in London, but we're not utterly outclassed."

"But don't you feel a great storm coming? Increasing havoc of the gods wreaked upon their pawns below?"

"Oh, I always feel a great storm coming." Beatrice chuckled. "It's my doom. I'm falling back into the melancholic patterns of my childhood. Once a Hamlet, always a Hamlet."

"This is hardly about woman's frailty, Miss Smith," he argued. "Or Shakespearean hubris."

Beatrice grimaced at his tone, her eyes wide and her nostrils flared. "Must you have *no* humour in you whatsoever?"

"I'm talking of grave danger. My Instinct feels it and has since Cairo. You remember my trepidations. They have not lessened. You might make light of me, but you don't feel what I do. I lie with them pressing like a demon down upon my chest, compressing the air in my lungs—"

"But your Instinct remains unclear! I do not deal in

abstractions, Mr. Wasil-Tipton. Corporeal or incorporeal, I deal in what stares me down face-to-face. Until you give me more than 'a feeling in your bones of inclement weather,' I cannot sit entertaining your apocalypse-mongering.

"And *you!*" She turned her fury out the window to the mad-eyed ghost of a highwayman who was loath to leave the Hampstead heath he haunted and rode alongside their carriage, brandishing a phantom knife he once used to relieve travelers of their purses or lives. "Find another maiden to frighten; you'll not get a rise out of me." She blasted the spectre with blue fire, and his ghost horse reared and charged away. For a moment she regretted the action, but the carriage driver, thankfully a man who had no evident sensitivities, seemed not to notice anything amiss.

She hopped down from the conveyance when it jolted to a stop outside a great gate. Charging through without thought or deference, she ran into the middle of Highgate Cemetery, tripping past eerily lit mausoleums, obelisks and angels, a place lit in part by marble reflecting moonlight upon surrounding sandstone. However, the true lamps of the necropolis were the cluster of luminous grey dead who swayed and flapped their sagging mouths at a crossroads of cemetery paths.

"I'm sure these poor souls would agree with my sentiments, were we able to hear them," Ibrahim said mildly, catching up. Then he admonished the ghosts with a Buddhist proverb about detachment, addressing in particular those sprits clinging too tight to specific monuments. They were likely attached to their bodies in the same way.

Beatrice ignored him, knowing her anger and frustration came from helplessness. Instead she worked her fire to best advantage. It was not enough.

The rest soon arrived. The ritual remained bogged down; they had a bit of trouble corralling their energy and focusing it, and it was as if they chanted their cantus from a faraway canyon where an echo muddied the effect. Still, while it was not perfect they were able to get the task accomplished.

When the ghostly crowd was thinned to a few floating spectres—the remaining dead were scattered or quiet enough not to attract mortal attention when living family members came in the morning to grieve and lay flowers—Beatrice gestured her companions back to their carriages. Mopping her brow with a kerchief, she said, "I do agree, Ibrahim, that a Guard likely fights best in the city it calls home, not transplanted elsewhere. One always fights harder for one's home, does one not?"

"You'd consider Cairo your home, then?" He sounded surprised. "The city first in your heart, though not of your people?"

"Indeed. A golden home of richest beauty," she said earnestly, staring at him.

Ibrahim's generally nonexpressive face showed something new: subtle pride and distinct pleasure. It made him even more handsome. The moment eased into something pleasant.

On the way back, she and Ibrahim shared the carriage they'd brought from the academy. Staring out the window, not far from Highgate, Beatrice espied a grand estate, back from the road a distance, its uppermost eaves silhouetted against the moonlit sky. Uninhabited, it had no lanterns lit at the gate nor any blazing at the doorstep. No curtains were drawn, the shutters were open, windows on both sides of the estate walls revealing a wide emptiness within. No. Not entirely empty. Something lent illumination, a shifting within. Beatrice called sharply to the driver, who halted at the estate's gravel walk.

"What is it?" Ibrahim asked.

"That house is calling us," Beatrice replied. "Something's inside; look at the light." She hopped down from the carriage and strode toward the wide and undressed windows, eerie colours emanating from within.

★ ★ ★

Persephone had stumbled, dizzy and bleeding, into the mortal world. She had been at the messy business of pins again but now she landed on the floor of an empty house to recover. Grand, regal, with Gothic detailing, it appeared to have just been finished or renovated. Out the front windows rolled an impressive heath. Behind, a small grove of trees and a stable.

With no idea where she was, she had to assume this was a place of import. The Liminal must have brought her here to heal for a reason. The sky looked like England. The air tasted so. She allowed herself a moment of pleasure. This country had become as much a home as any place ever, because it was where hope lived.

Her head and heart heavy, she lay on the floor and allowed the miasma of Whisper-world despair to drain away, the strain of leaving her blood in such deep, dark places. It felt violating, ugly, hopeless. Only faith in her visions kept her from entirely losing her mind to shadow, and the best way to cleanse the tainted air in her lungs was through tears. She felt warmth course down her cheeks, and quicksilver pooled in her palm.

Her tears formed a ring. A small, delicate silver ring in the shape of a feather, its quill meeting its tip.

"Oh," she murmured. "That's quite nice . . ."

Then she curled up on the floor of the empty foyer to recover.

★ ★ ★

"Wait here," Ibrahim instructed the driver.

Following Beatrice, who was halfway up the walk, he

caught her at the door. She let the heavy knocker lift and fall. No answer. Trying the lock, she found it open and stepped through. The inside of the home proved empty, but there was light down the hall.

The two made their way toward it. At the end of the corridor they found Persephone lying huddled upon the parlour floor, her face expressionless and yet her eyes pouring strange reflective tears. It was her light that filled the room with different colours.

"My Lady." Beatrice stepped closer.

The goddess looked up, startled, then relaxed again, laying her face back upon the smooth wooden slats. "Oh, hello, Beatrice, Ibrahim, how good of you to come," she said, her voice small.

"What . . . what are you doing here?"

"This is a special house. I'd like to live here. I want to be here. I care so very much about the mortal world and what happens here. But *you* are more than mortal. You are The Guard. And here I am thinking only of someone who is *not* a Guard! I don't know who he is—only a first name and a face in visions. I've seen him, but he's not here. I don't know. There are so many things I don't know. Don't mind me; pouring my warm blood onto cold stones is so very taxing. I need to rest."

There on the floor she curled up again and closed her eyes, loosing an ugly, rattling cough into her arm, then sniffling. Apart from the maturity of her body, she looked like a helpless, gorgeous child.

"My Lady." Beatrice bent and reached out as if to press comfortingly upon her shoulder. The goddess held up her hand to halt her.

"Please. I . . . I simply need to rest. I heal in this world. Do not worry. Please go."

Not knowing what else to do, Beatrice walked away. Ibrahim silently followed, closing the door behind them. He hadn't said a single word, so when Beatrice turned to him, she was shocked to find tears in his eyes.

He cleared his throat. "To see an angel so distract . . . It shakes a man to the core. If a being so lost is what protects the afterlife of mortals, The Guard in particular, then what have we to look forward to?"

Beatrice set her jaw. "She's right. She needs to take her next step, do something different, take another form like Phoenix and the Muses do. She needs to do it before she's no mind left to use. I just hope she knows *how*."

★ ★ ★

Persephone heard them leave, as she had requested. She couldn't bring herself to move and so kept gazing at the back of the house. It was such a beautiful dwelling, but empty, waiting. She lay upon the floor and begged for a sign. Since the Liminal had been taking strange interest in her of late, she hoped it might answer. If not the Liminal, then perhaps her own visionary gifts might channel a moment to rejuvenate her . . .

She did not wait long. Her eyes clouded as a vision filled her. The night was suddenly day, and there was a man at the door, looking out to the garden behind. He was tall and sharp-featured with a mop of black hair and black frock coat. It was him. Alexi. And this grand house was his? His eyes were dark, but they sparkled fondly, a contrast to his set jaw and pursed lips. This brooding man had found joy in something.

He stared and moved onto the veranda. Persephone turned and again saw herself in the garden. Well, not herself. Bright white, colourless, eerie; that self she saw only with her own eyes. But that young mirrored self was smiling. She was deliriously happy as she ran to him.

The vision made her weep: Alexi embracing a porcelain creature that the world would deem strange. Yet he was enraptured, drawing back to kiss her softly, passionately. Persephone's body ached with a fire her ghostly beloved could not quench, a need that had not been tended for millennia. She wanted to be touched again, kissed again. Like *that.*

Alexi scooped up the girl and carried her into the house and Persephone wanted to be her more than anything in the world. The vision faded away. The house again lay empty.

"Laws of the mortal world, as your laws are different than that which governs me," Persephone prayed, "be with me now. Show me the ways in which I may serve you, you, my dark-haired destiny. You are Phoenix and he is you. I *see* you. Come to me."

She felt so tired. *So* tired. She curled tighter into a ball, clutching the ring that had been made from her tears and closing her eyes, knowing she would just rest a bit. But the next thing she knew, she was roused by carriages clattering outside. She didn't know how long she'd been sleeping, but it was bright out and Beatrice and Ibrahim had left at dusk. That had been kind of them to visit. How had they found her? Her recollection was hazy. She wondered if she should be ashamed of her frailty.

There was nothing to be done for it. They'd seen her powerful plenty of times, too.

She glided to the window to see about the ruckus. A family was arriving. There were trunks and parcels, and a tall, distinguished man with dark features and a slight German accent had disembarked from the first carriage. He was helping a similarly striking woman down. They looked so familiar . . .

A black-haired youth was descending from the second carriage, an adolescent garbed in dark clothes suited to someone much older. He turned before she could catch his face and helped down a young lady. Surely she was the daughter of the fine couple from the first carriage; their striking grace and compelling airs were all of a piece.

The girl stared up at the estate, her thin face shifting from stern to enthralled. Hiking up her layered grey skirts, she darted toward the front stoop and her boots clipped upon the flagstones. The boy turned to follow.

A sound tore from Persephone's throat, a gasp of gratefulness, joy and hope. Birds in the garden began to sing.

"It's you," she breathed. Her heart was in her throat. He had come home to her, just as she had begged last night. "Dear one, it's you . . ."

Of course, it would not do for the family to arrive to find her. Not in her present form. For that reason, she glided up the banister and watched from above.

"Alexi!" the girl called as the two ran inside the empty house and began cursory, excited inspections. "There's a grand study on this side. Father will be so pleased. Father can't use all these shelves for his books alone, so surely there's room for your collection, too. And your desk."

"I should hope so," Alexi replied. His lofty voice held hardly a trace of his father's German accent, and neither did his sister's, meaning they'd been in England for a while. So, why hadn't she found him before? How long had they been close but so far apart?

She watched as he poked his head into each downstairs room, glancing out the bay window below the stairs, moving with purpose and determination. He was a born Leader. Persephone desperately wanted his dark eyes to find hers and for him to know her for who she was, to love her instantly as she loved him, but she would not interfere. Not until she could be certain the time was right.

The young man turned to address the man at the door. "Quite satisfactory, Father. A good choice of property, indeed." He nodded, and his quiet mother offered a slight smile while she slid her arm into her husband's.

"As it shall be yours one day, I suppose it ought to meet with your approval, young master," his father said. "As you shall own all you survey, I hope it stands up to your inspection." There was an odd dynamic between youth and sire.

Alexi turned to the stairs. "You'd best be at my heels to pick a room, Alexandra, else I'll choose a closet for you."

The girl shrieked with an excited giggle, darting up the stairs and looking down. "Wait for me! Oh, Alexi! Just look at the foyer, why, it's large enough to dance in. I'll teach you to waltz."

Alexi stared down from the banister with disdain. "I'm going to be an academic. What need have I for dancing?"

"You will thank me for it one day, you mark my words," Alexandra declared. When Alexi shrugged and turned away, she darted up to the landing after him and chased him down the hall.

Persephone moved herself out of sight, gliding onto a balcony, perching and watching, becoming even more like pure light, letting the sun blend her body with the sky. She watched fondly as brother and sister moved in and out of the rooms, staring out the windows, and her breath caught when Alexi's dark eyes stared through her. Perhaps it was wistfulness that made her see such longing in those intelligent eyes, a particular longing for the future. A new life was indeed about to begin for Alexi's family, whether they knew it or not. She would keep the others ignorant, but perhaps Alexi could know . . .

There was a loud beating of wings, and Alexi's eyes flew to the ravens alighting on the tree beside her. A squawk sounded at Persephone's ear, and she turned, maintaining her invisibility. Regal and large, one raven stared at her, its black eyes oddly sentient. Persephone reached out her hand.

"Hello, herald," she murmured as the bird leaned toward her fingertips. "Shall you help us? We've much to do to knit the new family together."

The bird gave a rasping cry.

The wind picked up, and a patch of plumage on the raven's breast burned a sudden, shocking blue. The sight was a surprise, and a rush of powerful, intoxicating hope seized Persephone's slender body. Suddenly she was more certain than ever that sometime very soon Alexi would indeed become Leader.

He had moved on to another room, so Persephone entered the house again, taking care to remain unseen. Moving to the parlour she found a familiar figure at the wide windows there. Alexi's grandmother was stern, stoic and powerful in her own right. Had Persephone and Phoenix imagined her stare when they stood on the Liminal edge? There was something inexplicable about this woman.

She spoke in rapid Russian. "When will you make him a Leader? I've demanded your attention."

Persephone felt her heart leap into her throat. She said nothing.

The grandmother continued. "I know who you are. He told me the light changes. That there's a distinct floral scent and a sour undercurrent. Something jarring. Pomegranate, yes? I know you are here even if I cannot see you."

Persephone only hesitated a moment. Sliding back her robe from her head she became visible and said, "Hello. This is most unexpected."

The corner of Alexi's grandmother's mouth twisted. "Yes, you are likely only known to a select few. A special six."

Persephone felt her breath catch. Alexi hadn't been taken yet, so he couldn't know any of this. He couldn't have told her. How did this commoner, an uninitiated, know the secrets of—

"Moscow. Dmitri. He was a brilliant Leader, was he not?"

Persephone gaped.

"I know. The Guard is not supposed to share The Grand Work with any uninitiated. My name is Katarina Novodevichy, and I was *not* a member of that Moscow Guard. But I loved

Dmitri Sergeyevna more than life itself. I could not have him. Not by your decree but by that of my country. I was born of high class. He, a stable boy. The Grand Work made a stable boy into a king, and I will forever worship you for it."

Katarina's eyes misted, and for a moment she was far away. "Dmitri and I loved each other since childhood. The night before I married an aristocrat I never loved, I presented myself to him. I prayed for a child to come from that sacred night together, a testament to true love foiled by cruel mortal constraints and imprisoning society. A child did. *Irina*, Alexi's mother. Dmitri never knew.

"It was best that way. It would have killed him to be away from her, and he had his Work. Irina was a gentle but frightened child; she had none of her father's strength. But now I have a grandson. Such a boy—he is magnificent and you know it. So, when will it happen?"

Persephone stood, stunned. "Soon," she finally said. "I believe it will happen soon."

"Good. Then I can rest in peace. I live only for the moment my grandson inherits his glory, and then these weary bones can rest. Dmitri will come for me, and our spirits will not pass on but instead travel the world in eternal adventure, together at last. I've seen to it Alexi will be well provided for, but it's up to you to make sure my firebird ascends his throne."

Katarina walked away, leaving Persephone to contemplate the wonderful webs that mortals could spin. Apparently even gods could be drawn into them.

Chapter Twenty

Ibrahim was pulled from a disturbing treatise on industrialization as Ahmed shot up from the chair in which he'd been dozing. The two of them had taken to the library in the "Apollo" wing, as it was here that Ibrahim was most comfortable. Here he was surrounded by his true friends: books. The collected volumes were prodigious. That produced a feeling that sufficed for contentment, though his blood was increasingly restless and his Instinct churned with dread.

"The dream again? The war in the ground?"

"No." Ahmed shook his head. "This time just a sense. I could hardly see anything, but the word 'betrayal' kept echoing in my mind, over and over again, like some thunderous bell. I fear there is a veritable battalion of betrayals ahead, and I don't know what that means. Do the bells of dread toll for us, or for the goddess? What does your Instinct tell you?"

"My feelings are muddy. They concur with your visions. But for us . . . Which of us I cannot say."

"Then it must not be about us. It's about the future." Ahmed paused. "Often those with gifts see more of others than themselves. All we can do is share our prophecies and dreams. The great mysteries must use us as they will."

Ibrahim shook his head, baffled by the genuine acceptance on Ahmed's face. "You see such horrors, and yet you remain the most joyful soul I've ever known. How can you welcome those visions and remain so unscarred?"

Ahmed shrugged. "One must meet Darkness with joy. It lessens his power. That is the simplest element of my gift, which I do not question. I lead a simpler existence for that. You could make the same choice."

Ibrahim chuckled, helpless.

"What?" Ahmed asked. "I hardly ever see such a face on you. What is it? Did I say something amusing?"

"I'm just . . . I am not built as you." Ibrahim shook his head. "But I am very glad to know you, Ahmed. The world is better because you are in it."

Ahmed's smile was radiant. "True friendship is life's greatest commission. That, and true love. You have allowed yourself the former, and I am honoured. Blessed by it, even. But now you must allow yourself the latter. You don't have far to look."

Ibrahim quickly turned the tables. This was disquieting territory. "Your commission, surely, is Verena. It's obvious. You're sickening together."

Ahmed looked taken aback, but when Ibrahim offered a slight smile he gave a joyous laugh. "Yes, she is heaven!"

And then they mused, as they often did, on beautiful women. Ahmed waxed rhapsodic on Verena, and Ibrahim spoke only in vague terms, theorizing about hypothetical females lest Ahmed force him into saying something about someone he was far too nervous and frightened to admit he adored.

★ ★ ★

As Persephone finished placing her blood on yet another seal, she knew better than to linger. She went right to the Liminal edge that would whisk her away to safely heal. After the last journey, she trusted it like never before. But at that gorgeous proscenium she found she had company.

"Aodhan. I didn't expect to see you here. Are you keeping safe? How?"

"I don't stray far. Darkness and his minions don't like it here, I've noticed."

"And we'd like to keep it that way. They don't understand this place. They fear it, and we must keep them fearing it."

Aodhan nodded, dazed. "I keep staring into this void, and sometimes I'll glimpse something. I think it wants to tell me something . . ."

"Ask it." Persephone gestured, the motion casting the light of her colours forward like ripples through a still stream. "Ask the Liminal what it wants you to see. It listens closely to those who were mortal."

Obedient, Aodhan turned. "Tell me. Show me."

Apparently a request was all that was needed. A scene leaped to life, though the clock above the proscenium remained still, meaning mortal time remained unchanged.

"Where is that?" Aodhan breathed, staring at a massive, sprawling, sparkling, shifting city.

"Welcome to London," Persephone replied, glancing at the Liminal clock for confirmation. "It is the year 1867."

From her experience, it looked like morning on the crowded docks of the Thames. An overfilled boat tumbled passengers out onto the landing, but the Liminal seemed to focus upon a disembarking family. From their clothing, they appeared without much means. The father's face hard, the mother's aglow with excitement and fear. The daughter glanced around in unabashed wonder.

"Oh," Aodhan breathed, staring. The adolescent woman, her hair in a golden braid down her back, was broad-shouldered and sturdy with fair skin and an engaging face. Then she smiled and was radiant. "Why, she's so much like my Brigid," he breathed, a tear rolling down his phantom cheek.

"Who was Brigid?" Persephone asked.

"A lass from the village. She wasn't Guard. I . . . I saw her nearly every day when the market was on, from a wee lad into my old age. She was such a good woman, a right saint. I was too afraid that she'd think The Grand Work was witchcraft to ever say more than a few words to her. But, oh, how she'd talk to me. And how her eyes would smile. *That* smile." He pointed at the young woman whose eyes were still drinking in London. "She never married, Brigid. She never did. I wonder . . ."

The girl's eyes, a rich green-hazel, seemed to stare right at him. Both Aodhan and Persephone caught their breath. It was like the moment before, with Katarina Novodevichy and Alexi. Was this girl, too, fated for something more than her means might normally offer?

Aodhan exhaled, a soft, amazed sound. His hand lifted, glowing with a Healer's light.

"The circle is complete," came a distinct whisper. "They are assembled. It is time."

Aodhan cocked his head, and all Persephone's shifting colour drained. She was just as ghostly as he for a moment; then a flush brought out rose hues again.

"I know that voice," Aodhan murmured.

"It's the Muse—your Muse, the Healer." Persephone choked. She began to wring her hands.

"But it never speaks. Only in death do they speak, or during . . ."

"The Taking. The changing of The Guard. It's happening again, now, in London."

"But didn't you take a set in Cairo?"

"Yes, and transported them to London. I suppose the Muses need something more—"

"We cannot ask our current hosts to relinquish their beloved Cairo," came the Muse's breathy explanation. "Their hesitancy shows in their Work. We require those who call *London* home, in their hearts and until their end of days." Floating into view was its hazy, incredible form, all starlight and music, glimmer and spirit. The being floated before Aodhan's face, across the

Liminal threshold, and the great wind picked up that always signaled a new taking. It turned toward Persephone. "Are you coming, my Lady?"

Persephone swallowed. "Of course."

Aodhan stammered. "B-but this is—"

"Unprecedented," Persephone and the Healer Muse chorused.

"What of this girl?" Aodhan asked, reaching out a desperate, glowing hand toward those bustling docks beyond. "What do you intend for her?"

"She will be a Healer like you. She will need your help. She is too young, but she will do. All too young, they all must do." The Muse turned to Persephone. "Especially your pet, my Lady."

It laughed, a tinkling sound. "Come. I'm the first to go. Your Phoenix will be reeling, but we will soon begin and he'll have no choice but to follow."

★ ★ ★

The day had not begun like any other. It began much like the day they were possessed, the day they were made The Guard, an uneasy day where the wind was restless. This time Beatrice knew what the odd wind was. But she couldn't be sure what it was up to. They had already been found, she and her companions. What was that force looking for now?

It wasn't the Pull that drew her to Westminster Bridge. Not exactly. It was pain. What had begun like a familiar beating of wings in her veins had become a bird struggling, now panicking to get out. Their Muses were rebelling.

Ibrahim and Verena stood at the crest of the bridge.

"The lack of our native soil is taking its toll, surely. Just like Ibrahim said," Verena suggested quietly, mournfully. She stared at Beatrice, puzzled. "And yet for you this *is* your native soil. Do you feel the pain I feel in my veins?"

Beatrice stared at her, then at silent Ibrahim, who appeared nauseated with worry. "I'd never denounce my heritage, but Cairo is my home," she replied. "Yes, there is a fire inside me, a pain I've never felt. The sensation of our possession but in reverse."

Verena whimpered. "Are our gifts faltering? Perhaps none of this was meant to be."

"No, it's what I was afraid it would be," Ibrahim said.

Beatrice shrugged. "None of this has proven predictable. Even our Lady couldn't be sure what event would beget what. All we know is that something is about to change."

"Where, then, is she? Where is our Lady?" Verena asked.

The others of The Guard appeared, drawn by the same call. All six stood on the bank of the Thames as Verena's uneasy query was answered. A light arrived at the scene. The goddess.

"Something is about to happen," she breathed. She appeared overwhelmed. And excited.

"Why, thank you," Ibrahim muttered. "I'd never have guessed."

"We are in an unprecedented age," Persephone went on. "Prophecy is at hand."

And then it came—an explosion—the light of the goddess was all around them. It was familiar, warm. Then they realized it was not her light but one they'd never actually seen; this light had overtaken them once, unawares. It had possessed them. The six stared at the glow, absorbing the sight of what had just been inside them, a shimmering iridescence beside the light and wash of Phoenix fire.

Beatrice felt it rip from her veins. She stumbled forward onto Ibrahim's outstretched arm. The others were shaken, too.

She saw them wince or recoil, and soon the Muses, vaguely humanoid forms if sparkling and effervescent, were all torn free. They stared down at their former hosts. Faces were not discernable, though their energies seemed kind, loving, pleased. But they were moving on. So soon. So soon when one expected they'd come not to leave. Those spirits and their accompanying mass of winged blue fire tore off through London.

"Unprecedented," Persephone murmured, staring longingly after them. Then she whirled upon the six mortals left behind. "I'm sorry, I must go," she said. And she vanished.

Belle began to cry. "I do not understand."

"It would seem we were useless. The spirits are finding better candidates," Ibrahim stated, his voice hard, his expression conflicted.

"Now what?" George asked. A mad smirk toyed at his mouth.

Perhaps, Beatrice agreed, it *was* best to laugh. Was it not best to be rid of this burden they'd not quite grasped? Yet was something still expected of them? And what of their lives? What would fill the resulting void?

Chapter Twenty-one

He was studying in Mr. Absolom's secret laboratory when it happened, far progressed into what he hoped would become a revelation of a multiple alchemical chain reactions. The revelation provided was of a far different nature.

Alexi Rychman had been a lonely child, prone to obsessive reading and study. At age seven, his mother, a timid woman, proclaimed him too intent and intelligent for her comfort. He spoke rarely to her, and to his father, instead reserving his limited energy for socialization to his sister and grandmother. It was his apprenticeship with Mr. Absolom that had drawn his family to London from Germany eight years ago, and he distinctly felt his parents resented him for it. But Katarina Novodevichy had given the family all the comfortable wealth they had, and it was she who made the decisions. He had therefore strived to live up to her expectations, and he had succeeded by all estimations.

As he supposed many intelligent children did, Alexi found numbers, powders, charts and books more agreeable than people. There were few moments when he cast detachment aside, but during these he would smile at his grandmother and she would grow misty-eyed. Katarina would say something in Russian about the grandfather he never knew and claim that there was hope for him yet, if he remembered to turn that rare, gentle, beautiful look upon those who mattered. She had always been his champion, though. His earliest memory was of her staring at him with an intent look he supposed he'd learned from her, murmuring that he would grow up to be very powerful. He didn't mind the thought, but neither did he take it for granted.

On this fateful day, something very powerful indeed was making itself known. Alexi heard a rush of wings, felt a strong breeze and for just a moment thought that perhaps his powders were indeed blazing the trail to a new discovery. But it was not the powders.

"Hello, Leader," came a firm male voice, surrounding him in a strange language he somehow understood. He looked up and saw fire. Blue fire. "This is the only time you will hear my voice, so listen close. You are a chosen one. *The* chosen one. What tops the alchemical pyramid? Me. The Grand Work begins, and the vendetta shall end with you. Treat her well and make us proud." These cryptic words were accompanied by an incredible sensation of power, joy, wisdom, balance and freedom. An ancient, righteous fury told him he was now a defense against evil, a mortal angel in a grand tradition . . .

His logical sense reacted aggressively. Terror struck him and he jumped back, pressing hands down his black suit as if brushing off the intruder. It was too strange, whatever was happening to his body. But something dulled his fear of this overtaking energy, the sudden knowledge that at the heart of it, whatever now held him in thrall was inherently good. What exactly it *was,* however, remained to be seen and examined. He had to get to Westminster Bridge. It was a sudden imperative.

For his solitary heart now beat with the echoes of others.

He looked at his laboratory table and was suddenly sad. What about the great work he'd been studying? Would alchemy be supplanted by this requisite Grand Work? Was he no longer his own man? Was his love of science to be sacrificed on the altar of a sudden new duty?

Greatness. Was this what his grandmother imagined? So often she spoke in riddles, he had no idea what she knew and did not. The idea of her having foreseen this was daunting if at the same time encouraging. But, he would overcome all the challenges of this new fate. Even the new sights.

It was the myriad dead that unsettled him most, more than hearing voices or seeing fire. There were ghosts *everywhere.*

"That will take some getting used to," he muttered, squinting in the bleary grey haze of the day, his vision lit further by the luminescent dead. Their countless forms floated amid the busy streets, in bustling doorways, docks and grand, carriage-filled avenues, and they turned to him, bowing as if he were royalty.

He moved from Absolom's offices on Baker Street, his wide eyes filled with phantasmal sights. He was walking slowly to a new life, and his mind felt as though it were being superimposed with directives, that a force was urging him forward like a bridled horse to Westminster. Then, secondarily, desire burgeoned in Bloomsbury, something important awaited him there, too: in his blood a treasure map burned where mysteries called to him in voices that he could not deny.

With every step, ghosts bowed to him. The word "Leader" echoed in his ears like a betrothal promise, and he had a sudden and startling certainty that by the time he reached Westminster Bridge and connected with those faint heartbeats that thrummed just beyond his own pounding pulse, he would have left part of his boyhood behind him in order to don the mantle of a man.

★ ★ ★

Persephone stood with her robes up about her head, hidden from even the most skilled mortal eye. She kept to the shadows, watched as the fire overtook him.

His intent young face displayed a new gravity as well as

the wonder and other striking qualities she recognized from her visions. She listened for his heart, felt it throb and thrum with new force, new feelings of wonder and terror. Such was always the case, but never before had so much been on the line, and never before did she have such personal investment in the Leader. But everything in the mortal nineteenth century had brought her to this moment, to this boy named Alexi who would become the man upon which she would stake eternity.

As she followed him out into the bustling, dirty, gorgeous streets of London, she saw that there had never been a better time to weave the fabrics of two disparate worlds together. Gazing about the manic city, she felt a thrill of anticipation. Theatres sported billings of mediums and magicians; bookstands teemed with tracts on spiritualism and séances. Lecture halls were filled with afterlife postulation, still other theatres offered the *vampir,* the classical, the mythological. Paintings, sculptures, prints, cards, all depicting gods like her, were mixed in among the velvet and cigars, were fawned upon by the educated and the merely titillated.

It was right that she would choose this world as her own. This gilded age understood sumptuous, glorious beauty, the rites and righteousness of spring. It also understood the dark, purgatorial whispers that had come to define the other part of her existence. She could here, as a mortal, be a child of two worlds. She would bathe in the glorious fires of he who would pull a star from the sky, choosing to live freely in the light. This grim and glorious age was hers, it was her chance to live, love and die as mortals did. This era was tailor-made for her and for The Grand Work. Provided she could follow through with the task whose exact details yet eluded her.

Westminster was hazy, the wind odd. Because of the Muses. The blue-breasted raven had come, hovering over five of the six chosen mortals, examining them as they planted themselves, one by one in a circle on the embankment side, waiting for the last, waiting for their Leader. Persephone took them all in, still invisible to them.

They watched Alexi approach. The five were nervous, excited and . . . too young. But, time wasn't on anyone's side. A tall and spindly if elegant brunette, the sharp girl from the Quaker meetinghouse, shifted on her feet. She drank Alexi in as if he were ambrosia. She was the girl Ibrahim had rightly pinned as Intuition.

Alexi arrived and spoke in a mature voice. "Good day. My name is Alexi Rychman, and this has turned into the strangest day of my life."

The spindly brunette and he gazed at each other, he the Leader, she his second-in-command. She blushed. Persephone's heart sank for her, this Intuition who must live heartbroken, for she was not the woman of Alexi's future.

"Hello, Alexi," the girl said. "I'm Rebecca, and I feel the same."

"Elijah," spoke up a thin, blue-eyed blond boy garbed in striped satin finery that bordered on the absurd. He, the Memory, and the Artist regarded each other with subtle curiosity.

"Josephine," came a voice with a soft French accent. Its owner was a gorgeous brunette, two shocks of white hair framing her youthful face. Persephone wondered if the Taking had caused them. Sometimes the process had effects: eyes changed colour, mortals grew more beautiful, more intelligent, more fearsome, whatever traits heightened their powers.

Alexi had been compelling from the first, but as Leader his presence was inescapable. Persephone nearly threw back her robes, aching to again be held by a powerful creature of goodness and wisdom. When Darkness held her, she knew only misery and pain. She ached to be touched by such a magnetic, inimitable man.

She hardly remembered what it felt like. The thought was

overwhelming. But Persephone had to stop losing herself in him, not when there were more introductions to make, a new Guard to cherish and love—

"Michael," chimed in a sturdy boy with a grin that rivaled Ahmed's. The Heart, a strapping, broad-shouldered youth with ruddy cheeks and the contagious smile that distinguished Hearts from all others, he stared at Rebecca as if dazzled by her prim grace. His oceanic blue eyes were full of wonder.

"Lucretia Marie O'Shannon Connor," said an Irish accent. A dusky blonde girl stared at the cobblestones, her hair falling to hide what was a fair but frightened face. Her plain dress bespoke modest means. This was the Healer, the one Aodhan had seen. "I suppose you could call me Jane if that's easier," she murmured with a shrug.

The blond boy laughed. "I'll say."

Alexi pursed his lips, then interrupted, his voice firm. "And here I thought all my life I'd be a scientist. It seems forces at large have other plans. I don't suppose any of you has the slightest idea what we're supposed to *do*?"

Everyone shook their heads.

Give it time, Persephone wanted to urge. *Trust your instincts.* But that was for them to know, not to be told. She walked a fine line with every Guard; they had to learn to trust their own burgeoning talent in order to truly own their Muses' gifts.

Alexi continued. "Then let me ask a mad question. Does anyone, all of a sudden, see ghosts?"

"Yes!" everyone chorused. Their relief was palpable.

"Can you hear them speak?"

"No," came the universal reply.

"Neither can I, thank God, or we'd never have another moment's peace." Alexi glanced around, giving a sigh of confusion. Persephone had witnessed many a Taking, and the scripts were always similar, the mortals struggling to comprehend. So many foreign sensations.

The raven above fixed its black eyes upon her, seeing as animals usually did past the robes that hid Persephone. Rebecca pointed to the bird, and the group followed it toward Bloomsbury. It was good that this Guard had a familiar to join them; they'd need all the help they could muster.

The city engulfed them. On they walked, toward the grand edifice that had changed into Athens Academy, Persephone trailing behind. Encouraged by the knowledge rioting like wildfire through their young bodies, they followed their herald all the way to their destination. The empty building would open to students within the year, but for now it was theirs. The sacred space awaited them.

Persephone was struck by a sudden fear. Where were Beatrice and *her* Guard? What were they experiencing? Were they in their upstairs rooms here at Athens, feeling suddenly, strangely hollow? This was unprecedented, to have one Guard replaced with another in this manner, and she was certain there would be great confusion if they met. Perhaps bitterness, seeing as their glorious commissions had gone sour so soon. No, the two groups needed to steer clear of each other.

She'd make sure of it. The only way to do so was to release Beatrice's Guard from service and get them back their lives. But, Beatrice she'd need. Beatrice had become an integral part of the equation, and there was work yet to be done. At the very least there was the annunciation of the new Guard to be handled.

Alexi had already begun to master the Phoenix fire. He was proficient enough to open the sacred space, and it was there that she moved to reveal herself, to name each of their individual powers. Like she always did. But, this time was different. This time was Prophecy. This time would be the last.

Opening a portal between the worlds, she stood upon that threshold, framed by the darkness that was the Whisper-world. The jaws of The Guard dropped in wonder.

"My beloveds," she began. "I've not much time, but I must inaugurate you as I have done since your circle began The Grand Work in ancient times. There has never been a more crucial age than this one—this century, this city. Your world is filled with new ideas, new science, new ideas on God and the body . . . and, most important, spirits. There's never been such talk of spirits."

She turned to Alexi, gazing upon him while willing him to know her heart. To them she appeared a prismatic, powerful angel, but inside she was terribly nervous. She could feel the tears in her eyes. "Alexi, you are Leader here. Inside you lives what's left of my true love, the first phoenix born of ancient times. His great power was only splintered, not destroyed. It is your tool. You control the element and are born again within it. My love lives in you, worthy Alexi, and you will fight Darkness by bearing the eternal flame of our vendetta."

She turned to the others and gave them their own instructions, assigning them their duties. But then the script changed. She thought of Darkness's threat, how he'd rip the worlds apart for her. She did not doubt that.

"Hold fast, for the struggle will worsen," she warned. "Darkness will seek to destroy the barrier between worlds. To fight this, Prophecy must be fulfilled. A seventh member must join you. She will come as your peer to create a new dawn."

Persephone glanced behind her, wincing, feeling the Whisper-world lurch in her blood, demanding that she step back into the darkness rather than stand precarious on the ledge. But the threshold itself was different. It sparkled and sparked with a very particular, familiar light. Liminal energy was here. The Liminal was present at this annunciation; it was taking a stake, as it was sometimes wont to do. It had an opinion about how things should be run, and the winds of change were set to blow.

At her discomfort, Alexi rushed forward. She would

normally have welcomed his aid, but she stilled him with a hand. "You must understand," she breathed. "Once the seventh joins you, it will mean war."

"Who are you?" Alexi asked.

The yearning in his voice made her ache—and smile. But the words she meant to say weren't delivered as planned. "I hope you will know her when she comes, Alexi, my love. I hope she will know you, too."

She was unable to say "I." That word was for some reason barred from her lips.

Well, it wasn't exactly "she." Whomever they met would be Persephone as mortal flesh remade her. Something was cautioning her words, allowing Prophecy to indeed take on a life of its own. The interference was troubling, for she desperately wanted assurances that no sacrifice of The Grand Work would be in vain, wanted to offer young Alexi Rychman promises of love and happiness, promises his grandmother had demanded for him, nay, called down the very gods to assure. But here she realized what the Liminal was doing. It, in its infinite wisdom, wanted Prophecy played out entirely by mortals. All would be left to chance and will.

She wanted desperately to tell Alexi not to worry, that she'd come to him soon and with everything he needed. The words did not come out that way at all.

"Await her," she continued, following a script she hadn't written. "But beware. She'll not come with answers but be lost, confused. I have put protections in place, but she will be threatened and seeking refuge. There shall be tricks, betrayals and second guesses. Caution, beloved. Mortal hearts make mistakes. Choose your seventh carefully, for if you choose the false prophet, the end of your world shall follow."

She heard her words, knew they were correct and felt her insides twist with anxiety. All she could promise was hope. Not herself. Not the girl she had seen. Just hope. And she had to hope he would fall in love with her like a normal mortal man would, albeit a man thrown into extraordinary circumstances.

She immediately regretted what she'd begun to cherish. This could lead to madness! She'd been running after phantom visions. But, a new leaf had been turned. Pandora's box was open. Hope was the only thing left inside.

"A sign!" the Heart insisted, that sturdy, amiable Michael. "Surely there will be a sign. When will she come? How will we know what to fight against?"

"You'll be led to fight the machinations of Darkness by instinct. But, you shall not always be fighting," she assured them, knowing there was yet time. "You are also as you were. Your mortal lives and thoughts remain unchanged, though they are augmented by spirits."

She thought a moment, wondering what she could promise them. What had been consistent in her visions? The hands of the Liminal clock had palsied in her visions, so nothing was certain. But, doors. In the end it was all about doors and paths between worlds.

"Look for a door. Something like this"—she gestured about her—"should be your gauge. But don't go in." She gave the Whisper-world a baleful glance. "You wouldn't want to come here. You'll see this threshold together, all of you. I cannot say precisely when your seventh will come. I'm powerful, but only the great cosmos is omnipotent. But, she will be placed in your path. And once she is, you won't have much time before a terrible storm."

In the distance Persephone heard barking. The dog. He sniffed a threshold held open too long and moved to guard it.

She heard Alexi ask her name. They always asked her name, The Guard. They had a right, but it was such a terribly limiting thing. "It hardly matters. We've had so many names through the years, all of us."

And yet, to mortals a name was so important. Staring at

Alexi, at his worried, amazed face, she was compelled to offer one final caution. If she couldn't give him certainty, at least she could give him this: "Please be careful. Listen to your instincts and stay together. A war is coming, but it isn't what you think. Hell isn't down, it's around us, pressing inward. But your seventh will be there when it comes, or she will have died in vain."

"Died?" Alexi cried.

"One must die to live again," she murmured. Then she blew him a kiss as the portal snapped shut. She could keep it open no longer, not with the Whisper-world monsters on their way, and she was again left in shadow.

She sighed and slid to the ground, her back against the stone wall, her head in her hands. Moisture kissed her skin with dread. She'd not thought of death until the word left her lips. But, she supposed, it was her turn to be a phoenix and rise from ashes.

Chapter Twenty-two

There was havoc on the street where The Great Work had ripped free from Beatrice and her Guard. Beatrice opened her mouth to exclaim but could not. Stilled by surprise, pain or protest, she watched as a trail of blue fire and the glimmering, iridescent forms of the Phoenix fire and its attendant Muses swept into the air and scattered in a burst of angelic music. The Muses spread out across the city; the flame congealed into a large ball over the Thames. Like a growing azure sun, it suddenly burst into a wide-winged, glorious birdlike form.

Beatrice found her voice and shouted up at the great avian vision. "What? No parting words for your unwitting servants?"

The immense cerulean bird descended. A rumbling voice of thunder and stars, wind and sage calm poured forth. "We're sorry. We forget mortal courtesy. You justly deserve every accolade, but our commission draws us onward. You have served valiantly and are rewarded with an early end to your duty. Go in peace."

The departing Muses darted to and fro, visible in the sky before making dizzying dives toward what must be assumed were new captures. The six Guard of Cairo could only watch in surprise. Beatrice wondered if her fellows felt as she did: hollow, torn, wounded, empty and confused like a child suddenly left alone in a crowd.

If their powers had left them, their ability to see the dead had not. In fact, the dead seemed more present than ever—and drawn to the river. It was as if they, too, sensed the great shift and were confused by it. But, not as confused as the Cairo Guard.

Ibrahim moved toward Beatrice, staring. He reached for her, as if she could steady him, and she yearned to take his outstretched hand, rare as such an offer was. But this moment of subtle, aching camaraderie was cut swiftly short, for Beatrice felt a sudden chill that rippled through them like a seizure.

Ibrahim whirled, his eyes wide and his bronze skin pallid. "Careful, we're vulnerable. Oh, no, this is the moment!" he wailed. "The moment of warning!"

A skeletal form appeared, the one in a rotting robe, the one that had followed them from Egypt. Its jaw sagging in a constant scream or some dreadful song, it had been looking for an opportunity all along. This was it.

Ibrahim tried to intercede. "Verena!" he cried, throwing himself before her as if to stop a bullet or sword, but the transparent spirit wanted none of him. It sought a more delicate, vulnerable target, as had been foreseen.

The phantasm hurled itself atop Verena, who cried out and collapsed. Her beautiful face was instantly grey and glowing. She had become a darkly luminous case, endangered.

Ahmed dove to catch her just before she dashed her head on the cobbles. With surprising strength, he lifted her and turned to the others. "We must get her to a doctor," he said in Arabic.

George shook his head. "No English doctor can treat this."

"To the academy, then," Ibrahim growled. "To the infirmary. If Muses are off to find a new Guard, they sure as hell better bring them back to us—and we can tell them a thing or two then. Ahmed, you're going to trip on her skirts. Allow me," he commanded.

His height giving him advantage, he lifted Verena away from the Sufi. Beatrice noticed how the muscles of his neck strained and his knuckles went white. Ibrahim was holding on for dear life, and Verena was shaking violently in his hold. The odd entourage set off, bearing her sickly body among them.

"They're looking at us," George remarked, watching Londoners stare at their motley cadre as they moved swiftly toward the sandstone edifice that had sheltered them since their arrival.

"I'm sorry, I can't turn them away," Belle said mournfully. She held up her hands, which did nothing to passersby but make them mutter that she was a lunatic. She kept her tears silent, knowing they were of no aid. George grabbed her hand and dragged her along.

Beatrice fought back fury. Somewhere in this city, right now, was a new Guard who could help. They might be crossing paths, missing one another by a few streets, and she couldn't count on the Muses or Phoenix to speak up. But, she didn't have time to be angry, not with fate or the Muses, or with Phoenix or his beloved. She only had time for a prayer, supposing one couldn't hurt at a time like this, and so she offered it up to some unknowable divinity with a higher purview than those with whom they'd already dealt; a prayer that begged for something to trust and believe in.

They were to be tested further. Ascending the stairs of Athens, the school still boarded and not scheduled to open for another few months, they felt pressed back, as if a great hand kept them at a distance. The air by the door crackled and was threaded by lightning. A dim blue shimmer appeared, as if they had reached some sort of sorcerous barrier.

"What the hell is that?" George barked.

Beatrice's stomach fell and her anger soared. "The goddess put a protective barrier over the academy, presumably to keep out the wrong sorts."

Ibrahim growled. "We are no longer The Guard, and in our arms we have *exactly* the wrong sort."

The two of them shared a look of helpless fury. If they

had struggled with The Grand Work before, they'd never felt so grievously wronged. And they weren't even the person *possessed*.

With Athens off limits, a chapel down the street seemed the safest bet. In a side annex, a sickroom. Their coterie ducked into the shadowed nave, grateful for empty pews bereft of inquisitive priests. Ibrahim laid Verena on one with a velvet cushion. "We'll move her to the sickroom once she's stable. But we've more anonymity here at the moment."

Verena's body lurched and her lungs rattled, the mysterious and horrible fluids that seemed inherent to possession welling from her eyes and down her nose. Ahmed, unflinching, wiped it away with the sleeve of his tunic. Beatrice tore the hem of her skirt to provide more fabric, and Belle drifted over and did the same. Then she walked away, unable to see her friend in such a state.

Beatrice sat and held Verena's shaking feet. Ahmed took her head in his lap, and Ibrahim knelt upon a padded cushion meant for prostration. It seemed oddly fitting in that moment.

"Can you say something to keep it at bay?" Beatrice asked, feeling useless. There was no power in her fingertips, which yet itched to cast out demons. She wondered if this phantom feeling of power was what amputees suffered, this awful yet certain feeling of something that was no longer there.

Ibrahim could not stop staring at Verena. "I . . . I've nothing. My library is gone," he said. He looked as helpless as Beatrice felt.

Verena's head was on Ahmed's lap, her body stiff and rigid on the pew. The Sufi launched into a recitation of Rumi, hoping to ease her pain or at least distract her from it. No one could tell if it was working.

Ibrahim jumped up. "I'll go to the Athens library. If I do not have a library here"—he tapped his temple—"I shall re-create it."

Ahmed kept reciting poetry, offering verses he had written for Verena. If she liked or was flattered by his verses, she said nothing, only shuddered and wept noxious fluid. Ahmed wept as well.

It was not long before Ibrahim returned from the Athens library carrying an armload of tomes on faith and beauty. He took over for Ahmed, whose voice was growing increasingly faint. Ibrahim's was sure and clear, and the passages he chose were intelligently to the point. Beatrice had never found herself admiring him more. This might not cast out the demon, but it clearly kept the horrific thing from progressing in its evil work; they were not seeing in Verena the full extent of damage her Guard had seen in others during their short time of service.

Beatrice turned to George, nodding to Belle. The young French girl could not handle the scene; her tears would not stop. "You can take her elsewhere. She doesn't have to see this, there's nothing she can do. It's all right, we'll await the others."

"No," Belle murmured. "The . . . *new ones.* I want to see them, too."

"Then sit and calm yourself," Beatrice said firmly. "There is no sense in you suffering in addition."

Belle nodded, moving to a baptismal alcove opposite where she sat stiff vigil upon a tomb. George flanked her, a silent sentinel much like the statue of the saint that bore his name, the patron of England who stood in grim marble triumph at the entrance to this place of worship.

Beatrice squeezed Verena's hand. "The goddess gave you a kiss of life, remember? Don't you dare forget it. That must count for something," she said. But, truthfully, she felt they could only count on one another. Mortals were best looking out for themselves.

While she was in a mood for prayer, she said one for the new Guard, too, the poor fools.

★ ★ ★

Everything inside Alexi's body screamed for him to remain with his new friends; everything in his heart screamed for the love of that unnamed goddess. His sensibilities were reeling and he just wanted to go home. He listened to those.

There was madness when he finally arrived at his family estate. His sister was broken in a heap on the floor, and his grandmother was wheezing like she was about to die of fright. The house looked like a storm had cut a distinct swath through it, glass broken, vases overturned, doors unhinged. He tried to ask his grandmother what had happened, but all she could offer were mad notions of demons and great winds tearing through the house, unspoken intimations of witchcraft. She was staring at him in that intent way of hers.

"There's something different about you," she murmured. Eyes wide, she exclaimed in Russian: "The firebird—that's it. A darkness comes, my boy. You must light the darkness with your fire." That cryptic instruction became her last words. She did not breathe again.

Alexi sat crumpled on the floor, staring at the bodies of those most precious to him. The help came, made wailing noises that were anything but helpful, and went about sending for a doctor. They also shouted that a bed should be made up for the departed Katarina.

"What's happened?" whispered Alexandra.

His sister was paralyzed, but she stared at Alexi, clearly trying to figure out what was different about him that their grandmother somehow knew. He wanted to answer with the only reply he had—"We're haunted, we're bloody cursed!"— but before he could, his head seared as if someone had split his skull. Gasping, he recoiled, and Alexandra put her hand to her mouth and did not say another word.

The staff was buzzing about. They took Alexandra off to her

bed, sending for more pillows to prop her against. They were just carrying off Katarina's dead body as Alexi struggled to his feet, backing away. "I'm so sorry, I must go," he murmured and knew he'd never forget the helpless, frightened look on his sister's pallid face.

He turned, feeling sick. The Pull had him, and it dragged him with claws on his heart back toward Bloomsbury, back to the heart of the city. He should not, it seemed, have left his fellows. Everything and everyone he and the rest of The Guard once loved was now haunted and cursed, but he had no time to grieve. He was the firebird. He was Leader, so he'd better rise to the challenge. If he did not, his curse would surely worsen.

* * *

Verena's body shuddered. A strange sound was on her lips, as if the creature inside were trying to manipulate her. It sounded like a growl. Or a barking dog. Belle wept softly against the baptismal font, George's hand on her shoulder white-knuckled but comforting. Time inched by. Ibrahim was on to another tome.

"Move her to the clinic," Beatrice instructed. "If they don't come, there may be something a nurse can do. We're right here, maybe someone can help us."

There was general, if limited, agreement. A great tumult sounded as their entourage entered the sickroom, and just as Beatrice was arguing with the nurse that, yes, all five of them were indeed family of the victim, there came a sound and the door was flung open. Beatrice held her breath. A young man, tall and black-haired, striking-featured and dressed in fine but austere clothes, made his entrance.

A wind picked up all around, a strange music in her mind that Beatrice knew well. The newcomer charged forward, blue fire trailing from his outstretched hands. So, they had come. The new Guard. Dear God, they were young, even the Leader. Fourteen, fifteen, perhaps? But his spirit was strong, Beatrice could tell. There was something timeless about him. Blue fire poured from his hands, and his fellows stared at him in a mixture of awe and fear.

New. It's so new and will take some getting used to, she wanted to say, but her breath remained stilled in her throat. She couldn't even hail the newcomers, so entranced was she by the Leader. Beatrice wondered for a moment if she had ever looked that fearsome, so full of power, so *unbelievable.* Perhaps The Grand Work would always amaze, no matter who wielded it. She hadn't ever seen herself charge onto a scene, but she had to admit this was impressive.

"Luminous," the Leader murmured, "I believe we call this a luminous case. A possession with intent to harm." The five youngsters gathered around, terrified acolytes.

Beatrice opened her mouth to say, *Yes, luminous! Help us, you hapless fools, then run for your lives! Damn this Work, it's nothing but a curse!* But again, no words escaped her.

She glanced at her fellows, but all they could do was stare, too, at these newcomers, Guard to Guard. Ahmed and Ibrahim stepped back from Verena's bedside, as if clearing the way. Beatrice tried to get Ibrahim's attention, to see if he could shout the declamation she herself could not, but he was staring at the tall, spindly brunette at the new Leader's side who was assessing the situation with a sharp, undaunted gaze. The Thompson girl was Intuition indeed.

A thin blond boy in fine if foppish clothes stepped close and stared with apprehension at each of Beatrice's assembled company, and at the two baffled nurses. "And I make them forget we're here . . . *how?*" he asked.

"I wasn't given a guidebook, Lord Withersby. Use your hands," the leader retorted.

Beatrice smirked despite herself, staring as the young lord

waved a hand in front of them. It didn't really do anything, but seeing as the Cairo Guard were all frozen and strangely unable to participate, that was a moot point. Perhaps it was best, after all, that they were pacified, standing there staring like dullards. Beatrice had received no help when leading The Grand Work for the first time, so why should they?

A dark-blonde woman in a plain dress, blushing, knelt by Verena's bedside. "I'm so sorry for yer pain," she murmured in a soft Irish brogue. "My name is Jane, and I'll try an' help you like Alexi said." She rallied herself with a meek smile and held up her hand, which glowed with a slight white luminescence.

Though it was pale, new and untrained, Verena seemed to recognize the light. She likely wanted to welcome this young woman as a sister but was kept a world away. Still, her pained expression eased, as did the tears coursing from her eyes.

The Healer, Jane, put her hand on Verena's forehead, and Verena's body was racked with a new seizure—the London Guard had hardly come to their first charge as experts. The work was progressing, however, and Alexi urged his power outward, commanding the Phoenix fire to contain and extract the offending spirit. Beatrice prayed he could finish the job.

She wanted to assure this young Alexi to stay steady, to tell him that results were not immediate. The impassivity of his face was belied by his eyes, the expression in those coal black pools indicated a riptide joy of newfound power.

She couldn't possibly know what he was thinking, feeling or expecting, of course. Nor could she really help. No one could tell you about The Grand Work. You had to feel it. You had to own it for yourself. Beatrice was suddenly sure this was why none of them could come forward offering instruction, guidance, encouragement or reprimands; that would only get in the way. Because, as the goddess had said, there were never two Guards. A Guard was always on its own. Something had stilled their tongues to make sure of it.

The Intuition glided forward, a surprising air of elegant, refined grace about her for one so young. The Grand Work had aged them years in a single day, severed their innocence and youth. Beatrice remembered the very same happening to her.

"Lord Withersby," the Intuition began crisply, "if you and your touch might offer us some clue about the offender, I might be able to wield my newfound library to best effect."

Lord Withersby glanced down and said, "Indeed, Miss Thompson, indeed." He took a step closer to Verena, angling past Jane and bending over her to speak softly to the charge. "My, you *are* beautiful, miss! Whatever brought you to England, this land of dreary grey, when you are a queen of a golden kingdom?"

"Miss Belledoux," Alexi called, "as you've not had time to produce a studio full of fine work, what do your Artistic instincts tell you about how you might be of service?"

A gorgeous brunette had come forward, staring at Withersby but snapping to attention as Alexi addressed her. She thought a moment, smiled and darted out of the clinic. Returning swiftly, having procured a golden icon of a dove from the adjoining chapel, she kissed it softly and rejoined the circle.

Beatrice watched, fascinated. She glanced at Belle, who was furrowing her brow as the Memory touched Verena's hand and winced in pain.

"Victim's name? Verena. Attacker violent," Withersby murmured. "Towers, shouting from towers . . . It's so angry, it has followed us, waiting for us . . ."

It was a muezzin, Beatrice yearned to say. *It followed us here, here where everything changed, here where the dead so terribly outnumber you . . .*

Perhaps there was divine commonality in the air, bringing them together despite themselves, for Miss Thompson began a verse Beatrice recognized instantly. Rumi. Ibrahim and Ahmed had tears in their eyes as she spoke it with clarion confidence, and so did a strapping young lad who was rotating around his fellows and touching their collars. It seemed the new Heart was an amiable, ruddy-cheeked and bushy-haired man who was the sort you instantly wanted to be your friend.

The Heart bowed his head and bestowed his gift. "Lovely verse, Miss Thompson."

"Thank you, Mr. Carroll," the Intuition replied. Oddly, he blushed.

In the tumult Beatrice hadn't noticed that the air near them shone with a strange but distinct light. And there was a vague, familiar scent of flowers, too. The goddess was here, hidden from view, managing the situation. *That's* why they were paralyzed, she realized, because Persephone likely knew they would tell these poor sots to run for their bloody lives. She was assuring that the new Guard learned The Grand Work in their own way, undisturbed.

The new Artist had lashed the icon procured from the chapel to the bedpost near Verena's head. She moved with fluid grace to Alexi's side, and Beatrice noticed George gaping at her. She *was* beautiful.

"Pardon me," she said with gentle deference. She lifted up the Leader's hand, cupping its ball of blue fire, and blew the flames toward the dove. The fire nestled into the heart of the bird, and the icon lit, luminous from the inside, becoming a magic talisman. She stepped close and shifted Verena's head. "Gaze on that, dear," she murmured in a lilting French accent.

Verena's rolling gaze steadied, now that she had a point upon which to focus her strength. Beatrice wanted to gaze on that icon, too. The Grand Work was affecting them in the way they'd always affected others. At least in part.

"Simple, brilliant," said Withersby, the Memory, gazing at the dove now illuminated with power. He turned to the

Artist and gave her a wide, appreciative smile. Miss Belledoux, flushing, was clearly flattered by his approval.

It was happening, Beatrice saw. The couples were forming. She could see it in the way some of them looked at one another, saw the same thing she'd seen with her friends. Except for the Leader. He was not struck by anything or anyone besides his purpose; there seemed a wall around him. Being Leader of The Guard had made her more sensitive to such things.

The possessing spirit reacted, whipping at Verena, making her flail her limbs, refusing to go quietly into any good night. Alexi narrowed his eyes, undaunted by the challenge, and began to experiment with his new power. He pressed the fire closer, moving it in; then he withdrew, gauging what the spirit did in reaction.

He looked like a conductor, Beatrice decided, one whose music took the shape of blue fire. It made her wonder what The Grand Work sounded like to spirits. To The Guard it was always wonderful, and she could faintly hear the music of the stars playing in her ears, but the song was different than it had been when she directed it herself. How did the notes sound to spirits? Terrible, like death knells? Or was it sweet, a lullaby, seducing them toward Peace and away from infraction?

"Quietus," Alexi said. "Thus is our cantus. I assume it is in your minds as well as mine?"

A burst of song was affirmation, the air was thick with magic. Beatrice fought against those enthralling strains, fought to clear her mind of the cosmic lullaby of wind and stars so that she could shout that Quietus wasn't strong enough. But she couldn't. He'd have to learn on his own. This same spirit was the first her Guard had battled, there in a Cairo alley. They'd failed, and perhaps it had grown stronger for its success.

Verena shuddered and convulsed, causing more tears to fall among the women and the men's faces to harden. She screamed in pain as the spirit ripped free. It surprised them all, but Jane was immediately responsive with a healing hand. The spectre careened loose.

Alexi swiped at it with an impressive arc of fire, but it eluded him and vanished. "Damn!" He bellowed and flung open the clinic door, even rushing into the lane to chase the monstrosity, but it was gone. The new Guard had proven unable to destroy it, too.

Alexi reentered the sickroom, and Beatrice well remembered the frustration, shame and sense of failure evident on his face. "I didn't choose a strong enough spell," he said.

"I daresay we'll have another chance," the Intuition muttered, "with that one."

The Heart rallied them. "The lovely lady is alive," he said, staring down fondly at Verena. "That, at least, is cause for celebration. We have not failed our first act. The offender is gone. The rest we must leave to God. I just hope she heals completely."

Everyone nodded save Alexi, who did not seem convinced. None of them could be sure of the lasting wounds and scars left by hauntings. Beatrice certainly felt she'd never be the same for her experiences. No one in this room ever would.

"As you were!" Withersby cried to the room, waving his arms like a ridiculous puppeteer. It seemed to work for the nurses, who came to themselves, dazed, and who conveniently left the room. The others remained.

The former and present Guards stared at one another for a long, uncomfortable moment. Withersby waved his fingers again for good measure. Belle looked like she wanted to laugh. Or cry. Both, likely.

Alexi turned to stalk out of the room, a tormented scowl upon his young face. The Heart was by his side, asking his Leader, "What occurred in the hour since we parted? I feel your dread weight, what loss have you suffered?"

The Intuition was close by, too, concerned, and the rest filed out behind him. As they did Beatrice heard Alexi reply, his voice hard, "No matter. Life is but meetings and partings." And then they were gone.

She whirled to the corner where she assumed the goddess was standing, ready to scream. But there were no telltale signs of her. Good God, did The Grand Work cut its way into the world so ruthlessly each and every time? Who had poor Alexi lost today?

Belle's voice roused her to the moment: "What do we do with Verena? You heard what they said. We can't leave her here alone."

"Back to Athens with her then, and we keep watch until her dark night has completely passed," Beatrice replied.

"But the new Guard—"

"Came from all over the city. The sacred space may be in the school, but their homes are elsewhere. They cannot have settled in so quickly. I'm in no hurry to have them supplant us and send us packing. We were brought here first; we don't deserve to be shunted aside. Now we must see if we can enter." Beatrice hissed, turning to Ibrahim ruefully. "Forgive me if I ever seemed like I doubted you. But what were we to do?"

"Indeed. This fate has us round the neck," Ibrahim agreed.

He didn't appear angry with her. Relief surged in her veins; The Grand Work had been trial by fire, and as Leader she was responsible for their successes and failures. And, now all guidance had been removed. She didn't know what next to expect. None could. Even the divinities seemed surprised, struggling to catch up.

She didn't care about anything so much as Verena. That, and having a few words with the goddess, who was likely off following her precious new pets. Beatrice had to admit, if only to herself, that the new Guard were good, if young. Quite good.

Chapter Twenty-three

As Beatrice hoped, with Verena's possession removed, the crackling, invisible barrier to Athens vanished. Within the hour their patient lay more comfortably convalescing in her upper-floor apartments, far from the comings and goings of any workers below. Ahmed and Ibrahim sat attendant at her side. Belle and George had run off to their café, the only ones who now had something in London to fall back on.

Beatrice was too full of raw emotion to sit still, and so she stalked to the third-floor seal. "Why did you leave me?" she cried out to the Phoenix entombed within. She had never felt an emptiness like she now suffered. Despite the fact Ibrahim had reached out for her hand like a true friend or . . .

Blue fire coursed around her ankles, as if happy to see her, and Beatrice scowled, wondering if it was a trick. The fire, and Persephone, had been fickle. Did this little show of affection hope to keep her mollified? "Some good you were out there on the bridge," she murmured, kicking at the flames with her boot. "Fair-weather fire."

She looked around, waiting for the light to be different, waiting for that scent of flowers. "Our Lady, you owe us an apology," she hissed through clenched teeth. The goddess said on the ship that they need but ask for her. Would she come now?

The light did indeed change, and Beatrice whirled. "Where were you when we needed you?!" she cried. She didn't worry if she appeared raving; there were no workers here due to the lateness of the hour, and she wouldn't have cared if there were.

Persephone stared. "I . . . was visiting with the new Guard, as I always do."

"Are we not still your Guard? Are we not still in your damnable service?"

Persephone blinked. "You are still my beloveds, but you are no longer The Guard. It all happened so quickly. I did not think there could be two Guards, but I'd hoped—"

"So now we're dispensable. We abandoned our homes, our lives, followed you blindly here to be cast aside thus?" Beatrice shrieked. "What if she died? What if Verena died?"

"I would not have allowed that. I gave her the kiss of life."

"And a bloody lot of good that did her, lying there, alive but possessed by a fiend."

"She did not die," Persephone repeated. "Danger surrounds the Work, there's no cure for—"

"You could have warned us that, should any of our Muses leave, what we once fought would take its place!"

Phoenix fire crackled around Beatrice's feet. Perhaps she was calling it with righteous anger and it was responding. The azure flames soothed her heart and mind, and she could not credit her powers entirely fled. They stood upon his grave, and an echo of him would always exist in her as it would always exist at his tomb. Yet, she felt compelled to reject him as her Guard had been rejected, to seethe with injured fury instead.

"I would never wish harm upon you," Persephone said. "I don't claim to understand all the particulars, how The Guard are chosen and when. That's up to the Muses and to Phoenix—"

"Have you ever asked? Have you ever thought beyond your own immediate fancy? Your whims?"

"There needed to be a changing," the goddess insisted. "Even if there's no precedent. None of this has happened before; never two Guards, never on one soil. I felt a need, a possibility . . . I've not always been on hand, coming and going as I must between worlds. And the bloodletting distracts me—"

Beatrice would have none of her excuses. "Beloved Verena nearly died tonight, senselessly, away from her home. Why, if those poor young wretches are the chosen ones, why weren't they chosen in the first place? Why involve us at all?"

"Because it simply wasn't time," was Persephone's reply. She looked regretful, but only a bit. Beatrice was convinced the goddess, regardless if she loved them or not, simply did not understand mortals and perhaps never could.

"The Muses found you first, you of proper age. When Darkness moved against all Guard spirits, things changed. Moving the Phoenix fire here to London, things changed again. This new Guard, they're so young . . . Guards are never that young. They're adults usually when they're taken, and they weren't all here in London. So many things weren't in place—"

Beatrice glared. "You just fell in love with a mortal boy, that's all. So all the important things you neglected don't matter."

"It is true that I fell in love with a mortal boy," Persephone replied. "He is a magnificent young man."

Pacing the fiery seal, Beatrice threw her hands in the air. "You're unquestionably one of those divinities of old if nothing else matters but one twist of your lovelorn fate. The gods are nothing but petty creatures after all. And, what is fate? Life is full of accidents and trials. If a goddess is clueless . . . God help us all. Or, *mankind* help us all, rather, because it's clear to me that no one greater is listening or helping. No one knows a damn thing about any greater plan. Being your 'chosen' simply means people I care about suffer. If you had been honest about that from the first, I might have more respect for you now."

In the face of Beatrice's wounded fury, Persephone

maintained her calm. "I am a force, but not an omnipotent one. I told you what I was—"

"No, you never said you were an accomplice to near murder," Beatrice spat.

She stormed past the goddess and up to her chamber on the uppermost floor. That small room housed all that was left of her identity, her shell of an existence. It had been a temporary lodging for a life of oddity, but now what? There was nothing.

Beatrice collapsed upon her bed and wept, her world shattered. She hadn't realized what being Leader had given her, how it had fed her adventuresome spirit. How important it had made her feel. How it gave her beautiful, extraordinary friends. How she thrilled in living an unconventional life, and how it gave her, like the goddess had once implied, the purpose in life she'd once so craved.

"Dear Verena!" Beatrice's tears were hot on her cheeks. "You were not one to question this fate. And Ahmed. If he yet loses you . . . oh, how his light will dim. What shall we do when our light has gone? What are we now?"

A wave of grief threatened to drown her. Standing in the sacred space, basking in the Power and the Light was an experience never to be replicated, nothing short of bliss. And The Grand Work had made a family, however odd the pairing. The six of them all truly loved one another, deep below their layers of armour. Beatrice was not fond of loss. She'd had enough, and she didn't want to be severed and lonely again. But she was no visionary to see an alternate future.

Bright colours appeared at the foot of Beatrice's bed. "I told you, you are my beloveds," whispered Persephone. "You will always be my beloveds."

Beatrice scrambled back. "Get out of my room. I did not invite you. You have no use for us, and I have no use for you."

"I need you," Persephone replied. "There is work yet to be done."

"Get your precious new Guard to do it."

"Beatrice, I need you. I *will* need you. And I trust you. There is no more precious thing than trust," the goddess added.

They stared each other down. Beatrice felt her nostrils flaring, and her fists clenched her bedclothes. "At the moment I don't trust you. I'm inclined to hate you."

Persephone stared at her, her aura cycling colours. "I know. I wish you didn't."

"Why couldn't we speak to them? To our own fellows? To another Guard! It was as if we were physically gagged. What's the sense in that? How does that help any of us?"

"I couldn't risk having you frighten them," Persephone replied. "It was manipulative of me, I know. But at the moment none of you are fond of The Grand Work. While I cannot blame you, I couldn't have you turning them against their destiny on the very first day it was given. I paid for it, though." She lifted her sleeve to show what looked like burn marks on her forearm. "All magic costs me these days."

"What, I should pity you your scars? What if Verena died? What if she *yet* dies? What scar will you show me then?"

Persephone rose and paced the room. "I'm doing the best I can with a life I didn't choose either!" she cried, and Beatrice realized there was never something so disturbing as a nervous deity. "Everything I attempt is to protect the Balance, the Muses and Phoenix. To protect what remains of my beloved. The Whisper-world is making its own decisions, and I've no choice but to keep up with Prophecy as best I can. I struggle to understand my own part! To understand and to do my best when others have controlled and punished me for eternity."

That much seemed true. If Beatrice held any hatred for the goddess, she hated Darkness more.

"You've every right to be angry," Persephone allowed. "The

Grand Work places you at the threshold of life and death, endangering your lives and the lives of all those around you. But for all The Grand Work takes, it also gives. It saves the lives, hearts and minds of many whom it touches." She moved to the door. "I owe you every thanks for your service. I do love you—all of you—and I hope you know it. And I'm fighting to make sure all of you will remain free. Now I'm going to see Verena."

Beatrice's small voice stopped her at the door. "Couldn't The Grand Work have *asked* us if we wanted this? Couldn't you ask for volunteers instead?"

Persephone stared at her. Hard. "If we did, what would you say?"

Beatrice wanted to denounce the Work, to say that she wanted nothing to do with it. But, would she really have refused? Even knowing what she did?

The goddess shook her head when Beatrice scowled. "You were chosen because you'd say yes anyway." Then she turned and glided down the hallway.

Beatrice gave chase. If further apologies would be made, she wanted to hear them. She followed the goddess to the correct door, Persephone apparently knowing Verena's location without being told. Perhaps she wasn't lying that her heart was still tied to them. Inside, Verena was unconscious. Ibrahim stared at Persephone with steely defiance, a glare that screamed he'd known better, that he had warned of this, a tortured expression of self-loathing and fury.

"You. You chose your precious English Guard," he growled. "You, the Muses, the fire, you all chose them over us and left us defenseless. What could we have done to stop this?" He indicated Verena's limp body.

Persephone shook her head. "I did not choose them over you. But I had to be there for the annunciation—as I was for yours. And this new Guard is charged with a grave responsibility that you were not."

Verena woke with a heartbreaking cry. It both gave Beatrice hope and filled her with fear.

"I want to go home," the girl begged, first in Arabic, but seeing Beatrice she repeated it in English for emphasis though she'd understood it perfectly well, looking next at Ibrahim and Ahmed. "Please take me home." She saw the goddess. If she was angry, she chose not to show it. "Now that you've no need for us, I'd like to go back. To Cairo."

"I want you comfortable and happy." The goddess glanced at Beatrice, who clenched her jaw. "I've work for some of you but not all. I could of course use each of you in this unprecedented time, but Cairo can have you back. I shall not be too covetous."

She turned to Ahmed and the others. "Go in peace, and know that I am with you in spirit"—her voice faltered—"even when I fail you, as I've failed every Guard that has come before. I am sorry for your suffering, and I promise to give everything I have to make it right." Her lovely face hard with conviction and desperation, she opened a trembling hand and summoned a portal to the Whisper-world. Vanishing through, she left them with a disturbing whisper. "All my blood. All my blood until I'm finally free."

Beatrice shuddered. Ahmed paced nearby, nervous like she'd never seen him. Ibrahim was staring at her. Despite the goddess's welcome apology, it seemed none of them had gleaned any answers. Dismissed or not, they still had no idea of their next move.

★ ★ ★

Sometime later, after a cup of tea alone in her rooms, Beatrice had calmed herself. There came a knock on her door and she called, "Yes?"

Ibrahim entered. Beatrice was glad she had composed

herself, as he seemed to be completely under control. He was looking characteristically stoic. "As you heard, Verena wants to go home. I think she should do so as soon as possible. It may mean life or death for her. It's all she'll speak of." His eyes were haunted. "Ahmed won't leave her side. He'll make the journey with her once we've seen her safely through a few nights."

Beatrice didn't answer, she just sat in silence. What was there to say?

Ibrahim turned and stared out the window at the greying sky. "What on earth are we to make of this? What do we do now?"

"The rest of you are free. Myself, I'm not sure."

"Why do you say so?"

Beatrice sighed. "I vented my spleen upon our Lady before she came down to you. When I did, she intimated that there was work yet to be done, and that I'm the one to do it."

"And . . . me?"

"I've no idea. Ask her yourself," Beatrice retorted. If they were no longer The Guard, she was no longer their Leader.

Ibrahim set his jaw, which she saw and regretted. "I'm sorry," she began. "You're the last person who should bear my frustrations. You know I don't like our fate any more than you do. Not knowing where to go, what or who to—" A sudden realization occurred to her, and her heart dropped into her stomach. Would he want to stay and help or would he hurry off? She turned away, hurrying to make herself another cup of tea, rejoicing in how that ritual masked every awkwardness. "And you? I . . . assume you will return to Cairo if nothing holds you here in England."

She tried to voice her question nonchalantly, but her mind voiced a torrent her lips dared not utter. *Oh, God. Stay, or ask me to come with you.* She felt ashamed at her intense yearning but there was nothing to be done for it. The company of Ibrahim Wasil-Tipton was something she craved. Whether he took an

English name or not, whether he wore tunics or fine English suits, she craved his eloquent words, his weighty stare, his compelling presence. She had from the first.

Ibrahim was evaluating her. She felt his regard and worked to keep her face blank, kept it fixed upon her cup and saucer.

"I . . . have not decided," he said quietly, then surprised her with, "What do you feel I should do?"

Oh, don't make me beg you. Don't put this upon me.

He was asking for her opinion? Dared she give it? Why was it her responsibility to knock down the walls he'd built up, to ask him to stay with her? It wasn't, and so she continued their maddening volley of detachment instead. "The great Ibrahim Wasil-Tipton is deferring to my judgment?" Straightening her spine, she turned and gave him a smirk. "Are you feeling quite well?"

Ibrahim eyed her. A corner of his mouth turned up, surprising her, and they stood there in silence, smirking at each other. Beatrice hoped he was as intoxicated and engaged by the game as she. Their relationship always held a subtle dance of power.

"I'll tell you in the morning," he replied. Then he stepped forward, grabbed her hand at her side, pressed it, and with both hands brought it up to his lips.

Proper or no, she rejoiced that she was not wearing gloves. She could feel the exquisite truth of his full, perfect lips atop her hand, and time stopped as his dark eyes rose to meet hers. His kiss continued. As it did, her left hand, holding cup and saucer, began to tremble.

A sound escaped her that was part choke, part gasp, part cry of exquisite bliss, a sound that revealed too much of her inner emotion, but she couldn't apologize for it. She gained in this moment all that she had been yearning for, but until now she had not known how much. It made her struggle to maintain any composure at all. Just this token, this glimpse behind the mask of his stoic, impassive character was a moment of aching intimacy revealing so much more than words . . . She felt a blush bloom on her cheeks like Phoenix fire.

He lifted his mouth away but kept hold of her hand, reaching for the still-shaking saucer and setting it gently aside, taking up that trembling hand in his as well. "You have been a very good Leader in the time allotted you, Miss Smith. It has been strange but a true honour to serve at your side."

And with that quiet compliment, he lowered her hands, turned and walked away. Beatrice was left thunderstruck, with only the sound of her pounding heart in her ears.

Chapter Twenty-four

The core of Phoenix lay listless in the Athens bricks, fiery and formless. He allowed himself to trickle out and course across the foyer floor, pacing like he used to do in corporeal form, always in concentric circles when pondering a great problem.

He'd almost forgotten how it felt to press firm feet upon the Earth. Floating did not satisfy. Still, he floated round the marble floor, now and then pausing in an almost-human form, a ghost of blue fire, before slipping back into simple, low-licking flames. He couldn't be too active, lest he wake up the young man to whom he was so tightly bound.

She was right, there hadn't been another Leader quite so like him. Young Alexi Rychman was everything that Persephone had hoped, a fiercely intelligent mortal with more raw promise and potential than they'd ever encountered. And Phoenix had liked all his Leaders a great deal. But this one was so similar to him as to be uncanny.

He sensed something, and he wondered if Persephone knew it as well. Though the Liminal had brought them both incredible sights, she was the visionary. But being buried here in Athens rather than in the bower she had originally fashioned him attuned him to new things. Here in Athens Academy, where so much would come to pass, where Prophecy would be unveiled and their great war would be wrought, here he could feel the crossroads.

She couldn't know, surely. If she knew what would soon come to pass, she would never be so excited, so full of life like he'd missed in her for centuries. Not if she knew all the details. She had been a divinity since the beginning of time, and such was how she'd always see herself. But, she had to take mortal form or she was going to fall apart. There was no choice anymore. There hadn't been for some time.

Yes, if she took a mortal shape, she'd no longer be bound to shadow. The problem was when to tell her what she'd lose in doing so. When to confront the particular reality of her future? Would such a realization break her? She needed her strength to knit the worlds and plant the seeds for rebirth; there was no time for a breakdown.

Perhaps he wouldn't tell her. Perhaps it wasn't his duty to tell her. It wasn't as though he was lying when they spoke about the future, but he also wasn't telling her the complete truth she herself refused to see. If he said nothing, it would still happen. She'd pass into her new world none the wiser. Not her, nor her new form—

Exactly. She'd be gone forever. The lover he'd known, cradled, cherished and trusted, the creature who'd trusted him, she'd be gone forever as he knew her. Any recourse she might have, he'd be denying her. And, if he didn't tell the truth, he was no longer the god he once was.

He'd have to tell her that she would remember nothing in this transition. That she would, in effect, die. She wouldn't come into this world all full of power, knowledge and glory like she'd hoped. The girl in that vision was a stranger to them both.

But when she did come, Phoenix pledged that he in turn would sink so deep into the farthest reaches of Alexi Rychman's mind that only his powerful fire would remain. As that ghostly girl of her vision would house spectral whispers of his beloved, so would he fade into Alexi's great shadow. They two ancients would offer up their gifts and let go, allowing mortals to take their places and live reborn in the love that gods once knew. But this could come to light only when it was too late to turn back, because going forward was the only option.

* * *

Beatrice rose with the sun and noticed a note slid under her door. Upon first seeing it, a blush burned her cheeks. She bit her lip and picked it up.

The script was easily recognizable, from that hand which so easily wrote in the beautiful sweep of Arabic as it did in English. Though The Grand Work had aged her sensibilities, she was still a young woman. In this moment, her heart was as impossibly fragile, thrilled and fanciful as those of the girls they were intending for this academy. And it was not disappointed.

Speaking with Ahmed, I have decided to help him see Verena safely home. It is the only appropriate action, especially given our summary dismissal. I have no sense of the goddess needing me or the others again. That said, I shall write you anon. After making sure they've all they need in Cairo, we shall speak of Egypt and of England. We shall come to an agreement on what is to be done.

Safe travels with the goddess, whatever madness she has planned. Tell me if there is some way I may yet be of service. And, take care of yourself. I don't want anything to happen to someone as important as you.

Warmly,
Ibrahim

Beatrice's pulse raced as she read and reread the note. For a man as cool as Ibrahim, these words were quite the change. *Warmly. As important as you.* The grey sky over London now seemed as golden as Cairo. If Ibrahim would yet be the light of her life, she didn't care which sky she spent it under.

★ ★ ★

Alexi Rychman stood in his study contemplating dark and dismal things. His grandmother's funeral had been hard on him. She was the person for whom he'd strived. Now all he had to replace her was supernatural madness.

A light across the room caught his gaze. There at his doorway stood the most breathtaking young woman, impossibly beautiful, luminous and subtly shifting colours as if lit by a rotating prism. His heart leaped into his throat and he felt his command of the universe shatter.

"It's you," he breathed.

"I've been watching," she confessed shyly, immensely powerful and yet somehow eternally youthful, naive. "I shouldn't, but I have."

"And you haven't made yourself known?" he asked, trying not to sound hurt. He could muster no craft when he spoke with her, no artifice or maturity; she drew from him raw, unfettered emotion, as if he'd known her all his life. There had been an immediate intimacy when she first appeared. She'd explained Prophecy to The Guard, but she'd disarmed him and charmed her way into his heart by merely saying his name.

"I've been trying to be good," the goddess breathed. "And to get on with the next phase of our plan so that I may come to you, in form newly refreshed, to take up our destinies. But I, a coward, can't bear the idea that if something goes wrong, I may never see you again."

She grabbed him by the hand, which felt encased in light, in gentle, humming fire more potent than the flames he these days commanded. He was a careful youth, quiet, hermetic and, as his friends insisted, always brooding. But with this woman, with her he felt alive, happy and eager. With her, this supernatural calling seemed no curse but a blessing.

With a start he realized she'd led him into his bedroom. Heat flooded him at the idea of them in so intimate a space.

"I shouldn't do this," she continued in an aching murmur.

Alexi's body nearly convulsed with desire at the thought of the something they shouldn't do. "Do what?" He meant to sound inviting but only sounded like an overwhelmed boy.

She sighed ruefully. "I must be going. We must begin. We must bring Prophecy to light. I've never done it before, you know."

Alexi trembled.

"Taken a mortal body to break Darkness's bonds," she clarified. "We're long overdue for these bold and dire acts, you and I. I was just waiting for the right time. You. You're the right one. I choose you. Now, and in the future. I will choose you."

She leaned in, and it was like a sunbeam broke upon Alexi's face. The soft, warm press of her lips against his sent crashing waves of pleasure across his body. It was his first kiss, and she bestowed it tenderly, gently. He found he was frozen, unable to take her in his arms as he wished, and all he could do was drink in the sensation of her lips questing over his. They danced over and across his sharp cheekbones, and her murmur in his ear caused frissons down his body.

"Nothing is as exciting as a stolen kiss, is it?"

She drew back and blushed, an action Alexi found wondrous. She was impossibly feminine, the ageless, timeless Girl. Her impish smile was inviting, her shifting and overpowering shades of beauty dizzying. Alexi wondered how he was so lucky.

"Furtively given and taken out of sight from watching eyes," she continued. "Illicitness is half the thrill of desire. Perhaps our situation in the future will be similar. Perhaps *you'll* steal *my* kisses next time. I shouldn't be here now, but I cannot help myself," the goddess continued. "I've never met another mortal more like him, you know."

"Who?" Alexi breathed, confused.

"Phoenix. My love of long ago. Before I was taken under." Her voice broke, and Alexi dared place his hand upon hers. "Your destined will love you as much as I do. She'll come with my heart."

"Love me?" Alexi stammered, reeling. "How can you say that? You don't even know me." He saw his expression darken, reflected in the wide mirrors of her eyes, for he was unable to entirely ignore the struggle imposed upon him by The Grand Work. "You think you know my destiny, and that of my new friends, but do you know *me?*"

She traced a luminous finger down his cheek. "I have a way of knowing souls, Alexi Rychman. Yours is worthy and true. The Grand Work has its curses, but I promise you joy."

The words were compelling. Then her face contorted with desperation, and she trembled before him. "Please. Do me one favor. Touch me," she begged. "You can't know how I've hungered for a kind touch, a true *touch*. Phoenix, now a ghost, cannot touch me. I simply need to be *held* again, and I'd like for it to be you who gives me that gift."

Alexi's head spun. His senses were afire, logic was of no use; he knew he'd do anything to ease her pain. His loneliness, the awkward demands of The Grand Work, these were nothing compared to his need to be this woman's champion. He seized her in his arms and kissed her again; clumsily, lovingly. She whimpered and surrendered.

He sank with her onto the bed, his trembling hands beginning to wander, her gasps urging him on. A girlish goddess, a mortal young man—these were foundations for a classic, beautiful tale. Becoming the conquering hero, sure and dominating, was a sudden intoxicant, and yet more youth drained away from Alexi. The growl of an aroused man took the place of boyish innocence.

The sound made the goddess smile. She shifted against him. His bed was all light and colour, she was all beauty and his for the taking.

But he was a gentleman, and this was not how a gentleman behaved. Even if he were drunk on a goddess's passionate words, even if stolen kisses with a divinity should supersede all rules of propriety in the first place. He sat up. His heart pounded in his ears.

"You are *so* like him!" She giggled. "My love never did anything without my express permission."

"Do I have your permission?" he choked, lust threatening to undo any and every principle.

"You'll have permission when the time is right."

She touched his temple in a ritualistic way. It was not the touch of passion for which he'd hoped, and he cursed gentlemen and everything for which they stood. He moved to take her in his arms again, but her fingertip on his temple held him away.

"What are you doing?" he asked.

The sudden sadness on her face doused his excitement. "I can't let you remember this dalliance of ours. I want you to know what it's like to truly fall in love. Like a mortal, with a mortal. Not like this, not by such charms. This isn't real. You're under my spell," she stated. "I have seen visions, and I want them for you. I'm a goddess. A scene like this will come, in time, but it will come honestly. Without magic. Yet wholly magical."

"No, please," he begged. He was not accustomed to knowing his desires let alone articulating them. "Don't take these moments from me."

"In part they will live here." Her fingertips, glowing and prismatic, slid past his vest, inside his shirt and across his skin, over his heart. He felt something flutter and land there, inside: a seething longing, a fierce strength to tend that fire. "Steel your heart until your destined beloved comes. When you're sure, you may unleash these floodgates upon her. But be patient. Be cautious. It will not be easy. For any of us. Darkness will look to drive a wedge between."

Her eyes filled with silver tears. He took her in his arms, this time without fumbling, this time sure of himself. But she drew back with a gasp, her lips breaking the deep kiss to land again upon his ear.

"Eternity awaits, my love," she murmured. Then all the room was light. She was gone from his arms like a vanishing ghost.

Alexi returned to his senses. Hearing his sister calling his name, he descended the stairs and entered the parlour.

"What were you doing? I thought I heard voices," said Alexandra, shifting her wheelchair.

Alexi tried to remember. All he could remember was light. Blinding white light. Nothing else. His heart hurt, but it was beating with fierce determination. "Muttering to myself, as usual," he replied.

Turning to gaze out the window, he saw a host of flowers had bloomed in the garden below. Had there always been so many flowers? Staring out at them, he felt three overwhelming sensations. First was loss, second was loneliness, but third was the belief that someday, despite this hollow pain, he would be provided for. Guided by something beyond his control.

★ ★ ★

Beatrice sat staring dreamily out the window. Persephone appeared at her side, a swooning jolt of light, colour and the scent of flowers.

"Ah, *love!*" the goddess exclaimed, grabbing her hand and dragging her to her feet. "I say. There is nothing so delicious as a man's first kiss!"

Beatrice raised an eyebrow at the goddess's rapture, even though she felt the contagious, bubbling glee and wanted to give over to it, to share the bliss that had been Ibrahim's lips on her hand . . . Instead she muttered, "Having fun with your new pet, I take it?"

Persephone sobered, not answering. "I was looking for the others, for Verena. Have the rest gone to the docks already? So swiftly departed for Egypt and home? Will you not say good-bye? Where is your second?" the goddess exclaimed. "Come, come, go with me, we must do just that!"

She was dressed in the style of the day—wide skirts, capped sleeves and tapered cuffs—but the fabric was grandly, absurdly red. Playing at mortal, she clearly relished in the costuming, however ill-advised. The lengths of garish crimson silk made Beatrice wince.

"I admit, my Lady, that I've been in a reverie. I lost track of the hour, and the boat may have already departed. But, come now, I'd not dare be seen with you looking like that."

"Forgive me, I don't really know what's in fashion." The goddess giggled. "But I adore the colour . . ." She peered at Beatrice. "You seem nervous, but you're blushing. Wait! I know that look. I'm sure I'm wearing it, too."

Beatrice composed herself and countered, "Are you? Are we feeling the same thing? I worry still for Verena, about her health and her travel home, Ahmed and Ibrahim traveling with her. I'm heartbroken to see our coterie break apart. No thanks to you. Don't you have things to do in the Whisper-world? Like pour your blood onto some stones?" Her tone was perhaps colder than was entirely necessary.

The goddess blinked. Seeing such an expressive, earnest

soul hurt was a terrible sight and Beatrice felt an apology immediately spring to her lips, but she bit it back. She did say, "I'm still rather upset with this whole turn, my Lady."

Persephone nodded. "Of course. I'm reeling from it just as you are. I declared a prophecy to the new Guard that felt as though it were being fashioned *for* me, not *of* me—the words changed on my very lips! I'm not sure how in control of my destiny I am. Not at all, I fear. The future is as foggy as London."

"How comforting," Beatrice muttered.

The goddess shrugged and regained her earlier joie de vivre. "Let's see the boat off. I want to wave from the docks and send my love with all those who cross the oceans!"

Beatrice sighed. She could not refuse the goddess's enthusiasm—or her own desire to drink in Ibrahim's visage once more. When next they spoke, it would indeed be of a future, preferably on golden sands rather than foggy shores.

The journey to portside was quick, and the goddess espied the steamer out the carriage window. Flinging open the door, she slid herself and her heaps of crimson silk out onto the stones. Beatrice noticed her motions bore a slight awkwardness, as if she were stiff or in pain. Perhaps she had come to heal bloody wounds indeed.

Ahmed was visible at the prow of the Peninsular steamer, his compact body shifting to drink in every departing sight, and his dark face lit with a smile upon seeing them as the goddess nearly dragged Beatrice right to the dock edge. He ran along the rails, shouting down, "Oh, my Lady, you're here!" He seemed not to harbour the anger of the rest of them did, which was odd, considering his love for Verena. But anger simply wasn't in his ingredients.

"Please," he called, heedless of the Londoners who turned to him with wary glances. The information was too important.

"The visions keep coming. I've seen betrayals that lie ahead. I don't know how far, but I feel it in my heart that those who love you will betray you. They won't be able to help it. Please be careful. Be wary of all. Betrayals will come from close by, from within your coterie; they won't mean it, so be wary. There is beauty ahead but so much pain beside."

Ibrahim appeared at the rail, staring down. Beatrice's heart skipped a beat. He did not notice her at first; he was eyeing Persephone and her costume, and in turn Ahmed, who saw fit to continue making a bit of a scene, warily.

Ahmed continued, "I know this defies Ibrahim's rational mind. I've been driving him mad with it. Our powers gone, my visions remain. I must be heard. The war in the ground. The dead have no place to go. You can't close every door . . . ?" He clutched his cap in his hand and ran his hand through his hair, disheveling it.

Persephone nodded and she did not need to speak loudly for her voice to carry. "You are heard and appreciated, Ahmed, though I do not yet see what it is you see."

"Because you are too focused on what is directly in front of you. I, objective, can see further," Ahmed insisted.

"I do not doubt it and will make sure your words are recorded," the goddess assured him. "That is all I can do." She faced Ibrahim, who was standing more stiffly now, staring down as if his eyes could burn holes in the dock. Beatrice was now the object of his attention, and they both clenched their fists at their sides. The tension was palpable—delicious, Beatrice thought.

"Oh, for God's sake. Go kiss him, will you?" the goddess said with a chuckle. She batted an elegant hand. "The damned propriety of this age. Thank God we divinities aren't bound by such ridiculous constraints!" She moved off to stand on a little platform, waving and blowing kisses to the departing passengers, leaving Beatrice to blush furiously on the dock.

Above, Beatrice saw Ibrahim's lips curve; he was surely imagining what Persephone might have said to make her lose her composure, her, the stoic Miss Smith. But the boat was pulling away and there was no time to run up or down gangplanks for such a dramatic display as the goddess suggested.

Ibrahim put his hand to his heart, staring at her all the while. She couldn't breathe, could only return the stare. She felt her eyes well with tears, and while she doubted he would appreciate a simpering woman, he was far enough away not to hear the little hitches of her breath. She placed her hand on her heart, too, and she hoped with every bit of that pounding instrument that what it signified was a compact. A vow. Somehow, for two such stubborn souls, a departure might have been the only thing that could have brought it out of them.

The ship shifted, turned, and so did Ibrahim, walking away, his elegant form in a tunic and long coat vanishing into the ship interior; Beatrice supposed he did not think it practical to linger in aching sentiment. It was only a matter of time before they could move their lives forward. Together, she hoped. She let her tears fall, allowed a final gasp of breath, dabbed at her face with a kerchief and moved to the goddess's side.

A bit of a crowd had formed around Persephone, still waving and sending kisses. Beatrice sniffled and laughed, saying, "You look as if you know and love every single one of us mortals."

"I do! In my way." She hopped down, wobbled a bit. Making a face she said, "Shoes." Then she held out her arm.

Beatrice took it. It was damnably impossible to stay angry with the creature.

"Now. What's to be done with you two?" the goddess asked. "Are you returning to Cairo, or is he coming back for you?"

"I . . . I don't know. It's yet to be determined." Beatrice felt a wave of trepidation. "I suppose it depends how long you're keeping me."

"Not too much longer, else I ruin everything. Come then.

We'll have to buy you some beautiful stationery for love letters."

Beatrice made a tiny noise. "That's presumptuous!"

"No. One should always be writing love letters," the goddess declared. "One can never write enough of them."

Beatrice wasn't certain if it was fate, but the route they took back to Bloomsbury and Athens held a small shop selling all things epistolary. Next door sat a jewelry shop. Persephone seemed unsurprised.

The goddess felt for a chain around her neck and lifted out an elegant silver ring of a feather, the one she'd held in her hand while curled upon that empty estate floor. "I'd like to do something with this," she said. "I'll meet you out front in a bit." Then she vanished into the jewelry shop.

Beatrice nodded. Going into the stationer's, it wasn't long before she reemerged with a set that had her dreaming of better days and times. The idea that a composed man like Ibrahim might be more forthcoming in letters than in person, that the written word might better reveal a guarded heart, was a titillating new prospect.

Persephone reemerged, and Beatrice noticed the jeweler placing the lovely, thin silver band in the window. It had apparently been traded for a bronze locket the goddess now flashed in her hand.

"Talismans," the goddess stated. "Can never have enough of these, either. Love letters and talismans. Come, escort me to the grave of my love. There is much to be done."

They traveled back to Athens. Ascending to the third floor, Beatrice and Persephone cordoned off the appropriate foyer with velvet rope. While the goddess was masquerading as a mortal, it wouldn't do for any administrators, workmen or teachers to see this strange display while they went about their work.

The goddess bent and began murmuring, placing her new bronze locket at the centre of the seal. A bit of blue fire reached up to kiss her cheek, and being nearby, Beatrice again felt that fire's phantom heat, which coursed through her body and made her ache. She supposed it would always affect her like this, like the smoke of opium did an addict.

"We must take every precaution," Beatrice heard the goddess say over Phoenix's remains. "Your fire and my blood—precious alchemy. Together they will break down the walls, knit the worlds and set the army free." She lifted the locket, and it was awash with bluish flame. Persephone hung it around her neck.

She turned to Beatrice, and her magical glamour faded, her garish crimson dress fading into the usual diaphanous robes, but this time the robes were laced with red silken patterns that corresponded to wounds.

The goddess fought showing her pain, but she could not hold back a cough against her robes. More blood pooled at the corner of her mouth. As she dabbed at it with her sleeve, Beatrice watched a spot of fabric turn to crimson silk. The dye was blood. What the mortal world made beautiful silk originated in the Whisper-world as blood. Beatrice felt a stab of empathy.

Persephone was sick, indeed; a consumptive goddess. She was, Beatrice thought mordantly, the very epitome of Victorian beauty. This was oddly her age, after all. And this age would claim her.

Yet the sleeve of her divine robes took what was terrible and made it into something valuable. Persephone tore it free, a long crimson strip, and wound the lovely length around her neck, shimmering, bold and beautiful. She turned to Beatrice with a grin, fluttering the accessory.

"I'll have to offer this to Alexi—a bit of flair, a spot of passion. I fear he wears too much black, so *serious* for such a young man! And you, I feared the same for you, but love quite becomes you, Beatrice. Go! Write your letter!"

She threw out her hand, and the Whisper-world opened, the portal edges sparking with a particular light. A moment later she vanished. Beatrice chuckled despite herself, unable to feel wholly lost when at last her heart's time was at hand.

★ ★ ★

Persephone found herself at the Liminal edge. Aodhan was there, dreamy-eyed. He bowed his head to her, and his grey face darkened in a blush.

"Cannot help it," he murmured. "My Jane, she has me in thrall and I cannot stop watching. Her guardian, her champion—I shall be both.

"Her gift grows stronger by the day," he continued. "But I'll have to find ways to help her. They're so young, all of them. We weren't this young."

Persephone shook her head. "You were not. But everything has changed."

"How are they faring as a group? How is the Leader?"

It was her turn to blush, and Persephone fondled the crimson swath about her neck, the fabric refusing to be anything but what her magic had made it; sumptuous silk. "He's terribly serious. But my mortal self will find him delicious once she sees the passion within him." She shook her head and gathered herself. "But I dally. The Liminal is wise, and I am grateful we are here together, Aodhan. I will need your help."

"Anything, my Lady."

"There will come a time when the barrier between Whisper and mortal worlds will come undone. I believe I've routed the paths onto the very stones of Athens Academy. There we will fight, for there are enough Guard spirits to win. Now, finally. It is time."

Aodhan nodded, pleased, eager to defy the will of Darkness at any opportunity.

Persephone continued, able to explain further only that which she knew. "I'm taking a body. A mortal body. Likely that body must enter this world to see The Guards' prison break open. But if something should happen . . ." She stared at the Liminal, which crackled lightning across its surface, asserting its power, reminding her nothing was certain, that there were details she couldn't predict.

"Take this," she said, handing Aodhan the locket. "It is full of Phoenix fire. I would a Leader wielded it, but I'm not sure who I'll have to spare, should the Cairo Guard, fate forbid, get caught up by Darkness. Be my eyes, my assurance. I do hope Beatrice will help when it's time, but I don't know how much more I can ask of her, and from them. I know I ask too much from you. From all of you."

"The Grand Work is both too much and not enough, everything and nothing at once," Aodhan replied. "But I'm not sure any of us would trade it. Not even those imprisoned."

Persephone wrung her hands. "I will set them free."

"We'll make sure of it. I promise."

Chapter Twenty-five

The Peninsular liner reached the open ocean and traveled without incident. They encountered no troublesome spots, though they still saw spectres, only the usual hangers-on, but the day they were scheduled to dock in Alexandria, it was Ibrahim's turn for a vision.

Not a vision, a nightmare. An echo of his Instinct remained—perhaps phantom imprints of their earlier power would live on in each of them, Ibrahim considered—and the sense of inevitable doom again seized him.

Beatrice and he stood, aged many years, side by side like husband and wife.

While fear of deep emotions had him once chafing at the idea, frightened to lose what little of himself he felt he owned if he allowed even a portion of his heart to another, he found he did not mind the concept now that the vacating Grand Work forced him to consider what life would be like *without* Beatrice Smith. Now their standing side by side seemed correct. They complemented each other. Not just as Leader and second, but in life, mind and heart.

She took his hand; he cherished the sensation. Then she died.

In death, her beautiful blonde colours, her fair face blushing with healthy amounts of sun and wind, turned grey. Ibrahim's heart was sundered. There was an open rectangle of a portal before them, and it whispered. The Whisper-world was aptly named, and it called for Beatrice. By name.

Her lovely face had not much changed; those piercing blue

eyes were now a dull silver, but they still stared upon him with affection. That beautiful smile he had silently adored was at last his. But it was too late. She was dead. Dead.

Surely, he would be the death of her. Could there be any other meaning? He brought ill luck, it would seem, to all his friends. He was a curse. He would be the death of the woman he had come slowly but surely to love, and that seemed as clear as the difference between day and night. And his dread-filled heart wondered if there was a single thing he could do to stop it.

His cry upon rising woke Ahmed, and they both sat up. They'd fallen asleep in chairs in Verena's room. She had taken a turn for the worse upon the ship, perhaps because the roll of the sea reminded her of the vicious pitch of the possessor she'd battled. What the event had felt like, she did not say. Ibrahim could only assume it had been terrible.

Both men turned to find the goddess standing at the head of Verena's bed. Perhaps their fear had summoned her. She was keeping watch, stroking Verena's brow, murmuring that she was sorry. The sense that the goddess truly meant it and had been caught by surprise eased Ibrahim's residual stirring of anger.

She evaluated his expression. "Nightmare or vision?"

"Both," Ibrahim replied.

"Do you want to tell me about it?"

Ibrahim sighed. "I doubt there is anything you can do. You've done quite enough."

She bit her lip and did not press him.

Ahmed, eyes wide, was in the throes of a different vision. Something new. When it had come upon him Ibrahim could not be sure, they had all been lost to their private nightmares. "My Lady! I see a black-haired girl and fire. Furrowed ground, dug, terrible, muddy—there's so much death, terrible noises, monsters, machines . . . All inevitable," he sobbed. "The girl says, as if she's speaking to me, 'We couldn't have stopped this. None of us could. All we can do is ease the pain. What little we can do, we must. To ease just an eddy of this ocean of pain . . . ' Does this mean anything to you, my Lady?"

Persephone blinked as the Sufi leaned toward her. "Alas. I've no reference for it, dear Ahmed. My visions have been insular: of Alexi, of the woman I must become. Nothing epic and dreadful like that, with people I don't know."

She frowned, placing her hand on her abdomen as if there was a terrible ache from deep within. "I wonder," she murmured, "if she could be of my lineage, that dark-haired girl. If a creature like me could bear a child. Not in this form. The rot of the Whisper-world has eaten me alive from the inside out. There could be no father, either. Phoenix could not impregnate me by fire, and nothing of Darkness would ever take to life within me, even if I allowed it."

Ahmed hung on her every word. Ibrahim felt equally entranced, but confused as well. He had little understanding of what games these gods played.

Sadness overwhelmed Persephone, her colours dimming. "I couldn't dare hope—" She choked and shook her head. "No. I can't say I comprehend your visions. I'm sorry."

"What of The Guard? Can't the women conceive?" Ahmed asked. "Maybe one of them . . . ?"

Persephone was further stricken. "None have. Their bodies are full—with Muse, with fire; there's no room to spare. Perhaps the Muses even stop it. You live and work at the threshold of life and death, a dangerous place for a child. And it would change the priorities of the parent. One cannot be the servant of two masters."

He sensed Ahmed's disappointment, and Ibrahim shuddered. While he couldn't disagree that such a policy was likely best for all involved, it was a further sacrifice for The Guard. Yet another forfeiture.

The goddess remarked with a shred of hope, "I cannot say, but your case of limited service may be different. It is . . ."

"Unprecedented," Ibrahim finished for her. They all nodded, silent.

Ahmed smiled wearily. "You know, I wish you *were* omnipotent."

Persephone joined him in the smile. "So I could give you answers to all that troubles you? Ah, but that would be untrue to the Sufi heart, which craves the divine mystery of which we two are a part. All your poetry would be gone."

Ahmed sighed. "You are wise."

Verena woke with a cry. It was a tortured sound, and Ibrahim stormed out of the room, unable to bear more sadness. He felt sure he brought nightmares upon the wind of his remaining Instinct, visions that could not be altered. His intuition had done nothing to keep them from harm, and now he had even less power with which to work. His vision of Beatrice's death, a death that he felt certain his presence assured, refused to leave his mind's eye.

He fled back to his cramped quarters, leaving Ahmed and the goddess to deal with Verena. There, at a small writing desk in the corner, his world went as grey as the Whisper-world. He must write a letter he would forever regret, for it might keep alive the woman who had become his treasure.

★ ★ ★

In the deep press of the Whisper-world, Persephone broke from an obligatory promenade, a ritual that surpassed unbearable since the burning of the field. She never deigned to take his flesh-then-bone hand anymore, but she did occasionally walk, if only to keep him from sensing that she was plotting.

He'd insisted on a journey round the stone tower that was the prison for her most beloved mortals. She backed away, staring sadly at that black spire, and made another silent pledge to save The Guard. Beatrice would hold her to it, whatever she became, and rightly so, this was all her fault.

"What if," Darkness growled, "I didn't let you go above anymore?"

"How ever would I heal?" was her reply. "Your hold over me would cease once there's nothing left to hold."

The words gave her strength, because that was exactly what she intended. Quitting his company, she felt the cool stones of the Whisper-world warm beneath her feet as she fled him. Each step forward was leaving Darkness further behind, each step closer to her new dawn. He did not dare pursue her.

Persephone sought out the Liminal, but she felt the Gorgon following her down several corridors. At last she turned and addressed her, saying, "You really should take over. You want it, I do not." They stood outside the vast chamber where the Liminal sat waiting.

The Gorgon's eyes flashed bright green and hungry. "Gladly. I never understood why he wanted you, a simpering weakling."

Persephone shrugged. "Nor did I." It was good for the Gorgon to think her weak. To underestimate her. She didn't need to prove herself to anyone but her Guard and Phoenix.

She turned away, saying, "And now you must excuse me." She fled into the Liminal chamber knowing the Gorgon would not follow. While the Liminal did not exactly give Persephone a sense of ease, it seemed to truly terrify Darkness's minions; it was the one thing that did. For that reason she felt safe in being left alone.

There was a bitter, bloody taste in her mouth. Before the promenade she had been at her task, anointing more stones in the gory ritual and leaving pins prepared for the future battle between worlds. The work hurt increasingly, pressing her light against the darkness. At every door she felt beaten and ravaged. Here again upon the Liminal edge she let go of all facade. She yearned for something to cleanse the terrible palate of death; she needed her beautiful young beacon of hope.

The Liminal gave her access to her desire. The Rychman estate opened before her through the proscenium.

She entered the portal, gliding down a hallway on the other side and finding it oddly silent. Keeping her diaphanous cloak about, she patrolled the house in unseen reconnaissance.

Alexandra was in the parlour with embroidery, as was her custom after her fall. Alexi was likely caught up in the long hours that comprised his apprenticeship; she could feel nothing of the Pull that might draw him elsewhere. But, where were his parents? There were things missing, and the house looked oddly bare. Empty.

To the study she went, knowing it was Alexi's favourite haunt; she could await him there. But a freshly inked letter lay drying upon the desk. "Oh no," the goddess murmured as she read:

Alexi,

There is no easy way to write this letter, but you are a sensible lad and I'll be frank. There is something wrong with that house. Your mother cannot abide it. She is full of fanciful and ridiculous notions, as women often are, of hauntings and curses and such. I don't know about that, but I do know she's grown distract, and I can't delay in removing her from these premises. Since the day of the accident, things haven't been the same. Not with you, this home, even the city.

We leave this house to you. It comes from your grandmother's money, and while your mother says that woman cursed you, I think it quite a blessing that she should have left you such a fine estate. Mr. Absolom will look out for you, and he'll make sure you have a proper job as an academic or something of the sort.

It would likely be best if you don't ask after us. We're taking some of the staff and have employed in their stead a quiet, unobtrusive couple, the Wentworths, who are aware of the solicitors retained for your affairs. You shall lack for nothing but our presence. Take care, my boy, you've long been independent. You are the master of all you survey.

Sincerely,
Alfred Rychman

P.S. You'll have to tell Alexandra. We couldn't take her with us, not like she is, and we know you love her dearly. We've left her a maid, and you'll have plenty of funds with which to look after her—or you may choose to put her into a convalescent home should she prove a burden. Such is the unfortunate lot for women who can't serve their born purpose.

A silver tear splashed from the goddess's eyes onto the paper just as a voice came from the doorway. "It's you."

She glanced up to see him. He would have no memory of her other than the annunciation of Prophecy, so this was like him seeing her again for the first time. It was both heartbreaking and wondrous.

"Hello, Alexi," she said.

"It's you," he repeated. "What are you doing here? What are you reading?"

She had no choice but to hand it over.

★ ★ ★

Everything went slack as Alexi read: his senses, his face, his hands. He dropped the letter and stared at the beautiful creature before him who moved, prismatic and silent, to pick it up, set it upon the desk and reach out to touch his temple.

"What are you doing?" he asked hoarsely, trying to keep hold of himself.

"Easing the pain," she said.

He ducked her hand, his heart spasmodic, his fists clenching and unclenching. His mind spun. "Leave me alone! You must be a curse. Get out of my house!" Everything had gone wrong since he was chosen.

Turning, he stormed out, tearing through the back garden toward the line of brush and birch trees to plunge himself into briars and dim light, away from the cursed house. Would he could escape his fate so easily. He didn't know where to begin, with anger, with terror, with indignation that his beloved sister was relegated to no more than a dismissive postscript?

Anger. Anger was the appropriate response for abandonment with no more courtesy or explanation than a note, as if a personal encounter might be too much to ask, even from a father. He was left all alone with no more than a *Sincerely, Alfred Rychman.* If the Germans really were so cold, he was glad to count himself an Englishman.

Sadness struck. This had all happened because his parents were frightened. He thought of the things he and his Guard friends had seen thus far: poltergeists, séances gone awry, violent possessions and swarms of seething spirits. They were enough to unseat sanity. Everyone should be frightened of what floated unseen upon this earth. But to those who did not see, perhaps he was the nightmare instead.

Anger returned, but the violent pitch of his emotions made him sick to his stomach. He wished he owned reason and analytical prowess alone. Feelings he could do without.

Moving slowly back to the house, he entered the parlour, that first-floor respite of light and colour where his sister always sat. She turned upon hearing his step and wheeled herself toward the door.

"What is it, Alexi? Why so weary?"

"Mum and Dad are gone," he said quietly.

His sister gasped, but not because of his words. Following her eyes, Alexi turned. There she was, standing patiently behind him. The goddess.

"Who . . . *what* are you?" Alexandra breathed.

Alexi moved to grab the goddess, but she nimbly eluded him and glided to Alexandra's side. "You stay away from my family," Alexi hissed, trying to fight back sudden tears. He didn't want to be angry with her; he didn't know who she was, and yet he helplessly loved her. "You've done enough, thank you very much."

Alexandra began to panic. "Alexi, what is this? Who is this?"

The goddess addressed him. Placing a hand on Alexandra's head she said, "Let me help. Trust me, you'll thank me."

Alexi darted forward, but he stopped when a calm smile washed over his sister's face. A genuine smile. "Mum and Dad are gone?" Alexandra repeated. "That's all right. It was always you and I anyway, wasn't it Alexi? I'm not sure they ever wanted us. Now we can do whatever we please."

The prismatic goddess stared at Alexi, and her voice was calm. "Tell your sister whatever you need to tell her to keep her safe, and to make your life easier." Alexi opened his mouth to admonish her, but the goddess held up a hand. "You can take me elsewhere, rail at me all you like and scream that I've ruined your life, but right now you'd best attend Alexandra. I can only be here a short time, and we must make sure she won't break apart with the strain. For some mortals, ignorance can be bliss. Your sister is one of those."

Alexi gulped. His mother was right: he was a danger to those involved with him, at least those who were not part of The Grand Work. His sister did not deserve such a fate, but all he wanted was to assure her peace and safety, however he could.

"Alexandra, I'm buying you a little cottage not far from here. It will be far more peaceful than this dreary place. This house is cursed. *I'm* cursed," he added in a tone too tortured for a man so young.

"No," the prismatic goddess countered, speaking softly to Alexandra, her colourful hands lovingly stroking the young woman's head. "Your brother is an angel. A prophesied angel. But his work has its dangers, and he loves you so much that he needs you safe. Removed. Because he doesn't want you to be frightened of him. He doesn't want anyone to be frightened of him."

Her eyes pierced him to the core. Alexi choked and turned away, overcome.

"Yes, brother, of course. You must do what you must," Alexandra said quietly, as if in a dream. "Just come visit, please."

Alexi's throat worked, painfully dry, and he stared at his one true remaining friend in the world, the only remaining member of his family. "Of course, sister, of course."

But he could bear no more and turned and left the room.

★ ★ ★

Persephone bent, kissed Alexandra atop the head and brushed a hand over her wide eyes as if closing the lids of the deceased. The effect was similar. There was no sound as she exited the room into the empty hall, unsure where Alexi had wandered off to but determined to follow.

She closed the parlour doors behind her. Once she had, she loosed the cough she'd been holding inside, cupping pulp and blood in her hand. Her heart faltered. "Heavens," she murmured. Even helping humans with simple tricks of grace and peace taxed her like it never had before. How much had she left to give? She might fall apart before all the doors were knit together.

Moving into the garden, she placed her sullied hand over a white rose and turned it red. Her hand was now clean.

His voice startled her. "I'm supposed to trust you because Prophecy is going to make all this better?" He was standing on the veranda, leaning against the bricks of the back wall, his dark layers of coat, vest and shirt open and disheveled, as was the mop of black hair that Persephone's fingers itched to caress.

She cleared her throat and smiled, hoping her teeth were not stained with blood. "Yes. I'm going to make it better. I'm going to make it all up to you, Alexi, I promise. Though I will say this isn't my fault any more than it is yours."

"Then, whose?" He ground his teeth.

"Whose fault is it when buildings topple, when quakes rattle the earth or storms fell trees? Is it the hand of the heavens or is it just the way of things? With as much as you've now seen that you cannot explain, and with the knowledge that I am a divinity without absolute power, what answer would you give?"

"I didn't choose—"

"No, you didn't. But you were noticed. When someone gains notice for greatness, sometimes that gives them choices. Sometimes it takes choices away."

He stared at her stonily. She continued, gliding up the walk and gesturing that they sit on the bench. When he refused, she shrugged and took a seat, tucking her legs up and shifting so that she sat facing him, her glowing layers gathered in bunches like the absurd poufs and skirts so fashionable in his century.

"I was noticed once," she said. "It got me stolen away to a

place where I rot year after year. I didn't choose. So often we don't. Your Grand Work has its blessings and curses—"

"There are no blessings."

"No? What about those lives you've already saved? The glory that you feel in the Power and the Light? The true knowledge, in your very veins, that you work for good?" Persephone watched as Alexi's face twisted, an admission that she was right.

They existed in silence for a spell, her sitting, him standing. But there was only so long she was afforded.

"I'll come back," she promised, rising. He allowed her to place a kiss on his cheek as she passed. She didn't think she imagined his pleasure, and she watched his teeth clench, him battling whether to reach out and take her in his arms. Then she placed a sorcerous finger on his lips that would prevent him from speaking to his friends about the encounter, for it would only bring pain and confusion. She did not wish to complicate things, even if she could not help these dalliances.

Slipping from her neck the crimson fabric that was partly her excuse for coming, she said, "Take this. A spot of passionate colour in what must feel like a life of utter darkness."

She wound it around his neck as a cravat, and when she was done he was helpless to resist her kiss. In it, she planted a seed of peace. Then she vanished into the house, leaving him where he stood, staring out at the darkening garden and again forgetting the intimacy that had just been theirs.

Moving into the study, the goddess glanced at Alfred Rychman's letter upon the desk. She grimaced, saddened, but she was doing all she could.

Her head suddenly swam. A vision formed, a vision of this house. The ghostly girl, the woman, the mortal Persephone must become sat at a harpsichord. Alexi stood to her side, and they were older than when she'd first seen them. The pair was still striking, still filled with love, and it looked like some, what, thirty years had passed?

As her impossibly white hands played a tune, folded paper fell from somewhere within the keyboard. It fell on her boots, and she plucked it up and opened it with a frown.

There were two messages inside. The goddess recognized the first page immediately; it was the very note from Alexi's father that she'd just discovered. The second and third were a missive in an even more familiar hand that Persephone saw was her own.

The vision faded.

"Well, then . . ."

Persephone never argued with her visions. She plucked two blank sheets of paper from atop the blotter, took a fountain pen and went upstairs. There she would plant a missive to ease the future. She would leave the letters to be found at the appropriate time. Words of hope, of praise, of thanksgiving.

She would also include Ahmed's warnings of the war in the ground, to not close every door, to allow room for the dead. Whatever that meant. There were times when it was best to offer warnings. When mortals were warned, they kept better Guard.

Chapter Twenty-six

Alexi walked slowly toward Athens Academy and his Guard meeting, his mind hazy, numb. Yet, his heart was stubbornly beating, a fact that reminded him he was alive.

He recalled the facts of the letter from his father regarding his circumstances and responsibility, remembered that his sister had taken it surprisingly well. However, a part of his day felt as though it were missing and he couldn't determine why. Perhaps he had gotten so adept at not feeling things that his life simply happened: a variable was placed into his respective equation, he deduced the total and moved on, emotionless. It left a void, but emptiness was better than the alternative. How many years would it be before humanity escaped him altogether?

He also wondered when he'd taken to wearing a scarlet cravat. But he liked the look of it.

Turning the corner and seeing a weeping Jane, he was suddenly certain he retained some concept of human compassion. She looked up at him and blushed, then only wept harder as he drew near and placed a firm hand upon her shoulder.

She fell into a stammering torrent of words, her accent heightened by anxiety. "I'm sorry, Alexi, to be seen like this, but I'm beside m'self. I've nowhere to go. Mum said I'm useless if I won't marry or take a job—but I can't marry!" She blushed more. "We just can't! And the factories, ye can't just walk off the line if The Grand Work calls, so I've been kicked out. I don't know what to—"

"Jane," Alexi interrupted with gentle firmness. "You and

I will walk through Aldgate tomorrow and we shall find you a flat. Rebecca and I were just discussing how that area gets spiritually fitful, so having a Guard resident there would be an asset. Aldgate would suit you, wouldn't it?"

Her red, tearstained face showed excitement for a moment before falling again into terror. "But I've no money."

"You leave the money to me, and I don't want to hear one more word about it," he commanded, proffering her his breast-pocket handkerchief. "Ever. You are provided for, Miss Connor, and that is all there is to say."

She watched him, wide-eyed, and he realized that she was leaning on him a bit. He tried to exude the strength he felt was appropriate to his commission. While some tiny, forgotten part of him wished to be as tearful as his comrade, he was now Leader, so he tucked that miniscule creature away and chose to believe in stoicism.

"Thank you, Alexi," she breathed. "I . . . knew you could help me."

"Of course," he said. "Such is my job."

He offered Jane an arm as they ascended the steps to Athens, and as he heaved open the great front door admitted, "I've been similarly abandoned." The Irish girl turned in alarm, her warm heart ever ready to offer sympathy, so he quickly admitted, "Though not without recourse as you have been. Worry not a whit for me, Jane. But trust me. I have learned today that we, The Guard, are all the family we can rely on."

"Oh, aye, Alexi," Jane said. "That much seems true."

Her tears vanished, and her relief and gratitude made him realize that friends were indeed a blessing, and that helping them made his heart less heavy. He smiled—or gave the best approximation he could muster.

"While being Leader is my job, helping a friend is a pleasure. Tomorrow, at the tower gates at eleven, we'll find you a home. Tonight, stay at the academy. There's room in the ladies' dormitory. But only until Rebecca takes over; then she'll have this place crawling with as many girls as families will allow."

Inside they were met by their fellows. Spectral matters were discussed, and they were renewed by the Power and the Light. It was an uneventful meeting, but the rejuvenation was necessary. He found that the meditative ritual in the sacred space was going to be necessary every week, to recall them to their purpose, to remind them what was good in spite of all their youthful sacrifice. It filled him with great hope and alleviated the darkness within, much like the spot of crimson against his black attire.

However, upon returning home, after a silent dinner with his uncomplaining sister and the small retained house staff, Alexi realized that would not be enough. There was still something missing, forgotten, unrealized. He was still as empty as the vast estate left solely to him, and he didn't know how to find peace.

★ ★ ★

Beatrice waited out the weeks of the Peninsular steamer's journey in anxious delirium, reliving Ibrahim's kiss upon her hand, the look in his eyes, the hand on his heart. Frequenting Café La Belle et La Bête, she found the friendship of Belle and George did her heart good, as did the knowledge that George continued to paint. His work was as beautiful as ever. For all The Grand Work had required in sacrifice, it had also brought her a treasure. Such friendship as the Cairo Guard shared was priceless.

"Have you heard from Ibrahim?" Belle asked. It was a casual query every time they met.

"Belle, he can't rightly send a letter from the ship. Where would it go? He has to dock before the mail can set sail again in return. Patience," Beatrice replied, as if she were detached from the thought of him. As if their relationship was all still business. Ibrahim. She wondered if Belle knew how her heart pounded at the sound of that name. If so, her friend never let on and never made her feel small for it.

"George and I shall retire to the coast," the French girl announced. "Won't that be nice? We've been discussing it for some time. Well, since the others left, since we've no further responsibilities. We're thinking Grimsby. But, not yet. I've this odd feeling we're meant to stay here a bit, to do something with this building. We feel it the same way we felt we were supposed to buy the place. What does the goddess have in store for you?"

"I've no idea," Beatrice said. "She means to take a mortal body, but she'd best stop dallying with her precious new Leader and do it already. If we're all headed for Darkness's dread prison, we'd better get her war well underway."

Maybe then they'd be free to live their lives—and afterlives— in peace.

★ ★ ★

Alexi awoke to a great, bright, shifting light at the foot of his bed. It was his goddess. She'd returned to him. It had been weeks since she'd first given them their commission and he constantly wondered if he'd ever see her again.

Staring at her, the stolen memories suddenly flooded back, other meetings. Their conversations, their kisses, the lust and longing, the pain she'd taken away, the vague promises and discussions, it all came at him like a hail of sharp stones. The tsunami of accompanying questions, emotions and desires had him aroused, overwhelmed and scared all at once. He backed against the wall, taking his blankets with him, shaking his head as if she were a nightmare and not the beauty for which his entire body cried out.

"What . . . what have you done to me?" he gasped, half a mind to run from the room, half a mind to seize her. "Why do you do this to me? Why have you done it again and again?"

Her beautiful face was stricken. "I'm so sorry, Alexi, love." She moved forward and touched his cheek. His roiling, reeling sensibilities calmed to a dull throb in his throat, heart and other parts of himself he hoped he was gentleman enough to curb. "I take the memories when I go because it's best that way, I promise. We must stay focused. I can't have you pining for me, lovelorn and useless, that's why I take the memories. There are these seals, you see, so many of them, and there's grim work at those joints between worlds. But the work that must be done there hurts me, so I come to you for comfort."

He struggled with her words. "What sort of work? Work we might do together?" Alexi murmured, unable to deny her closeness, the intoxicating smell of wildflowers.

"Would that it were so now. But I'm almost finished! And then there will be work for us together, I promise," she breathed, her head tilting in an angle opposite.

The kiss was inevitable, elemental. But for all the riptide of passion he felt, something about her felt so fragile that he didn't dare release such violent sensations. The goddess was meant for savouring, for slow and delicious tasting. She was like no other creature and he could not expect the basest urges of mortal men to be appropriate, and so he denied them as best he could.

"Don't take the memory of you away," he begged as she broke from him and laid her head upon his shoulder. Her hands clutched him desperately. He recalled then that her beloved, who she said was like him, did not exist to touch or hold. She, too, was perhaps getting her fill before going off to live in echoes.

"I must," she replied, her voice calm, but she kept clutching. "I've seen visions. I see how you look. I want you to look at me in the future the same way you do now—fresh, new, amazed. My riddles will not change, so would you have me repeat them? Can you not trust my ways?"

"Not really," Alexi replied.

She chuckled. "You're wise."

"So you tell me." He smirked.

He could not judge her harshly, even recalling all she'd taken away. It was not in him to be angry with her, to be anything but loving, as inexplicable as their relationship had been from the start. She was life like he'd never known, light like he'd never seen, and he wouldn't waste it by drawing the curtains. Only a demon could do so. If he did that, he would be as bad as the one she could not escape.

"How long do you give me to sit and stare at you?" he asked. "This time."

"I can stop time for a bit."

"Then do so for as long as you can," he replied, and he drew her into his embrace. "You've said the one you loved and lost is a ghost and cannot touch you, and yet I hold him in my hands. I assume, then, that this is a gift," he remarked. He took one hand and stroked it slowly, achingly down her body, calling on the force he wielded.

Blue fire wreathing his fingertips, that single caress became countless variations. That familiar fire kissed her skin and made her weep for remembrance.

Her sighs filled Alexi with a tingling bliss. True carnality was bypassed, but simple but meaningful touches and sighs provided the same fulfillment that had never been so exquisite.

Not that Alexi had anything to compare this to. Nor would he remember this chaste bliss when the night was through, even if he took a future mortal woman in his arms, for the goddess would never allow the memories to linger.

★ ★ ★

Slipping sighing back into the Whisper-world, Persephone knew she indulged herself in Alexi's company too much, but she used his light, his love, to give her energy and take her to another seal. She was addicted to the promise of the future she glimpsed, and only it kept her sane. With so much of her essence, her heart, her focus, her magic shifting to London, England, there was hardly enough of it here to keep her safe. She needed to work faster and remain focused.

This time, as she sprinkled the deep crimson flow of her life force onto a dank stone pin rimmed in gold, the bleeding would not stop. She pressed her gauzy clothing to the wound she'd created, and more crimson silk was made. But she did not have much left to give.

Chapter Twenty-seven

Ibrahim stared at the letter. He did not want to send it. He had delayed for too long and she must know something was wrong. She, being who she was, stubborn woman, had not written to him either, but her damnable pride was for the best. Her letters would likely contain some sentiment that would make it harder to sever ties.

He needed to act. Steeling himself, he took the letter to the post, ignoring the bustling city around him. He ignored the ghosts, too, but as he returned home, his task accomplished, he put his head in his hands, numb, and felt like he had joined their incorporeal number.

★ ★ ★

In the months that had passed since Ibrahim's departure, Beatrice wandered the academy, feeling much like the school's attendant ghosts, wondering if anyone possibly felt as hollow as she. What was *he* feeling a continent away, damn him? She had not heard from any of her friends who'd returned to Cairo, and Belle had long since stopped asking after a letter. Beatrice's box of stationery sat opened but unused. She was too nervous to begin the dialogue they needed to have; there were thousands of things she wanted to say, but a terrible silence had overtaken her life and she was paralyzed by it.

The dark part of her was sure Ibrahim had found someone back in Cairo, something closer to his world. He deserved something delicate and beautiful, something Egyptian, if that was what he wanted, and surely that was the reason for his silence: he had found it. He was done with The Grand Work, so he was returning to his old life, whatever remained of it.

But, there was no forgetting The Grand Work, really, was there? She couldn't imagine a world where that was so. He was just choosing to forget *her*.

She felt herself fading, though she was still in the flower of youth. Duty was all she had, and so she wondered when the goddess might return. She had not seen Persephone since the day Ibrahim's boat sailed. All those who had been most compelling in her life were now oddly absent.

Occasionally she picked up a pen to write to Ibrahim, but every time she did, she realized she didn't know where to send the letter. Every day that passed made unclasping her heart all the more difficult to imagine, her pride all the more unwavering. It was a man's duty to reach out to a woman, to court her. Women who did otherwise appeared the eager fool.

She spent a growing amount of time peering at Alexi Rychman. The dark-haired youth and his Intuition, Miss Rebecca Thompson, came and went from the academy, occasionally trailed by the Heart, Michael. This third member of The Guard stared at Rebecca in the same way Rebecca stared at Alexi, a miserable triangle. Beatrice cursed The Grand Work on behalf of all of them.

Poor Rebecca. If Leaders and their seconds were often meant to be, Persephone's plan would rend the girl's heart asunder. The numbers would prove uneven, and the new Guard would face great pain. But she supposed ill treatment of the conscripted was hardly new.

The plan was moving along. Things seemed in place to assure that the two most valuable Guard would remain close to The Grand Work's power source. Rebecca made odes of "When I am headmistress . . ." and Alexi already laid claim to the largest, grandest office in Apollo Hall. He tore about with fastidious focus, always glancing around corners as if making sure he hadn't misplaced something. He wasn't nervous, he moved with sure and steady grace. And his pure, unadulterated aim was Prophecy; Beatrice could see it in his every move as she passed like a ghost just outside his notice. Prophecy seemed a mental slavery that he worshipped as a religion. She could not blame him, she supposed. The Grand Work did inspire, though it took so much in return.

Still, she envied him bitterly. She wanted to be useful again. There were moments when she could feel that phantom power of the Phoenix fire, and she wanted to clutch it inside her, to never let it go. But memory was all she had left.

Belle and George were excellent company, and they all rejoiced when finally they received a letter from Ahmed that he and Verena were wed. But the careful absence of Ibrahim from the letter and the subsequent discussion at the café was awkward and glaring.

Beatrice knew she was becoming a spectre of herself. Just as Ibrahim had become a baffling ghost in their memory. Without being a Leader and without her second-in-command, she was a living parody of that dark, shadowy world she'd once fought.

When the letter finally arrived, printed in the delicate script of the man who in the murmurs of her midnight hours she achingly called beloved, the change Beatrice felt was elemental. Like a giddy, anxious schoolgirl, she rushed to her rooms to open it. She hurriedly drank in the missive but stopped, a mournful sound catching in her throat.

Miss Smith,

I truly apologize for the delay in my missive. The words I must write are not easy ones to pen and I have waited to see if my mind might change. But, I am resolute. You and I were thrust into a most unlikely partnership, and I maintain that I respect how you have handled yourself. I have valued your presence in my life more than I dare say.

Growing up with the knowledge I was left on a doorstep has made me care for people cautiously. Losing the father I so luckily gained made fear of growing attached all the more ingrained. I hope you can understand this, and I hope you can therefore forgive the time I made our interactions difficult. I hope you can also comprehend that being abandoned by you is the greatest terror I've known.

And now I've seen it with my own eyes. I lost you. There is no other way to say it. As we came upon Cairo, so a vision came upon me. I trust it, for Ahmed and Verena have both confirmed that we have all retained echoes of our powers. In my vision you took a fatal turn, and I somehow know I was involved. *It was when you took my hand that you died.*

I cannot again go against what remains of my instinct and cast you unwittingly into harm's way; you are too valuable a commodity to play with. As much as I at first wished the fate of The Grand Work were otherwise, I now wish this vision were untrue and that you might deign to join me in Cairo. But I'll not risk your life upon it. I cannot. We must not be together, it seems the only way to keep you safe.

Beatrice, you deserve a life full of light and glory. I'll not have you turn Whisper-world grey before my eyes. Live well and be well, Miss Smith. I shall surely see you someday in some Great Beyond.

Sincerely,
Ibrahim Wasil-Tipton

The letter fluttered to the ground, dropped from her trembling hands.

She had not cried during this lengthy period of silence. A part of her had clung to the notion that letters got lost, that a decision about companionship and where to make a home wasn't something one wrote about lightly, that once the goddess had detailed her last duty she would be free to make her own decisions and could address Ibrahim then, ending their awkward silence either in person or by epistle. But now there was finality. A kiss on the hand was all she would ever receive. Lovers would be denied her. Such was her fate.

Black clouds were rolling in, and with every crack of thunder that broke over London, so too did Beatrice break. The letter had not been entirely cold, but neither could she comfort herself with its passion. Ibrahim was a man of fact. If he had emotions, he placed them too deep to cultivate. His disturbing vision was the last thing they would share.

A riotous thunderclap, then a sob, carrying with it all the grief from Jean's death Beatrice had never let flow. And this new heartbreak was worse than the first. Beatrice didn't remember the last time she'd wailed, if indeed she ever had, collapsing in tears upon the centre of her floor, but the recklessness of the storm inspired her own. Her world that had gone Cairo golden when he'd kissed her hand—a world turned London grey in his absence—now went Whisper-world black.

She didn't care how she might sound to anyone passing in the hall until she heard a timid knock. She stopped, but the knock came again. Then a male voice, slightly familiar. "Terribly sorry. I know it might seem impertinent, but I was just seeing my friend to her new rooms here at Athens and in passing . . . I just have to ask, miss, if you are all right."

"Fine," Beatrice barked. And yet she stood and moved to the door. There was no hole through which to look out and see the visitor who stood just on the other side.

The man again spoke gently. "If I'm not mistaken, that was the cry of a broken heart. You must forgive me, but hearts are my specialty. I just wanted you to know that you are not alone. No mortal is alone. Even if you can't see or feel them, there are angels all around."

The stranger on the other side of the door made her feel as though she were in a confessional, something doubly bizarre for an Anglican. Yet, there was something soothing in the intimate anonymity. Beatrice found herself confessing, "I . . . found out that someone I love cannot love me in return."

"Ah, how I understand you, miss," came the sad reply. "And there's hardly a pill more bitter. But God loves you, always."

"Are you a priest? If not, you should be. The church could use an advocate like you."

"Why, thank you, miss, and indeed I have chosen to serve the church. Michael Carroll, at your service. Should you ever need an ear or a reminder of angels, please think of me. Especially during the worst storms and the darkest nights of your soul. Rest well."

Beatrice shook her head and listened to his footfalls recede. Michael Carroll? Of course his voice was familiar. He was the new Heart. Though she no longer wielded any power, and Michael wouldn't have known her as anything but some resident of the growing academy, she would have connected with him anywhere. The Grand Work refused to be ignored.

The storm rumbled, and she wondered what would follow in its watery wake.

Chapter Twenty-eight

Young Alexi Rychman stared out the window of his home, master of a dark and empty estate. He was alone. Alexandra had been moved to her own quarters with a kind young maid who would be ever at her service, so this haunted house, if full of murmurs, strange tricks of the light and endless shadows, was as hollow and echoing as his soul.

The wind howled. It was a terrible storm like he'd never seen, one that seemed to speak of wrestling gods and that made his mind race and his heart pound. Was Prophecy afoot? He felt a moment of foolishness, thinking that inclement weather might have a whit to do with the supernatural. Then he felt the Pull, and The Grand Work dragged him out into the storm.

★ ★ ★

In the dark heart of the Whisper-world, Persephone had no accurate gauge of mortal time. She didn't want to ask the Liminal for verification; she didn't dare ask too many favours, especially when she hesitated in what was required. What even Phoenix had urged her on to do. But the time was at hand.

She had been away longer than was customary of late, had bled onto several seals but without healing herself again in the mortal world. This caused its own danger. Only two seals were left, then all were set to be kissed by fire when the moment was right—provided no forces from the Whisper-world disturbed them in the meantime. She had to trust in the plan that had been given her by instinct, vision and the Liminal. Then, on to glory.

Her yearning for the mortal world was stronger than ever, but the end was too close to turn back now. Two more final bursts of her life force and she could finally make the change, carry herself over into mortal flesh and become a body no longer broken or tied to Whisper-world prison.

She had to be desperately careful. This final push had brought difficulties. These complications worsened at the last seal, just as Persephone cast aside the sharp thorn that had reopened her tender wounds. Moaning in pain, she watched her blood drip onto the stones, a familiar ritual at this point. But this time she had company.

"You're such a weakling," the Gorgon hissed, turning a corridor and coming into view. She and the dog had been looking for an opportunity to pounce. It seemed they had found one.

Persephone turned and spat to mask her purpose with a mixture of blood, bile and pomegranate. She hoped she appeared to be having merely one of her fits, as she'd had for centuries.

"You're such a pest," the goddess countered, wiping her mouth with her begrimed robes.

"You know, he'd never know the difference if one day you just *completely* fell apart. Surely I could convince him of its inevitability. So, why don't I help you? I can just put you out of your misery if you let me. You want to die; you've been trying to kill yourself for so long. Let me help."

As the Gorgon drew close, her head of snakes hissed and snapped, two serpents projecting themselves long and limber to wrap around Persephone's wrists. Her face was beautiful as she stared at Persephone, her eyes shifting red then green then black. Past the white of her skin as it appeared to her eyes, Persephone could see her coloured aura shifting and reflecting upon the Gorgon's fair complexion, colours that remained bold and defiant.

Persephone spat in the Gorgon's face. "Don't you dare touch me!"

Luce hissed in pain, her grip weakened, and Persephone broke free, her forearms slippery with blood. The snakes' tongues lapped at her injuries, but Persephone batted them away.

The Gorgon growled, and behind her the dog began to bark, countless red eyes looming. It pounced, its body first one then a hundred mongrels, and Persephone screamed in pain and terror as a rain of teeth scored her flesh. The goddess focused her energy enough to create a slap of white light that threw the protean canine off and sent the snakes hissing and reeling backward. While she knew she could gather more light with which to fight, she could not participate in a full-on brawl lest she have nothing left to take her to the next world.

Too much of her was bleeding. But, the last seal had been prepared. If she could just find the strength to open a portal, to tumble back to the mortal world, she might recover enough to make a last stand. She had to do so quickly, and she had to maintain enough of her energy for the final phase.

She tried to flee, to move toward the beckoning Liminal light down the next corridor, but the Gorgon would not desist. She blocked Persephone's path, lashing out with all the fury that hatred and jealousy had fashioned. Those base things the Whisper-world magnified, giving monsters the upper hand. Serpents wrapped around Persephone, driving their fangs and forked tongues deep into her wounds, tasting just how weak she was.

Persephone screamed in genuine agony. She heard every restless ghost take up her cry and echo it. The very ground of the Whisper-world shuddered. Rocks began to fall, and the sound was deafening. The Whisper-world Groundskeeper would be appalled to see all his stonework and bone sculpture come tumbling, the poor wretch. The Gorgon seemed unconcerned with consequence.

Struggling in vain, Persephone couldn't believe this crazed lackey dared bring down a veritable apocalypse. But when the dog pounced again, she felt her consciousness slip and her light flicker.

This was not how she was supposed to end.

★ ★ ★

Back in London, Alexi and his Guard were ghost hunting. It was a rough case. The Pull had brought them to a grand inn outside the city proper, a stone edifice ringed with lush rose bushes and a tended lawn.

The storm was merciless, rain soaking them as they worked. Alexi wound fire around the irascible spirit of a man who'd died in one of London's last legal duels, but his was not the only spectre braving the storm. The sky was lit with a horde of luminous dead, all swaying, mouths open, as if offering proclamations or warnings. Not that The Guard could hear their wailing cries.

"Alexi," Rebecca called in alarm. She stood under a portico with an open notebook. She furiously scribbled down every particular of the situation, as was her custom.

"Yes?"

She pointed to the stone foundations lined with red rosebushes. "The roses."

"What about them?"

Her face was ashen. "They were white. When we arrived, these roses were all *white*."

Throwing a definitive punch of blue fire to stun the duelist spirit into submission, Alexi bent to touch the deep red blossoms. They were wet. He brought his fingers to his nose and took a step back. All the roses were covered in blood.

Josephine the Artist cried out. "Is this a sign of Prophecy?"

Alexi set his jaw. "Everything in our age is a sign of Prophecy."

He touched his blue fire-kissed palm to the open bloom, and the blood streaked to reveal a still-white petal beneath. As he made contact, the crimson began to roll away as if repelled. Too oily to be human, the gore dripped to the earth.

"So shall we heal the world," Michael intoned, staring at the subtle miracle. "Through blood and fire."

"So long as the world is not *too* awash in blood," Alexi retorted. "Every power has its limits."

He glanced at the sky filled with clustered dead and wondered at The Guard's ability to maintain balance. They felt dangerously close to a fulcrum. With such omens, he couldn't be sure of long-term success, even though the duelist's spirit appeared mollified. He used his cerulean fire to kiss clean the bushes.

Michael drew close. "'O day and night, but this is wondrous strange!'"

The quote echoed exactly Alexi's thoughts, so he responded in kind. "'And therefore as a stranger give it welcome. There are more things in heaven and earth, Horatio, than are dreamt of in your philosophy.'" Though he considered himself full of Horatio's rationality, Hamlet's line seemed fitting. The Grand Work forced him to be both skeptic and believer.

He twisted a bloody rose petal between his fingertips. "Perhaps the gods battle in some unseen place. If so, I wager the blood on these roses is hardly the half of it."

★ ★ ★

"WHAT. IS. HAPPENING?!!"

The walls of the Whisper-world, wet with blood and echoing with Persephone's agony, amplified Darkness's bellowing cry. Rocks, silt and Whisper-world muck went flying. The river crested with murmurs and wails.

A whistle ten times that of the largest steam train sounded, and the dog yelped and whined, withdrawing its hundred heads' teeth from the goddess's hair and flesh. Luce the Gorgon grumbled and unlashed her snakes, and Persephone collapsed onto the wet stones now drenched in her blood. Barely alive, she prayed she had enough strength to crawl to the Liminal edge and slip through. These wounds were catastrophic.

"She was trying to kill herself," Luce muttered to the regal, red-eyed shadows seething at the mouth of the corridor.

"She tried to kill me," Persephone gasped in rebuttal, her hands slipping in her own gore as she struggled to lift herself. It was the truth, and if she was to live, she needed help. The idea that Darkness might aid her was irony indeed.

Luce pouted as the shadows drew close. "You believe her?"

The Lord of Shadow stared at the both of them, Luce standing upright, Persephone groaning in pain as she once more collapsed upon the stones. "By the look of her. Yes. She could not have done this to herself."

Darkness's eyes, when he had them, regarded Persephone in horror. She must look a sight indeed. Luce began to creep backward, and it was correct that she should fear his wrath. He reached out a hand, and his bone fingers seized a cluster of her snakes and yanked. Hard. It was Luce's turn to shriek. Skins and scales slid down her face, her hair writhing and hissing.

The dog whimpered, its tails between its legs. Darkness whipped the shadows with a long, sharp lash that seared its chimerical hides.

While Darkness was administering his punishments, Persephone mustered all her strength and dignity to stand upright before him. She swayed and shook on her feet. "Th-thank you, my lord," she said, her body convulsing. Blood kept pouring from her wounds. "If you'll permit me . . . ."

"Go," he said, his voice like gravel. His beautiful face—then skull, then face—was tortured.

"It will take . . . some time away. To heal. I need to *heal*."

"I. Realize," he said.

Staring at him, at his reaction, she was almost tempted to tell him the truth. Wouldn't that be freeing? It seemed that now, while he was seeing her like this, he was perhaps willing—

No, there was no second-guessing Prophecy, least of all the nature of deities. The soul of Darkness was jealous and warped. He would never let her go for good. Her freedom she had yet to earn. Persephone moved toward the darkened corridor.

She saw the Liminal ahead as she left Darkness behind, and there she was reminded of true love. Phoenix. Blue fire surged forward, all that could be spared from the thick of a Guard fight; it came tearing up, wrapped blue cords around her, loving and trying to heal her. She basked in its warmth.

There was a witness. One of Luce's snakes, sheared verily in half, slithered along at Persephone's feet. The head and first third of it were fleshy, the latter part torn and skeletal. It extended its bloody forked tongue at the flowers by her feet, struggling to blossom one moment and dead the next.

"I'll see you again soon," the snake hissed. "And when I do, I'll finish what I started."

"I know you'll try, Luce," Persephone began simply, emboldened by the fire of her love and by sparking Liminal light. With a delirious surge, she ran to the swirling, misty Liminal wall and said, before tumbling through: "But I'll prove love's greater power and settle the score."

★ ★ ★

There came a horrible roar of thunder, and a black maw of a portal spat the goddess onto the foot of Beatrice's bed. Beatrice cried out in alarm, for Persephone was a dripping, bloody mess. Her face was lovely as ever, but it was haunted and full of a ferocity she'd never seen. The goddess tried to right herself, but her hands slipped on her begrimed gown. It was the most terrible sight Beatrice had ever beheld.

She couldn't help but rush to the goddess's side, to ease her back onto the bed. Beatrice felt thick warm blood course over her hands, and she bit back a gasp and stilled a disgusted shudder.

"No, no," Persephone protested. "I can't lie down. We've work to do and only a bit of—"

"My Lady, what happened? You've been away so long. You're in dire need of attention, so I'll find that blonde girl, the Healer—"

"No, no, we've no time! I must offer my last energies to my new form, I can't afford to convalesce—"

"My Lady, you're half-dead."

"I'll be better off if you *help* me!"

The goddess had clearly come from a fight, and she was set to begin another.

"It's time," she continued, breathing deep. Moment by moment, the blood, gore and sickly sweet scent of sour pomegranate seemed to lessen. The mortal world did her such good. "I need your help now and in the coming months. Will you come?" the goddess rasped. "I must speak to the point, Beatrice. Since you were so angry before, I need to know your choice now: do you accept the dangers that may yet come if you follow and aid me?"

Beatrice was too moved by the dire, terrible sight of her to refuse. "I accept."

It was time for her to again do something useful. Ibrahim had abandoned her, but the goddess needed her. The fire of purpose flowed through her veins. And with this resolve, she dressed. Oddly quiet save the wheeze in her lungs, the goddess waited on the bed in an attempt to recover.

"I understand now," Beatrice breathed, glancing at the calendar on the inside of her armoire. "How your sense of time differs. When you lose a person who had begun to define you . . . you just float."

The goddess nodded. While the blood on her gown had faded and its torn layers mended themselves, deep crimson still pooled on Beatrice's bedclothes and Persephone's lungs still rattled. She frowned and placed a hand on the covers, turning them entirely into red silk. "I'd give anything to spare you that hollow existence."

Beatrice shook her head. "The solution is not in your purview. I'd not take such charity if it were. Making someone love me who chose to forsake me with an unsubstantiated explanation—"

"Ibrahim?" interrupted the goddess. "Why?"

"Something about a nightmare."

Persephone sighed. "He senses the danger you are about to face. There *are* trials ahead, Beatrice Smith. I dearly trust and truly need you, but I also respect mortal choice. If you refuse me, I will try and make do." The goddess added earnestly, "If you choose to help me, your willing mortal choice will strengthen and empower all I ask. We shall see our reward doubled should we succeed."

Danger felt so much better than numbness. "You once told me we were chosen because we would say yes," Beatrice stated. It was true. "Are you recovered?"

The goddess smiled, grateful. "As much as I can be," she replied, rising. She trembled but no longer shook. "We must go. I'm sorry about the bedclothes. I know you hate that colour silk."

Beatrice couldn't help but chuckle at such a mundane concern. "Lead on, my Lady."

Persephone opened her hands. A tearing sound resulted. Beatrice's stomach dropped, and her head spun in a dizzy whirl. Suddenly they stood on a precipice high over a darkened London. The robes that had cleaned themselves were again bloodied and dripping; here, where there was no longer divine artifice. Here where the temperature was cold and the chill deadly.

The goddess steadied Beatrice with one hand and herself on the great frame of a wide void that looked out onto the mortal world. It reminded her of a stage, but Beatrice kept her Shakespearean quip, and her thousand questions, to herself.

Persephone spoke: "The Liminal must help me find the girl I'm to become in order to finally be done with this form. You, Beatrice, are one of the only mortals ever to see this threshold, which has proved the doom and salvation of countless numbers of your kind. This is the place from which fate's greatest commissions are wrought."

A flicker of familiar blue fire coursed round the edge of the Liminal frame and moved to kiss Persephone's cheek.

"My love," Persephone murmured. She breathed a sigh of happiness. "Are you here to watch me find her?"

"Indeed," rumbled the voice of Phoenix. Beatrice marveled at it, the rich baritone that had only once brushed her ear. "Alexi rests fitfully but in no need of me. I want to be with you when you go."

Persephone turned to face the Liminal. "Tell me what you want. I shall go where you bid me go. Tell me what sacrifice I must give."

Beatrice shivered. What could such an awesome threshold

ask? Hadn't this goddess and everyone who suffered with The Grand Work made sacrifice enough? What was this Liminal place?

A torrent of images played over the great space like pictures cast wide upon a canvas, villages and towns along northeastern England. Then, suddenly, a courtyard. The blur of images stilled. A clock high above them whirred. A barrel of numbers hovered between 1875 and 1878.

The scene revealed a girl *all* white—a little girl, with white hair, skin, ice-pale eyes, perhaps all of seven years old, alone in a brick courtyard—stared up at a ghost in Elizabethan garb from beneath a wide-brimmed hat. She spoke timidly: "Gregory, why do I see you and speak to you if others can't?"

"Because thou art special, my girl," the spirit replied.

"I'm not special. I am a . . . *freak.*" That's what the novices say when they think I can't hear them."

"You mustn't listen."

"I can't help it. It hurts. I'm so scared. I see things. Terrible things I don't understand. Reverend Mother says I'm not to speak to anyone of them."

"And thou shouldst not, dear girl. The world, I fear, shall not understand thee."

"It doesn't. But you do." The girl reached out her arms. Gregory, chuckling, tried to enclose her in his arms. Being incorporeal, he could not.

"I love you, Gregory, but I wish you could give me a real embrace. I want so badly to be touched," she said, displaying a quiet mournfulness far beyond her years.

"Someday, my girl, thou shalt gain a beloved. I swear this upon my bones."

The eerie girl looked up at him from beneath her wide-brimmed hat and smiled a hopeful, lovely smile that could make flowers grow. Then the Liminal shifted, showing them the exterior of the convent before its vast surface went dark.

"I . . . I won't *take* a young woman's body," Persephone breathed, seeming to have gleaned more than Beatrice, who remained confused, "but be born again. Born as a timid girl who doesn't remember who she is. That's why I couldn't say 'I' when declaring Prophecy! She doesn't remember a thing. She's all alone with ghosts, never touched . . . How is the life of a mortal freak any different from my life now?" she cried at the Liminal, clenching her fists. "Why can't I simply take a mortal body as I am; blaze down upon the Earth in glory, without a further lifetime of trial?"

Beatrice watched her. This was clearly new and heartbreaking knowledge.

"It is as I feared," Phoenix murmured.

Persephone whirled, droplets of blood flying everywhere. "As you feared?"

"Yes, but you must make a change, beloved, or you'll end up with nothing. Choose life while you still can. Before you're all bled out and nothing is left. You're decaying, my love. Go. You must, and there's no turning back."

"But you made me think—"

"I listened to your visions and you sounded so happy . . . What was I to do but encourage you no matter what?"

The goddess shook with terror. The Liminal registered and amplified her anxiety; its glassy portal shuddered, sparks at its edges. Lightning streaked across it, illuminating their surroundings as corridors with pillars made of skulls marching deep into the Whisper-world. The shadows between scurried and hissed. This was not a place Beatrice wanted to linger.

"I don't want to die!" Persephone cried. Her colours shifted and whirled, dizzying. Beatrice had never seen her so addled or unhinged. It was terrifying.

"You won't die," Phoenix assured her. "You'll live on, you've seen—"

"But I won't remember. It's as if I never existed."

"Tell me the alternative!" Phoenix bellowed. "Living like this? How long before you're nothing but rot, memory and misery? You *know* this, my love, you've known it since you first spilled your blood on these stones. How many times have we yearned for peace? First we must take these steps to free our Guard, and then we can perhaps at last earn the Great Beyond!"

Persephone balled her fists, her prismatic eyes going onyx and refusing to shift. Beatrice's blood ran cold. This was not a look for a goddess of beauty, hope and life; this was a look the Whisper-world had fashioned. Beatrice wanted to weep for this great, decaying force of beauty and life reduced to near madness, this divine force that seemed suddenly all too human.

The shadows lengthened, and more lightning forked across the Liminal. Its glassy surface practically went convex, as if reaching out for them. Beatrice felt a weight upon her blood. The Liminal threshold was straining, desirous of change. Behind them was a dank, dark labyrinth. She'd been in the shadow of death often enough to know it in her bones. Ahead she saw possibility.

"My Lady, we must go," Beatrice pleaded. "If Darkness comes to this edge—"

"Give me time," Persephone barked.

"You don't have it," Beatrice hissed. "Time isn't yours anymore. You're weak, and your immortality is fading." She dared grab hold of the goddess, squeezing her arms. "This is what you have prepared for, whether you knew everything or not."

Persephone seemed to come to her senses. Snapping from misery's stranglehold, she was again like a curious child. She importuned Phoenix, "But what will it feel like?"

"I don't know," his fire replied. "It will feel . . . mortal. But your death won't be painful like mine."

"I'm so sorry—"

"Stop. You've apologized for my death a million times. It's time to let go. We both must let go. Go unto the vessels awaiting us."

"I love you," she gasped.

Blue fire wrapped her tight. "So you do, and so you shall. And I shall love you in return. Eternity awaits."

Persephone turned to the Liminal edge once more, silver tears glistening. "Show me how to proceed. I know you require sacrifice, so tell me—"

"My Lady," Beatrice murmured in sad realization. "You *are* the sacrifice."

Persephone stood on the threshold, wavering. "So I am."

The shadows nearly exploded around them. A roaring sound, rattling bones. A flash of red. Darkness was nearly upon them. They had to go before he surmised what was happening.

"I beg you, Liminal, who needs me?" the goddess asked the portal in a small voice.

There was a sparking, answering light to counter the growing, powerful abyss. But the shadows were quickly closing in.

"Now!" Beatrice cried, and she grabbed hold of the goddess and threw them both into the void.

Chapter Twenty-nine

The roar grew deafening, a blaze of light, and Beatrice and Persephone tumbled forward, hard, onto stones. They hissed, sharply, opened their eyes and struggled to their feet. Then the two gasped, for they were surrounded by more blood. Fresh, human blood.

"Oh my," Persephone breathed, looking down at the source. Her fear seemed to vanish, replaced by the need to be luminous and strong for the woman before her whom the Liminal had apparently decided needed the intervention of a divinity. "Who did this to you, dear girl?" she asked. In the mortal world, the goddess was again clean, all swaths of red silk.

There was a broken woman in a threadbare dress lying at an angle impossible for the human body; broken but alive. She was young, lovely, redheaded and fair-skinned. Squinting, she stared up in wonder at the two women who had quite literally fallen from the sky, backlit as they were by a huge door. The Liminal remained open, and its light was strong at Beatrice's back. Its humming vibrations felt much like the Phoenix fire once had in her veins.

Beatrice turned, suddenly unable to look. The image mirrored Jean, lying in his own blood on the Cairo stones. A hand flew to her mouth.

"Bill," said the young woman. The woman gestured upward with her chin. "He's gone now, I suppose. Run. He's in the drink again. I-I don't think he quite meant to push me."

Beatrice glanced up. They were in the courtyard of an old inn, and three floors of whitewashed balconies rose above them, their timbers settling in uneven joints. There was no one there, the doors all closed and the shades drawn. An eerie, deadly hush had fallen.

Anger swelled in Beatrice's heart. No one had come to help this poor broken body. Would this woman have been left there to die alone, abandoned by cowards who feared danger or the law? Not that women fared well under the law, not when abusers were the ones more often protected. Damn the miseries and injustices of the Whisper-world, there was plenty of that and more on Earth.

"We are here to help," the goddess stated. Persephone's anxiety, pain and madness were entirely forgotten; all her attention was on this broken woman. Beatrice was oddly touched by this selflessness.

"Think of someplace important to you . . ." The goddess paused, cycling colours, intuiting something. "*Iris.* You're Iris, aren't you? Lovely name."

The young woman nodded, grateful to be known.

"Someplace safe, think of it *now*," the goddess continued, scooping the young woman into her arms. An instant later, the Liminal blazed bright and they were transported.

The sensation was whirling and light-filled, but when they touched down Beatrice was steady on her feet. They were in a stone room furnished only with a cot and a chair. The goddess did not blink or pause but laid the woman upon the cot.

She urged her patient back onto the pillows, imploring her to relax and lie still. The young woman obediently did so, and Persephone's prismatic shifts of light grew more subtle, less manic. Iris's blood vanished.

"Tell me about this place," Persephone said. She sat at the edge of the bed and brushed hair out of the young woman's face. "Tell me where we are, and all about you."

The young woman glanced around the room, down at her body, unsoiled and unbroken. She touched her abdomen, stared up at the goddess and spoke softly, in awe. "M-my name is Iris Parker, and we're in the north of England, where my family landed after a failed time in Ireland. This is the convent where they sent me before I ran off and fell in with sinners. Oh, Holy Mother, I beg your forgiveness of all my sins!"

"You are forgiven everything, child," Persephone said, assuming the identity Iris needed her to be. "A child named for the rainbow. Beautiful Iris, God loves you."

Beatrice hung back in the shadows as Iris began to weep; the scene was too sudden and intimate to disrupt.

"No need to cry, unless it is for joy," Persephone said with a smile. "You've been chosen for a great task."

"I have?" the young woman asked.

"Yes, Iris. You shall bring something great into the world. I give my rainbow unto you, and all my colours together shall be a bright and brilliant white."

This woman seemed so much younger than Beatrice, though they were about the same age. The responsibility of The Guard had put years between their hearts and minds. "Why me?" she asked.

"Because the heavens said you needed me," Persephone replied. "And I need you, too. Very much. You will bear a child."

The goddess stood. Her light brightened, though Beatrice remained in shadow and silently watched. She'd only seen such transparent emotion on the face of Ahmed, and she found herself caught off guard and inordinately touched by that of Iris. Perhaps by watching other people's emotions she encountered her own. Iris Parker's face lit, as if a child was all she'd ever wanted.

Persephone continued. "A child like no other, she will offer hearts peace, and she will triumph against Darkness despite obstacles and iniquity. She escapes a prison of her soul to be reborn in love. She will make a life of pain into a life of love, a life that she was denied."

The goddess wept as she spoke, glistening tears rolling down her cheek. She cupped her hand at her sternum, and Beatrice saw her palm glimmer silver wherever the tears pooled.

"Wh-what shall I call the child?" Iris breathed, not for a moment questioning her destiny. Beatrice wondered at that. Though, perhaps if she'd had her own life so obviously saved, she wouldn't question fate either.

The goddess blushed. "I ought to be more original, but I am too fond. Call her Persephone as . . . it is my favourite of all names. And when the girl is ready, she'll go and find the Power and the Light. It is destined. And now, dear girl, sleep. In the morning you will not be alone."

She opened her hand, and something trickled free that her tears had made manifest. It was a silver chain bearing a phoenix pendant, wings outstretched and fiery tail arched artfully. The bird refused to be consumed by fire, instead wielding it as a weapon. The silver faintly glowed.

Persephone kissed Iris's forehead and clasped the pendant about her neck. As the girl's eyes closed, heavy, the goddess crossed to Beatrice and said, "I need you to listen very carefully to what I'm about to say. If you fail, perhaps all we've done will be for naught."

Beatrice stared. Fear of her own limitations seized her and she echoed Iris: "Why me?"

The goddess returned her stare. "Why not you? Are you not capable of great things? Did you not think that, when you asked the heavens to clarify that most grand of all human questions, 'Why am I here, and what is my purpose,' that the heavens might actually respond?"

Beatrice swallowed. She had not. But she did not back down from the goddess's gaze.

Satisfied, Persephone continued. "I cannot be too careful. Darkness has sentinels and drastic measures. It's why I've never done this before. I've been too scared about what it might unleash upon the earth."

Beatrice shivered. "What sorts of things?"

"Terrible things. Hounds of hell that your lot thankfully has had never to deal with—and I pray he doesn't let loose. Horsemen, riding up from the river of Death itself. What you see as a violent storm, I see as dread horsemen riding the clouds and seeking to drown souls in an undertow of misery."

"Do you mean all these things will pursue poor Iris Parker?"

Persephone shook her head. "Time in the Whisper-world is different. Darkness will not perceive my absence right away, nor will he pinpoint one random mortal. Iris, and you, will be safe. Though, haunted. I fear you'll be quite haunted."

"But when he realizes you've abandoned—"

"Yes, Beatrice. There will be war."

"War." Beatrice's already cold blood froze at what sounded absurd. "*War* is a good time to cast aside divinity and become mortal?!"

"It's the only way, Beatrice. Phoenix was right. I cannot foil Darkness otherwise. A stranger can, so that stranger I shall become. I've been knitting the worlds, readying for the Phoenix fire and the time when that eerie little girl becomes a woman ready to receive her fate."

Beatrice was amazed by the change in the goddess's demeanor. All faltering youth and naive fear had evaporated, replaced by determination.

"For safety's sake," Persephone continued, "cover traces of her birth. Iris Parker should arrive at that convent in York, the one from the vision. The reverend mother there will know what to do because I'm about to proclaim it to her." She lifted up a different chain, this one with a silver key sparkling in the moonlight. "This key. From The Guard's sacred space it will reveal the terrain of the Whisper-world and the location of The Guard prison. Leave it in an empty, infant grave next to the real grave of Iris Parker."

Beatrice started. "Grave? But you've saved her."

"The girl in my visions is an orphan. I do not think Iris survives the birth," Persephone said sadly, staring at the woman. Moonlight fell upon her sleeping head like a halo.

"You've saved her only to kill her?"

"You saw me ask the Liminal what mortal needed me most. Who am I to question?"

Beatrice couldn't find words. This work defied right and wrong, joy and sadness, life and death. Fair or not, she could not question. The Liminal ruled. And Beatrice supposed dying alone in a heap of blood was far worse than dying as the mother of a prophecy. Iris could perhaps go more directly to that heaven for which she pined, feeling like one of its angels.

Persephone continued. "You must go now. Take Iris someplace safe. Not here where the Liminal deposited us; Whisper-world agents may trace the scent of me."

She shuddered and continued. "Don't bring her to London, either. Darkness's emissaries can sniff out The Guard if they try hard enough, and a vulnerable child will do them no good. I must come—*she* must come—to them as a woman ready to take up her mantle." The goddess looked away. "I thought I could come to him now, matured. I thought I'd simply take a body, remembering exactly who I am and what we're to do. Now I see the timing's off. In those first visions I just didn't see it, or realize. With her unusual pallor, the distance between their mortal ages . . . I should have tried sooner."

She couldn't mask the pain in her voice, but steeling herself she continued: "I'm going to go appear to that reverend mother and make sure that an odd child born like starlight and snow shall, when she is a woman, take her place with the gods at

Athens. And I'll pray that she's loved by he who is meant to love her. So, business to attend. I've prophecies to proclaim, and I must also . . . say good-bye."

Beatrice shook her head. "Be mindful of mortal time," she cautioned. "Remember you're not good at it."

"When it matters, I am." The goddess placed her hand on Beatrice's shoulder, and Beatrice felt how it trembled. "Can I trust you to remain here and wait for me?"

Beatrice swallowed and nodded. She had little else to live for. All else had abandoned her.

"I'll return before morning. Thank you. Thank you for pushing me out into this world. I needed it. I've needed you."

Beatrice nodded again. It was nice to be thanked and needed. It eased the sting of the bittersweet wound that had defined her life. Thinking of Persephone, she wondered if The Grand Work would also define her death.

Chapter Thirty

"This is the last time, Alexi," came a voice at his bedside.

Alexi looked up and saw a goddess. *The* goddess. Then came the crashing memories again, all the ones she'd taken away, along with all the pent-up passion. He winced, squeezed back the tears that were there anyway, the slamming of all those emotions back into his body like punches to the face and insides. Heart in his throat, he was unable to speak, clutching at his long grey nightclothes.

"Come," she said with a smile—that beautiful smile—and touched his temple.

Alexi blinked. They had been transported. He always felt as though he were in another world when he was with her, but this time he truly was.

A subtle, sweet scent filled the air. There was nothing in his view but a rolling purple heath and her, all light and colour and breathlessness. Heather rolled away from them in gently bending waves, rustling; a subtle-scented flower by itself, in a field their scent was powerful.

Eyes fixed upon him, she sank to her knees. This supplicating posture made him clench his fists, trying to control his need, and he sank down beside her.

She lay back. As she did, her diaphanous gown shifted about her like a glowing cloud. Stretching her limbs, shapely and relaxed, she closed her eyes, breathed in the heather and sighed.

Her colours were shifting slower and slower; her breathing was strained. Her health declined. How could a goddess grow ill? Perhaps there was a limit to how long a being of light could live as stolen goods in a dark world for which she was not meant. Alexi felt sure that was the truth.

"Heather," she said at last. "It can grow in dim, gloomy climes; its loveliness refuses to submit to shadow. It is a flower that represents me well."

He lay back beside her, close enough to feel her shifting temperatures, warm then cool, depending on the colour. Reaching out, he took her hand. Her delicate form was so near, he strained to stay sensible, was choked with fear of saying the wrong thing. And yet he could not help himself.

"If you leave," he murmured, "and take my memories from me, please do me the courtesy of taking my heart. Cut it from me. It's a pointless instrument without you." He tried to suppress desperation and speak with the dispassion he retained in his day-to-day life, but such detachment was impossible around her.

She shifted her head against a tuft of heather, staring up at him, smiling in that maddening way with love, pity and sorrow. "You'll need your heart. For her."

"For Prophecy? When you declared a seventh member to us, I felt sure that love was involved. Is this true?"

"Yes."

"Surely then, you?"

The goddess struggled. "Her breath will whisper of me. Her light will call down my strength. Her love will be boundless."

Alexi furrowed his brow. "But she will not be you?"

"She will be what you need, and you what she needs. Shall you yet argue? You break my heart as you fight me, eroding my resolve to do what I must. Would *you* so easily give up this life for the chance at another?"

Not expecting that, he sat stunned. Opening his mouth to express his heart only made things worse. He would say nothing. Choking back a torrent of declamations, he balled his fists in clumps of heather.

Her resulting chuckle was almost more maddening. "Oh, Alexi, look at you! Such impassioned intensity, my brooding, tormented hero. I daresay your enigmatic nature will make some young romantic fall quite helplessly and passionately in love with you."

Alexi frowned. When she giggled, his frown turned to a scowl.

"Have I offended you?" she breathed. "Oh, come now, such a face!"

"I'm practicing," he retorted.

She stared a moment before laughing gaily and running a hand through his mop of black hair. "There's hope for you yet."

"Well, I'd like to be fallen for helplessly and passionately, so I'll do whatever you suggest."

Persephone grinned. "You shall be successful. Hold me."

A Leader capable of giving sure instruction, he rarely received it. Now he obeyed. Covetously. He lay holding her close, breathing deeply and trying to catalog every last detail, even if those would be removed from his memory. In the moment his keenest desire was to do whatever she wanted. She yearned to be touched, and so he did, running fingertips over and along her. Everywhere. Doing this gave him transcendent pleasure, and he gave over to it. Again, the touch was not carnal but loving, but it most certainly satisfied.

And yet, his heart was not whole. He had been abandoned by his family. He was a young man to whom everyone looked for answers, from whom everyone asked something. He wanted something of his own.

"Promise me that when Prophecy comes she won't be taken away. Promise me something that's mine, a haven I can rely on.

If she, too, will be taken away, as you take yourself and these memories, I swear to you I'll go mad. Give me something I can *keep*."

"I have seen your future," the goddess replied. "I promise."

"So, why not tell me everything?"

"It's ruined if I do! The forces at work would punish us. Nor should I deny you the mortal joy, pain and wonder that is falling in love. You must make your own mistakes and fashion your own victories. You must be given the freedom of choice or none of it will take. Rest assured there is a plan. I shall live again in hope."

"If there is a plan, how are we to follow it?"

She fought back silver tears. "That is for you to learn. But, be careful. I've been warned of betrayals, that mortal hearts are fallible. I dare not pin your hopes on anything that may yet change, not when your capacity for choice is what makes Prophecy come true. Divine machinations must agree that two lonely mortals find and love each other on their own."

She kissed him. After a long, delicious moment he drew back. "You're here with me," he pleaded. "Why can't you just stay with me?"

"Because this form is tied to the Whisper-world. I am bound to two worlds, and I must break those bonds. Besides, what I have seen must come to pass. You *must* love your own kind." She leaned over him. "You'll be wonderful. You'll have something wonderful. I promise."

Before he could fight her final good-bye, all went black in deep sleep.

★ ★ ★

"I love you. She'll love you. Let me go," Persephone whispered. Then Alexi was slumbering.

Once she had returned him to his bed, she did not need to

be strong for him anymore. Her shoulders fell as she wept. "I need to change that letter."

Ascending the stairs, she wandered to the little room she had seen in her vision, withdrawing her previous note from its hiding place. Her silver tears wiped clean the ink, and she began again. She finished by folding and marking the letter *The Rychmans*, tucking it back where her vision had seen it fall upon snow-white feet.

Moving through the dark estate, she stood and gazed one last time upon Alexi at his bedside. As she did, blue fire began to pour out of him. It was Phoenix, amassing himself before her.

"I'm scared to die, my love," she whispered.

The voice of Phoenix was choked. "Oh, love, I'm as scared and devastated as you. I lose *this* you. I'll never see you like this again." His fire raced over her, trying to clutch her, to seize her in the form he had first and always loved. "When I settle into him next, I will give over to him. I will defer to him, have no control. Without you to command me, I'm only the fire he wields, nothing more. Now we must trust two mortals full of Power and Light to find each other. Like you and I once did."

"I know. It's what must be done. They must be left to it. They are so beautiful, he and she."

"We are so beautiful, you and I," Phoenix declared.

They stood in an aching good-bye that would birth a new dawn, murmuring their love as a mantra to strengthen their resolve. Eternity indeed awaited, perhaps Peace like they'd never known.

A bright light suffused the room, and the Liminal drew Persephone away. It was nearing the end of her, but she went willingly. Iris Parker, mother, instrument, awaited. As did a new dawn.

Phoenix sank back into Alexi. Doing so, he was absorbed, erased. At least until he and his beloved met again. When they would be called to be gods once more.

Chapter Thirty-one

Persephone's light woke Beatrice, whose head had slumped against the stone wall. It was still dark. Iris Parker slept, peaceful.

The goddess knelt. She took Beatrice's hand, captured her gaze with those prismatic eyes. "I pray that when all is said and done there may be no more need for a Guard, that the difficult questions of The Grand Work will never again plague mortals. In the meantime, do remember its goodness, its beauty. Remember this in the future, when the most harrowing things are asked of you."

Beatrice shuddered, wondering what ominous things were yet to be learned. Persephone kissed her hands briefly, then let go. A complex torrent passed over the goddess's face, emotions amplified by her youthful divinity.

"Remember blood and fire," she continued. "When you are called again, please come and help. The choice will be yours. Our fates are tied, Leader." The goddess's tears might have made many divine talismans had she caught them, but they rolled like tiny gems onto the floor and away, perhaps to sprout flowers in the field beyond. "I can't wait any longer else I'm truly a coward. To the undiscovered country!"

So, it came down to this instant, where things would change forever. Beatrice held her breath. Persephone moved to the foot of the bed, toward Iris Parker. Her colours shifted less rapidly.

"Let it, at last, in ending, begin," she breathed.

The room blazed with crackling threads of light that Beatrice recognized as those from the Liminal threshold and came alive with the music of heaven, choruses of angels praising all Persephone was and what she and her kind served. The light was too bright, and she had to close her eyes and look away.

"Oh! It *will* be beautiful," came a final, joyful epitaph. Then darkness and silence.

Beatrice opened her eyes. The light had drawn ghosts into the room, and they gazed at Iris in awe, in seeming confirmation that she was now a new mother-to-be. The room grew chill with their presence.

Beatrice sat wide-eyed in the corner. She couldn't be bothered with the spirits; they seemed harmless enough, and there was nothing she could do to deter them. Sleep eventually took her, when she could ponder what she had witnessed no longer.

At dawn she awoke. Pulling her chair to Iris Parker's bedside, she glanced at the ghosts and batted her hands at them. They remained staring, enraptured, Beatrice supposed, by the lovely young woman bearing an instrument of peace. Beatrice herself wondered at that, at the fate of the imminent child who might or might not have any concept of who she was, who she might become. The mortal child of an immortal being.

Iris woke with a start. Beatrice placed her hand on the young woman's forehead. "Do not be afraid," she said.

"For you bring great tidings?"

Beatrice's lips thinned at the recited scripture. "Something like that. My name is Beatrice. I'm here to see you safely to your final destination."

Iris nodded, looked around in amazement. She saw the ghosts. The room grew increasingly cold as more appeared, floating peacefully, watching, reverent. "Spirits! Like in the magazines! I've had stories read to me whenever anyone might humour me. I've always wanted to see a ghost like in those tales."

Beatrice herself wished she couldn't. Not when she could not do anything about them.

"You must wait here, Miss Parker, and rest. I shall fetch us some things in London, as our fates are now entwined." She shook her head and gave a weary chuckle. "My friends will think me dead. I'll return to you soon."

At the door, she turned. "If the spirits frighten you, hold to that pendant of yours. It is your guardian angel, the only power we have left."

"We've all the power of heaven," Iris breathed.

"You hold tight to that certainty, my dear." Beatrice wished she was as confident.

Chapter Thirty-two

Restless, Belle was near the door just as there came a knock upon it. Flinging it open revealed Beatrice beneath a wide umbrella that she wielded against the insistent rain.

"There you are!" the French girl cried in relief. Embracing her, she hurried Beatrice inside, took her accoutrements and immediately fussed over some tea. "I was very worried about you! You disappeared! What was I to think? Where were you?"

Beatrice replied, "The goddess whisked me away to the Whisper-world." Adjusting the folds of her traveling skirt to sit at the polished wooden bar she added, "And when the Whisper-world spat me back out again, I was in the north. I've only a moment. A packed trunk sits in a waiting carriage."

Belle gaped. "What? The Whisper-world? Isn't that forbidden? Isn't that supposed to drive you mad, going in there as a mortal? And, where are you going that you've packed a trunk?"

"There is a Whisper-world threshold few mortals see, a terrible, awesome place. And now I'm caring for a mother-to-be. Much is yet needed of me," Beatrice said into her cup. "No rest for the wicked."

"You're hardly wicked, and you're not making much sense. What was it like there?"

"At the edge of the Whisper-world? It was like a stage, a proscenium arch, and I sensed that from it all things may be possible—with sacrifice. That's the way of life we have come to understand, isn't it? Strange, awesome beauty; painful sacrifice.

I watched visions of the future, watched as our Lady realized she won't come again to this earth as herself but entirely wiped clean. Her powers must pass on in some form, but she, no. Not as herself. It was . . . difficult. And now she's gone."

"Who—?"

"The goddess is gone. A young woman is pregnant in the north, and I have to make sure she ends up at York. There she'll bear a mortal child—what's left of the goddess we knew. Then I must leave her to her fate."

Belle blinked. "The goddess is gone? She made mention of turning a new leaf, of a new dawn, but . . ." Tears appeared in her eyes. "Is there anything I can do?"

"No. The seeds of Prophecy are already being put into place. After this, even my role is limited. But first I must return to the side of young Iris Parker and make sure she arrives safely in York. Not that she will survive much longer. Her mortal coil will also be sacrificed to this Grand Work. A Work that gives and takes life so freely . . ."

Belle shook her head, dismayed. "Would you like me to go with you?"

Beatrice smiled. It was a wan look. "You're a dear, Belle. But no, I need to be on my own. This is my cross to bear, and I am unfit for company. But I did want to tell you. I wanted someone to know should I . . ."

Belle clutched her hand. "Being a Leader is an oft lonely fate."

Beatrice did not argue.

"Poor Iris," she murmured. "Full of loving faith. Such a joyous soul for such a hard life, she shames me with her fortitude, with her blind trust. I believe she knows she's going to die. She's right haunted. Ghosts flocked to her immediately, fascinated, knowing she holds something special. The spirits aren't malevolent but taxing. It's a good thing, too, as I've no power by which to guard her. Nothing but a talisman the goddess left before she passed on. *In.* Passed in, rather. Into mortality."

Beatrice spoke as if to herself, in a reverie, but her glazed eyes eventually focused back on her friend. "So, pray for me. For us. I don't know if I can trust in prayer, but I need *some* help as I take her to York. It's supposed to be far enough from London so that the child won't be caught up in Grand Work but close enough for her to come when she's a woman, ready to love and ready to take charge.

"Timid though," Beatrice added with a shudder. "She looked so timid. I pray that once she comes into The Guard's care, into the Leader's care, that she is bolstered, that those ice-blue eyes blaze with confident power. I'd hate to think that the fate of every Guard rests solely in those trembling, awkward, ghost-pale hands. But nothing's certain. We can plant seeds but the rains still have to come. Prophecy must have room to grow."

Belle blinked, lost. "I cannot presume to understand a word of this, but I can most certainly pray for a joyous result after all our sacrifices. Though, I'll be the first to say that my fate has been a blessing." Her blush indicated thoughts of George. "But tell me of your heart before you go. How *are* you?"

"I'm fine," Beatrice replied.

Belle just looked at her. She refilled Beatrice's tea. She kept looking.

"I'm fine," Beatrice repeated.

"You loved him," Belle accused. When Beatrice blinked then scowled, the French girl pursed her lips. "Oh, you and your pride. The look on your face when you showed me his letter said it all. All that we never said—"

"He is gone from my life. What more is there to say?"

Belle shrugged. "Your countryman Dickens claims that 'life is full of meetings and partings.' Even the new Leader says so."

"And?"

"He leaves out reunions."

"He's not coming back," Beatrice said sharply.

"Beatrice, you two are suited. Like it or not, you are. Elegant, stubborn, strong and true. If he doesn't come back, you must go to Cairo."

"I'm not about to chase him! He clearly doesn't care for me, and I don't want to hear another word about it." Beatrice turned. "It's good to see you, Belle. I'll return once the child is born and poor Iris Parker's body's in the ground."

She gave a choked noise, kissed Belle softly on the head, snatched her umbrella and fled back out into the rain.

Chapter Thirty-three

For Ibrahim, the passing months were hell.

An onlooker would surmise him a young man in control of his destiny, a savvy traveler and son of the world. Inside, he was filled with fear and regrets that were eating him alive. He had two choices: ignore the past year of his life, or embrace it as his defining hour and risk whatever was to come. Declare himself to a magnificent woman, despite his vision, and to see what she would say.

He had an inkling that she cared. Surely he couldn't have imagined it. But likely she cared no longer, not in the way he did. She was an Englishwoman, he an Egyptian and they'd damnably never spoken about this sort of thing, so what did he truly know? To love or not to love. That was the question. Hamlet-like, perhaps. How English.

Ahmed and Verena's company was ever pleasant, but watching them grow joyfully closer was its own agony. They never made him feel unwelcome, but there were moments of awkward sadness. Verena once dared ask of Beatrice. When Ibrahim made no reply, she was a subject not brought up again. But the Leader was there, silently, in all of their hearts. As were Belle and George. Their beloved circle was broken but still considered.

Ibrahim was there to celebrate when, beneath a particularly incredible moon, Verena agreed to be Ahmed's wife. When Ibrahim asked how they'd manage their different faiths, Ahmed pointedly reminded him that the Prophet said a man might marry any chaste woman "of the book"—those Abrahamic faiths included Jews and Christians as people of the book. Abraham. *Ibrahim*. Perhaps his namesake was telling.

"Besides," Ahmed exclaimed, "The Grand Work brings strangers together to weave new understandings. There are personal truths: our love truths, our respective faiths. Then there is the truth of our mutual love born within the Power and the Light. It would be a shame and its own sin to deny that, would it not?"

Ibrahim couldn't help but agree, though he was uncomfortable with the way Ahmed eyed him. Ahmed didn't need a Muse to be powerful; he was naturally adept at penetrating the human heart.

Months passed. Time blurred, and Ibrahim became numb. He did not allow himself to think of Beatrice. He was only jarred back into focus when, one evening, Ahmed spoke to the point. They stood on the balcony ledge of Ibrahim's rented rooms.

"Your vision. What you assume was Beatrice's death. We are not gods able to know the circumstances. You share little of your heart with me, but I read your eyes, the corners of your mouth, the tone of your voice . . . You're a different man here in Cairo without her. You're increasingly like the ghosts we once fought. The fact remains, you cannot take her hand in Cairo when she lives in England. And I do believe, no matter what you saw, that you should take her hand."

Ibrahim opened his mouth to protest, but Ahmed waved him off. At the same time, Verena entered with tea and said boldly, "Staring down death made me discard subtlety. Go back for her, you lovely fool."

"I can't." Ibrahim choked, as if the desert took hold of his throat. A painful, wrenching feeling. "The vision of Beatrice going death-scale grey . . . It is too terrible to tempt, to test. I believe she's safer if I remain far away."

No more was said on the subject, and time again blurred.

Months passed before she was again addressed, in a letter from Belle and George via Ahmed. In it, Belle wasted no time in getting to the point.

Mr. Wasil-Tipton,

I understand you wrote to our beloved Miss Smith and severed ties. While I think this cowardly, I trust you have reasons. Despite those, please understand what your prolonged absence has done. Beatrice is a ghost of what she once was. Her pride would never admit it, but as friend to both of you it's time someone was honest. She needs her pillar, her second-in-command.

I believe it is proper to tell you this. Beatrice is currently engaged in The Grand Work. The goddess as we knew her is no more. Did you feel the storms in Cairo, or do you shun the traces of our power like you do our Leader? They alert George and I to divine movements. The goddess will be born mortal. Ghosts swarm around her expectant mother, and Beatrice protects her far from London along the coast, then inland onto York. I asked if we could help, but she adamantly refused. I do not think she would refuse you.

Despite your vision, you do more harm than good by staying away. You could read to these ghosts, just as you did to Verena when our powers had gone. You could still be of service, keeping them civil and passive. Could you not try to be our Leader's companion—in any and every way she needs? She will take no other. Or are you truly as lost to us all as you would seem?

Here the script changed:

This is George. Must I paint you a picture of what is required? Don't be stupid. Hie thee back to England.

Ibrahim laughed. It felt so very good to laugh, to feel tears rimming his eyes with such happy release. Was his beloved truly so struck by his absence? It did not solve his fear of harming her, but he felt his insides twist, constrict and rejoice in all manner of exquisite pain.

Belle spoke truth; an echo of his previous power remained. Instinct flooded him. Assisting his Leader was the right thing to do. He'd foolishly donned a mantle of misery out of fear. He could help on this haunted journey of Persephone's transformation, and having seen the danger in advance, perhaps he could keep his treasure safe. He would be a coward not to return, bearing his words as a gentleman's sword and a brimming heart unto a worthy hand.

★ ★ ★

Alexi often wandered the streets as if looking for something, but only ghosts stared back. He could never remember what he sought, so in these moments he always ended at the same place.

Michael Carroll had small rooms in a parish-owned town house. Because Alexi quite frequently burst into them, he'd begun mulling wine as his father had always done for friends and family. It gave the two of them something to fiddle with, and a bit of alcohol seemed to take the edge off Alexi's middling powers of communication.

"Faith isn't something I can explain," Michael insisted. Alexi took a draught of wine. "You just have to *have* it, Alexi, and I think you do. Trust that. You're a good Leader."

Alexi said nothing. At these meetings, Michael uncannily knew what he needed to hear. A young man of two worlds, Alexi was a logical, rational mind confronted with the impossibility of his situation. He had two minds if one heart, and he wished the three would work more effectively in conjunction.

"Our fates will fall into place, Alexi. There are storms to come, for certain. We'll meet them. But whatever you do, keep yourself whole. You'll need all your logic as well as the Power and the Light; this is not just about the immortal but the mortal. Never give The Grand Work anything but your whole self; else we'll all end up in pieces."

Alexi yearned for wholeness to mend his disparate pieces, edges that chafed. He couldn't be sure who or what would provide the binding, but there was something. Someone? A key yet to turn a great lock.

Chapter Thirty-four

Belle opened the door of La Belle et La Bête to an insistent knock. She and George had spent a late night at the theatre; then, having to themselves a café full of wine had proven its dangers.

"Ibrahim!" she exclaimed, flinging wide the door. He was well-appointed in a new suit coat and vest, looking every bit the Englishman as he'd looked Egyptian in Cairo. But this man of two worlds worried on her doorstep.

She eyed him warily. "What are you doing here?"

"I was struck by your letter. I . . . I've come back."

Belle just stared, waiting for him to continue.

"I . . . am worried for Beatrice."

"You should be," Belle exclaimed, her French accent suited to scolding. "You should've seen her face after your letter after months of waiting, keeping her heart captive!" She gestured that he enter, for a teapot began to scream. "What are you going to do about it?"

"If her work is as you've said, then I agree that it remains my duty to offer assistance. I'll simply . . . be very careful. I won't ever take her hand in my own. In my vision I clutched her hand and she died."

Belle's eyes flashed. "You won't 'take her hand . . .' Metaphorically or literally? Vision or no, to base your future on that one detail is a bit absurd. Tell me the truth. Why you're really here."

"I told you. To help her."

"What changed?"

Ibrahim couldn't hold Belle's gaze. "Ahmed reminded me that visions may have multiple truths and variable interpretations." He cleared his throat and admitted, "Because, truth be told, I am miserable without her."

"That's better." Belle brightened so swiftly her aspect mirrored that of the goddess. "Tea?"

Ibrahim shook his head. "Women. You are enigmas."

"No, we're just always waiting for men to say the proper thing. Now and then you do. And upon such occasion, we rejoice." She slid a warm cup in a delicate saucer across the bar.

"What's all this racket before noon?" George called. His freckled face lit with happiness as he came into view. "Ho-ho, Ibrahim, my friend. You're back! Love it or hate it, The Grand Work can't keep us apart, even when we're done with it!" He came bounding down the stairs to pump Ibrahim's hand with a hard, jovial shake, and gave him a strong pat on the back for good measure.

Belle pulled out a notebook and launched into particulars before Ibrahim could ask. "Beatrice spoke of a general route—convents, safe places for two women. Along the east, ending likely inland at York. A Catholic convent. Can't be too many of those, so that narrows things down nicely." She scrawled names and locations.

"Did you . . . know I would come when you wrote?" Ibrahim was agog.

"I prayed you would. You should have seen her in your absence. I could have slapped you. I've never seen such hollow sadness on so regal a face."

"She was so visibly affected?" Ibrahim asked, trying to sound nonchalant.

Belle sighed, irritated. "Neither of you is capable of showing it when you're in the same room, but she's been heartbroken! Thorny and defensive . . ." Belle grinned. "If there's one thing I know, its love in all its many colours. She's *deeply* in love."

George grinned goofily as if this conversation were the best sport ever. Ibrahim pursed his lips, though his already careening sensibilities reeled anew. He tried to maintain his usual reserve; it would not do to come undone.

"The English think they invented civilization," Ibrahim muttered, "and the French think they invented love?"

Belle and George laughed heartily. "Of course!" Belle cried, kissing George full on the mouth. "And together we could rule the world with passion!"

Ibrahim cleared his throat again. There had been a great many thoughts of kissing on the return trip to Cairo, thoughts that had kept him up at night. He wondered that any human being could stand the idea of caring for someone, of needing someone, of wanting someone. Apart from James Tipton, he had been an independent, solitary person with few meaningful connections until The Grand Work. Now, a life alone would not satisfy. Not once one had the experience of being so peculiarly tied to other human souls. To such a soul as Beatrice Smith.

"My dear friend, has that golden skin of yours paled?" George laughed and then sobered, scowling, though his bright eyes still playfully twinkled. "I'm sorry. We should not be so sporting with you. This is a serious matter. The two of you. Serious people—"

"The two of us nothing. I returned because I'm compelled to assist her work," Ibrahim barked. Defensive. Terrified. They *were* suited.

"And so you shall," Belle said, producing a leather pocketbook full of banknotes from under the bar. "Take this." She glanced at George and added, "When I had my powers, George convinced me to withdraw a ridiculous amount from the bank when we first arrived and I've felt guilty about it ever since. Help me pay penance. Use it for travel. Buy Beatrice something lovely. Give it to orphans." She tore her annotated paper from the notebook, placed it atop the pocketbook and said, "Here are the names she cited. Now, go on with you."

Ibrahim nodded. "Thank you both, I shall see you anon. Together we all shall celebrate the culmination of The Grand Work. Whatever our parts in it may be."

In his pocket was the key to the Athens library, where he would gather his meager spectral weapons. A few more errands and he would be on his way.

★ ★ ★

Ibrahim gone, Belle waxed rhapsodic. "What will their reunion be like—reserved or tender? Will they greet each other with civility or passion?"

George leaned upon the bar, grinning. "Passion? They don't know the meaning of the word."

"Oh, don't underestimate the stoic," Belle giggled. "Behind closed doors their kisses are often the most torrid!"

While clearing fallen window-box petals in front of the café, she was still imagining the possibilities when she saw an unlikely couple turn down the street. Recognizing them instantly, she hid behind the door. It had been many months since their paths had first crossed.

The male, a lean, flaxen-haired youth with sharp features, was dressed finely to the point of gaudiness, while the olive-skinned, dark-haired girl beside him was dressed in more sensible garb. One English, one French. How familiar. Belle wondered if it was a common pattern; the coupling of Memory and Artist.

The Artist's beauty outshone Memory's wealth; her youth was belied only by the two jarring shocks of white hair framing her face. The Grand Work did leave its traces.

Memory looked around. Believing that he and the Artist were in no danger of being discovered, he closed the distance. His sharp features twisted into something devilish, rakish, something surprisingly attractive. "At last, a moment away from that tedious lot. I now gaze upon the only thing that makes this bloody Work bearable."

"Why, Lord Withersby, you flatter me." The Artist giggled, her olive skin flushed. Belle continued working with her broom while she eavesdropped.

"Flattery isn't always untrue. Come now, Josie— May I call you that?"

"Lord Withersby, you've been calling me Josie for months."

"Ah, so I've no manners. But, Josie, you're a balm to my misery. The six of us are to be joined for eternity, and I'd open my veins if not for you. Ruled by that brooding, insufferable Rychman? No title, no ancestral lands, yet he acts as if the heavens themselves opened to appoint him Leader."

"But, Elijah, the heavens did exactly that."

"Don't you play Rebecca and take his part! He doesn't have to be so haughty. I daresay he rubs it in, knowing I'd have twice his status were we not subject to this paranormal meddling!"

"His fine estate aside, a man's worth should be determined by his actions. By what he does." Josephine paused as Elijah loosened his cuffs and waistcoat, and she raised an eyebrow. "Or doesn't."

The French girl suddenly noticed Belle, and she and the Memory turned toward the door of the café. The Memory tipped his hat.

"Good afternoon, mademoiselle, don't mind us, we're simply discussing the more tedious details of our Grand Work—we're spectral police, you see, keeping ghouls at bay by rites and rituals, with inexplicable fire, with music and all manner of incredible trickery." He smiled, believing himself the revelator of great things that he would subsequently wipe from her mind. Lifting his hand, his pale eyes sparkling with preternatural light, he tried to do just that.

Belle grinned, playing along. She allowed her eyes to glaze. Not that she could have retorted if she wanted; the goddess's protective spell yet held.

The Memory turned back to the Artist, his expression triumphant, but she stared up at the sign above her head. "La Belle et La Bête . . ."

The Memory began down the lane, his fine boots clipping against the stones. The Artist lingered.

Belle acted as though she came back to herself, resumed sweeping, shook her head and turned. "Bonjour," she said. The other French girl lit up, and they exchanged a few pleasantries in their native language.

The Memory stopped and turned back, folding his arms. Josephine raised an eyebrow. "Since when is Lord Withersby so keen to return to his fellows? I thought you were taking me for refreshment."

"I had a place in mind," he replied.

When Josephine didn't move, Belle spoke in French. "Sometimes you don't know you're looking for something until you find it." She gestured down the stairs to the open door.

"Here, Lord Withersby," Josephine called. "Here."

When she entered, Lord Withersby, shrugging, traipsed after her. Cordial introductions were made as Belle seated them and procured them some fine French wine.

Josephine looked about appreciatively at the work on the walls, products of George's brush.

"My resident artist," Belle said with a blush, gesturing to the frames.

"Exquisite. Reminds me of someone." Josephine's dark eyes looked into her hazel ones.

"Funny, that," Belle said, pouring wine and holding back a smirk. "Do you like the place?"

"I'm quite taken with it," Josephine breathed.

It was an absurd charade. All of them were able to track the motions of the spirits inhabiting the bar, and there they all were, trying to pretend they couldn't see them. But Belle realized that this was a fated encounter.

"Business is hard, you know. It's a bit out of the way," she said.

Elijah and Josephine replied in chorus. "I like that about the place." Elijah turned his attention to the furnishings.

"Pardon me," Belle said. "I shouldn't be so forward, but I sense you're a lovely young couple, well-intentioned—"

Josephine blushed. "Oh, well, we're not a—"

"And so I'll get to the point. My partner and I plan to leave London. We're looking for someone to take over the place. Do think about it," Belle said.

Either they were there for the goings-on of Prophecy or they weren't. She left the pair with cups of tea and moved up the stairs, allowing them time with their thoughts. On the landing she found George, who'd been listening all the while.

"Leaving? Already?"

Belle shrugged. "I think they should have the place. I may have lost my power, but I certainly haven't lost my instincts."

George twisted to stare at the couple and shook his head again. "Poor sots," he whispered. "We had it easy, Belle, I see now. Those poor fools inherited the hard work for the rest of their bloody lives." He turned and went back to his room.

Unable to resist, Belle continued to spy. She hardly knew them, but she loved this new couple like kin. They *were* kin. Sad that they couldn't know it.

The Memory was leaning over the table excitedly. "Let me buy this place for you, Josie. It's much better than that sordid flat of yours, and it will give us a safe place to occupy ourselves. I can't stand sitting about that *school*. My class insists upon the finer things of life. I was meant for leisure not labour! In the name of dear Saint George and whatever French saint you choose, grant me this safe harbour instead of that echoing Athens institution. A Withersby simply doesn't know how to *exist* without a fine glass of wine. Come now, Josie—"

Josephine's laughter filled the room and Belle's heart. The Memory leaned close to her, trading his constant jokes for an earnest plea. "Let me do something for you, Josie. Don't let the Withersby fortune languish without ever having done something decent. Perhaps you won't allow me to express my thoughts for you in any other way but material goods, but . . ."

There came a pause. "Why? In what other ways would you express your thoughts?" Her tone was heavy with anticipation.

The Memory leaned forward, reaching out a long-fingered hand and cupping Josephine's cheek. He kissed her. It was a tentative kiss, but Belle felt it had been brewing from The Grand Work's commission. She knew the moment well; she'd wanted George in the same way from the very first. All was as it should be, even if the timing had been a bit off, for all of them.

The kiss deepened before Josephine broke away with a gasp. "We mustn't tell a soul about this!" she murmured. "Our stations, our work, it could never be—"

"What, caring for you must be as secret as the rest of my blasted fate?" The Memory scoffed. "Well, I couldn't tell my family, of course—"

Josephine gave him a sharp look. "I don't mean your family. I mean our motley circle. Poor Rebecca only has eyes for Alexi, Alexi only for himself and his work. Michael loves Rebecca, and Jane . . . Well, Jane baffles me. But we cannot be the lone pair—"

"The envy of all." Elijah chuckled.

"We mustn't drive such a wedge between us," Josephine said. "But you, Lord Withersby," she said, leaning close, "come from a class that is expert at keeping secrets."

"Just as you, my dear, are French. And I'll never let you forget it."

"Won't the others suspect, you buying me this place?"

Elijah shrugged. "I'll make Alexi pay half." He lifted his glass and said, "To La Belle et La Bête, our new home away from home!"

It was time; Belle went back downstairs. She rounded the corner just in time to see Elijah sweep Josephine into his arms and spin her about the floor. "We'll take it!" he cried.

Belle smiled. Inside, in her bones, she could feel a storm coming. But here was one safe haven, a place the goddess herself had even blessed, which was why it needed to be passed on.

Chapter Thirty-five

In truth, Beatrice wanted to be found. She wanted to feel she was joined with others in purpose, wanted the knowledge she had friends interested in her safety. For that reason, to her surprise, she missed the appearances of the goddess, random, mysterious, and unannounced. She doubted not that the goddess cared. She missed their maddening interplay.

Desired or not, however, no one was coming to find her, no herald or guardian angel. Lives had moved on. She'd been in London months ago. When young Iris Parker gave birth and passed on, Beatrice's time doing The Grand Work would be entirely forgotten.

For the thousandth time, she debated rushing back to London, finding Alexi Rychman and telling him exactly how it all would come to pass. At least, what little scraps she'd been given. But she also knew that nothing was set in stone. All the planning in the world couldn't make it so, and her tongue was yet shackled by the goddess's hypocritical magic.

Beatrice thought back to the Liminal edge, when the goddess realized she'd be unable to guide Alexi in the ways she'd hoped, unable to remember her lineage. As for Alexi, she couldn't begrudge his falling in love, or making it as natural as possible. True love could not be told to be true. True love was a path to be traveled or not. And seeds could be planted in a forest but there was always the fickle nature of rain.

What of her own heart? Had she fallen in love of her own volition, or had it been something else? Leaders and seconds often did, she remembered. But, no. She felt all the more keenly Ibrahim's loss now that her powers were gone, and he was a world away.

She took some comfort from her task as she and Iris made their way, every few weeks, farther south, convent by convent. Prophecy was progressing as well as it might.

On this day, the conversation was usual. "Good morning, Beatrice," Iris chirped as they took their tea and warm breakfast oats. "Are we relocating today?"

"If not today, tomorrow. We've grown weary of the ghosts of these walls, have we not? They grow more numerous each day, so fascinated with you! I daresay you're the spirit world's most popular mother."

"I wonder why that's so," Iris mused, then suddenly smiled. "No. I *know* why. It's because of my child, my Percy. Isn't that an endearing nickname for Persephone? I know it's a boy's name, but it will be special and unique like her. My child will be a child of peace. Of love. She will be the sort of girl who sets souls at ease. Human souls, and perhaps others, too. That's why the spirits flock here."

"I do believe you are correct," Beatrice replied, propping Iris against the headboard. "Are you feeling well?"

"Oh, heavy and stiff. Pain comes here and there. But, I think she's healthy. I'd know if she wasn't. I'm sure the pain comes from being raised from the dead to bear her," Iris added, with a surprising matter-of-factness. "And I know, Beatrice, that my time is short."

How awful. Beatrice opened her mouth to protest, but Iris continued joyfully.

"No, it's all right, I was saved for this purpose. I'm utterly at peace, Beatrice Smith, so don't you cry over me. You may cry for yourself, certainly, for I see your heart is heavy. You may tell me your troubles if you've a mind."

Beatrice fought back amazement at her perception. "No,

you keep your lovely mind and heart focused on that baby. Give her all your energy, and fill her tiny heart with love. She'll need all the love afforded her. It's a dark world into which she'll be born."

"She'll fill it with light," Iris promised.

"That she will. But she'll need your strength. She will likely be odd. Fragile."

"The meek shall inherit the earth."

"And so they shall," Beatrice murmured.

To herself, she wondered about the haunted. The dead, and hearts like her own. What would they inherit?

She kissed Iris on the forehead, because she could not help how fond she'd grown of her. Then she exited the room, envying the girl her faith, trust, joy and acceptance.

★ ★ ★

That afternoon, just as Beatrice was considering whether or not to set off or wait another day, there was a surprise as a sister came to their door. "There's a gentleman here to see you, Miss Smith. We aren't supposed to let men in, but he was so insistent, saying he's sought you for some time now, all down the English coast. He's just out in the hall, but, miss, he's a *foreigner!* I—"

Beatrice's heart convulsed in her chest, and she nearly pushed past the girl without another word. At the last moment she said, "Thank you, Novice Clarence, I'll see him."

Sticking her head out into the hallway, she found Ibrahim in a fine long suit coat and waistcoat looking every bit the Englishman, a look he'd donned at times during their work in London, shifting fluidly between different aspects of himself and the diverse worlds to which he'd grown accustomed. Though she cared not a whit what he wore about the countryside, he did look unbearably dashing. But more important, he'd come for her, after all. With a large stack of books.

She made herself scowl, though she knew her eyes must glow. "You may leave us, Novice Clarence. Mr. Wasil-Tipton here is a colleague, and we've business matters." The novice bobbed her head and vanished.

Beatrice folded her arms and opened her mouth to speak, but Ibrahim strode forward and interrupted, placing the volumes on a nearby ledge. "I assume you received my letter. I maintain that I must keep my distance so that I will not endanger you, but I am here to help. It was wrong of me to abandon you with work to be done." He smiled, patting the book spines. "And so, powers or no, the power of the word remains. And you have my word. I promise to be careful with it."

Beatrice stared. So, still fearing he'd be the death of her, he was all business. Still, it was so very good to see him.

She found herself replying with the curt and detached tone that she always used, the one that betrayed nothing of her heart. "I welcome your assistance. The haunting becomes unmanageable at times, and we must keep moving else the dead overrun the towns in which we stay. They hear of her or sense our charge, I cannot tell which. But, come and meet her. By the end of the month we move west into York and await the final days there."

She gestured to the room behind her. Ibrahim did not move. They shared a long, aching moment of mutual regard.

"It is . . . good to see you," Ibrahim murmured.

Beatrice felt her hard expression soften, her breath catch and her colour rise. "And you."

Ibrahim turned, lifted the stack of books and strode into the room. Iris sat up in bed, singing softly to herself. At his entrance, her mouth fell open.

"You're one, too!" she cried, raising both Beatrice's and

Ibrahim's eyebrows. "You, too, were saved from death to live a life of glory and service!" She smiled, radiant. "Don't be surprised, sir. I know things."

This effusive, unexpected greeting made Ibrahim chuckle, and Beatrice hurried to introduce them, thankful the dear girl didn't bat an eyelash at the entrance of a *foreigner*. "Iris Parker, Mr. Ibrahim Wasil . . . Have you been going by Tipton or no?"

"Yes, Tipton. But you may call me Ibrahim, Miss Parker. You remind me of a friend of ours. Ahmed. He, too, is full of joy and mysterious knowledge."

The girl stared at him. Then she said, "Iris then, please. We must all be friends here—friends brought together by wondrous fate, wondrous love." She saw his burden and exclaimed, "Books! Oh, you must promise to read to me, Ibrahim. I adore being read to. I never learned to read. The sisters tried during my first few years in the convent, but they said I've a handicap. Then I fell in with sinners and had no one to teach me. But, now I've found saints."

Ibrahim looked unsure what to say.

"Are you two friends, then?" Iris asked. "Beatrice sent for you?"

He shrugged. "I . . . I'm here to help. I understand you are plagued by spirits."

"Oh, they're no bother, really. They're kind. I think they're here for the baby. Did Beatrice tell you? She's very special. The baby. Beatrice, too, of course, but the baby was heralded by our Lady. Oh, where are you from? Do you have a Holy Mother in your land?"

Ibrahim smiled. "I am from Egypt. But I do know of our Lady."

"Egypt?" the girl repeated, wide-eyed. "What have you to do with ghosts to come from a full world away? Can you see them, too?"

"Yes, I can," he said, "and I think it might be best for you and the child not to be too long surrounded by them. The dead can be taxing. For that reason I've brought some . . . recommended reading." He moved his books to the room's desk, shifting through the spines. The titles were varied, books of worship, spiritual tracts and a few books of law. There were also many magazines.

He lifted up a thin volume. "*Household Words*. Dickens." He turned to Beatrice. "Do you think ghosts like ghost stories?"

Beatrice laughed despite herself, trying to fight back tears. She felt like Elinor in Austen's *Sense and Sensibility* after finding out Edward was free for her to love, having to leave the room and sob with happiness. She felt the urge to do just that. It was so good to just see Ibrahim, simply to be near him. All felt right with the world. Prophecy was unfolding like a flower.

Then the ghosts swooped in.

Iris shuddered at the sudden chill. The horde surrounded the bed like nurses around the dying, only these were not administering aid. Iris tried to pretend she wasn't startled, but the pendant around her neck went luminous. Beatrice believed it was the goddess's power trying to keep the girl safe. It wasn't that the ghosts were ill-intentioned, but their energy was frantic, overwhelming.

Ibrahim noticed this. "Well, I suppose I'll try my hand," he said, reaching for a book.

"Do choose Rumi, Ibrahim," Beatrice exclaimed. "I miss him as much as I miss the others. As much as I miss Cairo."

"You miss Cairo?"

"Of course I do, that hasn't changed. I miss our home," she replied.

Ibrahim's face lit up, and she was equally warmed by the expression as by the words he proceeded to read. For a moment they both seemed caught in the idea of *their* home.

The ghosts dispersed. It seemed that certain texts indeed retained power of their own, or perhaps Ibrahim retained some of what he'd been. Either way, the reading was effective. Iris breathed a bit easier, though she gave no complaint either way.

"That was lovely!" she said. "Would you deign to read some prayers to me? Do you believe in God, Mr. Wasil-Tip—*Ibrahim?* Do you mind?"

Ibrahim answered slowly. "In *God?* Let us say that Beatrice and I call ourselves people of spirit. We've a fairly wide notion of what that entails."

He lifted a Bible and began reading various annunciations. From that he moved to the Quran, for which Iris showed intense curiosity. She listened in awe until at last she fell into a peaceful sleep, convinced that there were angels of all faiths, goodness of many shapes and beauties.

Seeing Iris safely resting, the necessity of her rest determined their travel must wait. Beatrice motioned Ibrahim out into the hallway. She could wonder no longer about the fullness of his intent. "Do you plan to stay for the remainder of this duty? If so, then what?"

Ibrahim was nodding, but he paused. "I . . . don't know. I fear my vision."

"And yet you are here."

"I told you, I want to help."

Beatrice waited, her gaze daring him to say more.

He looked away. "Cairo was not the same without you. Still . . . I fear your life being cut short." He gestured to his head, then his heart. "I feel—"

"Ibrahim. It's been a harrowing, grim few months. I've seen wondrous, terrible things. The goddess was nearly destroyed doing what she intends, merging two worlds that should be kept separate. One day to the next, we're never guaranteed life.

But I don't believe taking your hand will do me in. I daresay what does me in will be something I agreed to when I believed I had nothing else."

Ibrahim said nothing.

"Tell me," she implored him. "The goddess once intimated something, and Iris repeated it. The day James Tipton died, do you believe The Grand Work saved your life?"

"I know it did."

Beatrice nodded, feeling phantom blue flame caress her heart. "And for that gift, for the gift of your life, The Grand Work is worth all its sacrifices. But"—she trembled as she dared prompt—"can we not choose how far we allow such sacrifices to rule our hearts?"

She stared at him, waiting for him to speak, to acknowledge his love for her. To acknowledge that they were meant for each other. She waited for him to say what she hoped he felt in his heart, what it seemed like his journey here proved. But though he stared back, and she thought she glimpsed something simmering in his expression, he said nothing.

Beatrice straightened her shoulders. "Do you have resources to find your way to an inn?" When Ibrahim nodded she said, "Then go. Sleep well, and we'll travel the final leg of our journey in the morrow."

At the door, she paused and turned back. "It is . . . *very* good to see you, Ibrahim. Good night."

That was the best she could manage to his face, though in her heart she said a thousand things more.

Chapter Thirty-six

The weeks that followed were both joyous and heart-wrenching. Ibrahim, Beatrice and Iris traveled together. The women stayed at convents, Ibrahim stayed at inns nearby. They did not speak again of feelings. At last they came to York and the Bar Convent, the Institute of the Blessed Virgin Mary. All was progressing according to divine decree. As one final assurance, they would not go to the Bar Convent until the very last moment, when Iris, in her state, could not possibly be turned away.

Drawing near the place, intending to make arrangements for them all at the inn across the street, Beatrice caught a glimmer in the air, something only eyes accustomed to strange sights could see. If the Liminal images were indeed true, she was seeing a bit of shelter over those Georgian convent walls; here was a thin, sparkling parasol under which a strangely beautiful, eerily white flower would magically grow.

Late that night, all was arranged. Ibrahim sat in the corner of Iris's room, reading as he had every night since joining them, both to entertain her and keep the ghosts at bay. Iris was a wonderful audience, laughing, sighing and crying as he read, occasionally hypothesizing and exclaiming, and if Beatrice wasn't mistaken, Ibrahim thoroughly enjoyed it. She yearned for him to turn that pleased gaze upon her, but alas their quiet amiability had not been replaced by passion. There was an impassable gulf Beatrice had no idea how to cross.

Ibrahim's set of *Household Words*, Mr. Dickens's popular magazine, contained a serialized novel by one Mrs. Gaskell, written over a decade prior. About an industrializing country and showcasing two very different worlds and stubborn persons, *North and South* was perfect, Iris having recently requested more Gaskell, having loved her ghost stories in magazines prior. They had nearly gone through Ibrahim's whole array of material.

There were moments when Ibrahim sat stiffly in one corner of the room and Beatrice sat stiffly in the other, Iris lying in rapture between them. During these periods Beatrice was struck on more than one level by the story, yearning for its two stubborn characters to give in to each other. Sitting opposite Ibrahim during the recitation became unbearable, a painful rapture where her whole body tensed as though one simple touch might entirely break her.

They neared the end of the tale. Ibrahim was reading the strained financial proposition from Margaret Hale upon John Thornton's mill, a conversation between two people who were desperately in love but who refused to show it.

"'*Mr. Lennox drew me out a proposal,*'" Ibrahim read quietly. "'*I wish he was here to explain it—showing that if you would take some money of mine, eighteen thousand and fifty-seven pounds, lying just at this moment unused in the bank, and bringing me in only two and a half percent—you could pay me much better interest and might go on working Marlborough Mills.* Her voice had cleared itself and become more steady. Mr. Thornton did not speak, and Miss Hale went on looking for some paper on which were written down the proposals for security; for she was most anxious to have it all looked upon in the light of a mere business arrangement, in which the principal advantage would be on her side.'"

Beatrice stood, agitated. She could hear no more.

Ibrahim glanced up, so she blushingly gazed down at Iris, mopping her brow, relieved and satisfied that the young woman was sleeping comfortably. She hurried to inform him, "She's dreaming. I daresay she'd not want to miss the ending of the tale, and we're not far from that, are we?" Beatrice could not meet his eyes.

"We are not."

"Shall Mr. Thornton and Miss Hale end their stubborn charade or no?" Beatrice drew a pained breath. "I suppose we'll have to see tomorrow. The end must come, just as it must for the goddess's own tale. At least, our part of it. Soon the child will come, which will mark the finale of our duty."

Ibrahim laid the magazine aside, his face thoughtful. He said nothing, just took up his tea.

Too much to bear. Beatrice fled to her rooms, needing to cool her face and be alone. The sooner this business was done, the better. Ibrahim would be relieved of all responsibility and could go back to Cairo, for clearly he had not come here to claim her. If he had, he'd have unclasped his heart at some point, rather than maintaining such maddening distance. Was he so afraid, still, that he would be the death of her? Had her words not combated that fear? How could such worries affect him? Life and death were ever precarious where The Grand Work was concerned. It was absurd.

She paced the room and didn't notice the door open or the figure standing tall in the archway until his voice arrested her: "'While she sought for this paper, her very heart-pulse was arrested by the tone in which Mr. Thornton spoke. His voice was hoarse, and trembling with tender passion as he said, *Margaret!*'"

Beatrice turned to see Ibrahim standing on the threshold, a smoldering light in his eyes, the magazine in his hand. He came into the room, stepped toward Beatrice as he kept reading. "'For an instant she looked up and then sought to veil her luminous eyes by dropping her forehead on her hands. Again, stepping nearer, he besought her with another tremulous eager call upon her name. *Margaret!*'"

Ibrahim drew nearer. She could feel the warm heat of him, could taste the scent of myrrh oil that faintly hung around him, exotic and delectable, could feel his breath on her cheek as he continued reading.

"'Still lower went the head; more closely hidden was the face, almost resting on the table before her. He came close to her. He knelt by her side, to bring his face to a level with her ear and whisper-panted out the words: *Take care. If you do not speak I shall claim you as my own in some strange presumptuous way. Send me away at once if I must go . . .*'" Here Ibrahim paused. He leaned in, his body brushing hers, and the final call was not Mr. Thornton's but his own.

"Beatrice . . ."

She turned her head, wondering if her eyes were luminous as Mrs. Gaskell had described. Her expression betrayed her anticipation, she was sure, for her body ached for his touch.

He lifted the magazine once more so that he might read it over her shoulder as he stood so unbearably close, his breath upon her ear. "'At that third call she turned her face, still covered with her small white hands, toward him, and laid it on his shoulder, hiding it even there; and it was too delicious to feel her soft cheek against his, for him to wish to see either deep blushes or loving eyes. He clasped her close. But they both kept silence.'"

Ibrahim dropped the magazine. He cupped her warm cheeks in his cool hands and pressed his lips gently but firmly to hers. The taste of tea, the smell of incense and priceless myrrh . . . The soft press of his lips grew hungrier. Mutual acquiescence had them clasping each other close and at long last giving in. This magnetism they'd senselessly fought was at an end; they were too close to resist crashing greedily against each other.

They drew back to breathe deep, to shudder, but they were unfinished.

"Mrs. Gaskell was a savant. Keep more silence with me,"

Beatrice whispered, then drew him into another kiss that sent them to the divan to press as close as bodies and layers of clothing would allow.

There remained no words. However, they did not keep silence. Sighs and soft gasps flew from Beatrice's lips until at last Ibrahim murmured upon her ear, bringing them back to themselves. "The man who raised me gave me every opportunity. He never forced me to be like him or his colleagues; he gave me fine upstanding examples of men and women within my culture who were business partners and wives, both devout and secular, sent me to school in my native tongue and planned that I would live as my people do. And I resented them all because none of them were truly like me. Nothing was truly mine."

Beatrice opened her mouth to say, *Then let me be yours.* Instead, her damnable pride had her saying; "I've always wondered if you resent *me.*"

"That's not what I'm trying to say, Beatrice," he hissed. "I never thought I was meant for love, for passion. Most certainly not with a woman like you." His breath was hot against her forehead. "In working with a woman like you, in deferring to a woman like you—"

"You've never deferred to me a moment in your life," she exclaimed.

"In *wanting* a woman like you." He traced a fingertip from her throat to the edge of her bodice, and Beatrice shivered with desire. "Perhaps it's time for us both to defer to the higher calling."

"And what might that be?" she breathed.

"Passion. Will you be mine, Miss Smith? Would you make a home with me? All that should have kept us apart, The Grand Work erased. Culturally, religiously, ideologically—it literally gave me new life. Would you give me, at last, a place to belong and someone to belong to?"

This was everything she'd wanted. Dared she trust it? "You no longer think you'll be the death of me? Aren't you afraid to take my hand?"

He ran his fingers up her body and pulled her fully against him. "Does it look now like I'm afraid to take your hand? The Grand Work may be the death of us all, but it already saved my life, saved me from that house fire on the day we were called. It is as you said. If we're living on borrowed time, we might as well live fully."

"Finally, we agree," she murmured, fully relaxing against him, feeling all the mortar of their stubborn walls turn to powder at their feet.

Physical vows were torturously slow and delicious in the making; gentle, sacred acts; delicate promises of the life they would yet share. For one night, the dread press of fate was abandoned for the duty of the heart.

Chapter Thirty-seven

A storm gathered. The clouds were black all around the convent where Iris Parker would breathe her last, but not above it. Iris, Beatrice and Ibrahim watched from the window of the inn.

Iris knew it was time. She called Beatrice over to write a letter to her daughter. Words of faith, love, assurance—and some instruction for good measure. Beatrice held Iris's hand when that was finished. Ibrahim kissed Iris's brow and Beatrice's in turn, and he allowed the women their silent vigil, not asking for direction until the pain came and they moved Iris to the convent as was foretold.

Ibrahim had been quiet and gentle since their passionate foray, but they'd spoken not a word of their future. Beatrice couldn't be troubled by it, not when Iris was her present concern and needed her aid.

The storm threatened to break above them as they left the inn, but Beatrice saw the sky sparkle with that particular light, a similar sheen, elusive to the eye, as the one that hung in spiritual protection over Athens. Blessings the goddess had left behind for her mortal charges.

"There is something of safety about that place," Iris gasped between the pain of her contractions. She allowed herself to be helped into the carriage that would take them the short distance necessary.

Beatrice nodded. "I do believe our Lady offered it a particular benediction."

The always swarming ghosts were agitated, billowing and swaying like sails in a squall. They hovered all around as the short journey was taken, and soon Ibrahim sat waiting in the carriage while Beatrice led Iris to the convent door. He sat with texts in hand. If she needed him, she'd call for him. But this was a woman's threshold.

Beatrice knocked boldly, Iris leaning upon her, gasping.

A young sister opened the door, eyes wide, her dress a simple grey with a coif. Beatrice didn't wait upon niceties.

"Hello, I'm Beatrice, this is Iris and she needs your help."

"You are the one whose coming was foretold," the sister murmured.

"Ah, it's good to be expected." Beatrice moved Iris into the plain foyer as the sister went for the mother superior.

The nun needn't have bothered. A plump, ruddy-cheeked woman, the picture of authoritarian kindness, was already rounding the corner. "So it is, so it is," she said.

The sisters provided Iris a room and the assistance of their precious few trained in such matters of the body. Beatrice was content that Iris was in good care. The general compassion and lack of prejudice was comforting, and it made her rethink any words of admonishment regarding the Church. It had its flaws, as did every institution. But here women's magic was rife. Though, they'd hardly call it magic. It was faith, firmly wielded.

Iris shared passionate prayers with the sisters. No one bothered Beatrice, no one asked her relation, no one hurried her away; they allowed her a chair in the corner where she sat with her hands pressed in anxiety. She wished Ibrahim could sit with her there and read soothing things of beauty but it would hardly have been proper. As unusual as this birth was, they couldn't attract any more undue attention.

After a time, when Iris's cries were too much to bear, Beatrice sought out the reverend mother in her office. She found her drawing up papers.

"She won't make it through the night," the nun murmured. She glanced up at Beatrice with calm gravity. This, Beatrice thought, was the perfect hand to grow an odd young girl into something substantive.

"I know this because it was foretold to me by the Holy Mother," the nun clarified. "Our Lady gave us particulars for the burial of the mother. Also, particulars for the child. We should cover her traces to be safe. It is uncommon, this night. Uncommon, this charge. But when the Lord decrees something and sends his messengers, so it shall be."

Beatrice gaped. How wondrous, when mortals could talk of such spectacular goings-on as simple fact, especially those not directly called into the service of The Grand Work. Goodness knows she had not gone so effortlessly into the good night of her fate.

Closing her mouth, she composed herself and spoke plainly. "I'll not subject your sisters to such melancholy work. If you could kindly supply me with two shovels, my colleague and I shall make sure a site is ready." Beatrice pulled banknotes from her reticule. "These shall pay for headstones. Thank you. I do believe, as odd as this is, and odd as this child shall be, that you are doing good."

"I agree." She eyed Beatrice. "Don't speak as though you doubt, though, Miss Smith. Speak as though you know. If you're confident good shall win, it will. If you doubt it, it won't. Do not leave room for darkness, lest it wedge its way in."

"You are wise, Reverend Mother."

"No, not personally. I allow for higher truths to flow through me. I am a vessel. So I shall give this child what I can and see that she journeys where the Holy Mother commanded. I promise."

"Thank you," Beatrice said.

She exited the convent to find the storm still held back its fury. Good, for there was a grim business yet to be done. She joined Ibrahim in the carriage.

Without a word between them, only an occasional bolstering nod, the two of them went to a small York graveyard. There they began to dig. The physical work felt good, exorcising demons of anxiety, knots of uncertainty and the grief of losing such a sweet soul as Iris Parker, and soon there were two graves set aside from the rest of the graveyard, one for a woman and one for an infant. The goddess's morbid requests.

Beatrice took a wooden box the size of a dead child, placed the letter from Iris and the key from the goddess into a metal container, closed the lid, laid it in the coffin that was in turn laid into the ground. Standing over the soil, she and Ibrahim said many different prayers. It would be well that this ground was blessed with wards against darkness, lest it have the wedge of which the reverend mother warned.

She and Ibrahim returned to the convent, and just as they entered Beatrice heard the scream of a newborn. Uncannily, almost immediately, it quieted.

Ibrahim waited respectfully in the reverend mother's office, as the mysterious chamber of childbirth was entirely off-limits to him. Beatrice rushed to Iris's side, stroking her hair and trying to ignore how much blood had been lost. A broken body that yet birthed a child was indeed a miracle; she tried to focus on miracles instead.

The attendant nun midwife cried out once the child was wiped clean. "Why, the girl's a ghost!"

"Let me see her," Iris murmured, all her strength gone but tears of love in her eyes. She ignored the two sisters in the room anxiously whispering that the child was a frightful omen.

"Hush," the reverend mother said, who had come to sit sentry in the corner. "This is a child of God and she will be raised as ours. Pallor aside, she is sacred to us, and I'll not hear one word against her."

"Thank you," Iris whispered. She gazed down at the precious bundle in her arms, the baby whose ice-blue eyes were staring fixedly, intelligently up at her. Iris said to Beatrice, "She's very special. See how she doesn't cry? See how gentle and peaceful a soul?"

"Beautiful," Beatrice choked out.

A host of spirits hovered at the edges of the room, making the cool room colder. Beatrice had never seen them so respectful; they hung silent, watching, listening. Perhaps worshipping. Neither Iris nor Beatrice acknowledged them, lest the lesser sisters think their strange charge further cursed.

"Give her the pendant, Beatrice, and my letter, please."

"She will be provided for," the reverend mother said, seeing Beatrice struggling for composure.

"And so it is finished," Iris murmured. She kissed her daughter on the forehead. The baby's tiny arm reached out, her tiny fist pressed against Iris's cheek. "Good-bye, Percy. Always remember, no matter what, you are a child of Power and Light. Unique as you look, you'll likely not think yourself powerful, but you must have faith. I did, and you were my reward."

She closed her eyes, and in the next moment Iris was gone. Simple. Peaceful. Beautiful, perhaps. In its way. In that very moment the storm clouds broke and the rain came. So did Beatrice's tears.

Everyone but Beatrice left the room. She curled over Iris's body, doubled over it as if by doing so she might yet catch a bit of that effervescent, wonderful spirit and hold it ever close to her bosom. Instead a cool draft encompassed her, and she looked up to find Iris's spirit, luminous and radiant, hovering, a veritable angel with all the joy and life it contained. The ghost stared alternately at Beatrice and at the tiny, colourless baby still cradled in her mortal shell's dead arms, then blew Beatrice and her child a kiss. The room grew blindingly bright, and Iris was gone. Just as the goddess had vanished.

Beatrice lifted the child into her arms, surprised by Percy's preternatural quiet, by her inquisitive, eerie eyes. But then again, the child was an elder soul than any could possibly know.

She hugged her tight, brushing away tears that had fallen into the baby's pearlescent hair. "Persephone Parker. You'd best make things right, young lady. You've a lot of work to do, do you hear me? Grow up fast, my girl. Grow up fast."

The baby made no sound but stared at her almost as if she understood. If not now, she would someday. She *had* to.

Beatrice brought the baby into the reverend mother's office and without a word handed the child over. Then she gestured to Ibrahim, who stared at the baby in awe. "I'll stay the night here. Tomorrow we are free."

Her voice shook. Ibrahim said nothing, as he knew there was nothing to say, just pressed her hand in support and love. She waved him gently off, and he went to spend the night at the inn. When it came, sleep came heavy.

She woke to the cry of the novices. At first Beatrice was afraid something was wrong, that the baby was ill, that any number of strange phenomena, the aftershock of divine interferences, was taking hold of the convent. But, no. Looking out her window at the bright dawn, at the storm clouds rolling away, pressed back by determined sunlight, Beatrice saw the gifts Iris Parker had left. Her tears flowed anew.

In the sky were a hundred rainbows.

Chapter Thirty-eight

Alexi slept fitfully through the terrible storm. His fingers felt wet, as if still soiled by those bloody roses from so many months prior, their grim oil impossible to wash away. But, midway through the night, the wind of The Grand Work burst through his room. There was the brief cry of a newborn, then a great and glorious peace as the cry quieted into a soft lullaby. It was a dream so powerful that his hands and heart were cleansed.

Awaking with tears on his cheeks and his heart beating wildly, he strained his eyes against the bright morning light. Out his window he found multiple rainbows in the sky, an impossible act of nature but a beautiful omen.

Throwing back his covers he found something even stranger: a talisman at the foot of his bed. A luminescent feather. He held it up to the light, and it reflected every colour as if the rainbows outside shone directly upon it. The goddess that had revealed herself to announce Prophecy came to mind, a goddess he'd kept close in hazy dreams never again fully realized.

"'From the flame of Phoenix, a feather did fall and Muses followed,'" he murmured. It was the mythology that bound them, words ingrained in his brain when he was first chosen by Phoenix.

He seized a notebook on his bedside table and began to write furiously. Something had been born today; his destiny was closer than ever. How long before it all reached fruition he couldn't know, but something of Prophecy had been completed. He wanted to tell the others and yet this joy felt so personal, so private. They couldn't possibly understand.

The feather in his pocket, Alexi was en route to a meeting when something glimmering caught his eye in the window of a small jewelry shop. He went over to examine it.

An elegant silver ring, one plain feather wrapped into a circle. A sudden, terrible pain seized his body and soul, an agony he'd never before felt. His mind flashed to a field of heather, his body felt a phantom embrace. A hand in his, being dragged away. Something wonderful, taken. Something stolen, leaving a hollow in his heart.

Shaking, he had to steady himself with his hand upon the bricks of the shop. A concerned customer clutched her purchase tight as she hurried off the doorstep, murmuring to her top-hatted escort, "Why, that young man looks *mad*." And then, in his ear sounded a whisper, a voice of an old familiar friend. Or lover.

"I promise."

Whatever had lurched and ached within him lost its breath in a sudden rush of hope, and his mind narrowed to that one word, and that word filled him. Promise?

He straightened himself, his waistcoat, his scarlet cravat. In a matter of moments the ring had been purchased, placed on a chain and was hidden beneath Alexi's layers. There it would lay against his heart for however long it took to find the mysterious provender he hungered for. That promise.

Everything about this age marched toward Prophecy.

★ ★ ★

Ibrahim gathered Beatrice from the convent. In solemn quiet they stood within the sparse room where she'd spent the night and prepared to leave York.

"Did you see the sky?" Beatrice asked.

Ibrahim nodded, touching her arm. "I did—heralds of a new dawn, releasing us to our lives."

Freedom. Was it possible? A gnawing feeling had Beatrice wondering what the goddess had meant by "blood and fire" in the midst of her final instructions. Such intense words had her wondering if The Grand Work would yet call her at some future date. She had a feeling it would, but maybe that was just a vestigial desire of the past. She now had everything she wanted. At least she hoped.

They'd made a connection, body and soul, she and Ibrahim, one that couldn't be denied. Yet there hadn't been a proposal. What was he waiting for? It wasn't as if she could ask.

A familiar ripping sound made them whirl. There before Beatrice stood an open, vertical rectangle, obscuring the bed and window behind. What lay visible beyond was her father's apartment building in Cairo.

"Home! Oh, Father . . ." Beatrice choked. It was only now she allowed herself to entertain how dearly she missed him. How she had missed the simple human interactions she'd known before being one of The Guard. Perhaps it was time to gather family back again and cherish each and every moment.

She and Ibrahim stood staring. A crackling, threading light coursed about the edge of the portal; Liminal light, it seemed.

Ibrahim asked the portal warily. "Are you here to carry us home? Is this the reward for a job well-done?"

The edges sparked and flickered, but the Liminal wasn't one for conversation.

Ibrahim approached and gingerly pushed his fingertips inside the portal. When he withdrew them he said, "It feels like the air of home."

Beatrice chuckled. "Well, it *would* beat weeks on a steamer. See? You'll take my hand and we'll go home. A much better vision. Not everything we fear comes to pass as we fear it."

The word "fear" seemed to strike and shudder through him and he stepped back. "Having escaped death, I do now fear it. I fear these thresholds, Bea. I have been warned of them."

"A portal, exactly like this?"

"Well no, not quite like this."

"Then shall you be ruled by fear? Or instead by your own decisions?" She asked gently, but firmly. A quality she knew he admired.

He considered her a moment, Cairo waiting patiently before them. "You know, one of the reasons I chafed against loving you was that a few of my countrymen once chided me for living among English people and permitting their company. Having been abandoned by Arab parents, it pained me to be shunned by more.

"And here I think upon the benediction of Ahmed Basri's smile, and the encouragement of our friends. I am that which I choose, as simple or as complicated as I may be. No other opinion has a right to that choice. Indeed, Miss Smith. My choices shall not be ruled by fear."

When Ibrahim offered his hand, she took it. They smiled and stepped through into warm golden light.

Chapter Thirty-nine

"Hello, Father."

Beatrice's greeting slipped tentatively across the threshold, whole worlds having passed since she'd last spoken those words, if only one of them noticed the distance.

Leonard Smith looked up from his clay fragments with a smile. The blue eyes she'd inherited sparkled. "Ah, Bea! Hello! Seems I haven't seen you in a while. School, wasn't it? Did it go well? Are you back, then?"

"Yes."

He stood, acknowledging the newcomer. "And who's this?"

Ibrahim stepped forward. "Ibrahim Wasil-Tipton, sir, at your service."

"Tipton. Tipton . . ." Mr. Smith's brow furrowed before he suddenly lit up. "Are you Father Tipton's boy, then?"

"Yes, sir, I am."

"What a good man, Tipton! One of the best I knew! What a shame; he's sorely missed. He spoke so fondly of you, said you were brilliant. I'm so sorry about what happened but am grateful you're alive. Have you met my daughter, Beatrice? Bea, you remember my telling you about the good father from England? Why, this is James Tipton's boy, Ibrahim."

"We've met, Father," Beatrice replied patiently. The Grand Work had made some people lovers and some strangers.

"Sit, both of you, I'll send for tea. I'm so glad you've come! Bea, the new dig, it's exquisite! I have to keep idiot tourists from tromping around in it, but the government's giving me permission to cordon it off."

"I look forward to seeing it."

"Oh, yes, do come," Mr. Smith enthused. His thoughts visibly shifted, trying to pierce the clouds of Belle's lingering magic. "Pardon me, my boy, why are you here?"

"I've something to ask."

Her father seemed not to hear. "Good, good. I'm so glad you've met my daughter. I always meant to invite Father Tipton over, Bea, and then, you know, you just take life for granted . . ." His eyes watered. "Then it's gone. But I'm so glad you've met. Isn't that fortuitous? How did you meet, anyway?"

"On the street," Ibrahim replied.

Beatrice looked down to hide a helpless smile. Her mind replayed the first moment he turned the corner outside Abu Serge. When his eyes had met hers, her breath had caught in her lungs and her heart skipped multiple beats. Her heart had reinvented itself in those stilled moments, having died and lived again.

"You see, Mr. Smith," Ibrahim continued. "I'm here to ask for your daughter's hand. Because on that fateful day, my life changed. I could have died that day. Yet I lived. I was saved. I was visited by an angel."

Bea looked at him, shocked by his pronouncement and by the softness of his tone. She'd never heard him use that voice apart from that night in the inn, Iris sleeping in the chamber across the hall.

"That angel was fated as mine," Ibrahim continued. "Heaven-sent. Against all odds."

Beatrice smiled, suddenly realizing that he hadn't meant the goddess. He'd meant her. This was even lovelier than she'd imagined.

Her father blinked. The young lovers sat, terribly anxious

at what he might say. They lived a new life now, one where Guard magic couldn't simply influence the world to do what they wanted. They were back to the permissions, proprieties and barriers of the age. She stared at her father, pleading with her eyes for him to be as open and loving as his friend Tipton seemed to have been.

Mr. Smith jumped up. "Ho-ho, Bea! I can't think of a better man than Jim Tipton, so the boy he so dearly loved . . . Why, I daresay you couldn't do better! Tell me, son, do you have an interest in the digs as your father did? Would you like to come along?" He bounded forward and clasped Ibrahim in an embrace.

Beatrice's hand flew to her mouth, grateful tears leaking from her eyes. Ibrahim tentatively returned the embrace, a bit shocked himself. Shrugging at Beatrice with an amazed little smile, he seemed utterly moved to be so effortlessly called son again.

"I would like that, Mr. Smith. Very much."

"We'll all go! A family expedition to relish and cherish the exquisite riches of this marvelous land!" His excitement couldn't be contained, and Beatrice was reminded that perhaps she should have simply trusted her father all along. He had raised her to be the woman that loved Ibrahim; why, then, wouldn't he feel the same? He threw wide the door and without a hint of propriety cried, "Scratch the tea. Champagne! There's going to be a wedding!"

★ ★ ★

There was indeed.

The ceremony was simple but powerful. Beatrice had heard so many declamations, heralds, prophecies and postulations coming from grand and terrible thresholds, all she wanted was a simple, quiet, meaningful pledge. So they had this, under a golden Cairo sun. Ahmed read Rumi, a poem on marriage. Verena sat beside Mr. Smith, who looked on, proud.

Belle and George even appeared. It was a surprise. They'd sent the pair an invitation but hadn't expected them to hop right on a steamer. But, Belle claimed she'd been ready for this and took all the credit for their relationship.

Beatrice felt for the first time since fire coursed her veins a settling sense of contentment.

"Welcome home, Bea," Ibrahim said, whisking his bride into their new flat. "Thank you," he said quietly, when Beatrice giggled and threw her arms around him. There were tears in his eyes.

Beatrice cocked her head to the side, waiting for an explanation.

"For choosing to make this home. For wanting Cairo. For wanting me. You did not have to."

Beatrice smiled. "Ah, yes, you and your choices. Home sometimes chooses us, you know."

"We are so blessed," Ibrahim murmured. "To be rid of it all. To have done our parts. To have the luxury of the home of our heart. I pray they all will find their way. I pray for a shining star. I pray for all of their passages home."

"Ibrahim prays for The Guard at last? For our dear Lady made flesh?"

Ibrahim nodded. "Most heartily for her."

This time it was she who paused with a shudder of fear. "Love, forgive me. Tasks may yet lie ahead for me. I'll know when, but I must always heed the call."

Ibrahim nodded. "And I shall help you always. No more regrets. We must remember that I live on borrowed time. Every moment with you is a blessing to be cherished. Never to be squandered in fear."

They had years they'd not have had otherwise. Without The

Guard, Ibrahim would have had no years at all, and Beatrice's life would be entirely otherwise. Likely locked in some Parisian flat, trapped by a family and a life with no adventure. Without the defining, all-encompassing purpose she'd craved. This The Grand Work had granted her, along with the simple joy of love.

Epilogue

Beatrice and Ibrahim enjoyed years of happiness, never forgetting the forces that had drawn them together. Every now and then Beatrice caught a fleeting sense, like a scent of flowers on the breeze, strains of faraway music, distant echoes of that young Miss Percy Parker and Alexi Rychman. When she felt her heart beat briefly with reverberations of those two hearts, she wished them every blessing. They'd need them.

Then came this moment. In her happy Cairo home, Prophecy came again to call. It was a sudden, eviscerating blow.

Beatrice realized what the goddess had meant by her knowing it would be time. It wasn't that one could ever actually be prepared for such a thing, but Guards had always been chosen for unparalleled instincts. There was also a roaring sound in the room, catching them surprised as she and Ibrahim sat, hands clasped, upon a divan by a blazing hearth.

The huge black rectangle opened, revealing a dim, dank maw beyond. Figures floated down the grey length of a seemingly endless corridor. A man stood in shadow with a faintly glowing hand. A familiar light . . . Was this someone waiting just for her? The door had opened for some fell purpose.

Beatrice voiced her dread realization as it entered her mind: "The Whisper-world . . . Oh, God. And it needs me inside. Her blood. I'm the one to bring the fire, to knit the worlds. To free all The Guard spirits. But from within." She felt a wave of anger swell within her. "How, if I've no power?"

A tiny lick of blue flame coursed around the edges of the portal. Familiar blue flame, an old friend coming to collect a promise she'd made to face dangers whenever they came. But this time she realized her entry into the Whisper-world would be more than that fleeting glimpse beside the goddess. She wasn't coming back. Not as she was, not to this world as she knew it. To do her job, she would have to pass. Like dear Iris.

Ibrahim, ever attentive, didn't need to ask what was happening. He knew this was his vision. "Eternity wouldn't be enough by your side," he declared. "No matter when this portal came for us, we'd want another day."

"It's not coming for you but for me," she hissed, anger cresting anew.

"But you remember my vision. We are hand in hand. You've work to do, but I am your second. When I came for you in York I made a pledge to never let you go. No matter the dangers, this vision be damned. Do you regret that I came for you?"

"No," she choked out.

"So we mustn't move forward in anger, as it is but duty that again comes for us," he continued. "Anger will chain us inside this drear place, but we must fight for a brighter dawn."

"But we could've done so much more."

"I daresay every living person feels the same, but in all things there comes a time for something new. For our Lady, for us."

Beatrice took a deep breath and exhaled just as slowly. There was no sense in waiting; the door would not close on its own. She extended a hand to her beloved, grateful for his fortitude, for the choices that had made him her husband. He took it. Now, as they'd stepped from England to Cairo, so would they step . . .

"To the undiscovered country?"

Ibrahim offered her a rare gift: a sweet chuckle. Boyish excitement was contained within it. He could not fear the beyond, not when they were together. Beatrice was bolstered by his strength.

"Eternity awaits," she murmured, stepping forward to the edge and hesitating. Juliet and Romeo, they were, uniting houses and taking a journey together. Unlike Juliet, however, Beatrice knew there was work to be done on the other side. Blood, fire and a captive army.

Ibrahim squeezed her hand. "I love you, Bea. And I will be here with you, now and for every adventure to come. I promise."

There was no promise she could believe save this one, not after all she had seen and done. Luckily, this was the only promise that mattered. They stepped forward into darkness and believed in the coming light.

THE BEGINNING

Leanna Renee Hieber's
Strangely Beautiful series concludes with

Miss Violet and the Great War

1895
The Rychman Estate, Hampstead Heath, London

Mrs. Persephone "Percy" Rychman started, stopping the waltz mid-chord as she felt something fall onto her bare feet. Shifting back the piano bench, she bent to find a letter.

"That's odd."

"What is?" asked Professor Alexi Rychman, who stood leaning against the wall in a state of delicious undress, staring hungrily at his wife. Moonlight filtered through the window.

"A letter. Addressed to 'the Rychmans.'" Percy lifted the missive and opened it.

Alexi took the contents and sat next to her to read. The first of the pages was a note from his father, leaving him the house at too young an age.

"I dimly recall this note." He scowled, his eyes flashing. "But this . . ." Behind it was another letter, written in a beautiful, feminine script.

Over his shoulder, Percy read aloud:

To the strangely beautiful woman I hope to become:
The hand that writes this is a hand that would take yours and
hold it if I could. As I am, I will pass on to become you, you

whom I see as a ghostly pale girl who stares at her prophesied husband with all the love he well deserves . . .

She gasped. "It's from *me*?"

"The goddess," Alexi whispered, taken again by old if blurred wounds. His shaking hand gestured for her to continue, and Percy took the letter and did. Her voice was true and clear.

Some have called me goddess, some have called me our Lady, some have called me angel. A force of nature, I answer to all. But of all my mortal names, I remain fondest of Persephone, which I hope you've taken in my honour.

What is built between you is strong. I have seen it, seen this very moment in a vision, the Liminal and fate willing, and so I leave this note for you. You are meant to hear it from me, a herald from your past affirming your present. I made a promise to Alexi, a promise he likely only remembers as an echo in his heart, but a promise that he will be loved, supported, adored. I believe that he is.

He comes from a lineage of Guard Leaders. The grandfather he never knew. He was intended for this destiny, if he yet had to walk it blindly. I see now that this must always be the way, for only through honest human choices can the power be effective. Only through mutually earned love is the old vendetta truly healed. Without that, the vendetta lives on.

I die. My form fails me; the last drops of my life force are bled onto the Whisper-world to set The Guard free. But you, dear girl, will set me free. You must live on, live well and love. No matter the storms, no matter the nightmares. You are my eyes, my heart, my light. You are the future I would wish for myself.

Good-bye, my beloveds. I give my light unto you and pray for Peace.

One final thing: Ahmed, the Heart of The Guard before

yours, warned of a war in the ground. "Do not close every door,"
he said. The dead must pass. I trust that you will know what
that means when the time comes.

Finished, there was a long silence before Percy registered
that she was aglow. Light shone at her bosom, a reactive
luminosity in times of danger or extreme emotion that was
borrowed from a goddess but sustained by a passionate mortal
heart. Its provenance stemmed from her kind soul.

She took hold of her husband, thinking again of the goddess
that was both her and not her. No matter how things had come
to pass, Alexi was her greatest gift.

"I was left so in the dark," he murmured. "We *both* were left
so in the dark." Alexi took the letter from Percy's trembling
hand and put it down. "If we'd just been told, all the trauma
of our coming together could have been avoided. All the
danger—"

Percy, particularly luminous in the moonlight, placed a
finger on her husband's lips. "You heard the goddess's words,
and I have maintained—and will always maintain—that
falling in love with you of my own accord was far better than
being told to do so. How else can one gain sure footing but to
stumble first along the way?"

He stared down at her, loving her more than life. "Again,
you prove wise beyond your years. My *goddess.*" He bent to kiss
her, then gestured to the sheet music. "You've a page left. One
cannot leave a waltz unfinished. It is unlucky."

"Says who?"

"Well, surely the Germans."

Percy smiled and resumed.

A ghostly movement down the hall caught Alexi's eye, and
he folded his arms, scowling. Percy noticed, and she followed
his gaze and stopped playing. A black-haired child in a white

nightgown shifted in and out of shadow. Her pale skin was luminous, and her ink black hair shone with an odd hint of purple. Her eyes glowed icy amethyst.

"Violet! What are you doing awake?" Percy called out.

The eight-year-old paused, stepping into the moonlight to make a calm reply. "Why, I was waltzing, Mother. What *else* is a girl to do when she hears a waltz?"

That haughty matter-of-factness she had inherited from her father, but he thankfully withheld a chuckle so as not to encourage her. Instead he cried, "Violet Jane Rychman, what on earth are you doing waltzing after midnight?" He strode briskly toward her, and the girl bit her lip and looked up at him a bit fearfully. "—Without inviting your father?" he added, whisking her up into his arms.

Her pale face lit with the staggering smile she had inherited from her mother, and she roared a giggle as he began to grandly waltz her about the foyer.

"Carry on, Percy, my dove, carry on! We must have music!"

Percy grinned and sat back down at the keyboard, playing and watching them over her shoulder. She beamed whenever they twirled by and blew her a kiss.

The waltz ended, and Percy moved to join them. Violet was returned to her room, ever filled, at the child's own request, with flowers. Both she and her mother had a particular way with plant life.

Alexi tucked his daughter under her white lace covers, and Percy and he sat on either side of the bed. As had become their custom, they clasped hands together over her. Violet placed her hands atop theirs.

"The truth is, I couldn't sleep for a nightmare," the child stated.

"Would you like to tell us about it?" Percy asked.

"It was a war. In the ground."

Percy turned to Alexi, trying to hide the unease on her face. Alexi, unruffled, placed his free hand fully atop their entwined fingers. "Don't you worry about any nightmares. Your mother and I are always here to protect you."

Percy nodded. "Oh, yes. Your father has protected me against the most terrible of nightmares indeed. The darkness won't find you."

"Promise?"

"We promise," they chorused.

Little Violet closed her eyes. "I'll dream of angels, then."

Kissing her daughter's head, Percy kept hold of Alexi's hand as they exited the room. "Will it ever end?" she murmured.

"It doesn't appear so," Alexi replied. "But I have you." He reached out and combed his fingers through her pearlescent hair, cupping her cheek. "And for you, for this family, I will suffer anything."

He smiled suddenly. "I believe I've strength enough for one last fight, should Phoenix again come to call and The Grand Work press us back into service. We have our promises and I intend to keep them."

Percy loosed a weary chuckle. "I've been quite enjoying retirement. But perhaps our daughter will outshine us all."

Alexi nodded. "Considering how she embodies our love, I daresay she will. Darkness can never again ascend the same throne. Light crowned us the victors, and while we yet live, we shall walk in its promise. No matter what dreams—or nightmares—may come."

Leanna graduated with a BFA in Theatre, a focus in the Victorian Era and a scholarship to study in London. She has adapted works of nineteenth-century literature for the stage and her one-act plays have been produced around the country. Her novella *Dark Nest* won the 2009 Prism Award for excellence in Futuristic, Fantasy or Paranormal Romance. *The Strangely Beautiful Tale of Miss Percy Parker* won double 2010 Prism Awards for Best Fantasy and Best First Book, the 2010 Orange County Book Buyer's Best Award (Young Adult category) and the rights have been sold for adaptation into a Broadway musical theatre production currently in development. A member of the Science Fiction and Fantasy Writers of America, Romance Writers of America and International Thriller Writers, she's thrilled to have been named RWA NYC's 2010 Author of the Year. A member of actors unions AEA, SAG and AFTRA, Leanna works often in film and television. A devotee of ghost stories and Goth clubs, she resides in New York City with her real-life hero and her beloved rescued lab rabbit Persebunny.

INTERACT WITH DORCHESTER ONLINE!

Want to learn more about your favorite books and authors?
Want to talk with other readers that like to read the same books as you?
Want to see up-to-the-minute Dorchester news?

VISIT DORCHESTER AT:
DorchesterPub.com
Twitter.com/DorchesterPub
Facebook.com (Search Pages)

DISCUSS DORCHESTER'S NOVELS AT:
Dorchester Forums at DorchesterPub.com
GoodReads.com
LibraryThing.com
Myspace.com/books
Shelfari.com
WeRead.com

9 781428 511163